PRAISE FOR ENEMY OF THE STATE

"In the world of black-ops thrillers, Mitch Rapp continues to be among the best of the best."
—*Booklist* (starred review)

"Series fans and newcomers alike will watch in wonder as Mitch Rapp executes a clever plan that leads to an explosive climax." —*Publishers Weekly*

"This novel perfectly combines geo-politics, covert operations, and the backstory of the characters. Readers can close their eyes and remember past books written by Vince Flynn and will not skip a beat with Kyle Mills at the helm." —*Crimespree Magazine*

PRAISE FOR ORDER TO KILL

"This series continues to be the best of the best in the high adventure, action-heavy thriller field. . . . Flynn's name, Flynn's characters, and Mills's skill will take this one to the top of the charts, territory already familiar to Mitch Rapp." —*Booklist* (starred review)

"Just as compelling as when Flynn was doing the writing. . . . Satisfied fans will hope that Mills will fulfill their continuing Mitch Rapp needs far into the future."
—*Publishers Weekly* (starred review)

"Flynn is a master, maybe *the* master, of thrillers in which the pages seem to turn themselves."
—Bookreporter.com

"What thriller readers live for: tense and dramatic with a nice twist." —*Kirkus Reviews*

PRAISE FOR THE SURVIVOR

THE LAST MAN • KILL SHOT • AMERICAN
ASSASSIN • PURSUIT OF HONOR •
EXTREME MEASURES • PROTECT AND
DEFEND • ACT OF TREASON • CONSENT
TO KILL • MEMORIAL DAY • EXECUTIVE
POWER • SEPARATION OF POWER •
THE THIRD OPTION • TRANSFER OF
POWER • TERM LIMITS

Novels by Vince Flynn

And by Kyle Mills

VINCE FLYNN

ENEMY OF THE STATE

A MITCH RAPP NOVEL
BY KYLE MILLS

POCKET BOOKS

New York   London   Toronto   Sydney   New Delhi

Pocket Books
An Imprint of Simon & Schuster, Inc.
1230 Avenue of the Americas
New York, NY 10020

First Pocket Books paperback edition August 2018

POCKET and colophon are registered trademarks of Simon & Schuster, Inc.

For information about special discounts for bulk purchases, please contact Simon & Schuster Special Sales at 1-866-506-1949 or business@simonandschuster.com.

The Simon & Schuster Speakers Bureau can bring authors to your live event. For more information, or to book an event, contact the Simon & Schuster Speakers Bureau at 1-866-248-3049 or visit our website at www.simonspeakers.com.

Manufactured in the United States of America

10   9   8   7   6   5   4   3   2   1

ISBN 978-1-4767-8351-2
ISBN 978-1-4767-8353-6 (pbk)
ISBN 978-1-4767-8354-3 (ebook)

ACKNOWLEDGMENTS

Once again, thanks to my agent Simon Lipskar for, well, everything he does. Sloan Harris for his ever steady hand on the tiller. Emily Bestler for her insight and for tolerating me when I climb on my soapbox. David Brown for tirelessly getting the word out. My mother for her unfailingly honest comments—were you smoking crack when you wrote that chapter? Ryan Steck for keeping me from losing my way in the details. My wife, Kim, for her increasingly practiced thriller eye and for everything else. And, finally, to Vince's fans for going out of their way to make me feel welcome.

ENEMY OF THE STATE

PRELUDE

I T was just after midnight and Rabat felt largely deserted. Prince Talal bin Musaid stared out at the densely packed residences built into the hills overlooking the city. His eye was attracted to a human outline ducking into an alley to his right, but through the glass of his Mercedes S-Class it didn't seem real. The layer of dust covering everything, the cracked façades, the ragged laundry hung out to dry—none of it had ever been part of his existence. This was the world of the faceless masses. The people he became aware of only when they failed to do his bidding.

Four days short of his thirty-ninth birthday, his life had become a blur of private jets, beautiful women, and luxury homes. London, Monaco, Paris, New York—they were indistinguishable to him now, existing only to house the opulent nightclubs and shops that he and his companions required. Exclusive places that precious few people knew about and even fewer would ever be admitted to.

He could still be coaxed back to Saudi Arabia when family politics demanded, but more and more it was a place to be avoided. A place of bitter memories, betrayals, and reminders of a birthright stolen from him.

His driver eased onto a side street barely wide enough to allow passage, and bin Musaid looked away from the concrete tenements lining it. The boredom and disdain he normally felt when surrounded with this kind of squalor had been drowned out by excitement and anticipation. No more waiting. No more words. This overwhelming sense of exhilaration could only be generated by one thing. Action.

He slid a suitcase filled with American dollars onto his lap and felt the satisfying heft. It was the unfamiliar weight of purpose, he knew. The weight of power.

He was the nephew of King Faisal, but had never been treated with the respect that position demanded. After his parents' untimely death, bin Musaid had been sent to Europe, where he was forced to absorb the insult of Western schooling. His teachers—many women—had not only refused to defer to his station but had lorded their authority over him in a pathetic effort to obscure their own inferior birth. They'd given him poor marks and reported back to the king with stories of women, liquor, and violence.

All of this would have been of little consequence, but Faisal sided with *them*—with the British infidels who mocked both the House of Saud and Allah himself. Bin Musaid had finally been called back to Saudi Arabia after a meaningless incident with a female student. She had been a typical Western whore and he had treated her accordingly, no better or worse than required. In any event, he had welcomed the opportunity to take his rightful place in the ruling class.

It was not to be, though. Instead of a respected government post, he had been shuttled into an endless series of menial tasks and obscure, low-level positions. The king spoke enthusiastically of his bright future when they were together but never took steps to make that future a reality. Betrayed by his own family, bin Musaid had finally left the country of his birth and cut ties to the degree possible without jeopardizing the flow of family money.

He knew now that none of it was of any importance. The Saudi Arabia that had rejected him was doomed. King Faisal was old and weak, a puppet of America who was losing control of the forces gaining power within his borders. He didn't understand the true destiny of his country. Instead of crumbling and besieged, the Saudi royalty should have been taking a place at the helm of the new caliphate. It was the House of Saud's privilege and responsibility to lead the forces of Islam as they exterminated their enemies throughout the world.

His driver leaned forward to search the darkness for a rare street sign.

"Left, you idiot," bin Musaid said.

He'd been poring over the maps and satellite images on Google for days, anticipating this moment. They would drive straight for another kilometer, where the street would dead end. From there he would continue on foot into the dark maze of souks that climbed even higher above the city. The journey would take approximately seven minutes at a pace designed not to attract undue attention from anyone he might pass. Finally he would arrive at his destination: a nondescript apartment building where an ISIS representative was waiting.

The money in the suitcase would be used to finance a large-scale attack inside the United States—something ISIS saw as critical to advancing their already wildly successful propaganda campaign. The lone-wolf attacks that they had inspired were unquestionably glorious but lacked sufficient weight in a country where mass shootings were a daily event.

It was critical that America's Muslims join the fight, but thus far they had been reticent—lulled into complacency by their prosperity and integration into the patchwork of immigrants and mutts that made up their adopted country. Cracks were beginning to form, though. America was already turning against its Muslim population. It just needed a final push for it to go from shunning Mohammed's followers to isolating, attacking, and discriminating against them. When that came to pass, there would be millions of young disaffected men ready to be recruited into the army of God.

Saudi Arabia's leadership had taken similar actions in the past. In fact, two of bin Musaid's older cousins had been directly involved in the financing and planning of 9/11. While bin Laden had become the face of that attack, it would have been utterly impossible without the support of other powerful men familiar with America's vulnerabilities.

The prince smiled in the darkness, remembering the video footage of the burning towers and the terrified Christians throwing themselves to their deaths. It wasn't those glorious images that lifted his spirits, though. It was that the American politicians had known about Saudi Arabia's involvement but had been too cowardly to take action. Instead, they had made a hasty backroom deal with King Faisal. He would crack down on the subversives and keep the oil flowing. In return, the Americans would ignore the fact that the attack had been carried out almost entirely by Saudi nationals and instead divert their people's attention with the punishing quagmires of Afghanistan and Iraq.

Those wars and the lingering effects of the West's financial collapse had divided the American people to a degree not seen since the Civil War. America was a wounded animal. And he had become the lion.

CHAPTER 1

MITCH Rapp tried to find a more comfortable position, but none was available. His helmet was jammed against the top of the fuselage and there was something sharp poking through the mesh seat just to the right of his spine.

Not exactly the CIA's G550, but then this aircraft hadn't exactly been designed to ferry government VIPs. Its only purpose was the insertion of select teams behind enemy lines, and in order to do that effectively it had to be small, fast, and stealthy. There was no pilot or cockpit, no cabin pressure or heat, and no light other than the dim glow from a computer screen to his right.

He glanced over and scanned the data it contained. Four hundred knots at 25,000 feet on a south-by-southeast heading. An infrared map moved lazily beneath the compass and numbers, tracking the ground. Near the bottom of the display, his target began to appear.

Al-Shirqat.

Despite everything he'd lived through—everything he'd done—there were very few places that held memories bad enough to make his palms sweat. In fact, only two. The place his wife had died and al-Shirqat.

A green light over the door flashed and he disconnected his mask from the aircraft's oxygen supply, immediately reattaching it to a low-volume tank on his wingsuit. Slipping out of his chair, he sat on the carbon fiber floor and lashed a small pack between his legs. The countdown had started and he waited until the door began to retract to lower his goggles. The outside air temperature was thirty below zero and the wind lashed at him as he fought his way to the inky black opening. When the countdown in his earpiece reached zero, he threw himself out, struggling to maintain a stable position as he accelerated into his free fall.

After a few seconds he was steady enough to glance at the screen strapped to his wrist. Along with altitude, it indicated direction and horizontal distance to his drop zone. Not that hitting it exactly was all that critical—it was a more or less randomly chosen spot about a mile from the edge of the ISIS-controlled city. His old mentor Stan Hurley had beaten precision into him during jump training, though. Rapp could still picture the man standing in the middle of the landing circle, staring skyward.

If you don't kick me in my head, I'm going to kick the shit out of yours.

Who would have thought he'd miss the old cuss so much?

Everything below him was dark, creating a disorienting sensation of floating in space. Saddam Hussein's former officers were becoming increasingly prominent in ISIS leadership and with their rise came a commensurate improvement in discipline. They'd completely blacked out al-Shirqat in an effort to reduce the effectiveness of U.S. bombing runs. Worse, a few mobile SAM units were being moved around the battered streets. Their functionality was unknown, but the knowledge that they were there was enough to prompt him to jump from altitude and come in sideways.

He pulled his chute about a thousand feet above the ground, releasing the pack between his legs and letting it drop onto the lanyard connected to him. With a few deft pulls on the chute's toggles, he came down directly on top of the planned target—a sandy knoll that offered him the high ground.

Rapp gathered the chute quickly and pulled off his goggles and helmet. He lay still for almost two minutes, listening. When he was satisfied that his arrival had gone unnoticed, he stripped down to a grimy pair of jeans and T-shirt, then dragged his pack to him.

It didn't contain much more than a shoulder holster with a Glock and silencer, two extra mags, some dried meat, and a shovel to bury everything else. Once that was done, there was little that would identify him as anything more than a local Iraqi who had been caught in the desert after sunset.

Without the screen on his wrist, he was forced to use the stars for navigation. Fortunately, they were just as effective now as they had been when explorers first set out to discover the world. He followed a southerly course, rubbing at his face to remove any marks left by his goggles. Based on weeks of overhead surveillance, he didn't expect to run into any security forces as he entered the city, but there was nothing certain in this business.

When Rapp reached the bombed-out buildings at the edge of town, he dropped to his stomach again. The men he was there for were farther toward the interior and he mentally reviewed the path through the city laid out by the Agency's cartographers.

When he'd escaped al-Shirqat last time, he'd been posing as an American ISIS recruit. The former Iraqi general controlling the area had devised a plan to use dirty bombs to take out Saudi Arabia's oil-producing capacity, destabilizing the world economy and leaving the Saudis vulnerable to a takeover by Islamic radicals. Rapp had managed to stop the plot, but not without the help of the local resistance.

Now the identities of those men had been discovered and ISIS was closing in on them. Most of the people at Langley thought he was crazy to come back, arguing that the risks far outweighed the rewards. And they were probably right. With one exception, the five young men Rapp was there to extract weren't good fighters. None were much use at gathering intelligence, either. Mostly they sat around making long political speeches that the others then heartily agreed with. But when he'd needed them, they'd stepped up. Fuck if he wouldn't do the same.

Unfortunately, that decision had forced him to put a reluctant Joe Maslick in charge of the Rabat, Morocco, operation. In the end, it was probably a good thing. The op wasn't all that complicated and Maslick needed some command experience whether he liked it or not.

Rapp closed his eyes for a moment, acknowledging that he was just stalling. He'd hoped never to have to return to this place, going so far as to try to convince the military to mount a major assault to take back the city. Predictably, they'd pushed back. It wasn't that they didn't think they could do it. With U.S. support, the Iraqi army was strong enough now to recapture it. The problem was that the locals didn't really see the Iraqi army as much different than ISIS. Just another occupying force to fight an endless guerrilla war against. Welcome to the Middle East.

Rapp stood and moved forward, slipping between two buildings and navigating by the light of a full moon. This area of town had taken a lot of battle damage and was largely uninhabited now. He'd been through it once before but hadn't bothered to commit it to memory.

After about five minutes of generally southward travel, he came to a collapsed building with little more than the east wall surviving. It was one of the landmarks he'd identified from a photo at Langley and he turned left, cutting diagonally across a cratered square.

By the time he made it to the far side, he was certain he was being tracked. There was a natural rhythm to the debris dislodging from the structures around him and now it was off just enough to stand out. The footfalls were random and careful, but to the practiced ear they were unmistakable.

He kept his pace casual, climbing over a burned car to gain access to the alley behind it. When he was certain he was obscured from view, he sidestepped into a gap in the wall to his right.

Whoever was behind him was disciplined—Rapp

would give him that. It was a full two minutes before he was able to pick out an intermittent shadow inching toward his position. He dug a shard of concrete from around a piece of rebar and threw it, creating a nearly inaudible clatter twenty yards to the south.

The footsteps faltered for a moment. Rapp retrieved his Glock and waited, barely breathing. A few seconds passed before the silhouette reappeared. The man it belonged to was an inch taller than him and a good six inches wider at the shoulder. He had an assault rifle strapped across his chest and was moving in a manner that suggested he was more than just another ISIS dipshit.

Rapp remained motionless in the darkness where he'd taken refuge, watching the man approach. When he walked past, Rapp stepped out and pressed his gun to the back of his head.

The man didn't cry out or even speak, instead coming to a halt and raising his hands. Rapp moved slowly around him, brushing the barrel of his Glock through the man's hair until it came to rest against his forehead.

"I remember you being less sloppy," Rapp said in Arabic.

"And I remember you looking like the wrong end of a goat."

Rapp pulled the gun back and the big man embraced him.

"Hold your face to the sky, my friend. Let me see you."

Rapp raised his chin to catch the moonlight and the Iraqi gripped Rapp's beard, moving his face around to see better.

"It's miraculous what you Americans can do," he said sincerely.

In order to not be recognized on his prior operation in al-Shirqat, Rapp had been forced to let Joe Maslick beat his face into something resembling raw meat. That was the only face Gaffar had ever seen—the broken, bleeding, and swollen one Maslick had created.

"More surgeries than I care to remember."

"Yes, but still . . . it's incredible."

"How are the others?"

"They're managing, but they aren't soldiers. Fear is a good motivator, but this . . ." He waved a hand around him. "The cold, the boredom, the lack of food. It is hard."

"How long have you been hiding out here?"

"Two weeks."

Rapp nodded. Often it wasn't the terror and exhaustion of combat that beat people down. It was everything in between.

"Come," Gaffar said. "I'll take you to them."

What was left of this part of town appeared to be uninhabited and of no interest to ISIS forces, but still it made sense to proceed carefully. They finally arrived at a massive concrete slab that had tipped against a crumbling wall. Gaffar picked up a rock and tapped it three times against what had once been a lamppost. A moment later the people Rapp had come for appeared at the entrance of the artificial cave.

On the left were two thin men who looked like computer geeks. One seemed to have lost his glasses and was squinting uselessly into the darkness. Mohammed, their leader, didn't seem too much worse for the wear and neither did his brother.

The Iraqi siblings were the only two men in the world that Rapp had a hard time looking in the eye, so he adjusted his gaze to the woman pressed against Mohammed's side.

"Who's she?"

"My wife."

"You got married?" Rapp said. "Interesting sense of timing."

"Shada was being auctioned off by ISIS. I've known her since we were children. I sold everything I had and used the money to buy her."

Rapp looked into her dark eyes, taking in the un-lined face and black, tangled hair. He had purchased Mohammed's sister under similar circumstances. This girl was younger and more fearful, but otherwise no different than Laleh had been.

The memory was accompanied by a painful con-striction in Rapp's chest and he pushed her image from his mind. It would come back, though. It always did.

"If there isn't room for me, I'll stay behind," she said as the silence drew out.

"No," one of the geeks said, a little too loudly. "If anyone is going to stay here, it should be him. He got us into this."

"Shut up!" Gaffar said in a harsh whisper. "We got ourselves into this. It's our country to fight for. Our people who have destroyed it. Not his."

He raised his hand to strike the man, but Rapp caught it.

"Look, all you have to do is hold it together for a little longer. Then this'll all be over."

He retrieved the food he'd brought and divided it among them. "Now eat up and gather your gear."

"Then she can come?" Mohammed said.

Rapp nodded. "Five minutes."

CHAPTER 2

JOE Maslick looked through the dirty windshield at the neighborhood around him. It was better lit than he would have expected but there were still plenty of shadowy corners to park in. At six foot one and 220 pounds, his ability to blend into this part of the world—hell, any part of the world—was crap.

Reason number forty-eight that he shouldn't be here.

Fortunately, it was late, and human activity was at a minimum. That wouldn't last forever, though. Before he knew it, early risers would start searching for their morning coffee, kids would begin the march to school, and vendors would begin positioning themselves to pick off the customers who preferred not to shop in the full heat of the day. Someone from that last group would undoubtedly bang on his window and ask him to move his car. But he wouldn't really know for sure, because he didn't speak Arabic.

Reason number forty-nine.

"Mas?" Bruno McGraw's voice over his earpiece. "You copy?"

"Go ahead."

"We've got a car bearing down on your position. Kinda unusual. Makes me think it might be our guy."

"Unusual how?"

"Shiny new Mercedes S-Class. Two men in front, one in back."

"So now terrorists are driving hundred-thousand-dollar cars?" he cracked to cover his nervousness. "Maybe we're fighting for the wrong side."

This whole op was fucked. His commander, Scott Coleman, was still recovering from almost being killed in Pakistan, and Rapp was off screwing around in Iraq. That left him squinting into the glare of the misplaced confidence of everyone from the director of the CIA on down.

"Might be a false alarm, but he's coming up on the Bani Street turn," McGraw said. "We'll see if he takes it."

Maslick had never wanted to be in charge of anything. When he'd joined Army Delta, he'd decided the way to live a happy life was to pick good leaders and do what they said. It's why he'd followed Coleman into the private sector and spent most of his career backing up Mitch Rapp. They did the thinking, he did the shooting. It was the fucking natural order of things.

"Yup. He's turning. Game on."

Maslick checked his fuel gauge. An eighth of an inch past full, just like it had been five minutes ago. He'd become obsessed with blowing this operation over something stupid and having to tell Rapp that he'd forgotten to charge his phone, or run out of gas, or brought the wrong map. It had gotten so bad that it was starting to interfere with his ability to think straight.

"Did you get any pictures?" he asked.

"Of the car, but nothing decent of the people inside. Too much reflection off the glass."

"Copy that," Maslick said, trying to calm down. This was a simple job, which was why it was given to him. A few months ago Rapp had gotten his hands on a rising ISIS star from Crimea. Hayk Alghani had been a con artist his whole life, spending most of his time in and out of jail or on the run. After one of his banking scams had gone bad, he'd run to Sevastopol and holed up in a tenement run by local gangsters. The European authorities got wind of it, though, and in a panic he'd bought a copy of *Islam for Dummies* and hightailed it to Syria. His history of financial and Internet scams had made him an instant hit and he'd moved up quickly. Unfortunately for him, so quickly that he'd attracted the attention of the CIA.

Rapp had snatched him outside of Berlin and he'd cracked after the first face slap—giving up everything he'd ever done and pledging his undying loyalty to America. Now he was in a run-down apartment less than a mile from where Maslick was parked, waiting for one of ISIS's top money couriers. A man known only as the Egyptian.

All Maslick had to do was stuff the Egyptian into his trunk and get him to an Agency black site in one piece. By all reports, the man always worked alone, was getting up there in years, and never carried a weapon. Ops didn't get much easier than that.

Now, though, they were looking at a guy in an S-Class with what sounded like bodyguards. Pretty much the fucking *opposite* of easy.

Headlights appeared at the end of the empty street

and began to approach. Maslick ducked down in the cramped seat, waiting for the vehicle to pass before rising again. Definitely a late-model S-Class. Even worse, it was riding a little too low on its shocks. Armor.

The brake lights came on and it eased left, disappearing from his line of sight.

"Wick," Maslick said into his throat mike. "They're coming your way."

"Roger that. I'm in position."

Wicker's vantage point was from the top of a building across from the one where the meeting was scheduled to take place. While Wick was undoubtedly one of the best snipers on the planet, his job at this point was just to observe. The goal was to capture and interrogate this asshole, not to kill him.

Maslick waited, noting that his heart rate was higher than it normally would be during a firefight. He didn't know shit about logistics, and while this op would have been a cakewalk for Coleman or Rapp, it had too many moving parts for him to keep track of. Instead of one target, there were three. Instead of a conventional vehicle, there was an armored Mercedes. Was it possible that these sons of bitches had backup? Maybe Wick wasn't the only shooter on high ground right now in Rabat.

Maslick was starting to sweat so badly it was going to be hard to hold a gun, something that had never happened to him before. Not in Afghanistan. Not in Iraq. Not even in that disaster in Pakistan.

Reason number fifty he shouldn't be running this op. Or was that fifty-one?

"The target's stopped," Wicker said. "One man getting out of the back. Doesn't look Egyptian to me. Full

Saudi getup—ten-thousand-dollar suit and a table-cloth on his head."

Maslick swore under his breath.

"I didn't copy that, Mas. Say again."

"Did you get a picture?"

"Yeah. Not perfect, but probably good enough for the cover of *Terrorist Prick* magazine."

Maslick slammed a hand against the steering wheel and then wiped at the sweat running down his forehead. Everything he'd been told by the analysts was now officially complete bullshit. This had just gone from a by-the-numbers rendition to an on-the-fly improvisation.

"Send it to Langley. See if we can get anything off facial recognition."

CHAPTER 3

RAPP glanced at the glowing hands of his battered Timex watch and then behind him into the darkness. While he couldn't see much, he could hear plenty. Dawn was bearing down on them and they were moving at half his worst-case pace with twice his worst-case noise. The plan was to be well into the open desert by sunrise. Clearly, that wasn't going to happen. Time to come up with a plan B.

Gaffar slipped around a fallen column and Rapp followed his bulky outline as it approached.

"I told you to stay in the back and sweep," he said when the Iraqi came alongside.

"I understand, but this isn't going well, Mitch. Ali is struggling and Yusef says he twisted his ankle. It's going to slow our progress further."

That seemed impossible. There were people in nursing homes who could have made it to the edge of town by now.

"How far into the desert do we need to travel, Mitch?"

"About fifteen kilometers. It wasn't hard for me to

drop close to town, but bringing a chopper in is too risky. There are too many patrols."

The rest of their people started trickling in after an excruciatingly long five minutes. The woman whose name he couldn't remember was first, keeping a reasonable pace. Not surprising. If anyone was motivated to get the hell out of al-Shirqat, it would be her. The perfunctory decapitation or firing squad ISIS would use to deal with the rest of them was downright humane compared with what they did to women.

"Tell me your name again," Rapp said quietly to her.

"Shada."

"Where's your husband, Shada?"

"Helping Yusef."

It took four more minutes for the rest of them to gather. Yusef was limping badly with an arm looped over Mohammed's shoulder for support. Rapp was accustomed to working with soldiers who would go to extraordinary and sometimes even counterproductive lengths to hide fatigue and weakness. Yusef, in contrast, seemed to be milking it.

The temptation to grab him by the hair and have a serious heart-to-heart about their current situation was overwhelming, but it would just make things worse. These were young civilians who had spent the last few weeks living out in the elements and the last few years living in hell. They were running on fumes, and when those fumes were exhausted, they wouldn't be able to switch over to determination or pride or loyalty to keep them going. They'd drop.

Rapp sank to one knee and motioned for the others to gather around him. "Change of plans. Trying to walk out of town and across fifteen kilometers of desert isn't going to happen. We're going to have to get a vehicle."

Quiet murmurs rose up. Predictably, most seemed enthusiastic about the idea.

"Don't get too excited," Rapp said. "We were going to slip out of town without getting anywhere near an ISIS patrol. Now we're going to have to go looking for one."

"Perhaps the rest of us should stay here," Yusef offered. "You could get a vehicle and come back to pick us up."

Gaffar reached out and slapped the young man hard in the back of the head. "Does he look like a bus driver to you?"

Rapp motioned for calm. "Because of all the debris, getting a truck back here isn't going to be possible. And even if it was, it would attract too much attention. We go together and we get out of here together. Understand?"

More murmurs. Less enthusiastic this time.

"Gaffar, what's our best bet for picking up a patrol?"

"If we go north about a kilometer, we'll get to the edge of the territory that's regularly patrolled. And it puts us in a good position to escape the city without being seen."

"Then lead us out. I'll take over at the rear."

Shada followed on Gaffar's heels, with the others respecting the intervals that Rapp had insisted on. Yusef, still leaning heavily on Mohammed, was the last to set out. Rapp paced them at a distance of thirty feet.

He kept an eye on his six, but the danger of being flanked was pretty minimal. His position at the end of the column was intended primarily as motivation and it seemed to be working. Every minute or so Yusef glanced back and each time his pace surged.

The buildings around them remained dark but were becoming less and less dilapidated. The rubble that made stealthy movement so difficult gave way to smooth dirt, and empty window frames evolved into ones protected by shutters and glass.

Rapp heard a gentle crack above and he swung his Glock in the direction of the sound. Sighting over the silencer, he spotted the outline of a cat leaping between a series of open rafters. Otherwise, everything was silent. ISIS had instituted curfew and blackout protocols, and the local population wasn't inclined to defy either.

There was a vague glow becoming visible to the north and he stopped, turning his head to try to pick it up in his more light-sensitive peripheral vision. It turned out to be unnecessary. The sound of a car engine began to emerge from the same direction.

Rapp accelerated to a jog, passing the others on his way to the front of their ragtag column. As expected, Gaffar had stopped, taking cover behind a shattered fountain.

"It's one street to the east," he said, as Rapp knelt and motioned for the others to hold their positions.

"Seems like they'll go for the edge of town and then double back on the street in front of us."

"That would be my guess, too."

"Then this is as good a place as any," Rapp said. "If the opposition looks manageable, we stop them here."

"And how do you define 'manageable'?"

Rapp examined the road and the buildings on either side. There wasn't much they could use to their advantage. Only surprise and the fact that the ISIS men would be unaccustomed to resistance from the locals.

"I assume you don't have a silencer."

"No. A revolver with five rounds. And a knife."

"In that case, anything over eight men will be risky."

"Eight? Are you sure?"

"You think we can handle more?"

"I was thinking less."

"Don't turn nervous on me, now, Gaffar. We'll flag them down and I'll go out there and try to make a few friends, get them to lower their guard. If you use my Glock, they're not going to hear much and they won't react right away. I—"

"No," Gaffar said firmly. "We both know this is a terrible plan. I will go. Your accent is not from this region and you're far more accurate than I am. Besides—and I mean no offense—you are not a man of great warmth. I, on the other hand, am loved by all."

"Is that right? I didn't know that about you."

"Ask anyone," he deadpanned as the hum of the ISIS patrol truck reemerged. "I have a very fine personality."

"Then let's put it to use," Rapp agreed. It was undoubtedly the better strategy, but his knee-jerk reaction was always to take on the most dangerous part of an op.

"Mohammed is armed also," Gaffar said. "Should we solicit his help?"

"Not a problem for me, but do you really want him shooting in your direction?"

"I suppose not."

Illumination from a single headlight began reflecting dimly off the buildings to their right, and Gaffar took a deep breath. It shook slightly when he let it out.

"You all right?"

"Of course."

He'd been Iraqi regular army, trained by the Americans, and was solid in every way. But strolling into a group of heavily armed ISIS psychopaths would be enough to shake anyone.

Rapp dug around in his jacket and pulled out a pack of Marlboros. He held them out along with a pack of matches.

Gaffar grinned. "You are truly a gift from God. May Allah smile on you."

"And you."

With that, the big man walked into the middle of the street and held up a hand in greeting, squinting into the glare of the truck bearing down on him. It began to brake and Gaffar watched with calculated boredom, cupping a hand around a lit match and bringing it to the cigarette in his mouth.

The pickup skidded to a stop about twenty feet in front of him and the men in the back jumped out. All were shouting and all had AKs aimed in Gaffar's direction.

The men in the cab were slower to abandon the vehicle, but when they did, Rapp was able to get an accurate head count. Seven. They were on.

"What are you doing out here?" the driver demanded. "It's curfew."

Gaffar tossed the match casually on the ground before taking a long drag on his cigarette. "General Masri sent me. We had intelligence that Mohammed

Qarni and his band were hiding out in the abandoned part of the city. I don't think it's true, though. I was able to find no trace of them."

He started forward, ignoring the weapons trained on him, and shook a cigarette out of the pack for the driver. He accepted and Gaffar lit a match.

"They may have fled the city," he continued. "If so, I suspect the desert will do my job for me."

He held the pack out and the men around him approached hesitantly. Rapp watched carefully over his suppressor, taking in how each of them moved, how they handled their weapons, their level of alertness. By the time they all had lit their cigarettes, he'd designated each one with a priority. Of course, the unpredictability of battle would inevitably throw a wrench into his order, but it made sense to go in with some guidelines.

Gaffar was playing it beautifully. Apparently he was serious about being likable. The conversation was flowing nicely, punctuated every few seconds with laughter. Rapp couldn't make out individual words anymore, but that was by design. Gaffar was speaking quietly enough to force the men to gather in close. A nice tight grouping, but one that was going to put him in the line of fire.

Rapp waited for another burst of laughter and fired two shots in quick succession. He abandoned his normal head shot—too obvious and messy—instead going for center of mass. He'd threaded the first rounds through the men with their backs to him and hit ones on the other side. The third shot was complicated by Gaffar's position in the group and took longer to line up than he would have liked. The two men he'd shot had nearly hit the ground when he finally squeezed the trigger and struck a man just below where his assault rifle was hanging across his torso.

The driver shouted a warning and Gaffar picked up on what was happening without missing a beat. He screamed something about Mohammed and his gang and pulled his weapon, firing in the wrong direction to reinforce the illusion of a shooter to the south.

They all followed suit, opening up on the windows of the building across the street. Chunks of wood, vaporized concrete, and shattered glass rained down as Rapp lined up on the back of the driver. A quick squeeze of the trigger dropped him. Leadership gone. Next he turned his weapon on a man from the back of the truck who had seemed unusually wary and athletic.

Gaffar suddenly jerked and went down hard. It was violent enough to make Rapp hesitate for a moment, concerned that there was a shooter unaccounted for. He quickly realized it was just for show. Gaffar was now on his back behind the three surviving men.

Rapp returned to his target and dropped the man just as one companion lost the back of his head to a round fired by Gaffar. The last man standing suddenly stopped shooting and looked around him, confused. A moment later Rapp put a bullet into his right temple.

Then everything went silent again.

Rapp motioned to the others before running into the street to gather weapons. "Are you injured?"

"I'm fine," Gaffar said, getting up and dusting himself off.

Rapp tossed him an AK before dumping the other guns into the bed of the pickup. By then Shada was behind him and he helped her over the gate. Gaffar jumped in next to her and began pulling the others over the side. Mohammed helped Yusef in before running for the passenger door of the cab.

By the time Rapp began accelerating up the road, Gaffar had the people in back holding their weapons in a way that would make them look enough like an ISIS patrol to fool the casual observer.

"There," Mohammed said, pointing through the windshield. "Turn left and swing around. We'll have a straight path out of the city."

Rapp did as he suggested but didn't otherwise acknowledge him. With a little luck, they would be on a chopper in an hour and he would never lay eyes on Mohammed Qarni again.

CHAPTER 4

HAYK Alghani stood at the edge of the window, looking down on the winding souk below. He'd seen the flash of headlights a few moments ago, but now they'd gone dark. The suddenness of it suggested not a passing vehicle but one that had stopped.

The dizziness he felt began to intensify, causing his stomach to churn nauseatingly. He gagged and was forced to run for the bathroom. Pulling open the cracked toilet lid, he vomited into its stained bowl. Not much longer, he told himself. Soon it would all be over.

Or would it?

There was no question that he had done this to himself, but it seemed like another life now. The arrogant young man who had fled authorities in Sevastopol to join ISIS no longer existed inside him. And perhaps never had.

As always in his life, his current problems had begun with a woman. She was beautiful and impassioned— a devout Muslim who thought about nothing but God and the struggle. Despite having abandoned Islam after leaving home as a teenager, he became infatuated with her unquestioning faith and unwavering sense of purpose. It was she who convinced him to flee into the welcoming arms of jihad. To give up his life of petty crime in favor of a far grander purpose: the creation of a new caliphate.

After a rushed marriage, they used contacts she'd made on the Internet to cross into Syria and then they were taken overland by ISIS representatives. To where, neither of them knew, but it didn't matter. They were out of the European authorities' reach and he was under the seductive spell of her beauty and her world of radical Islam. Wherever they ended up, they would fight for God against the evils of the West.

It was a simple matter to pinpoint the moment it had all gone wrong. They had been traveling for days, dodging Assad's death squads, Russian planes, and American drones. Sleep had consisted of fleeting moments in bombed-out ruins or caves. Finally, they arrived in an ISIS outpost beyond the infidels' reach. Mira went with a group of women to bathe. There she would have taken off her chador and been seen by them.

Later that day, he and Mira were separated from the rest of the recruits and put in a sweltering SUV that headed west across the desert. He started to become nervous when the driver refused to answer questions, but not Mira. Her certainty was unshakable. She believed that they had been chosen for some special purpose. That her destiny was to change the course of history.

When they were granted a personal audience with Mullah Sayid Halabi, she became even more ecstatic. To be brought before the man who was so loved by

Allah. Who struck such terror into the hearts of the Americans. It was an honor that even she had never considered. He remembered her pledging her endless devotion and the amusement in the pale blue eyes that Halabi had been gifted by ancient invaders of his homeland.

Her eyes had been very different. Dark and filled with the glory of God. That quickly turned to horror when she was informed that her role in the struggle would be as a member of Mullah Halabi's harem. Alghani could still hear her pleading with him to save her as she was dragged from the room. But there was nothing he could do.

Once she was gone, he'd found himself standing alone before the ISIS leader. The amusement was gone from his eyes. They now seemed dead. Like water pooled in the empty sockets of a skull.

He had quickly pledged his own emphatic allegiance to the mullah and expressed how proud he was to provide his young wife to the cause. When Halabi's men began to close in from behind, Alghani desperately tried to find something that would make those eyes come alive again. He finally struck on it when he mentioned his great skill in financial crimes. The subtle change in the mullah's expression made him speak even faster, boasting about his expertise in fraud, laundering, and concealing bank transactions from authorities. A motion from the mullah's hand stopped the advance of his men and changed Alghani's life forever.

He had spent more than a year in the service of Halabi, setting up financial networks and collecting money from sympathizers around the world, but particularly from Saudi Arabia. It was a squalid but bearable life right up until his existence came to the attention of the CIA.

Three months ago he'd been running a routine errand in Berlin's financial district when two men jumped him and pulled him into a van. He awoke naked on a concrete floor, with zip ties securing his hands and feet. There was no light and no sense of time. He shouted to his captors but got no answer. He pleaded. He begged. He even prayed. Finally, the cold, hunger, and isolation eclipsed his fear of the mullah and he offered anything—everything—for a brief moment of human contact.

It was then that he had met Mitch Rapp. The American had the same dead expression as Halabi and the same capacity for violence, but the similarities ended there. Where the ISIS leader was volatile, unpredictable, and cared for nothing but his own perceived stature in the eyes of his god, Rapp was infinitely rational. He knew his enemies and what was necessary to defeat them. The question was whether Alghani could assist him in his efforts or whether he would be more useful with a bullet in his head.

Without Mira, he had once again lost his faith. In the end, he was just a criminal. A self-serving little man who cared nothing for Islam or the caliphate. He just wanted to survive.

Rapp had given him that opportunity. After telling the CIA everything, he was returned to ISIS with orders to provide regular reports on the work he did for them. When he informed the Agency of the Rabat meeting, Rapp decided he wanted the courier. And in exchange, Alghani would be given his freedom.

There was a quiet knock on the front door and Alghani rinsed his mouth out before striding across the empty flat. He had barely turned the knob when a powerful man in a dark suit forced his way in. He moved quickly through the apartment, searching for anything amiss. Finally, he shoved Alghani against a wall and frisked him. The only thing he had was a phone and the man took it, removing the battery before dropping it on the floor. Satisfied that the flat was secure, he retreated to a corner and spoke into a microphone attached to his wrist.

A moment later another man entered. He was thin but had a belly that protruded over a belt that looked like it cost more than most people made in a year. Alghani took an involuntary step back and a satisfied smile curled the man's lips. Who were they? He was supposed to meet a lone courier. An Egyptian in his fifties who knew more about the individuals involved in financing ISIS than anyone but Mullah Halabi himself. Had the CIA betrayed him? Had the Mullah discovered his treachery? Were these men here to kill him?

Alghani took another step back, but then noticed the suitcase in the man's hand. Having had significant experience with these kinds of exchanges, he knew that it was the correct size to hold the amount of cash that was to change hands that day. One million U.S. dollars.

"You have the money?" Alghani asked, hoping to gain some understanding of his situation.

"Of course," the man said. "But I'm sorry that Mullah Halabi couldn't come personally. He and I have much to discuss. The creation of the caliphate and the spread of the one true religion is no small task. And the Western powers are no small opponent."

Alghani nodded submissively. He'd initially thought that the man was a wealthy Saudi businessman but he could now see that he was wrong. The regal posture, the comically exaggerated sense of self-importance, the recklessness of cutting out the Egyptian and handling this errand personally. A young prince.

Alghani had dealt with them many times, both in his current capacity and previously when he'd targeted them in a number of real estate scams. As near as he could tell, they were all the same. Useless, arrogant, stupid men who believed that their privileged birth put them above the rest of humanity. Qualities that made them attractive targets for graft and utterly blind to the fact that they would be the first to die in a caliphate led by Sayid Halabi.

In this instance, though, the royal's presence created an impossibly dangerous situation. He had promised Rapp the Egyptian courier. Not a pampered child. Would the CIA man think he had been duped? Would he revoke his promise of freedom in favor of a summary execution?

The man held out the suitcase. "A gift from me to your leader. The first step in drawing the Americans into a fight that they can never win."

Alghani accepted the case and confirmed its weight at around ten kilograms. He expected the young Saudi to turn and disappear from his life forever, but instead the idiot began to speak again.

"We'll battle the American cowards from without while simultaneously destroying them from within. I know them well. I was educated in the West and have many business interests in the United States. The American people are weak and easily manipulated. They see things in terms of five years. Perhaps ten. We understand that those time frames are meaningless. Allah is eternal and favors the patient. We will defeat them over the next fifty years. Or a hundred. Or even a thousand. As their society crumbles under the weight of its own wickedness and lack of cohesion, we will rise up to take their place."

"Praise be to Allah," Alghani responded, trying to comprehend why this pup wouldn't leave. What profit could there be in staying? Surely there were safer places that he could listen to himself talk.

"As I say, I know the Americans," he continued. "Better than they know themselves. I would like to offer my services to the mullah. If he wants to destroy the Westerners, he must first understand them. His background . . ." The Saudi's voice faded for a moment. ". . . would make that kind of understanding difficult."

Alghani had to struggle not to react. Halabi had been educated in madrassas likely financed by this man's own family. While the mullah indeed lacked direct experience with the West, he had retaken enormous amounts of territory lost by his predecessor and created a complex command and control structure that the world was only now beginning to understand. What had the pampered man-child standing in front of him ever accomplished? His only responsibility was to cash the checks provided to him and to try not to lose it all in Europe's casinos.

"I will pass on your generous offer to the mullah when I see him. I'm sure he would greatly value your counsel."

Like others of his kind, the man was easily flat-
tered. He smiled condescendingly and motioned to
his bodyguard. A moment later they were finally gone.

Alghani opened the briefcase and emptied the
bundles of American dollars on the floor before retrieving his phone and replacing the battery. He stood
by the window, peering out and trying to slow his
breathing. A few moments later he saw headlights
flash on and move away. When the darkness and silence had descended again, he made a move for the
door but stopped with his hand on the knob.

What should he do? Call Rapp's people and tell
them that the man he'd met with wasn't the one they'd
expected? Or should he just run? What would give
him the best chance of disappearing forever from the
gaze of Sayid Halabi and, even more important, from
the gaze of Mitch Rapp?

CHAPTER 5

R EPEAT that," Rapp said into his throat mike. "I lost you."

No response.

Despite having to deviate from the initial plan and take the truck, the operation was going pretty smoothly. Mohammed's lifelong familiarity with the area had gotten them on the road out of town without being seen and with no wrong turns. Al-Shirqat was five miles in Rapp's rearview mirror and he was estimating that they'd arrive at the LZ in another six. The road surface was better than his intel had suggested and the bottomed-out pickup was negotiating it with no significant problems. Its maximum speed wasn't much over thirty, but the wheels hadn't fallen off and all the gauges looked good.

"Marcus! Come in!"

"Hold . . ." came the static-ridden reply. "Trying to fix . . ."

Marcus Dumond was a computer hacker who would have been in prison if it weren't for Rapp intervening and giving him a job. Over the past couple of years he'd become increasingly involved in these kinds of operations and had proved his worth many times over. In a way, he was a victim of his success. He despised being involved in life-or-death situations and knew precisely nothing about military tactics. His grasp of technology, though, was second to none.

"Penetrating the army's jamming is a pain in my ass!" he said when he came back on the comm. The military was doing everything it could to keep electronic communications down in ISIS-held territory, and Dumond had set up a narrow encrypted band to cut through. Unfortunately, its effectiveness was spotty.

"I've got you back," Rapp said, slamming into a deep rut that the feeble headlight hadn't picked up. He glanced back to confirm the people riding in the bed hadn't been thrown out. Gaffar anticipated his concern and gave a few encouraging slaps on top of the cab.

"The good news is that the chopper's on schedule," Dumond said.

"And the bad news?"

"You've got a patrol coming at you from the north. Same road."

"How far out?"

"Call it two miles. You should be seeing their lights pretty soon."

"Any detours I can take?"

"None. Can you just go off road a hundred yards? They'll drive right by."

"We'd be lucky to make it ten feet before we bog down."

"They probably won't do any better, then. Go as

far as you can and then move fast to the LZ on foot. They'll probably see your truck and come after you, but, traveling as the crow flies, you'd just have to stay ahead of them for about four miles. Mostly flat terrain with a few moderately rocky sections."

An easy task if he'd been with Coleman's team, but this crew would get chased down inside of five minutes.

"Not a chance."

"Then I'm out of ideas, Mitch. I can tell you this, though: if you keep on like you are, you're going to run right into them."

Rapp swore under his breath. "What's happening in town?"

"I've got the drone over top of you, so my view isn't as good. They've definitely found the mess you made and have patrols converging on the area. One vehicle seems to be tracking your path out of the city somehow, but too slow to be a problem for you."

Not necessarily true, Rapp knew. While the U.S. had been successful at shutting down cell and satellite communication in the area, they hadn't been able to do much about short-range radio. It was possible that the patrol ahead of them knew what was happening in town and was looking for them.

"Understood. Stand by."

Rapp looked over at Mohammed and switched to Arabic. "We've got a patrol coming in our direction."

"A patrol?" he said, twisting in his seat. "What do you mean? There are no turns off this road. They—"

"Calm down. We're going to be fine. You're probably going to have to take over driving, though. Just stay on the road and follow the directions I gave you to the LZ."

"I don't understand." His words came out in a barely comprehensible jumble. "Why would I have to drive? What are you going to do? Where will you be?"

Rapp ignored him, instead banging a fist on the window behind him. A moment later Gaffar leaned around and stuck his bearded face in the open driver's-side window.

"Do we have a problem, Mitch?"

"Maybe. Maybe not. There's a patrol coming down on us. Tell everyone to look friendly."

He nodded and pulled back into the bed to get his people in line.

"Mitch . . ." Mohammed started.

"Not now," Rapp responded. A slight glow was becoming visible in the distance, but it wasn't the approaching patrol that made him grip the wheel tighter. It was Mohammed's face in his peripheral vision.

"I need to ask you a question."

Rapp remained silent, hoping that the young Iraqi would lose his train of thought as the threat of the men coming at them increased. Not surprisingly, the opposite was the case. Mohammed didn't want to leave this world without knowing how his sister had died.

"What happened to Laleh, Mitch? General Mustafa was stabbed to death and we found her body lying next to his with a gunshot wound to the chest. You were there, weren't you? When she was killed?"

Again Rapp didn't answer. The oncoming patrol vehicle wasn't going to save him, though. It seemed to be moving in slow motion.

"She had a knife," he said finally. "I didn't see it. She attacked Mustafa."

Mohammed nodded, a vengeful smile just barely

visible in the glow of the gauges. "My brother thought it was you who had killed that pig. But I knew. Laleh was the strongest of us. Ever since we were children."

Rapp pressed harder on the accelerator, but the truck wouldn't respond. Even downhill, thirty-five miles an hour was all it would give him.

The silence between them lasted only a few seconds before Mohammed broke it. "So one of General Mustafa's guards shot her?"

Rapp knew he could lie. No one would ever know. He was the only living witness to what had happened.

"Mitch?"

"It wasn't one of the guards." He'd known this conversation was inevitable when he'd come back for Mohammed and his people. And he'd made his decision about what to say long before he'd set out for Iraq. Laleh deserved to have her story known. Her real story.

"Who then?"

"I shot her. The general was bleeding out on the floor. His guards were going to take her."

He wasn't sure how Mohammed would react but was surprised when he just sank a little deeper in his seat.

Where the fuck was that patrol? Anything would be better than having to sit here and talk about Laleh. He was just starting to be able to sleep through the night without her memory jerking him awake.

"I know what ISIS does to women who defy them," Mohammed said finally. "Like you, I've witnessed it personally. And I've seen what's left of their bodies after."

He put a hand on Rapp's shoulder. "Me and my

brother are the only people left from my family. And on behalf of both of us, I want to thank you for having the courage to do what had to be done. I know how hard it would be for an American. Even one like you."

A set of headlights appeared from over a rise in front of them and Rapp tried to determine whether the road's shoulder was solid enough to divert onto if the oncoming patrol tried to block them. Not a chance. The sand had drifted into a soft ridge alongside the roadbed and ahead it grew into a low cliff.

"What are we going to do?" Mohammed asked.

"Nothing. For now, just sit there."

The intensity of the headlights grew until Rapp had to pull down the visor in an effort to protect what night vision he had. He eased as far right as he could and hovered a foot over the brake in case the patrol turned sideways in the road. At one hundred yards it became clear that the vehicle was similar to their own—a small pickup with two men in the cab and more standing in the bed. Unless the driver was an idiot, he would resist the urge to do anything sudden out of fear of throwing his men into the road.

At fifty yards Mohammed reached for the pistol in his waistband. "Are you sure we shouldn't—"

"Don't do *anything*."

He heard Gaffar shout a greeting that wasn't returned. The men in the truck just stared at them as they passed. Rapp drifted back to the center of the road, focused on the rearview mirror. Twenty-five yards. Fifty . . .

Suddenly the men in the bed of the ISIS truck crouched to steady themselves.

"Shit . . ."

"What?" Mohammed twisted around in time to see the truck skid ninety degrees to a stop.

Rapp shoved the accelerator to the floor without much effect as the truck behind them struggled to turn around without getting bogged down.

"Take the wheel," he said, throwing open the door and stepping onto the running board. He found Gaffar already in motion, gathering mags from the terrified people around him.

"All right, listen to me," Rapp said to Mohammed as the man slid into the driver's seat. "We're going to start up the hill and when we circle behind that cliff, you're going to slow down enough for me and Gaffar to jump. Use the parking brake—we don't want the brake lights to go on. Do you understand?"

He gave a jerky nod, keeping his hands locked around the wheel at two and ten o'clock. Rapp swung into the bed and accepted an assault rifle along with three magazines.

"What's the plan?" Gaffar shouted over the wind.

"We're getting out. You take the high ground to the east of the road. I'll set up in the sand to the west. You shoot first—drive them to me."

Gaffar nodded.

The patrol vehicle finally managed to turn around and its engine was audible as the driver pushed it to the limit. Unlike the little service vehicle they were stuck in, the one chasing them was a late-model Toyota Tacoma. By the time Mohammed got them around the cliff and started to slow, the patrol truck had already cut the distance between them in half.

Velocity was hard to judge in the dark, monochromatic landscape, so Rapp looked through the back window, waiting for the speedometer to reach fifteen miles an hour. When it did, he threw his AK over the side and jumped out after it, clearing the road and landing in the softer sand at its edge. Gaffar, heavier and less athletic, came up short and hit harder, rolling across the road surface before coming to a stop.

Rapp scooped up both weapons and ran to him.

"You alive?"

"I'm fine," he said, rising unsteadily.

Rapp grabbed the man's hands and jerked back on them. Gaffar managed to resist and maintain his balance without too much difficulty. He was just shaken up. No damage done.

Rapp handed over one of the weapons. There wasn't much time. The approaching engine was getting louder.

The Iraqi ran toward the cliff at the edge of the road while Rapp retreated into the desert on the other side. He glanced back and saw Gaffar scrambling to high ground, looking solid and making decent time. The glare of headlights was growing in intensity, increasing the sense of urgency but also allowing Rapp to move more quickly over the uneven ground. He crested a small sand drift and dropped to his stomach on the other side.

Aiming into the oncoming headlights wouldn't be optimal, but Gaffar didn't have to be all that precise. He just needed to put the fear of God into these pricks.

The truck rounded the corner fast enough to lift onto two wheels. It had barely managed to straighten out when Gaffar opened up on the windshield. Unfortunately, the men in back were well braced and the truck didn't roll. Instead it just lost power and slowed as the driver slumped against the steering wheel. The men in the bed leapt out as the vehicle began to grind against the cliff. There were eight of them and all looked uninjured. By contrast, both men in the cab appeared to be either dead or incapacitated.

Four went for the cliff, taking cover directly below Gaffar, where they would be invisible to him. The others were running directly at Rapp. Gaffar took one out when he was still fifteen yards away, but it was a lucky shot. The truck's headlights had been damaged by its impact with the cliff and Gaffar wasn't going to be able to reliably hit crouched, running men in the moonlight.

Rapp's earpiece crackled to life, but this time it wasn't Marcus Dumond. The voice belonged to Fred Mason, his go-to chopper pilot on operations like these. "Mitch, I'm inbound and I'm seeing a lot of commotion to the southwest. Are you kicking up dust over there?"

"That's an affirmative."

"You need help?"

The three remaining men had closed to within ten feet and Rapp fired, sweeping across them. Two dropped immediately, but one made it a few more steps, before falling into the sand right in front of Rapp.

"No. Continue on your heading. Your cargo should be arriving at the LZ in about fifteen."

"What about you?"

"We'll play that by ear."

The men huddled at the base of the cliff had seen the flashes of his rifle and began pummeling the dune Rapp was ensconced behind. The body in front of him jerked with bullet impacts and Rapp slithered back a few feet before starting to crawl south. After a few seconds, the guns went silent. The terrorists would have no way to confirm a kill and would want to conserve their ammunition. After covering fifty yards, Rapp slung the rifle across his back and darted across the road. The scramble up the cliff took longer than it should have, but he had to remain silent. Not because of the assholes behind the truck, though. Because of Gaffar. They had no way to communicate and he was going to be looking for anyone coming up behind him.

Rapp swung well into the desert before cutting back. Moving slowly and focusing on every footfall, it took another three minutes before he spotted Gaffar lying at the edge of the cliff. Rapp came up directly from behind and put a hand on the man's back.

He jerked and started to spin, but Rapp held him to the ground. "Relax. It's me."

The Arab let out a long, wavering breath as Rapp dropped next to him. "Don't ever do that again."

"They're not moving?"

"No. They seem suspiciously comfortable where they are. I think we can assume that they've called for help."

Rapp nodded in the darkness. "How fast are you on foot?"

"Middle of my graduating class in the army."

So not very fast.

Rapp activated his throat mike. "Marcus, you copy?"

"Yeah, I'm here."

"Have you got a bead on us?"

"You're kind of hard to miss."

"Do we have incoming?"

"Four trucks. All full. ETA to your position is probably ten minutes."

"Can you reliably track a man in the desert?"

"With thermal. Sure."

"Okay, I'm handing my radio over to Gaffar. You're going to have to give him instructions on how to get to the LZ from here. He doesn't speak English, though, so call down for a translator."

"Okay, Mitch. No problem."

"Fred," Rapp said. "Are you copying this?"

"Affirmative."

"Give me a sitrep."

"I have eyes on your people and I'm getting ready to land."

"Pick them up and get back in the air. Then stand by."

"Roger that."

He removed his earpiece and throat mike, handing them to Gaffar. "Your heading is due east to the LZ. It's going to be about eight kilometers over moderately difficult terrain. Keep a reasonable pace. Don't blow yourself up and don't fall in any holes."

"What are you going to do?"

"Keep these guys down long enough to give you a head start."

"No. I won't leave you here. We should—"

"You'll be too slow for me out there. Go now and I'll catch you."

The Arab reluctantly turned and crawled a few yards before getting to his feet and accelerating to a careful jog.

Rapp settled into the silence. The wind was completely dead and nothing around him moved. He was completely on his own. A pleasant change from the babysitting he'd been doing over the last few hours.

He didn't have to wait long for the illusion of peacefulness to be shattered. Not by the sound of oncoming trucks but by a quiet rustling from below. A moment later he saw the dark outline of a man break cover for a split second and then jerk back. Rapp just sat there. A few moments later the man showed himself again. This time for a bit longer. Again Rapp did nothing.

Finally the shadow came out from behind the truck and began skirting the cliff. Rapp gave him a long leash, hoping that his companions would get overconfident and follow. When he started climbing toward Rapp's position, though, it became clear that the other surviving men had decided to sit tight and wait for reinforcements.

Rapp fired a single shot, hitting the man in the stomach and sending him toppling back to the road. A few shouts followed but no one was stupid enough to go to the aid of their wounded companion. Not a big surprise, but it had been worth a try.

A few minutes passed quietly before headlights appeared to the south. Rapp watched them as excited voices once again became audible below. Four vehicles coming fast. Whatever Gaffar's head start was, it would have to be enough.

Rapp stood and began running into the desert as the convoy continued to bear down. He figured he was about doubling Gaffar's pace, slowed slightly by the fact that the only way for him to navigate to the LZ was to follow the man's tracks in the moonlight.

He'd only made it about five hundred yards when the shooting started. It sounded like the reinforcements had arrived and that all of them were firing on full auto. No point in looking back. He assumed that they'd pulverize the top of the cliff he'd been staked out on and then charged en masse. ISIS was not known for its subtlety.

He covered another quarter mile before temporarily losing Gaffar's footprints on a rocky plateau. The man was smart enough not to change direction, and Rapp picked them up again in the sand on the other side.

The news wasn't all good, though. Behind, he could see no fewer than ten flashlights coming his way. The lead one was using the advantage of artificial illumination to good effect and actually seemed to be closing. Rapp considered abandoning Gaffar's tracks in favor of speed, but it wasn't time for that yet. There was a whole lot of desert out there.

To the east, a dull glow was starting on the horizon. The light improved his speed, but it also robbed him of his cover—something that became evident when shots sounded behind him. He glanced back and estimated the distance to the closest chaser at more than six hundred yards. A doable shot with the right equipment and training, but they seemed to have neither. Just a little youthful jihadi enthusiasm.

The question was how long this was going to go on. Did Marcus have a position on him? Was Fred willing to fly in on a force of probably thirty armed men?

His question was answered a moment later when the thump of rotors became audible ahead. With the sunlight angling in, he was able to pick up his pace to the maximum his lungs would allow, increasing the gap between him and his pursuers. If he could gain some ground, the chopper would be able to touch down long enough to get him aboard.

Apparently, Mason didn't want to wait. He passed overhead, banking north as the sound of his door gun shook the air. Rapp glanced back and saw the arcing laser light of the tracers sweeping across the ISIS force. He kept pushing, dropping his rifle to get rid of as much weight as possible as he angled down a steep slope. It was a risky move that could give ISIS the high ground, but if he moved fast enough, it would provide temporary cover.

The door gun went silent, replaced by the roar of rotors. The chopper came in low enough for him to feel the pressure of its downdraft. The skids were still two feet above the ground when Rapp dove through the open door. Mason started climbing again as Mohammed pulled Rapp the rest of the way inside and Gaffar opened up with the door gun again. The terrorists managed to get off a few shots, but none came anywhere near them as they turned toward the sunrise.

CHAPTER 6

"THE Saudi and his men are back in the car and on the move," Charlie Wicker said over Maslick's earpiece. "Alghani is hauling ass to the north. He's got the case, but it looks too light to have anything in it."

"Copy that. Let me know when I should go."

"Probably about a minute."

"Copy."

Maslick would have preferred to take the courier during his meeting with Alghani, but there were too many uncontrollable factors. The apartment building had no fewer than thirty residents packed into it, including nine women and twelve kids. Worse, the souk where it was located was too narrow for a vehicle. That would have forced them to go in on foot and then drag their target back to the car. While it was true that there wasn't much activity on the street at this hour, it was also true that Murphy's Law ruled the business he'd chosen.

The plan they'd landed on was pretty simple, which was the only kind worth dealing with as far as he was concerned. There was just one way out for the courier—

a road that was barely wide enough for a single car. Maslick would pull out in front of the Mercedes and Bruno McGraw would come in from behind. When they were directly beneath Wick's rooftop position, they'd box the target vehicle in, snatch this son of a bitch, and be gone. The whole thing had been slated to take less than a minute and with a little luck would go completely unnoticed.

But now that elegant little plan had been blown to shit. Instead of a scrawny middle-aged Egyptian in a tin can of a car, he was dealing with three men—two undoubtedly armed—barricaded in an armored vehicle.

"Mas, you're a go," Wicker said over his earpiece.

He started the vehicle and moved out into the dark road. A man with a wheeled cart was coming in his direction, apparently getting an early start on setting up for the morning's shoppers. Maslick eased to the right of the vendor, grinding off part of his side-view mirror on one of the buildings crowding the asphalt. Fuck it. It was a rental.

"Okay, Mas. You're about a hundred yards ahead, paralleling them. Maintain your speed after the turn and you should be good."

He stayed on course for another twenty-five yards and then took a left, keeping the vehicle at a leisurely fifteen miles an hour as he closed on a T in the road.

"You're good. He's still fifty yards out. Bruno's coming up behind him."

"Roger that." Maslick turned right and was immediately dazzled by the glare of headlights in his rearview mirror.

With the new reality on the ground, there was no

way they were going to be able to quietly box in their target. Instead, Maslick was going to have to slam on his brakes and let the Mercedes ram him from behind. It wouldn't be enough to injure anyone inside, but the airbag deployment would slow down any reaction, and Wick had ammunition that would penetrate the windshield. That would leave the man in back undefended, but accessing him was still going to be a noisy and potentially time-consuming trick.

So, while they could still achieve their objective of getting the courier—though apparently the wrong one—they were going to leave two smashed cars and two dead men instead of just the brief disturbance he'd planned on. Not ideal, but also not enough to call it off. It wasn't like Rapp hadn't broken a few dishes on these kinds of ops in the past.

"Mas, do you copy?" Wick again.

"Yeah. Go ahead."

"We got a hit on that picture I sent to Langley. Seventy-nine percent probability that the guy in the back of that car is His Royal Shithead, Prince Talal bin Musaid of Saudi Arabia."

"You've got to be kidding me."

"Nope."

Maslick started to sweat again despite the cool air flowing through the window. The target was only twenty yards behind him now, approaching fast. Time was running out. In less than an eighth of a mile, the constricted corridor would open up and the powerful Mercedes would go by him like he was stopped in the road.

So now they weren't just talking about a messy snatch-and-grab, they were talking about a messy snatch-and-grab of a Saudi royal. Bad, but still not a disaster. There were about a thousand of these anonymous princes roaming the world, so he wasn't going to get his panties too bunched up about it. His job was to deliver a ISIS moneyman. What Rapp and Irene Kennedy did with him was their business.

They were right on his tail now and he could see the outline of the two men in the front seats of the Mercedes. Maslick suddenly realized that it was possible—probable, really—that they were just guards employed by the Saudi embassy to cart around visiting VIPs. Not terrorists. Not criminals. Just a couple former soldiers making a living.

"Mas, we've got some more intel coming in. Bin Musaid's thirty-nine. Wife and two kids who live in Riyadh, but he seems to get around—the U.S., Canada, Europe. He's worked for the Saudi government in the past, but not for a few years. No known job right now."

Mas was feeling increasingly uncertain. "That seems like a lot of detail for us to have on some random prince."

"That's probably because he's not some random prince. He's King Faisal's nephew."

"What? Repeat that."

"I said the Agency probably has all this intel because he's King Faisal's nephew. His dead sister's son, it looks like."

Fuck!

In his rearview mirror, he could see Bruno McGraw taking up a position thirty feet behind the Mercedes. Maslick was having trouble focusing on the image, though. It was being pushed from his mind by the thought that he was about to kill two innocent embassy workers and grab the nephew of the king of one of America's primary allies in the Middle East. This had just gone from dealing with some bitching from the Moroccans to a major international incident with two counts of murder thrown in for good measure. Then, of course, there would be the official protests to the UN. The American politicians making grandstanding speeches about the out-of-control CIA. The calls for Irene Kennedy's resignation. And him standing right in the middle of all of it.

"Mas," Bruno McGraw said over his earpiece. "What are we doing? You're coming up to the end of the road."

Maslick reached for the phone on his dashboard, but there was no time to get authorization. His foot hovered over the brake for a moment then shoved down on the accelerator instead.

"Abort. I repeat, abort. Wick, go get the money from that apartment. Bruno, peel off east. We'll rendezvous at the airstrip in two."

CHAPTER 7

THE CIA's Gulfstream G550 was on its final approach, heading into the setting sun as it descended toward the treetops. Rapp was stretched out on the sofa with his phone pressed to his ear.

"When you say 'ready,' Mitch, what exactly do you mean?"

"I mean that my car is parked next to the fucking airstrip like you promised."

This landing site was Rapp's go-to when flying into the D.C. area. Quiet and out of the way, but still less than an hour from his house.

"Yeah . . . about that," Craig Bailer responded nervously. "Gunter isn't done with the subwoofer."

"Who's Gunter?"

"The Swiss dude making your sub. Look, Mitch. The guy's an artist and you can't rush artists. Trust me, man. It's gonna to be worth the wait. Not only are you finally going to have a kick-ass stereo, but I've also knocked forty kilos off the Kevlar without any effect on integrity. Plus, you're going to have built-in encrypted phone and Internet."

"How's that going to help me on my forty-mile walk home?"

"I told Claudia it wouldn't be done. Are you two—"

Rapp disconnected the call.

His efforts to get his life together had been just successful enough to remind him that having a life was a monumental pain in the ass. After his wife had been killed he'd jettisoned almost everything—family, friends, possessions. And while the existence that remained had been admittedly empty, it had also been wonderfully simple. A sparse one-bedroom apartment, a flawless backup team, and work. The lack of extraneous moving parts kept everything rolling along with a satisfying precision.

Rapp sat up and looked out the window. The deserted airfield was a powerful reminder of the fact that the simplicity he'd become so comfortably numb to was gone. Cheerfully and thoroughly shredded by Claudia Gould.

Her husband had been one of the top private contractors in the world until Stan Hurley ripped his throat out. Rapp had set Claudia and her daughter up with clean identities and a new life in South Africa, but it hadn't lasted. The Russians tracked them down and forced him to pull them out. In return for helping finish the construction of his new house, he'd let the two of them move in. It was a temporary accommodation that was turning out to be not so temporary.

So now he and Claudia had settled into an uncomfortably platonic cohabitation that was starting to feel like a low-grade Cold War. He was always able to find an excuse not to send them back to Cape Town, but couldn't seem to dig up the courage to commit.

Even after so many years, the death of his wife was a raw, bleeding wound. The years had proved that there wasn't much that could kill him. Living through another loss like that, though, might.

Which brought him back to the empty airfield. Was Claudia making some kind of statement by not being there? Was she telling him that he needed to either make a move or walk away? It would be a fair point, though out of character. Her style was to have it out face-to-face. And why not? She was a deadly opponent in those kinds of confrontations.

The wheels touched down and Rapp went forward, grabbing his duffle and opening the door. He jumped out and immediately turned away from the cockpit. The pilots hadn't seen his face and he preferred to keep it that way.

The Gulfstream immediately took to the air again, leaving him standing among the lengthening shadows. His cell was in his pocket but he didn't want to use it. Had he completely missed the fact that his relationship with Claudia had deteriorated to the point that she'd leave him there? Or was she just forcing him to sit and think about his situation for a while? Either way, she was justified. He was blowing it.

A vehicle appeared in the distance, but it wasn't Claudia's Audi Q5. Rapp's hand moved closer to the Glock beneath his jacket but then fell to his side when he recognized the SUV belonging to Scott Coleman. It rolled to a stop and Rapp tossed his duffel inside before slipping into the passenger seat.

"How'd it go?" Coleman asked.

"Everyone got out."

"Did you pass along my job offer to Gaffar?"

Rapp shook his head. "Turns out he was an artist before he was a soldier. He wants to learn English and go to work for an advertising agency."

"No shit . . ."

Rapp watched the deliberate movement of Coleman's arm as he put the vehicle in gear. The injuries the former SEAL had suffered in Pakistan were far worse than Rapp's own. It was a minor miracle that he was alive and a major one that he could walk. He was working on his rehab full-time, but the slow progress had left yet another glitch in Rapp's well-oiled machine. Coleman's outfit, SEAL Demolition and Salvage, had been his primary backup for years. With its founder out of commission, they had been forced to put a reluctant Joe Maslick in charge. And while Mas was a hell of an operator, he was no Scott Coleman.

"Where's Claudia?" Rapp said. There was no point in hiding from the subject.

"Apparently there's a sleepover at your house tonight and she has her hands full."

He was surprised at the relief he felt. She hadn't been expecting to have to pick him up and it was entirely plausible that Anna had friends over. Maybe this wasn't her drawing a line in the sand.

"So why are *you* here?"

"Somebody had to come and get your ass."

That story sounded a bit thin. Sitting for extended periods of time was hard for him, and he had people he could have sent. There was more to this and it wasn't hard to guess what it was.

"What happened in Rabat?" Rapp said.

Coleman didn't immediately answer, instead accelerating up the road. "There was a problem."

"Are any of our guys hurt?"

"Nah. They're all fine."

"And the Egyptian?"

"There was no Egyptian, Mitch. Our intel was bad. The courier was a Saudi prince."

"Do we have him?"

"So, the thing is—"

"Do we have him?"

"No."

"Why the fuck not?"

"He was traveling in an armored vehicle and there were two guards with—"

"You're telling me that Mas, Bruno, and Wick can't handle two guards and a little armor?"

"What I'm telling you is that the prince in question is Faisal's nephew."

"I don't give a shit who he is. I told—"

"Mitch, please! Let me finish. We threw Mas headlong into this and told him it was a nobody ISIS courier. He didn't feel like he had the authority to make the call and there wasn't time to get to Irene."

"So he just walked away?"

"In a nutshell, yeah."

Rapp tried to control his anger. The Saudis had gotten pass after pass. They were an antidemocratic monarchy, the world's largest supporter of terrorist organizations, and funded the countless madrassas that churned out an endless stream of radicals to replace the ones he killed. And now King Faisal's worthless nephew was rolling around Morocco with a briefcase full of cash earmarked for ISIS?

"Do we have proof?"

"That it was bin Musaid? Not ironclad, but we have a pretty decent photo taken through Wick's scope."

"Where is he now?"

"He hasn't popped back up on our radar yet. We're watching—"

"I mean Maslick."

"Oh . . . Somewhere in Europe. He's afraid to come back. He doesn't want to face you."

They drove in silence for a good five minutes before Coleman spoke again. "You keep avoiding the subject, but we can't anymore. We've got to talk about finding a replacement for me until I can get my shit together. You need reliable backup and I guarantee if you put Mas in charge of anything again, he's going to quit. I don't want it to be my fault if another op goes south or if you get shot up. I'd never hear the end of it from Irene."

Rapp knew he was right. The hope had been that Coleman would bounce back in a few months, but that wasn't happening. It could easily be another year. Or, as much as no one wanted to face the possibility, it could be never.

"It's your organization, Scott. Not mine. You can do what you want."

Coleman seemed to relax a little. "But it's your ass out there. I need you to be comfortable with who I pick."

"Do you have any ideas?"

"Mike Nash and I have been doing some spitballing. We've turned up a few names and he's digging a little deeper for me. We've also been talking about splitting the job in two. Maybe having a separate field commander and logistics person."

"So you'd handle logistics, then?"

The former SEAL shook his head. "I've got more on my plate than I can deal with right now."

Rapp felt increasingly uncomfortable with the conversation. The more they talked about a replacement, the more it felt like Coleman wasn't coming back. They'd been together for years. In many ways they'd grown up together in the business. Beyond the friendship they'd forged, there was a level of trust that he didn't see being able to build with someone new.

Coleman seemed to read his mind—another facet of their relationship that was going to be hard to replace. "It's just for a little while, Mitch. I need this, okay? I'm stressing out that you or one of my guys is going to get killed. I don't need that right now."

"When's Mike going to have some recommendations?"

"Next day or two. He's working on the ops side. I'm dealing with logistics."

"And?"

Again Coleman didn't immediately answer, instead focusing on getting around a truck creeping along the rural highway. He seemed to be building up to something, but Rapp had no idea what it could be.

"It's hard not to think about Claudia," the former SEAL said finally.

For the second time since he'd gotten in the car, Rapp found himself having to control his anger. Normally he wouldn't bother, but Coleman was struggling. He'd gone from being one of the best operators in the world to barely being able to roll out of bed in the morning. He felt like he'd abandoned his comrades and was terrified that he might live the rest of his life getting winded buying groceries.

"No," Rapp said. "She's already risking enough just being near me."

"To be clear here, Mitch, I didn't approach her. She approached me. And we both know that a big part of Louis Gould's success was her doing most of the thinking for him."

"We're done with this subject, Scott."

Coleman shrugged. "All right. As far as I'm concerned, it's a dead issue. But I'm not sure Claudia's going to feel the same way."

CHAPTER 8

Prince Talal bin Musaid stepped into the Learjet 75's cool interior and frowned at the pilot bowing to him from the cockpit door. He'd never seen the man before, but it mattered little. The pilots he'd been provided in the past had been adequate and he had no reason to believe that this one would be any different.

"Welcome, Your Highness. All is ready for your return to Riyadh."

"Make me a drink," bin Musaid said, and then went to the back, taking a seat.

He watched disinterestedly as the pilot closed the door and then rushed to pour a single malt for his only passenger.

"Do I have your permission to lift off?" he said, handing bin Musaid the drink with another bow.

The prince nodded and took a sip from the crystal glass. Not his preferred brand but it would do for the relatively short flight. He savored the dark liquor without guilt as he did women, drugs, and gambling. Why not? He had been shut out of his rightful place by old men fearful of his youth and vitality. Certainly Allah would understand him taking solace in these meaningless vices until the order of things changed. Until the storm that was brewing in the Middle East finally destroyed the Western appeasers who infested the region.

As the engines spooled up, he wondered idly what had happened to the money he'd provided ISIS. Was it being passed along their elaborate network on its way to America? Had it been laundered and deposited in a legitimate financial institution? Was it already in the hands of the devout men who would use it for a glorious attack?

What would the target be? An American sports stadium? One of the country's decadent commercial centers? The Capitol building during a meeting of its congress?

Freedom made the Americans weak. How could a society protect itself unless the greater men took charge of every aspect? How could a society be truly exceptional when it was at the mercy of the whims of the mob?

His own country was slowly succumbing to a similar fate, he knew. King Faisal and the leaders who had come before him had turned their backs on Allah. The old man had retreated behind the walls of his depraved palace, emerging occasionally to falsely proclaim his devotion to subjects who were beginning to see through his lies. He had abandoned the almighty power of God long ago, replacing it with the power of America.

Like all bargains with the devil, though, this one was beginning to unravel. The vast network of conservative madrassas financed by the House of Saud were no longer blinding the people to its excesses, but instead showing them the truth. The king was now faced with an impossible situation. His strategy of publicly condemning the U.S. while privately supporting its battle against fundamentalist Islamic forces was beginning to fail. And the Americans were finally waking up to the fact that the billions they spent on Saudi oil was being used to create terrorists whom they then had to spend billions fighting.

This increasing dysfunction had culminated in the recent action ISIS had taken against his own country. They had acquired radioactive material from Pakistan and attempted to use it to irradiate Saudi Arabia's oil-producing region. In the ensuing economic chaos, Faisal and his lackeys would have fled to the West, leaving the forces of true Islam to take control of not only Saudi Arabia but the trillions of dollars' worth of sophisticated weapons the Americans had sold its military.

It was a magnificent plan, but one that had not succeeded. The murderer Mitch Rapp had thwarted the attack. Now King Faisal was bowing and scraping even more to the Americans—begging men like Rapp to provide enough stability to protect him in the last few years of his life. After that, Faisal cared little about what happened to his country and the religion that should have been under his protection.

The plane accelerated a bit abruptly up the runway and bin Musaid struggled to keep his drink from spilling. He was about to shout an insult in the direction of the cockpit but then reconsidered. He would soon rise to a position from which he would lead the

Arab people. A king of kings acting as God's representative on earth. Personally interacting with this man was beneath him. A brief mention to one of his people when they landed would ensure the pilot never worked again.

Bin Musaid's phone rang and he glanced down to see the recently appointed Saudi intelligence chief Aali Nassar's name on the screen. He ignored it.

Nassar was undoubtedly strong and had proven intelligent enough to identify bin Musaid as an ally, but he was also a commoner. It was a fact that he seemed to be forgetting as his power grew. While his machinations were unquestionably impressive, they were entirely for the benefit of the next generation of Saudi aristocrats. When bin Musaid took his rightful seat as the head of the House of Saud, he would of course reward Nassar's efforts lavishly. But he would also forcefully remind the man that he was a servant. A valuable one, to be sure, but a servant nonetheless.

The plane leveled out and the pilot immediately made his way back to him.

"Your Highness, Aali Nassar is trying to contact you. He wonders if perhaps your phone is not functioning properly?"

Bin Musaid stared up at the man. "My phone is functioning perfectly."

"I don't understand, Your Highness. You—"

"I'm not interested in what you do or do not understand!"

Knowing that he'd been dismissed, the pilot retreated back to the cockpit. Before bin Musaid could take another sip of his drink, though, he had returned. This time with a phone in his hand.

"I'm sorry, but I'm told it's urgent."

Bin Musaid let out a frustrated breath and snatched the phone.

"What?"

"You went personally? You were to leave the money for the Egyptian and let him make the exchange!"

"You'd do well to watch your tone when you speak to me, Aali. It was my money and I wanted to meet the man taking it."

"Watch my tone? Idiot!"

"You know nothing of this!" bin Musaid shouted. "You sit in your office in Riyadh using other people's funds and labor to advance your plans. You would be able to do nothing—you would *be* nothing—without the support of my family."

"It never occurred to you that you could be seen? That your involvement might be discovered?"

"Impossible."

"You drove there in a car provided by the embassy! Do you have any idea what your thoughtless arrogance has put at risk? Have you—"

Bin Musaid disconnected the call and threw the phone against the bulkhead. Who was Aali Nassar to speak to him like that? He was a pauper. One of the thousands of meaningless bureaucrats who infested Saudi Arabia's government payroll. The fact that he had temporarily gained the favor of the useless old woman who was their king had caused him to become drunk with self-importance.

The pilot apparently had a second phone, because it began ringing almost immediately. Surely he would not be stupid enough to bring it back again. Bin Musaid swallowed what was left of his drink and went to the galley to pour himself a second. A third and fourth would probably also be necessary to soften both the memory of that conversation and the fact that he was being forced to return to Riyadh.

He'd spend only the number of days required to keep up appearances. The moment his familial obligations were fulfilled, he would leave again. Perhaps for New York. He had an interesting woman there and a sudden yearning to walk among the godless inhabitants of that country. To revel in their ignorance of what was to come.

"Allahu Akbar!"

The sudden shout from the pilot was followed by the nose of the plane dipping violently and the fuselage beginning to vibrate. Bin Musaid lurched for the cockpit but the angle of descent continued to steepen. A moment later he was weightless, feeling panic grip him as the aircraft dropped below the clouds and revealed the earth rushing toward them.

He screamed but it came out as more of a whimper, swallowed up by the sound of rushing air and the deafening whine of the engines. The sensation of weight returned suddenly and he hit the floor, rolling through the food, dishes, and liquor bottles strewn across it before slamming into a table.

Gravity continued to increase until bin Musaid's body felt as though it was being pressed to the floor by the hand of God. The breath went out of him and urine ran down his leg as his universe contracted until it consisted only of blinding sunlight, the deafening roar in his ears, and the unbearable force of gravity.

Then, as quickly as it had started, it was over.

The pressure subsided and the scream of the engines returned to the reassuring hum he had spent so much of his life surrounded by. Blue, unwavering sky glowed beyond the windows and he fixated on it, gulping air as he tried unsuccessfully to stand. The pilot appeared, hovering over him for a moment before dropping a phone onto his chest. Bin Musaid took it in a shaking hand and put it to his ear. A moment later Aali Nassar's voice came on.

"Do we understand each other, Your Highness?"

CHAPTER 9

"Let's see if they finally added me to this thing," Coleman said, sticking his arm through the open window and pressing his thumb against the scanner. After a brief delay, the gate in front of them began to open.

Rapp's subdivision was situated in a rural area outside of Washington, D.C., and had originally consisted of ten large home sites to be sold off at market price. His obscenely rich brother had swooped in and bought the other nine, leaving Rapp with a hundred acres on the top of a butte surrounded by farmland. It was a nice gesture but had the effect of making his house too remote. The 9th Armored Division could roll up to his gate and go unnoticed for a week.

Ever the idea man, Steven had sold off the luxury lots to Rapp's friends and colleagues for a dollar apiece. A retired Secret Service man had already broken ground on one to the north, and Mike Nash's wife had finally decided on one to the east.

"That's mine," Coleman said, pointing through the windshield at a wooded knoll next to the barn that Anna was preparing for the pony she was certain would be arriving for her birthday. "I'm thinking Western contemporary. Something that'll give me a little class, you know?"

Rapp nodded silently. It wasn't a solution that he'd have come up with on his own, but it was the kind of out-of-the-box thinking that had his brother edging up on billionaire status. Within two years Rapp would be surrounded by shooters completely loyal to him, as well as a few kids around Anna's age. A perfect scenario for everyone involved. All he had to do now was not screw it up.

They came over a small rise and the spotlit wall surrounding his house came into view. The copper gate swung back as they approached and Rapp frowned. Claudia had undoubtedly activated it based on the security camera displays. With the glare of the headlights, though, it would be impossible for her to see through the windshield to confirm their identities. He'd have to talk to her about that.

The modern, single-level house had been designed mostly by his late wife. His only demand was that it have no exterior windows. She and her architect had done an incredible job of camouflaging the thick walls, reinforced roof, and defensive positions.

Coleman swung the vehicle in a circle and came to a stop next to a spectacularly ugly sculpture that Claudia loved.

"Looks like a Skycrane lost its grip on a Hyundai and it landed in your yard," the former SEAL said.

Rapp ignored the comment and stepped out into the cool night. He slammed the door and leaned through the open window. "You coming in?"

Coleman shook his head. "I hear you've got twelve little girls in there. That's an opposing force I'd prefer to avoid."

Instead of turning away, Rapp continued to grip the edge of the car door. "Things are going good?"

"Better every day. They say I might be able to jog a quarter mile on the track next month. Anything to get me out of that lap pool, you know?"

Rapp started to pull back but then stopped when Coleman leaned painfully across the seat toward him. "I have one more thing to say about Claudia."

"You're pushing it, Scott."

"What are you going to do? Hit a man who walks with a cane?"

"Maybe."

"You need to put yourself in her shoes for a minute, Mitch. If your wife had lived and you'd had a kid, would you have given everything up? The rush? The satisfaction of doing something you're good at? Would you have just turned yourself into a stay-at-home father? Because that's what you're asking her to do."

"Good night, Scott."

Rapp watched him pull through the gate and then started for the front door. The normally spotless entryway was strewn with shoes, tiny backpacks, and a trail of colorful Legos that for some reason led into the powder room.

Much of the house consisted of floor-to-ceiling glass that looked into an elaborately landscaped courtyard. He crossed it and used a sliding door to access the industrial kitchen the architect had convinced him he needed. The dark-haired woman inside wedged one last pan in the dishwasher and spun toward him. Her hair was a bit unkempt and she had a smear of something that might have been mustard on one cheek, but she was still stunning.

Rapp indicated to the dishes stacked everywhere. "I take it the rumors of a sleepover are true."

"You may want to go back to Iraq where it's safe," she said, striding across the stone floor and throwing her arms around him.

He returned the embrace hesitantly. Whenever they touched, he felt the same confusing combination of adrenaline and peace. The fact that he was becoming increasingly dependent on that sensation worried him. Those kinds of addictions never worked out well.

She pulled away and went back to cleaning. "Have you eaten? I'm sorry. I haven't had a minute to make you anything."

He took a seat at the large island and searched the dishes piled on it, finally selecting a hot dog with a tiny nibble out of one end. "I'm fine. Looks like you've had your hands full."

"You have no idea," she said, switching to the French she preferred. "Your operation went well? All of your friends are safe?"

"More improvisation than I would have liked," he responded, taking a bite of the cold hot dog. "But everyone's in one piece."

"And Joe? Things went well with his first command?"

It felt strange talking about these kinds of things with her. He'd done everything possible to keep his work hidden from his wife. But Claudia had been part of a similar world for years. She understood what he was dealing with. What was at stake.

"Could've been better."

She stopped loading dishes into the sink and turned toward him. "Everyone's okay, though, right?"

He reached for a bag of potato chips. "Yeah, but it was a bust."

"Really? What happened?"

He examined her as she leaned against the sink. It was an odd question. While they were in the habit of discussing his work in general terms, he never went into specifics and she knew better than to ask. What had changed?

One of the pillars of effective interrogation was knowing more than your opponent thought you did. He had a feeling that he was on the wrong side of that now. Had Coleman given her details about Maslick's failed operation in the hope that he could recruit her? No way. The former SEAL was famously tight-lipped. And that left only one possibility.

Irene.

"Just some bad luck," Rapp said.

She fixed her almond-shaped eyes on him in a way that suggested she knew that she'd overplayed her hand. "Nothing could have been done?"

"Act of God," Rapp said, going out of his way to be as vague as possible. He recognized that the conversation was inevitable, but at least he could make her work for it.

She finally admitted defeat. "Did Scott talk to you about me?"

"Yes."

"You're a very infuriating man to have a conversation with."

He finished the hot dog. "Really?"

"I'm thinking about buying another sculpture for the front," she said. "This one's much larger."

He fought back a grin. "Okay. Truce. Scott and I talked, but I don't think it's a good idea."

"Why not?"

"Because it's dangerous enough just being around me without getting involved in my business. And because Anna needs you here."

"It's not operations, Mitch. You know that. And you also know that you're putting too much pressure on Joe and Marcus. You're going to break them."

"Claudia—"

"I'm not finished."

"Fine. Continue."

"You have a life. A purpose. Challenges. I love being with Anna. But I can't *just* do that. What happens in a few years when she doesn't want her mother hovering over her every minute? You say Joe's operation didn't go well. Let me ask you something. And I want an honest answer. Would it have been different if I'd been involved?"

The answer was a solid *Probably*. She was talented and incredibly exacting. It was possible that she could have IDed the prince well before things got critical and almost certain that she'd have been maintaining a reliable link to Langley.

"I don't know," Rapp said.

"But maybe."

"Yeah. Maybe."

"I can help keep you and Scott's people safe. From his office. Not from the field."

"I just have a bad feeling about this, Claudia. I understand what you're saying, but there are a lot of jobs out there that don't involve so many fireworks. Why not get one of those?"

"You can't tell me who I can and cannot work for, Mitch."

That was true. She was essentially his roommate—a fact that was very much not lost on her. Why was it always the strong, defiant women he was attracted to? A doormat would make his life so much easier.

"Can we continue this conversation later?" he asked.

"Is that a delaying tactic or are we really going to continue later?"

Between her and Coleman, it was like stereo bitching.

"Just let me just take a shower and sleep on it, okay? We'll pick it up again when we've taken back control of the house."

The fact that she returned to the dishes suggested she was satisfied, so he grabbed the bag of chips and started toward the master suite. On the way, though, he stopped in Anna's open doorway. The girls were all dead asleep—on the bed, on the floor, sprawled across stuffed animals. A powerful reminder that, outside of his world, everyday life kept marching on. In a way, this was what he fought for. Sleepovers.

CHAPTER 10

SOLDIERS scurried from Aali Nassar's path, focusing on erecting temporary living quarters, servicing vehicles, and preparing weapons. They were mounting a counterterrorism operation against a top ISIS leader across the border in Iraq. It was likely that Nassar's assistant had called ahead to warn the base commander of his mood and that it would be best to give the Saudi intelligence chief a wide berth.

Nassar was still in a rage about what had happened in Rabat. Talal bin Musaid had been tasked with the simplest of endeavors, but he hadn't been able to do even that. Instead, this meaningless pup had jeopardized everything Nassar had accomplished over the past six months.

He could feel the men's gaze on him as he walked along the dirt road, their eyes shining with admiration and desert sun. The fact that he had been chosen to replace Prince Khaled bin Abdullah as the head of the General Intelligence Directorate was all but unheard-of and gave each of these soldiers the hope that they, too, could rise above their common births.

Prior to Nassar's promotion, high government positions had typically been held by royals. The exception
was the energy ministry, which the king quietly acknowledged was too important to trust to one of the
half-wits that made up the House of Saud.

Now, though, the forces of radical Islam were mass-
ing at the gates, threatening not only the common
man but the monarchs who lorded over them. With
his family no longer immune to the danger posed by
the jihadists they'd created, King Faisal had decided
that a certain level of competence would be required
to maintain order.

An improbably young man in a colonel's uniform
appeared from a tent and, instead of attempting to
avoid Nassar, rushed to meet him. Maheer Bazzi had
recently been promoted to lead Saudi Arabia's special forces. While insufferably eager and loyal, he was
wholly unqualified for the position. King Faisal had
felt obligated to reward the man for his role in saving
Saudi Arabia's oil fields from an attack orchestrated
by ISIS. The fact that Bazzi was likely complicit in the
murder of his predecessor by Mitch Rapp was something the king was apparently willing to overlook.

"Director Nassar," the man said, stopping to give
a crisp salute. "It's a pleasure to see you, sir. Are you
aware that the king is on his way here?"

Nassar had been informed of that fact only an hour
ago and, despite the efforts of his staff, was still in the
dark as to why. The aging monarch rarely left the walls
of his palace anymore. What matter could be urgent
enough for him to venture out into the world that he
had become so fearful of?

"His Highness and I have matters to discuss and

this was a convenient time and location," Nassar said, being careful to hide his contempt for the young colonel. He was a tepid Muslim with little guile or ambition beyond simple service to his king and country. Nassar's people had found nothing with which to blackmail him, and he would likely be immune to offers of money, women, or power.

That, combined with the fact that he'd gained the king's favor, made him a man to be rid of at the earliest opportunity. Fortunately, that opportunity was about to present itself.

"Is everything ready?" Nassar asked as jet engines became audible to the east. He didn't bother to look, confident that the source of the sound was Faisal's Airbus A380. Despite being only an hour's drive from Riyadh, the geriatric fool had flown. Undoubtedly out of fear of leaving the lavish ministrations of his wives and doctors.

"Yes, sir. Intelligence has confirmed that General al-Omari is en route slightly ahead of schedule."

"Will that be a problem?"

Bazzi shook his head. "I was prepared for variations in our timetable. We'll be wheels up a half hour earlier than planned, but it won't affect any of the other operational parameters."

Nassar gave a barely perceptible nod. Dabir al-Omari was near the top of ISIS's command structure. Before the invasion of Iraq, he had been one of Saddam Hussein's most talented young officers and now he was adding his strategic genius to Mullah Sayid Halabi's messianic charisma. Capturing him would be a devastating blow to the terrorist group and a service that Colonel Bazzi was anxious to perform for his beloved king.

"I have every confidence in you," Nassar started. "But I've decided to personally oversee this operation."

"But, sir, the general will be traveling with a significant security force. There's no way I can guarantee your safety. Please allow—"

"I understand. Neither I nor the king hold you responsible for my safety." He forced a smile and clapped the younger man on the shoulder. "I think you'll find my men quite useful and I assure you that I can take care of myself."

The Airbus passing overhead drowned out Bazzi's response and Nassar began walking toward the runway, feeling his sense of agitation increase with every step. If anything, he had been overcautious in his efforts to undermine the authority of the country's monarchy. Was it possible that his actions had been discovered? The likelihood seemed remote. But even if the king had unwittingly stumbled upon some faint trail, nothing would lead to Nassar personally. Still, the damage to his plans could be considerable.

A group of soldiers double-timed a set of steps to the plane and Nassar climbed them as one of Faisal's security men opened the door. He stepped aside and bowed his head respectfully.

"His Highness is waiting for you at the back, Director."

Nassar passed through the opulent interior and found King Faisal sitting alone on a sectional sofa near the rear bulkhead. There was an oxygen mask next to him but the tank it was attached to was tastefully hidden. Eighty-six years of life and hundreds of thousands of American cigarettes had left the man with emphysema and congestive heart failure. But as near as Nassar's people could tell, maddeningly free of cancer.

"It's my understanding that preparations for tomorrow's operation are proceeding acceptably," Faisal said, dispensing with the formalities he'd reveled in as a younger man. With so few breaths left, he now tried to use them wisely.

"This is my understanding as well, Your Highness."

"I also hear that you've decided to involve yourself personally."

"You are indeed well-informed."

"Do you think it's wise?"

"The risk to me is minimal and the importance of this operation can't be overstated. If we move quickly, the capture or assassination of Mullah Halabi is within the realm of possibility."

"Is that something that we would handle ourselves?"

"No, Highness. I think it would be much wiser to have the Americans take the lead."

Faisal nodded, his blue-hued lips pursed into a perceptible frown. It had been the king's strategy for decades—let the West protect his privilege while he quietly undermined them. It wouldn't work for much longer, though, and Faisal knew this better than anyone. He was one of the smartest royals and had the impressive distinction of being perhaps the most selfish. He saw the growing power of the jihadists and understood the horrors that a confrontation would bring. He just wanted to make sure that confrontation didn't occur until he was gone.

"And what of the other matter?"

"You're referring to Tha'labah?"

"You know I am."

Tha'labah was a Saudi blogger who despised the monarchy and was becoming increasingly bold in airing that distaste.

"It's an issue we're still studying, Excellency."

"'Studying'? If Khaled was still in charge of our intelligence efforts, this problem would have been resolved long ago."

It was hard to argue the point. Prince Khaled, in addition to being a complete idiot, had been almost comically heavy-handed. He liked to make an example of anyone who defied the royal family with a public trial and an even more public execution. Unfortunately, with every agitator killed, a thousand more were created.

"May I remind you that this is precisely why you found it necessary to remove Khaled, Your Highness. Any overt action against Tha'labah will only martyr him. News of his death will spread across social media like wildfire, consuming everyone who reads it."

"But he's associated with ISIS!" Faisal protested. "And you tell me there's nothing we can do?"

The old fool was incapable of understanding the world that had grown up around him. Affiliations were fluid at best, meaningless marketing declarations at worst. ISIS was as much an idea as an organization. An idea that was infecting Saudi Arabia's youth like it had the youth of Iraq and Syria. An idea that would soon overwhelm everything.

"Discretion is why you hired me, Your Majesty. And so that your family could be insulated from these things."

"What about the Americans?"

"They won't act against Tha'labah. Freedom of speech is one of their most dearly held values."

Faisal finally reached for his oxygen mask and continued to stare at his intelligence chief while gulping from it. With falling oil prices, he could no longer provide sufficient entitlements to keep his people docile. They were beginning to turn on him, fueled by the fanaticism beat into them by the Wahhabi madrassas he'd built to blind them.

His relationship with the West was all that stood between him and his own people. Unfortunately, the Americans had begun to tire of spending billions supporting a country that was anathema to everything they stood for. Worse, terrorism was becoming more important to them than oil, and Saudi Arabia was among the largest exporters of both.

ISIS could be defeated. It was a trivial matter, really. But the idea that it represented would not be so easily vanquished. With ISIS gone, what would fill the vacuum left behind? History had answered this question countless times. Eventually, extremist forces had their day. The only question was whether Saudi Arabia would lead those forces or be consumed by them.

The king removed his oxygen mask and allowed his withered frame to sink deeper into the sofa. "The President of the United States has demanded a meeting with our ambassador. No information has been provided as to the reason. This is unprecedented. Do you have any thoughts as to what would prompt such a request?"

"None whatsoever," Nassar said, but his mind immediately went to Prince bin Musaid's actions in Morocco.

"The ambassador is quite worried. He believes that the lack of an agenda is intentional. That they don't want to give him the ability to prepare."

It seemed obvious to the point of being self-evident, but then, Saudi Arabia's ambassador to America was a drooling moron. Unfortunately, he was also King Faisal's cousin.

"Would you like me to attend that meeting, Your Highness?"

The king smiled. "I assumed that you would resist, Aali."

Normally he would have, but if there was any chance that the Americans had information on what had happened in Rabat, it would be unwise to let the ambassador go alone to that meeting.

"I am yours to command as always," Nassar said.

"You've never met President Alexander, have you?"

"No, Highness."

For a man in his position, he had met very few Americans—something that was by design and not chance. He hated their arrogance. Their obsession with peace and money. They had traded the privilege of serving their god for order, comfort, and pleasure.

President Joshua Alexander took this one step further. He had been attacking the Saudi way of life since he was a young politician—trying to transform the kingdom into a modern, secular blend of Eastern and Western values. To force the followers of Allah to make the same bargain with the devil that his own countrymen had.

"Perhaps this would be a good time."

"It would be my honor, Your Highness."

Faisal nodded regally. "Success in your action

against General al-Omari should be enough to put us in a position of strength with regard to the Americans."

He covered his mouth with the mask again. His next words were muffled but still intelligible. "Yes . . . al-Omari's head will keep the Americans docile for a bit longer . . ."

CHAPTER 11

"And that?" Irene Kennedy said, pointing to a partially completed stone dome.

The afternoon had turned warm and the sky was marred by only a few white clouds to the east. Claudia had just mowed the lawn with a John Deere tractor that was her new favorite possession, and the scent of freshly cut grass still hung in the air.

"Pizza oven, I think."

Kennedy took an austere sip of her wine, trying to hide her smile.

"What?"

"Most of us would have bet against Mitch Rapp ever owning a pizza oven."

"Maybe I'm less of a one-trick pony than you thought."

Her smile broadened. "The house is magnificent, Mitch. So is the location. I can see why you chose it."

"There are still a few lots left if you're interested. I think I could convince Steven to give you half off. Fifty cents."

She shook her head. "Thank you, but I'm a city girl at heart. I'll just hope you invite me back."

Rapp nodded and took a less austere pull on his beer. In some ways they had become like siblings. Despite that, they rarely saw each other outside of work. Their lives were in a constant state of chaos and the normal things that normal people did tended to get lost in it. Even now, the reason she and her teenage son were there wasn't because of him. It was because of Claudia.

He heard Anna walk up behind him and felt a tug on his pants leg.

"Can I take Tommy to see the barn?"

He glanced at Kennedy but she turned away, pretending to examine the landscaping. His reflex was to tell Anna to ask her mother but he fought it. Kennedy was testing him.

"Sure. But there's still a lot of construction equipment in there and I don't want you to get anywhere near it, okay?"

She grinned and then looked up at Kennedy. "Mom wants me to ask you if you want another glass of wine."

"No, thank you, dear. One's my limit."

With that, Anna sprinted toward Kennedy's son, who was standing in front of the sculpture near the gate, studying it with a slightly cocked head.

"Tommy!" Rapp shouted. "You're in charge. Don't do anything that'll make me want to snap your neck!"

The teen gave him two thumbs up and jogged toward the gate, playfully nudging at Anna as she ran.

Kennedy watched them start up the road, not speaking again until they disappeared into the trees. "Terrifying, aren't they? I make life-or-death decisions every day and more often than not it's Tommy that I lie awake at night worrying about."

"Yeah. I'm not sure I'm doing a very good job making the transition."

"Really? My understanding is that you're doing a wonderful job."

"Did Claudia tell you that?"

Her only answer was another dainty sip from her wineglass.

"What's happening with the little prince?" Rapp said, changing the subject to one he was more comfortable with.

"The president's called a meeting with the Saudi ambassador."

"You're not going to get anything from that idiot. No one tells him anything."

"I agree. But I understand that he's bringing Aali Nassar along."

"The new intelligence chief? Interesting. Have you dealt with him yet?"

"Not personally. But I can tell you he's very different from his predecessor. Strong, intelligent, and ambitious."

"Is that better than Khaled's stupid, radical, and misogynistic? Or is it worse?"

"Having a counterpart like Nassar in Saudi Arabia could be very helpful. Or it could be very dangerous. Unfortunately, where the Middle East is concerned, it's usually the latter. I've been included in the meeting, so I'll be able to give you a better assessment after."

"And what's the tone of this meeting going to be?"

She considered her response for a moment. "The

president's angry. In fact, this may be as angry as I've ever seen him."

Rapp could very much sympathize. The redacted twenty-eight pages from the report that detailed Saudi involvement in 9/11 was only the tip of the iceberg. The Agency had been told to bury everything else they'd found on the subject. King Faisal had been left to handle the many coconspirators in his government as he saw fit. Stability and the flow of oil were preserved, but it was a decision that Rapp had been violently opposed to. At the time, though, he'd been a young operative with very little to say about decisions at that level.

"And do you feel the same, Irene?"

"Angry? Yes. But I'd be surprised if Faisal knows anything about his nephew's activities. Even you have to admit that after 9/11, the Saudi government has been an imperfect but reasonably cooperative partner in the war against terrorism."

"Faisal's on his last leg, though. The man spends most of his time holed up in his palace with oxygen tubes up his nose."

She nodded thoughtfully. "He'll be gone soon and we'll have a whole new set of challenges to deal with. That's for another day, though. The question we have to answer now is whether Rabat was an isolated incident or whether there's a greater conspiracy. The people looking to fill the vacuum Faisal's death creates may also be looking to generate closer ties with the young radicals gaining power in the region."

"Maybe I made a mistake, Irene. Maybe I should have let ISIS irradiate Faisal's shithole of a country. How many times are we going to have to go through this with them? We let them off the hook for the most deadly terrorist attack in U.S. history and now here we are again. It's starting to sound like a broken record."

"You didn't make a mistake. We still have a significant amount of influence on the Saudis and letting the country fall to ISIS would have been a disaster."

"Sometimes I wonder. Every day it seems to get worse. It may be that we have to let it all burn down before we can rebuild it."

"Possibly. But I don't think we're there quite yet, Mitch. I still see a few rays of hope."

"You must have better eyesight than I do. So you think you'll actually be able to resolve anything in the meeting with Nassar?"

"Probably not. I assume the Saudis will just deny everything and we don't have much in the way of hard evidence. It would have been convenient if we'd actually *captured* bin Musaid . . ."

She fell silent but kept looking directly at him.

"Go ahead, Irene. Say it."

"Okay, I will. You need to replace Scott. Not forever. Just until he's fit for duty again. I heard he's thinking about splitting his job into operations and logistics. That's an intriguing idea."

As if on cue, Claudia appeared from the front of the house, holding a fresh beer for him. She handed it over and smiled warmly. "Dinner will be about another half hour. So, what are we talking about?"

CHAPTER 12

IRONICALLY, the house had once been the property of a U.S. contractor charged with the hopeless task of rebuilding Iraq. America's politicians had once again made the mistake of judging this part of the world by their own standard. They believed that the natural state of humanity was justice and that it would reign if the pockets of wickedness were eradicated. In truth, the natural state of humanity was chaos. The Americans had just managed to hold it at bay over most of their short history.

Colonel Maheer Bazzi crawled forward to get a better view of the property. The compound was constructed of stone and ancient beams, built into the cliff behind it. Trees sprouted in front of the stacked rock perimeter wall and vines clung to the gray stone, nearly obscuring it. Through the haze of his night-vision scope, the property looked abandoned, but it was just an illusion created to ward off American drones.

Bazzi swept his scope right and spotted a man creeping up on the empty space where a gate had once been. Four additional armed men were angling in from the north and two more, invisible from his current position, would be coming in from the east. None were from his teams, though. They all belonged to Aali Nassar.

Bazzi had protested to the king, but it had been pointless. Faisal had become a man of compromise in his twilight years. While Bazzi remained in command of the assault, Nassar's elite ops team would carry it out.

It was true that Nassar treated him with respect, but Bazzi was fully aware that it was only a pretense created to please the king. Nassar dismissed him as inexperienced and hated him for his history of cooperation with the Americans. Further, Nassar believed that he had witnessed and covered up Mitch Rapp's killing of Saudi Arabia's former special operations commander.

These suspicions, far from suggesting that Nassar was paranoid, were just another example of his competence. All were in fact true. While the American government was hopeless, Mitch Rapp had an encyclopedic knowledge of the Middle East and what had to be done to tame it.

There was evidence that finally, with so many failures behind them, the politicians were starting to listen to him. As Bazzi saw it, this was the only hope for his country. Left to the backstabbing machinations of Faisal's successors, the kingdom would descend into an endless civil war that would wipe it from the map.

Nassar, while unquestionably a force of nature, was a fundamentally twisted man. A man of all-consuming ambition and an almost sociopathic lack of patriotism.

While he had managed to convince the king of his fealty, it was clear that he cared nothing for the man, the
kingdom he ruled, or his thirty million subjects.

And so Bazzi found himself adopting the unchar-
acteristic strategy of leading from behind. As little as
he trusted Aali Nassar, he trusted Nassar's men even
less.

The team was finally in position, and Bazzi was
about to authorize the assault, but it turned out to
be unnecessary. They began without his order. He
watched them flood into the compound, losing sight
of most as they fanned out behind the wall. The muffled crack of suppressed assault rifles was joined by
the undisciplined growl of fully automatic weapons as
General al-Omari's men tried to resist the incursion.

Bazzi started down the loose slope, forcing himself to keep an unconscionably slow pace. His normal
practice was to run toward battle, but he suspected
that his survival depended on reining in that instinct.
In fact, he would have preferred to be relieved of his
duties with regard to this operation, but such a request
would have been an insult to the king.

The gunfire fell silent when he was still fifty meters
from the wall and he activated his throat mike. "Has
the courtyard been secured?"

There was no response.

"I repeat. Has the—"

"It's secure," came the curt response.

Bazzi moved through the gap in the wall cautiously,
scanning the moonlit courtyard. Nassar's men were
in evidence on all sides, having taken control of every
strategic position. The bodies of three armed men
were facedown in the dirt.

"Any injuries?"

"None."

The sound of machine-gun fire erupted to Bazzi's right and he dove headlong to the ground, rolling into a position that allowed him to swing his Heckler & Koch G36 toward muzzle flashes coming from a stand of trees fifteen meters away. He depressed the trigger and felt the buck of his weapon as he returned fire. A shadowy figure burst from cover, using the eruptions of dust created by his bullets to refine his aim. The impacts made it to within five centimeters of Bazzi before he managed to hit the man in the chest and spin him into an ancient well.

The silence descended again and he searched the darkness, seeing no one but Nassar's men looking down at him. None had fired a single shot.

It was clear that his continued existence depended on learning a whole new set of survival skills. He was no longer a simple special forces captain. He was a favorite of the king and, as such, a reluctant player in the power struggle that was to come.

Bazzi moved toward the men gathering at the front door of the massive house. Again he hung back, waiting for them to enter before he followed. They needed to move quickly. There would be more security men inside and all would be running for defensible positions. Nassar's team couldn't afford to get bogged down. They needed to get General al-Omari on a chopper before ISIS reinforcements arrived.

He kept Nassar's men in front of him but doubted they would do anything overt. Allowing one of General al-Omari's men to kill him was very different than doing the job themselves. One day it might come to that as Nassar continued to push against the limitations of his low birth, but for now it was unlikely that he was prepared to murder the head of Saudi Arabia's special forces.

They continued down the hallway, coming to a set of stairs that demanded a split in their forces. It was obvious that he wasn't really in command, so he didn't bother to give orders. He wished that he could just retreat back outside of the wall, but King Faisal would want a detailed description of the operation. His duty was clear and he carried it out, choosing to follow the men who continued along the ground floor and letting the other team take the steps.

A sudden flash to their right was followed by the earsplitting shock wave of a grenade. The two lead men crumpled as the two behind them began trading fire with an assailant or assailants in a room ahead. Bazzi instinctively sprinted up behind them, sliding on his hip toward the downed men. One had been hit in the neck by shrapnel and was trying unsuccessfully to speak through blood-spattered lips. Despite his relative youth, Bazzi had seen men in a similar condition before. He wouldn't live. The other man was still down, but his flak jacket had taken most of the shrapnel. Bazzi dragged him to an empty room, keeping watch behind him more for Nassar's men than al-Omari's. It was a situation where friendly-fire casualties could be easily explained away.

There was a second door in the room and he shoved it open, checking the hallway before slipping into it alone. The sound of gunfire continued, increasingly muffled as he cleared the rooms lining the passage. Most consisted of nothing but four stone walls, but the last two were decorated with opulent bedroom furniture. Finally, he arrived at a locked door near the back. Nassar's men were still pinned down behind him and he fired at the latch, deciding he'd rather go in alone than with backup handpicked by Saudi Arabia's intelligence chief.

Bazzi stood to the side and gave the door a gentle push. A moment later three shots sounded, passing harmlessly by and hitting the wall on the other side of the hallway. He risked a quick glance inside and was able to make out detail from the moonlight coming through an unshuttered window. The furniture was even more grandiose than in the prior rooms and the space was much more expansive—probably ten meters square. The shooter had taken cover behind a bed and seemed to be armed with a handgun. Almost certainly the general making a last attempt to protect himself and his family.

"Surrender, General! If you do, I promise your wife and children will not be harmed."

Two more shots came through the open doorway and Bazzi slipped his weapon around the jamb, firing a short burst into the bed's dense wood frame.

"Come in here where I can see you, Saudi coward!"

Bazzi pulled back. "Be reasonable, General."

"You think I'll let you take me?"

"If you force me to kill you, your family will be interrogated in your place. What kind of man would allow this to happen?"

Bazzi slipped his weapon around the doorjamb again, this time sighting over it. Al-Omari held his fire. Muffled whispers were audible behind the bed and he finally tossed the gun onto the mattress and stood with his hands in the air.

"I have him," Bazzi said into his radio.

The shooting at the other end of the hall had stopped and he could hear the sound of booted feet running toward him. A moment later Nassar's men had surrounded al-Omari and his family.

"Bind them and bring them into the courtyard," Bazzi said. "I'll call in the helicopter."

"Understood," Aali Nassar said. "ETA less than one minute."

The operation had gone reasonably well. Al-Omari and his family had been secured without injury and at the cost of only one of his men. Bazzi had survived, which was suboptimal, but having him die during the assault was less critical than it would have been convenient. The young military commander would just have to be dealt with more directly.

The pilot switched on a spotlight and Nassar could see al-Omari's compound below. The only place flat enough to land was the courtyard, and the pilot set down inside the walls, kicking up a dense cloud of dust that enveloped the young colonel running crouched toward the aircraft.

He stopped short when he saw Nassar jump out, his gaze flicking from the intelligence director's face to the suitcase in his hand.

"Director Nassar. What are you doing here? I was told that we were to bring al-Omari to Medina."

"There's been a change of plans," Nassar said. "We'll begin our interrogation here."

"Sir, this location isn't secure. By now the locals will be aware of our presence."

"But that's precisely the problem, isn't it, Colonel?

News that we've captured al-Omari will travel quickly, and any intelligence he provides us will become useless at the same rate. If we have any hope of finding the whereabouts of Mullah Halabi quickly enough to take him, it will have to happen here." He paused. "If you're frightened, I can arrange for my helicopter to take you to a safer location."

"That won't be necessary," Bazzi said, leaving off the requisite "sir" as an act of pointless defiance. "May I carry your case?"

Nassar gave it to him, smiling imperceptibly as the man moved off with what he undoubtedly assumed were the implements necessary to extract information from their captive.

Nassar followed the young officer through the building and into a back bedroom where General al-Omari was secured to a chair. His wife and children were huddled in a corner.

"Take his family outside," Nassar ordered.

Two of his men ushered them out and another two remained, keeping their guns trained on the helpless Iraqi.

"Aali Nassar," the man said, and then spat on the floor. "What brings you this far from your comfortable home? And who will lick King Faisal's ass while you're gone?"

"Your reputation for bravado is well-earned, I see."

"As is your reputation for drama."

Nassar drew his firearm and aimed it at al-Omari's head. The general stared back defiantly while the increasingly nervous Colonel Bazzi looked on.

"Sir, I need clarification. I was told that we were to get this man and his family back to Saudi Arabia.

I understand that time is of the essence, but we're in danger here, and if we're attacked, we risk not getting any intelligence at all."

Nassar nodded silently and then adjusted his aim, firing a single round into Bazzi's forehead. The man collapsed onto the stone floor, a dark pool of blood fanning out around his head. Nassar fired a second shot, hitting the dead man in the thigh and then another in the neck. It would make the precision of the kill shot easier to explain away.

"Cut the general loose and leave us," Nassar said, holstering his weapon. One of his men severed the flex-cuffs holding al-Omari and then he and his comrade disappeared down the hallway.

"What is this?" the general said, too confused even to stand.

Nassar gazed down at the man who could legitimately be described as his ISIS counterpart. Al-Omari was hardly a brilliant man, but he didn't need to be. That was Mullah Halabi's role, and it was one he filled well. Al-Omari needed only to be competent enough to carry out the mullah's orders, and indeed he had proved to be more than up to the task. The combination of the two men was extraordinarily dangerous. More so than even the vaunted Irene Kennedy understood.

"We both know that the Saudi royalty won't survive the death of King Faisal, General. He's refused to groom a successor and the government will collapse under the weight of the power struggle. The Americans know that the royals in line are cretins and it's unlikely that they'll support any of the candidates."

"That's why you're here? To tell me things I already know?"

"I'm here because the rise of a caliphate that spans the Middle East is inevitable. And I believe that ISIS has an excellent chance of being the organization that ushers in that era. The mullah's plans display great wisdom and vision."

"Really?" al-Omari said, his voice gaining strength. "And what are those plans, Aali?"

"ISIS will eventually succeed in a massive attack on the U.S. and you will use that to turn the American population against its Muslim countrymen. As they're increasingly marginalized, ghettoized, and persecuted, they will rise up. This will continue the trend of America turning inward. Combined with their increased energy production, they will come to the realization that they have no compelling strategic interest in the Middle East anymore. They'll withdraw and Mullah Halabi will be free to take control of the entire Islamic world."

"Very clever," al-Omari said. "But enough with speeches. You want something."

"Of course," Nassar responded. "Your recent attack on Saudi Arabia would have destroyed the country's oil supply and with it the country itself. This was unwise. We have unparalleled military, intelligence, and financial resources. In fact, I think you recently enjoyed the fruits of the latter through the efforts of Prince bin Musaid."

"You were behind that?"

"Did you really think that an idiot like bin Musaid could have initiated something like that on his own? I have an extensive network of royals and wealthy private citizens sympathetic to your cause. And I'm willing to coordinate their efforts to help you."

"The king will discover what you're doing and ex-ecute you."

"The king will do nothing but die."

"You'll kill him?"

Nassar shook his head. "The years are doing it for me."

"And what do you want in return?"

"That's something for me and Mullah Halabi to discuss face-to-face."

Nassar opened the suitcase, enjoying the general's expression when he saw the euros stacked inside. "I'd like you to deliver my request for a meeting along with this gift."

"And if I refuse?"

On the surface it seemed like an odd question from a man in his position, but it was expected. He would reasonably see Nassar as a threat—as a man with far greater training, intellect, and resources than he him-self had. And while taking the general's place might become necessary in the future, it made sense to allay al-Omari's fears for the time being.

"I believe that you and I can work very effectively together, General. Me from Saudi Arabia and you at Mullah Halabi's side."

CHAPTER 13

RAPP pulled into the underground parking lot at CIA headquarters and briefly slammed the Charger's accelerator to the floor. The engine was powerful enough to shove him back into the racing seat but incapable of drowning out Radiohead's new album. He would never admit it to Craig Bailer, but the car actually had been worth the wait. The sound system was as good as any he'd ever heard, the armor's reduction in weight was immediately noticeable, and the annoying turbo lag was gone. Finding something to complain about was going to be a challenge.

He blasted by a few startled men in business suits before slamming on the stellar brakes and turning onto a ramp that led deeper into the garage. As was his custom, he passed by his assigned space and selected one at random. State-of-the-art armor or no, there was no way in hell he was going to park in a space with his name stenciled on it.

He jogged across the asphalt and slipped into a private elevator, leaning against the back wall as it ferried him to the seventh floor. Normally he avoided Langley like the plague, but Mike Nash was pretty much glued to his office these days. He'd become Irene Kennedy's go-to for dealing with Congress and the press, making it difficult for him to stray far from the Beltway for more than a few hours at a time. Besides, if Rapp had stayed home, he would have gotten roped into talking to Claudia about Coleman's job.

"I hear the Iraq op went off without too many problems," the former Marine said when Rapp entered his office.

Rapp dropped into a chair and put his feet up on Nash's desk. "But not so much Rabat."

"Yeah. Mas is back stateside, but he's lying low. Scott and I both told him you're over it, but he won't listen. He needs to hear it from you."

Nash was forever playing the diplomat. In this case, though, he was probably right.

"I'll call him on my way home."

That seemed to satisfy him and he pulled a folder from his drawer. The purpose of this meeting wasn't to talk about Joe Maslick but to find a temporary replacement for Coleman on the ops side. Rapp wasn't particularly optimistic, but it was something he was going to have to face. Sitting around and hoping for Coleman to miraculously heal wasn't working out.

"I think we've put together some solid candidates," Nash said. The hint of nervousness in his voice suggested that he wasn't sure Rapp would agree.

"Go ahead."

"Let's kick it off with Gary Fielder."

"The guy with brain damage?"

"It's not *brain damage*, Mitch. He has a congenital

neurological condition that makes it impossible for him to feel fear. It's a thing. People have written papers about it."

"No."

"That's it? No? Gary's a solid operator with years of combat experience."

"I can anticipate what a brave soldier will do in a given situation," Rapp said. "But someone who can't even conceptualize fear? Unpredictable."

"But—"

"Move on."

"Fine. You don't want Gary, forget Gary. Anthony Staton."

"How old is that guy?"

"Not as old as Scott."

"Weren't his hips shot?"

"Got a replacement. You're still due for a knee."

Rapp shook his head. "I've got nothing but respect for Tony, but you've picked the only guy on the planet who's full of more lead than me."

"I figured you'd say that, but it was worth a shot. Pun intended. Here's an out-of-the-box one. The Japanese said they'd lend us Yoshi. Don't tell me *that* guy isn't solid."

"He eats nails," Rapp agreed. "But I can only understand about half of what he says and that goes to ten percent when he's on a radio."

Nash let out a long breath and shuffled through the folder for a few seconds. "So, I'm not going to be able to sell you Chet Washington."

"No."

"Or Seth."

"Hell no."

"Brandon Tra—"

"No."

Nash closed the file. "I get the feeling you're doing this to me on purpose."

"If Scott's replacement fucks up, you'll be fine. But I'll be dead."

"Okay. Fair enough. What would you say if I told you I have an operator who's so good that even you'd steer around him if you had the chance. Rudimentary Arabic, but pretty well-connected in the region. And as a bonus, he's easy to get along with and speaks fluent Russian."

"I'd say you have my attention."

"Grisha Azarov."

Rapp just stared at him, not sure he'd heard right. "You want me to replace Scott with the man who did this to him?"

Nash held his hands up in a plea for peace. "Not my idea, Mitch. That name came straight from Scott. He's worried about you and he's worried about his guys. Figures Azarov's the best."

"So that's all you've got?"

"Pretty much, yeah."

Rapp pushed himself straighter in his chair. "Maslick's a good man. His first command was a little rocky, but none of us could say ours went much better. He'll get his feet under him."

"He's going to quit, Mitch. I'm telling you, if you put him in charge again, he's going to walk."

"I'll talk to him. What about logistics?"

"We haven't worked on it."

"What do you mean? Why not?"

"You already know the answer to that, man. Scott

wants Claudia. Irene wants Claudia. And Claudia wants Claudia. You might be picking up a pattern here. A certain name that keeps coming up?"

"She isn't getting involved."

"Then we've just managed to get absolutely nowhere."

"I'll convince Mas to take the ops job and you'll get me some names for logistics."

"I'd rather not, Mitch. If I do, Claudia's going to find out and then she's going to tell my wife and I'm going to catch hell."

Rapp started for the door. "I don't give a shit what you'd rather not do and I don't give a shit what Irene thinks. You and Scott have forty-eight hours to get me that list."

CHAPTER 14

W HEN Irene Kennedy entered the Oval Office, President Alexander was looking through the window at the sunlit landscape beyond. Normally he would have turned to greet her, displaying the southern hospitality that he was famous for. Today he didn't acknowledge her at all.

For a politician, Alexander was a surprisingly reasonable and honorable man. His opponents tried to use his good looks and dimpled, million-dollar smile to paint him as naïve and weak. Those accusations couldn't be further from the truth. He was an extremely intelligent and pragmatic man who cared deeply about his country. Like everyone in his position, he occasionally did the wrong thing for political reasons, but at least he did it reluctantly and with a strong grasp of the consequences.

The American people would be shocked to know that their affable leader's greatest flaw wasn't naïveté or weakness. It was rage. Instead of brief flashes of anger or occasional sarcasm to blow off steam, he bottled it up and eventually exploded. Kennedy had never spoken directly to the man about it, but the topic had once come up at a cocktail party she'd attended with the president's aging mother. According to her, he'd been that way since he was a toddler.

Kennedy took a seat in front of his desk. As always, a steaming cup of tea was waiting for her on a side table. "Good afternoon, Mr. President."

He didn't respond, undoubtedly preoccupied with the meeting he was about to host. Of all the problems he had to deal with, Saudi Arabia was perhaps the one he despised most. It was a country with sufficient resources to provide prosperous lives for its citizens and be a force for good throughout the region. Instead, those resources had been used to enrich a handful of monarchs and to promote the cycle of violence and misery that the Middle East was currently mired in. There were enough horrifying problems facing the world without having to spend blood and treasure trying to deal with the self-inflicted ones.

When the president finally took a seat, he wore the relaxed smile the world was so familiar with. "Irene. A rare pleasure. You seem to be sending Mike Nash to deal with us politicians these days."

Alexander was fond of ribbing the people who worked for him, but there was always a serious side to his jokes. A response was always required and it was best if it was an honest one.

"He's good at it, sir."

Alexander nodded. "Watch out for him, Irene. I don't think he wants your chair, but I wouldn't be surprised if one day he's sitting in mine."

Her eyebrows rose slightly. It wasn't something she'd ever considered, but now that she thought about it, Alexander was right. He always was when it came to politics.

"I'm certain I'd enjoy working for him almost as much as I've enjoyed working for you."

That was her subtle dig. Alexander hated to be patronized.

"Stop buttering me up, Irene. I already feel like a turkey about to get shoved in the oven."

She reached for her tea, relieved that the level of tension had diminished slightly.

"Did you hear that the ambassador's begged off?" Alexander said. "Some bullshit story about having food poisoning. So we're just getting Nassar."

"I'm not entirely surprised, sir. Calling an emergency meeting with no clear agenda is going to worry King Faisal and he's aware that Ambassador Alawwad is . . ." Her voice faded for a moment. ". . . less than capable."

"He's a mental defective. But my understanding is that Aali Nassar isn't. What do we know about him?"

"He's a former army officer with a significant amount of combat experience. He was educated at Oxford as part of a scholarship program King Faisal put into place for the exceptional children of working-class Saudis. In his early thirties, he moved from the military to Saudi intelligence, where he's enjoyed a distinguished career, culminating with him replacing Prince Khaled as the head of the General Intelligence Directorate."

"Religious?"

"He had a strict Muslim upbringing and gives every impression of maintaining those beliefs. Having said that, he's also practical and ambitious. So it's hard to determine how much of his religious conviction is real and how much is just a reflection of what's expected."

"Another politician in the making."

"Possibly."

Alexander leaned back in his chair and appraised her for a moment. "I'm suspicious about them suddenly flying Nassar in for this meeting. Do they know about Prince bin Musaid's visit to Morocco? Do they suspect that we tracked him there?"

"I don't think we should jump to conclusions," Kennedy said. "Right now, all evidence suggests that King Faisal has lived up to his post-9/11 agreement with us. We're not seeing any pattern of government-sponsored terrorism or support coming from the royal family."

"Until now."

"Yes, sir. But Prince bin Musaid is hardly a member of the power elite. I'd categorize him more as a black sheep."

"So a disgruntled little prick who doesn't think he's getting his due is lashing out."

"Until we have evidence to the contrary, it makes sense to assume that's the case."

"You're always the voice of reason, Irene. I don't know how you do it."

"I've always been an optimist, sir."

He actually laughed at that. The levity didn't last long though. His secretary poked her head in and announced the arrival of Aali Nassar.

"Send him in."

Kennedy had never been in the same room with the Saudi but now she could see that he was an impressive figure. Probably six foot two, with the square shoulders and narrow waist of a soldier despite being in his early sixties. His beard was dark and neatly trimmed, topped with close-cropped hair graying at the temples. He smiled politely and reached for the president's hand.

"It's a great honor, sir. Please allow me to apologize on behalf of Ambassador Alawwad for his absence. He's quite ill."

"Let me know if there's anything I can do."

"That won't be necessary. Your country's excellent medical personnel have things well in hand." His accent was more British than Middle Eastern—the result of his years studying in England.

When Alexander released his hand, Nassar turned toward Kennedy. "Dr. Kennedy. After speaking so many times on the telephone, it's a pleasure to finally meet you in person."

"I'm glad you happened to be coming our way, Director Nassar."

His dark eyes flashed almost imperceptibly at her words. They both knew very well that the timing of his trip was no accident.

"Have a seat," Alexander said. Nassar selected a leather wingback chair and watched silently as Kennedy and the president took up positions adjacent.

"I don't see any reason to beat around the bush," Alexander said. "We have information that Prince Talal bin Musaid recently went to Morocco to provide a million U.S. dollars in cash to an ISIS representative."

Kennedy watched the man's reaction carefully. For a moment there was none at all. Clearly he was calculating how to respond. The question was whether he had been aware of bin Musaid's actions or if this was a complete surprise. To his credit, she was unable to determine that from his expression.

"I'm sorry, Mr. President, but I find that difficult to believe. Who gave you this information?"

"We had a team there with orders to capture the man delivering the payment."

"Are you saying you have the prince in custody?"

It was a surprising question. Obviously, Nassar would know if the king's nephew had disappeared in Morocco. In light of that, it came off as a bit of a taunt. The president didn't react, so maybe Kennedy was in luck. Maybe he missed it.

"Our team was concerned that taking him could create an international incident and made the decision to stand down."

"Then I don't understand. Is this just speculation? Because our government and our royalty are as dedicated to the war on terrorism as anyone in the world. And that war has been extremely effective."

"Like your recent operation against General al-Omari?"

That quashed her hope that Alexander had missed Nassar's provocation.

"Our operation went flawlessly," Nassar responded. "Unfortunately, al-Omari wasn't there."

Alexander turned toward her. "Is that our understanding, Irene?"

This was a dangerous and unnecessary game of brinksmanship—one she didn't want to be dragged into. "The intelligence on the general's location was accurate."

"And yet I was there," Nassar countered. "It seems

likely that your intelligence was flawed. I think we would both agree that this is hardly uncommon where the Middle East is concerned."

He hadn't bothered to veil that insult.

"Certainty is difficult to come by," she said before the president could rejoin the conversation. The anger was visible in his eyes and he needed a moment to gain control of it.

"I believe that your accusation against Prince bin Musaid is an example of that lack of certainty," Nassar said. "Who were these witnesses? Private contractors in your employ? These men are little more than mercenaries and as such have very little credibility. Do you have any actual evidence to present?"

"We have a photograph," she said.

"Really? And is this photograph conclusive?"

It was clear that no photograph would be considered conclusive by this man. Certainly not one taken through a scope in marginal light.

"Director Nassar," Kennedy said, grateful that the president was allowing her to lead. "Incontrovertible proof may not be available, but this isn't a trial. We're allies. This is hardly something we would want to keep from you. It's possible that he's funding another attack on your own country."

"Frankly, I find that insulting."

"Be that as it may, it appears that he was using an embassy vehicle and embassy bodyguards to take him to the meeting. We can provide you with times and routes. I don't think it will be difficult for you to corroborate what we're telling you."

"The fact that the prince might have been in Morocco and might have taken a car out is hardly going to corroborate this outrageous and unsubstantiated accusation. Who was it that he was supposed to be meeting?"

"A man with a history of handling ISIS's financial matters."

"And is he in custody? Can he corroborate your story?"

"He is not," Kennedy said, unwilling to reveal that they'd turned Hayk Alghani.

"Then I'm not sure why I was even called into this meeting."

The president had finally reached his limit and Kennedy winced at the violence with which he threw himself forward in his chair. "First of all, you weren't called to this meeting. Alawwad was. And second, you're well aware of our agreement that your government will not aid or tolerate the aiding of extremist groups."

"And in return, you are to support us and our efforts to stamp out threats to the monarchy. To be frank, we've begun to question your continued commitment. Your support of Israel, your overtures toward Iran, your increased focus on—"

"I think you may be overstating what was promised by my predecessor," Alexander said, barely holding his anger in check. "We agreed to keep the extent of your government's complicity in 9/11 quiet and help you keep it from happening again. Not that we were going to become your servants on the world stage. Despite Saudi Arabia having the third largest defense budget in the world, *Norway* has flown more sorties against ISIS than you have. And every time they—or *we*—do, you quietly talk about the Christian Crusaders pounding at your gates. And we tolerate it. But if your royals are starting to get directly involved in terrorism again, that's crossing the line."

"It seems, then, that neither of us has an ideal partner in this relationship, Mr. President. But, as imperfect as it is, it is a relationship that will persist. If all the facts surrounding 9/11 were to come out, it would unquestionably be very damaging to my country. But I think the American people would be less concerned with our actions than your government's efforts to keep those actions secret from them. And while you didn't forge this agreement, you would very quickly become the face of it."

The president seemed frozen and Kennedy had no idea what he was going to do. She'd never witnessed a foreign bureaucrat openly threaten the President of the United States.

It was clear that there was no way to deescalate the situation. The only course of action she could come up with was to counter Nassar's unprecedented move with one of her own.

"It's been a pleasure meeting you, Director," she said, unilaterally ending the president's meeting. "I'm certain that you'll handle this matter with the thoroughness you're known for."

When Alexander didn't stand, Nassar just nodded in his direction and made his way to the exit. Kennedy half expected Alexander to explode when the soundproof door clicked shut, but he just sat there. She took a seat in the chair that Nassar had just abandoned, hoping to erase some of the memory of his presence.

A very long minute passed before Alexander spoke. "Did he just tell me to go fuck myself?"

"I think you're overreacting, sir. I—"

"You're patronizing me again, Irene. And this time I'm not laughing."

"Sir, please hear me out. Director Nassar isn't a diplomat. He's a soldier and a spy who's stepped into a very difficult situation. The Middle East is imploding, King Faisal is dying, and—"

"The Middle East is imploding because those Saudi sons of bitches have been pumping up religious fundamentalism to hide the fact that they're robbing their people blind. And when they aren't busy with that, they're doing everything they can to tank oil prices in an effort to wipe out our energy industry—"

"But that isn't Director Nassar's doing. It—"

"I'm not done! We don't want to forget that Saudi women have virtually no rights and that the government still executes people for witchcraft. Our relationship has always been a stain on our moral authority and dignity, but it was necessary. Is it still?"

She remembered that Mitch Rapp had recently asked something very similar.

"On balance, I'm convinced that it is, sir."

"The devil you know. Is that what you're saying, Irene? Let me ask you something. What if this goes beyond bin Musaid? What if King Faisal is too old and sick to keep tabs on what his people are doing anymore?"

"It's something we need to look into."

Alexander just stared into the distance. "Faisal won't do anything. He has a soft spot for that little asshole. His dead sister's son, right? And even if he didn't, we both know that he's just running out the clock. Waiting to die so he can leave his problems to someone else."

"I'd say that's an accurate assessment."

"What about Nassar? It seems like the king's putting a lot of faith in him. You said he was ambitious. Is he ambitious enough to be thinking about who's going to take over when the old man's gone? Because when I look at the front-runners, I see a pack of complete dipshits."

"Overthrowing the Saudi monarchy would be no small task, sir. But it's something we'll include in our analysis."

"Your analysis," Alexander said, and then laughed bitterly. "I can't wait."

CHAPTER 15

"TWENTY-SIX! Come on, Mitch! You can do thirty!"

Based on the daggerlike pain coming from an old elbow injury, thirty would probably be a bad idea. Anna groaned theatrically when he dropped off the pull-up bar and worked his right arm around. The gym Claudia had installed in the basement was incredible—better than anything inside of fifty miles. The fact that the lap pool bisected it was a little inconvenient, but she liked the way it reflected the glass-fronted wine cellar along the north wall. Who was he to argue?

"You could have done more," Anna complained.

"And you could end up in the pool."

He started chasing her, and she squealed with delight as she ducked through a squat rack. He nearly had her cornered when Claudia's voice rose up behind him.

"I bought you all this equipment and this is what you do with it?"

They froze, both looking a little guilty when they finally turned toward her.

"I went to tuck you in and you weren't there. It's after nine."

"There's no clock down here, Mom."

Claudia looked around the expansive room, discovering that her daughter was right. "That's no excuse. Now march. When I get up there, your teeth better be brushed and you better be under the covers."

"Okay," she said. As she passed Rapp, she gave him a hard jab in the leg and then darted away. He would have liked to chase her up the stairs, but it would be too obvious. He'd avoided being alone with Claudia for about as long as he could.

"She's never going to get to sleep now."

"Sorry. But there really isn't a clock down here."

"There will be tomorrow," she assured him. "Would now be a good time to talk?"

"Well, I'm in the middle of working out," he said, immediately regretting it.

"Is that what you two were doing? Working out?"

Checkmate.

"I guess I can cut it short."

"Thank you."

They just stared at each other for a few seconds. This was her pet subject. If she was waiting for him to start, they were going to be here for a long time.

"I need to *do* something, Mitch. After finishing your house, my life has lost its sense of direction. I love being Anna's mother—it's the most important thing in the world to me. But it can't be the only thing."

"You take care of me, too."

"You would be fine in a tent in Afghanistan," she said, and then waved a hand around her. "Does any of this even matter to you?"

"A few months ago I would have said no," he said honestly. "That shithole I was living in kept the rain off my head as well as any place. But now? Yeah. It matters."

"And us? Me and Anna?"

He thought about her question for a long time, finally realizing that he'd been wrong. He didn't really give a shit about the house. The concrete, glass, and overpriced furniture weren't what made it home. Claudia and Anna were.

Claudia slid back beneath the sheets, pressing her naked body against Rapp's. The pace of her breathing increased for a moment but then returned to the gentle rhythm he'd been listening to for the last three hours.

The point of no return with her—and with Anna—had now been crossed. He thought about his wife and how much he'd loved her. About his unborn child and what that child would have meant to him. And, of course, about Claudia's role in their deaths.

Were they looking down on him right now? And if so, what were they feeling? Betrayal? Anger at the fact that every day their memory lost a little bit of sharpness? Or relief that he'd finally moved on?

Ironically, the hours they'd just spent creating a seismic shift in their relationship had also allowed him to once again delay the conversation about her going to work for Coleman. Giving orders was no longer an option—if it really ever had been. Maybe tomorrow she'd make the observation that Scott paid better than the Agency and that maybe *he* should be the one to stay home with Anna.

The phone rang, and he snatched it off the night-stand in an effort not to wake the woman who was no longer sharing just his house. "Yeah. What?"

"Sorry about the hour, Mitch. Do you have a min-ute?"

His instinct was to bolt upright in bed, but he couldn't do that anymore, either. A call in the middle of the night from the President of the United States now only rated sliding carefully off the mattress and padding into the bathroom.

"I'm sorry, sir," he said, closing the door behind him. "Of course I do."

"Shit. You weren't alone. This is obviously a bad time..."

Incredibly bad. But not as bad as a couple of hours ago. "It's fine, sir. Is there a problem?"

"There's always a problem. That's the life we've cho-sen, right?"

His voice had a strange undertone that Rapp hadn't heard before. Frustration and anger, sure. But there seemed to be something hidden beneath. Something that even this consummate politician couldn't hide.

"I suppose so, sir."

"There's something I need to talk to you about. But not over the phone."

"Do you want to schedule a meeting for later this morning?"

"Honestly, it's not a conversation I want to be seen having, either."

Rapp was intrigued but also a little guarded. He'd been in this business a long time and the president had never called him personally to set up a completely black meeting. He tended to use Irene Kennedy as an intermediary. Best not to be seen with a man whose job description no one ever spoke about but everyone understood.

"It seems like we're both awake, sir. How about now? With no traffic I can be there in less than an hour."

"I don't want to take you away from anything," he said, although it was clear that it was exactly what he wanted.

"Not a problem."

"Thank you, Mitch."

Rapp disconnected the call and slipped into the bedroom to find some clothes. When he came out of the closet and started for the hallway, Claudia called after him. "Mitch? Who was that?"

"Work. I've got to run out."

"When are you going to be back?"

"A few hours," he said, wincing a bit.

"Oh," she responded, sounding like she'd thought he was going to say a few months. "There's a sticky on the refrigerator. Could you pick up the things on it? Anna doesn't have anything for breakfast."

"Sure."

And then she was asleep again.

That was it? His late wife would have been wide-awake, cross-examining him about where he was going, who he was meeting, and why it couldn't wait until after sunrise.

Some of the tension he'd felt over the past few hours started to dissipate. Maybe this could actually work.

CHAPTER 16

RAPP pulled Claudia's Q5 up to the White House gate, rolling down the window as a guard approached.

"Morning, Charlie."

The man studied Rapp for a moment and then checked his clipboard. "I don't see you on the list, Mitch."

It was a long-standing joke between them. His name was never on the list.

"Just open the damn gate and go back to your coffee."

He grinned, as he always did, and let Rapp through.

President Alexander hadn't been kidding when he said he wanted to keep this meeting quiet. No security was in evidence, and the lights indicating power to the surveillance cameras were conspicuously dark.

He walked through the semidarkness to the Oval Office's partially open door. The president was at his desk, scanning a document through metal-rimmed reading glasses.

"Sir?"

"Come on in," Alexander said. "Close the door behind you."

Rapp did as instructed and then took a seat in front of the man's desk.

"Can I get you anything, Mitch?"

"I'm fine."

The relaxed façade that Alexander normally kept between him and the world was showing cracks. Not that this was unusual during their meetings. If Rapp was at the White House, something had gone very wrong. On this particular morning, though, the cracks seemed dangerously deep.

"I assume you're aware of what happened in Morocco with Prince bin Musaid?"

"I'm sorry about that. With Scott out of action, we're spread pretty thin."

He nodded. "And you're aware of my meeting with Aali Nassar?"

"Irene mentioned it."

"And how did she characterize that meeting?"

"As less than ideal."

"So she didn't tell you that he unzipped his fly and told America to get on its knees?"

Actually, in her own sterile way, she had.

"Nassar isn't a diplomat. He—"

"Don't start. I already got that speech from your boss."

Alexander began pacing around the room, forcing Rapp to scoot his chair around to keep eyes on him.

"I assume you're also aware of the deal that was made with the Saudi government after 9/11."

Rapp nodded. In fact, he was far more aware than Alexander was. While the administration at the time had ordered the CIA to drop the matter, the director had interpreted those orders loosely. The Agency had quietly continued to gather intel, which was now squirreled away on an encrypted drive accessible only by Irene Kennedy. The specific names, dates, and bank account numbers in that file were no longer of much practical use—the players were largely dead or headed for nursing homes. What was still relevant was the portrait of a country playing both sides hard, counting on oil reserves and radical Islam to keep it intact.

"I know something about it," Rapp replied.

"So do you think bin Musaid's a lone wolf? An anomaly that got by the king?"

"I don't have enough information to make that call."

"Then speculate."

Rapp thought about it for a moment. "I'd be surprised if Faisal was involved. He just wants to keep the shit from hitting the fan until after he's dead. As far as the prince is concerned, he's a useless prick who thinks he's being unfairly passed over by the family. This could just be a tantrum."

Alexander continued to pace, considering what he'd just heard. "I thought the same thing. But what if it's not? My concern is that bin Musaid isn't smart enough to do something like this on his own. How did he make these contacts? How did he set up the meeting? Neither thing is rocket science, but it would take a certain amount of persistence and initiative that he's never demonstrated."

The president's anger seemed to be on an unstoppable upward trajectory. Rapp had heard rumors about Alexander's temper but had never known anyone who'd experienced it firsthand.

"That deal was one of the biggest mistakes this country ever made," the president said, spinning toward Rapp. "Those royal motherfuckers don't give a shit about anyone but themselves. They'd destroy their own country, America, the world, and anything else they can get their hands on for another gold-plated Rolls-Royce."

The volume of his voice had risen to the point that Rapp glanced over at the door to make sure he'd pulled it all the way closed.

"What if this is just the tip of the iceberg, Mitch? Faisal's going to be dead inside of two years and his successor is going to have the power to decide who he's going to back. The radicals or us."

"More likely they'll just try to keep limping along, playing it down the middle."

"Unacceptable!" the president yelled.

"Sir, I think you should call—"

"I am *not* going to be the man who ushered in another decade of those pricks sitting around London nightclubs while our guys bleed in the sand defending them. They're either with us or they're against us. And if they choose the second one, I'm going to squash them like fucking bugs."

Rapp rarely found himself in the position of being the voice of reason, but things were getting out of hand. "This is something you should sit down and talk to Irene about. She can—"

"You think I've lost my mind, don't you?" Alexander said.

"No, sir. But I'm not sure why I'm here."

"Then let me tell you. You're here because it's time for us to put the fear of Allah into these sons of bitches."

"Can you be more specific?"

"I could slap the harshest economic sanctions in history on their country and you know what those royal assholes would do? Fly to Paris and drown their sorrows in ten-thousand-dollar bottles of wine while their people starved. The only way we're going to get them to fall into line is by creating a penalty that *they* feel. From now on, I want them to know that it's *their* asses on the line."

"And how would you propose we do that?"

Alexander looked like he was going to make a move for the chair behind his desk, but chose the one next to Rapp instead. "I think you need to have a talk with Prince bin Musaid and at the end of that talk I think he needs to be dead."

"Sir?"

"You heard me."

"I'm not sure I did."

"I want you to find out if this goes any further and I want you to make the point that no one is off-limits."

"And how would I make that point?"

"By killing those people, too. It was suggested to another prince once that it's better to be feared than loved. When the new Saudi administration comes in, I want it to be clear that when America says jump, the only appropriate response is to ask how high."

Spent, Alexander leaned back in his chair. "You're surprised."

"That's a lot of plain talk coming from a politician."

"Then, while I'm on a roll, let me give you some more. This conversation never happened. The CIA can't be involved in any way. If you decide to do this and you get caught, I'll abandon you so fast, it'll make your head spin. The Saudis need to know I'm responsible, but they can't be able to prove it."

"Understood."

"So what do you think?"

Rapp shrugged noncommittally. "Obviously, you're playing my tune. But then, you know that or you wouldn't have called me."

Alexander smiled, the storm apparently over. "Let me give you a piece of advice, Mitch. You should tell me to go fuck myself. Then we can forget this conversation ever happened and talk about the Redskins' chances this season."

When Rapp exited the building, he discovered that Claudia's car was gone. The White House wasn't exactly a high-crime area and that could mean only one thing.

His suspicions were confirmed when a Lincoln Navigator glided up in front of him. He opened the back door and slid inside.

"You're up early, Irene."

As always, she looked impeccable—gray suit, dark hair pulled back, and shoes meticulously polished. "I couldn't sleep."

The silence stretched out between them as they pulled onto a quiet Pennsylvania Avenue. Finally, she broke it.

"The president's angry about bin Musaid and the Saudi government."

"Really?"

"The subject didn't come up?"

Rapp shook his head. "He just wanted my thoughts on the White House football pool."

It was a statement that would make the discussion he'd just had completely clear without making her complicit.

"Alexander's a good man. I've been lucky in my career. We both have. We've worked for smart, reasonable administrations."

"Yeah."

"But he's still a politician."

"You're not telling me anything I don't know, Irene."

"He won't just turn his back on you," she continued. "Neutrality won't play well on the international stage. He'll do everything in his power to track you down. And capturing you won't be the goal. America can't risk you being questioned."

"Uh-huh."

She looked out the window, watching the buildings pass by for a few moments. "I understand that things are going well with Claudia."

He wasn't sure what she meant by that. Could she know? The woman had an intuition that inspired confidence when it was working for you but was infuriating when it was turned against you. He remained silent.

"You have the beginnings of a good life, Mitch. And while I'm not here to suggest that you slow down, I'd recommend that you avoid running off any cliffs. Just for a while, until you figure out what you want for yourself and for the people around you."

"Then tell me he's wrong, Irene. Tell me that *I'm* wrong. I've always listened to you."

She just kept looking out the window. Finally, Rapp saw Claudia's Q5 parallel parked at the edge of the street. The driver stopped beside it and, in an unusual gesture, Kennedy held out a hand to Rapp. "Whatever you decide, Mitch, good luck with it."

By the time Rapp pulled up in front of his house, the sun had cleared the horizon. He hadn't driven directly home, taking the long way to give himself time to think. What conclusions he'd come to, though, he wasn't sure.

Anna met him in the entry, still wearing her pajamas and rubbing at her eyes. "Did you get me my oatmeal?"

He held up a grocery bag. "Go get ready for school. I'll make it for you."

"No," she protested. "Let Mom do it."

"Fine. But put it in gear. You're going to be late."

She disappeared up the hallway, and he crossed through the interior courtyard to the kitchen. Claudia was standing by the refrigerator, carefully extracting coffee from a machine that looked like it had been designed by NASA.

"How was your meeting?" she asked.

"What meeting? I just went to the store."

"Ah," she said, sliding a cup of Peruvian dark roast toward him. As always, it was spectacular.

"There are some things I need to deal with," he said as she began the elaborate process of filling her own cup.

"The problems you learned about at the Food Lion?"

"Yeah. Those."

"How long will you be gone?"

He wasn't sure how to answer. This job was unlike anything he'd ever taken on. He worked at the extreme edges of the U.S. intelligence apparatus but he was still part of it. Disregarding orders was very different from not having any orders.

"Awhile."

She slid onto a stool and stared at him, picking up on his unusual reticence. "Off the books?"

"Worse."

"Completely black?"

He took a sip of his coffee. Fuck. He couldn't believe he was about to do this.

"Keep going."

She clapped her hands together excitedly. "A rogue operation?"

He gave a hesitant nod.

"So, a criminal enterprise," she said, not bothering to hide her glee. "And only one of the people at this table knows how to be a criminal."

CHAPTER 17

A ALI Nassar glanced at his watch. Four in the morning.

Through the window he could see the refueling truck as it approached his jet and the glow of the airport beyond. Individual lights were ringed with a distinct haze, and he blinked his eyes in an effort to clear them. It was no use. Sleep had been impossible since his meeting with the American president, and fatigue was starting to take its toll.

There was little question that his performance in the Oval Office had been stupid and careless. He'd allowed his hatred for Joshua Alexander and the country he represented to overpower his reason. What should have been a careful political denial had become a battle of wills between him and the man purported to be the most powerful in the world. The temptation to demonstrate his disdain and to watch the man sputter like an impotent fool had been too strong.

He told himself that there was nothing the president could do—that the economic and geopolitical ramifications of acting against Saudi Arabia would be too great. Kennedy would undoubtedly counsel her country's leader that the meeting was an unimportant example of a bureaucrat untrained in the complexities of politics. And he would likely listen. But what about the more violent and volatile elements of the American government? Those led by Mitch Rapp?

Nassar had significantly increased Prince bin Musaid's security, but Musaid was still an obvious target for the CIA and, as such, a potential liability. Would they be that bold? While bin Musaid was an idiot, he was the only living connection King Faisal had with the sister he'd favored above all others.

A man in overalls appeared in the jet's open doorway and spoke briefly to one of Nassar's security detail before disappearing again.

"Sir, the refueling hose has become jammed and they're concerned it could cause a fire. We're being asked to deplane until they can get the problem resolved."

"How long?"

"It should be no more than a few minutes, but they're unwilling to start the process of freeing the hose until the plane is empty."

Nassar let out a frustrated breath but then started for the door. Getting delayed in West Africa wasn't an option. He might still have time to take advantage of Alexander's paralysis and get to Faisal before he was informed about what had happened. It wouldn't be hard to soften the impact. The old fool trusted him.

Nassar followed his two security men across the tarmac to a small building along its edge. They were well away from the main terminal, and the darkness increased as they distanced themselves from the plane. It took a few seconds for his man to find the light switch, but once it was on he ushered Nassar inside.

It was little more than a shed full of rusting equipment and Nassar stopped just beyond the threshold. "This is unacceptable. Find me another place to wait. Clear out a gate in the—"

He fell silent when he saw a shadow move near the back. A moment later three men stepped into the harsh light of the overhead bulb. Nassar's reaction time, honed by years in the Saudi special forces, had been dulled only slightly by age. In this instance, though, his confusion caused him to hesitate. It was clear that none of the men were local. Two were wearing desert fatigues and scarves wrapped around their faces, but he didn't focus on them. It was the man in the center who captured his attention. He was Nassar's height and weight, with the same neat hair and tight beard. Moreover, he was wearing a suit and a pair of aviator sunglasses that were identical to ones that Nassar had left in the plane.

The Saudi spun toward the still open door and was nearly through when one of his guards grabbed him from behind. Instead of protecting him, he slammed Nassar facedown on the greasy floorboards.

A blinding flash at the main terminal was followed by the rumble of an explosion and a burst of machine-gun fire. Again he found himself in the unusual position of being unable to decipher what was happening. Had his guard anticipated the blast and shoved him down to protect him? Or had he been betrayed?

The answer came a moment later when two of the men he'd seen at the back of the shed dropped on top of him. Outside, a vehicle with a mounted gun was coming their way, firing random bursts at aircraft as it passed. The man dressed like Nassar joined Nassar's guards and started for the door.

"You're working for the CIA!" he shouted after them. "Stop this now or your families will pay the price! I will—"

One of the men grabbed him by the hair and yanked his head back, silencing him with a piece of tape. Flexcuffs were looped around his wrists as he watched his guards run across the tarmac with his doppelgänger, firing their handguns at the approaching truck. Another explosion rocked the terminal as they leapt into his jet and closed the door. The fuel hose had been detached and the plane immediately began taxiing with the truck in pursuit. It was an obvious diversion—the gunner was going wide with every shot. By the time the plane finally took to the air, Nassar was struggling to breathe. It wasn't the tape over his mouth, though. It was the realization of what was to come.

He had only himself to blame. He'd been blinded by his own arrogance and the intensity of his hatred for the Americans. He'd believed them to be too weak to move against him like this. And now that miscalculation would cost him a slow death at the hands of Mitch Rapp.

CHAPTER 18

"ARE you sure this is it?" Claudia leaned into the dashboard and examined the decaying buildings closing in on them from both sides. Around the turn of the century, the brick and stone structures had been used to build locomotives, but now most were abandoned.

"I'm sure," Rapp said.

He turned and drove alongside the blackened shell of a building, picking his way along a cobblestone street that was more mud than stone. The Charger's recently upgraded suspension handled it all without breaking a sweat.

"Kind of a depressing neighborhood," Claudia said, returning to the computer in her lap.

"Where do we stand?" Rapp asked.

"In a good place, I think. That was a very thorough list of Prince bin Musaid's bank accounts and passwords. Did Marcus give it to you?"

"Let's just say that it happened to be sitting on his desk when I walked by."

"A wonderful stroke of luck," she said, tapping a few keys. "I've been able to confirm that they're all active and use them as a starting point to track down a few more of the prince's assets."

"Really? Things Marcus missed?"

She nodded. "Offshore accounts and shell corporations, mostly. The money from them was laundered through financial institutions not friendly to the U.S. Mostly Iran, Syria, and North Korea."

"Not a problem for you, though."

She shrugged. "I've used the same networks in the past."

"So you're confident you have all of it?"

"Unless he has significant amounts of cash hidden somewhere, but I doubt that's the case. In my experience, men like him trust financial institutions. They have no reason not to."

"Yet," Rapp added.

"Yet," she agreed.

"Do you have a secure connection?"

"Via 4G."

"Then transfer the money."

"Now?"

"Yeah."

She smiled broadly and typed in a few more commands, finally hitting the ENTER key with a flourish.

"Well?"

"Don't be impatient. These things take time. . . . Yes. There."

She held up the laptop so he could see the screen. Their newly formed company, Orion Consulting, now had bank balances that totaled just over seventy million dollars.

"That should keep you in ammunition and unfashionable leather jackets for a while."

"So we've completely emptied bin Musaid's accounts?"

"Down to the equivalent of twenty-eight thousand U.S. dollars."

"Why did you leave him twenty-eight grand?"

"So the banks don't close the accounts and notify him."

"Does he have overdraft protection on any of them?"

"Yes. Two."

"Okay, max out his overdrafts and get me that last twenty-eight grand."

She worked for a few seconds more. "Done. I think you Americans would say that Prince Talal bin Musaid is officially fucked. He has multiple large mortgages and other loans, salaried staff, and various taxes coming due—none of which he'll be capable of paying. He has whatever cash he keeps on hand. After that's gone, he won't even be able to buy groceries."

"And you're still confident that you can keep tabs on him?"

"My guess is he'll run to Europe. He has a successful brother there who's distanced himself from Saudi Arabia and the monarchy. When the prince discovers his accounts have been drained, I suspect he'll go to him for money, advice, and protection."

With a little luck, that's exactly what would happen. It was impossible to know if Nassar and Faisal would tell the little prince that the CIA was onto him, but bin Musaid would be smart enough to realize that this wasn't just some random hack. And when he made that connection, he'd start wondering if a foreign government was behind draining his accounts. More important, he'd start wondering what his life was worth in Saudi Arabia. How far would the king stick his neck out to protect one of his dumbass nephews? It wasn't like he had a shortage of them.

"Once bin Musaid's outside of Saudi Arabia, he'll be isolated and easier to deal with. We just need to—"

Claudia's phone started to ring and she held up a finger before picking up.

"Bonjour, chérie!"

Anna. Rapp frowned, reminding himself that these kinds of interruptions were part of his life now. That didn't mean they weren't going to take some getting used to, though.

"Yes, of course you can. It sounds like fun. How high? Well, you should be very careful, yes? Remember what happened last time."

She was staying with Irene and being largely cared for by her son, with whom she'd developed an immediate rapport. It turned out that Tommy had always wanted a little sister and was being a startlingly good sport about the new demands on his time and teenage dignity.

"Yes, of course. Soon. Don't run if it's wet."

She hung up and Rapp glanced over. "How's she doing?"

"Oh, fine. Her life has always been chaotic. She's used to it. Sometimes I wonder if she'd get bored if she was ever forced into a routine."

"And you?"

"Me?"

"How's your new routine working out?"

"Wonderfully so far."

"You can back out anytime."

"Why would I want to do that?"

"I can think of about a hundred reasons. I never want you to feel like you're trapped in this, Claudia. If it starts looking hairier than you're comfortable with, or even if you just want to get back to Anna, you can walk anytime. You don't owe me anything."

"Stop worrying, Mitch. This isn't the first time I've done this kind of work."

They pulled up next to a group of parked cars that included Scott Coleman's SUV and got out, walking toward an unadorned steel door. There was a single button above a brass plate printed with "SD&S, Inc."—previously "SEAL Demolition and Salvage." When Coleman moved his offices, he'd decided to use the acronym. It was as vague as he could go and still get his deliveries.

Rapp hit the bell and the door buzzed, letting them through. The interior was better appointed than anyone would guess from outside. Freshly painted walls, exposed brick, and carefully preserved industrial hardware further obscured the organization's real purpose in the veneer of a San Francisco tech firm.

"We're in the conference room!" Coleman shouted from the back.

Rapp and Claudia started down a hallway lined with offices that ranged from the OCD neatness of the one occupied by Charlie Wicker to the disaster of take-out food trays and partially disassembled weapons that belonged to Bruno McGraw.

The conference room was completely nondescript other than the people surrounding the table. Most were former spec ops—Coleman, McGraw, Joe Maslick, and Wick. The exception was Bebe McCade, whose grandmotherly look hid the fact that she was probably the planet's top surveillance operative.

Claudia gave Rapp a subtle nudge and he singled out Maslick for a nodded greeting. It was the first time he'd seen the man since before the Morocco op, and the former Delta operator was apparently still on edge. As usual, Claudia was right and he relaxed visibly in response to the gesture.

Rapp stood at the head of the table, aware that everyone probably assumed that he was going to announce his decision to allow Claudia to take over Coleman's logistics role. What he was actually there to do would be a hell of a lot harder.

"Earlier this morning, I gave Irene my letter of resignation," he said.

The expected stunned silence ensued. Finally, Coleman managed to speak. "What are you talking about?"

"I'm talking about the fact that the injuries I got on our last op are worse than the docs told me and I've had to admit that I can't do the job the way it needs to be done. I want to be clear, though. You guys aren't out. Cary Donahue is going to replace me and he wants you as his primary backup. All of you know him, and I know that all of you have the same respect for him that I do."

"Can I have Claudia for logistics?" Coleman said with a calmness that seemed a little ominous.

"No," she responded. "Mitch and I are going to be doing some traveling."

"Really? Traveling? Let me guess. Bird-watching in New Zealand? Maybe a little boogie boarding in Hawaii?"

"I don't—"

"This is bullshit!" Coleman said, flinging the pad in front of him against the wall. "Mitch Rapp is quitting the CIA because he got a few bruises in Pakistan? What the fuck are you even talking about?" He grabbed the cane next to his chair and held it up. "Look at me."

"I've got some things I need to work out," Rapp said.

"Yeah? Like what?" Coleman used the cane to point to the people around the table. "We've all bled for you, Mitch. And now you come in here and tell us some bullshit story about walking off into the sunset?"

A few of Coleman's men actually scooted back a bit, but he just kept staring Rapp in the eye. He obviously believed that, after everything they'd been through together, he deserved better. And he was right.

"I need to go somewhere you and your boys can't follow, Scott."

"When have we ever complained?"

"Couldn't be worse than the shit that went down in Nigeria," Bruno McGraw said, and everyone nodded in agreement.

"What are we talking about here?" Wicker asked. "Beyond black? What's the worst that could happen? I end up dead? Or on the run from the FBI? Fuck it. I'm in." That drew more nods.

"You're the best in the world at what you do and it's been my privilege to serve with you," Rapp said.

"But now you need to show Cary the same loyalty you showed me."

He gestured toward the door and Claudia started for the hallway, looking a bit choked up. He felt the same way, but refused to show it. "Thank you for everything you've done. And good luck."

CHAPTER 19

AALI Nassar regained consciousness slowly, becoming aware of the hum of a car engine and crunch of tires on a dirt road. He was blindfolded and his hands were secured behind his back, but they hadn't yet arrived at what he assumed would be his final destination. The lingering rage at the betrayal of his men had turned cold with fear. Was there an opportunity for escape? It had been many years since he'd been in combat, but the training was still part of him. How many men were in the car? No one spoke, but he could smell their sweat. The heat was a clue. The windows were closed. Did it mean they were on a busy road? There was no sound filtering in from outside, but that didn't mean the landscape they were traveling was empty.

He had no idea of their speed, but he did have a good sense of what awaited him at the end of this journey. Could he reach the lock without alerting anyone that he was conscious? The handle? If he was able to throw himself through the door, would he survive? Did it matter?

A quick death from trauma would undoubtedly be preferable to what Mitch Rapp had planned for him.

Nassar began to turn, keeping his movements agonizingly slow and straining his ears for any reaction. He'd made it less than a centimeter when the vehicle slowed and came to a stop. The door he was leaning against was yanked open and he was pulled violently through.

"We know you're awake, Director," a disembodied voice said. "Walk or I'll saw your legs off myself."

Nassar got his numb feet beneath him and began stumbling forward with men holding him on either side. The sound of a door opening was followed by him tripping over the threshold and nearly falling face-first to the floor.

The blindfold was removed and he squinted against the light. The concrete cell he had been expecting wasn't in evidence. Instead he was in a large room with exposed wood walls and utilitarian architecture that gave no hints as to his location. The man looking down on him, though, was easily recognized.

He was sitting on a raised platform haphazardly draped with colorful rugs. His clothing was traditional and all black, with a headdress that covered his hair but left his bearded face exposed. Not Mitch Rapp. Instead, Nassar found himself in the presence of Mullah Sayid Halabi. The leader of ISIS.

"Good evening, Director. It's my understanding that you wanted to see me."

Nassar met the pale blue eyes of the mullah with the required deference. In his peripheral vision he could see men lined up on either side of him. General al-Omari was to Halabi's right, but the others were only intermittently identifiable. Largely former Iraqi officers and advisors to Saddam Hussein.

"Yes," he said, the residual effects of the drug he'd been given making it difficult to form words. Thank Allah that his mind was clear.

"To what purpose?"

"To negotiate an alliance between ISIS and Saudi Arabia."

"You speak for the king, then?" Halabi said, though it was obvious that he knew the answer.

"No. The king and the royalty have turned their backs on Islam."

"I see. Then you speak for yourself. For your own ambitions."

"My ambition is only that the caliphate succeed. And that Saudi Arabia act in service to that goal."

The mullah remained silent, making it clear that he expected a more complete response. And that the content of that response would determine whether Nassar lived or died.

"ISIS's attack on Saudi Arabia's oil fields and the fact that it was thwarted by Mitch Rapp has strengthened King Faisal's allegiance to America."

The mullah's eyes narrowed but it was impossible to know if it was the result of his hatred for the CIA man or the mention of his plan's failure. The question was how plainly to speak in the man's presence. He had surrounded himself with competent advisors, but did he listen to them?

"That action, if it had succeeded, would have created chaos in the region that you could have brought order to. But it was a plan with drawbacks. It would have left ISIS in control, but of what? A fractured and

violent land with thousands of factions being supported by Americans, Russians, Europeans, and even
Asians. Consolidating that into a cohesive Islamic
state with the ability to effectively administer its internal affairs and defend itself from outside forces would
have been difficult if not impossible."

"But you can solve these problems," Halabi said.

"Solve them? No. But right now you have Saudi
Arabia, a country with one of the most powerful militaries in the region, increasingly dedicated to your
destruction. Faisal has refused to name a successor,
but I can tell you that every man in line is weak and
corrupt. The question is: Who will pull the new king's
strings? You or the Americans?"

Halabi scanned the faces of his advisors before
answering. "Then you want my help in increasing
your influence in Saudi Arabia so that in turn you
can influence who succeeds Faisal. Or perhaps your
ambitions are grander? Perhaps you see the end of
the Saudi monarchy and yourself as the leader of that
country."

Nassar lowered his head submissively. "Whatever
would serve you most effectively."

Halabi's unblinking eyes were suddenly filled with
amusement. As though they had examined Nassar's
soul and found it laughably trivial.

"State your case plainly, Director. I have to return
you to your home as quickly as possible. My men
won't be able to hide your absence for much longer."

Nassar felt some of the tension drain from him
at the acknowledgment that he wouldn't die in this
place. A significant amount of that tension remained,
though, at the realization that the Saudi guards he'd

thought were loyal to him were in fact servants of Halabi. How far did the mullah's tentacles reach into the Saudi government?

"I request that you table any plans for terrorist acts on Saudi soil and that you provide me with the tools to shut down the majority of social media attacks on the royalty. I have the ear of the king, but I'm forced to share it with America's CIA. I need to show him that they're unnecessary—indeed, that they're counterproductive. He has to be confident that I, and I alone, have power to defend his dynasty."

"And what would I receive in return? Surely not just the promise of your loyalty at some future date."

"I understand that it's your plan to hit the Americans hard inside their borders. To cause them to lash out at their Muslim citizens in a way that makes them susceptible to recruitment and that turns America's allies against it. My agency is one of the primary sources of intelligence on Muslim immigrants and refugees entering America. It would be a simple matter to alter that intelligence in a way that would allow your agents to infiltrate the country. Further, we have knowledge of poorly defended targets that have the potential to cause significant disruptions—power transfer stations, dams, commercial and retail centers, to name only a few. And finally, we are informed of the vast majority of CIA operations. We can tell you almost immediately about—"

"And you have money," Halabi interjected.

The Americans had become quite skilled at tracking wire transfers and confiscating bank accounts. Combined with the crackdown on ISIS oil sales, they were squeezing the organization. Fighters had taken pay cuts, equipment was failing, and the web of graft that kept local leaders docile was breaking down.

"Of course. Many of the Saudis who have supported your efforts have done so at my bidding. Prince bin Musaid, for instance."

"Not a successful exchange."

"How so? It's my understanding that the prince delivered the money to your man. Did you not receive it?"

Halabi didn't answer and his silence was intriguing. According to Irene Kennedy, the ISIS contact hadn't been captured. Had he been turned? Was it he who had informed the CIA about the exchange? It seemed likely, but Nassar decided it would be unwise to point that out in his present situation.

When the mullah spoke again, he changed the subject. "This insight into the CIA's operations that you speak of. I question how much the Americans really share with you. I think you're overestimating your usefulness. Give me an example of something you know that I don't."

Nassar smiled. It was a question he was well prepared for. "Of course. General al-Omari's home isn't the only one that's been discovered." He indicated with his head toward Fares Wazir, a man who had spent years as an executive in Saddam Hussein's secret police. "The Mossad has located General Wazir's base of operations, and the U.S. is planning a raid to capture him in two days' time."

"Impossible!" Wazir said. "I—"

"You and your family have taken over the top floor of a building in Tal Afar," Nassar said in a calculatedly bored tone. "A few blocks north of the city center, as I recall."

That shut the man up. More important, the information seemed to please Mullah Halabi. He had passed the man's first test.

"I've enjoyed our conversation, Director Nassar. But, as I've said, it's important that you return home. I'll expect a payment of five million euros by later this week. We'll contact you with the exchange site."

"Five million?" Nassar said. "With all due respect, there are certain complexi—"

A cloth bag was pulled over his head, and a moment later he was being dragged from the building.

CHAPTER 20

HERE'S your chardonnay and a sparkling water," the waitress said.

Claudia reached for the wineglass with a visibly shaking hand.

The otherwise empty deck looked out over flowering trees and a field of boulders jutting from the sea. Rapp could hear the waves crashing against stone, but the spectacular view was at his back. Normally, he preferred to have a wall behind him, but the ones that made up this mostly outdoor restaurant were just flimsy partitions. Nothing that would stop a bullet.

Not that he was expecting any gunfire on that particular day, but it wasn't out of the question. Grisha Azarov, the man they were there to see, was unquestionably the most dangerous opponent he'd ever faced. After nearly killing Scott Coleman, he'd faced down Rapp in a battle that had been far more desperate than the CIA man would have liked. While Rapp had won, a win on that particular day had involved getting thrown from an oil rig with his hair literally on fire. He wouldn't survive many more victories like that one.

"Where is he?" Claudia said before draining half her glass in one gulp. "We've been in Costa Rica for two days and this is our second afternoon eating at this restaurant. Is it possible that he doesn't know we're here?"

"He knows."

Claudia's late husband had been one of the world's top contract killers and he'd been terrified of Azarov. It was a fear that he'd left deeply imprinted on her and one that Rapp couldn't resist using as a test. So far, she was passing with a solid B plus.

"That dress looks great on you," he said, trying to ease the tension a bit.

She polished off the rest of her wine. "It's my favorite. The one I'd like to be buried in. Seemed appropriate."

Rapp caught the waitress's attention, pointed to Claudia's empty glass, and held up two fingers.

"Where is he?" Claudia repeated. "He's probably watching us. Waiting. Making us sweat."

"I think that's just the humidity."

"So *now* you get a sense of humor?"

The waitress arrived and set a full glass down in front of Claudia. She was about to give Rapp the other but he indicated that they were both for her.

"Just trying to lighten the mood."

"Well, stop."

He smiled reassuringly while he watched Grisha Azarov get out of his truck and start walking up behind her. The fact that he wasn't alone was a good sign. He and Cara Hansen had been virtually inseparable since he'd resigned from the service of Russia's president. She was a thirty-year-old American surf instructor with the expected athletic figure, unkempt blond hair, and perpetual half sunburn. Her barely perceptible smile looked both permanent and entirely sincere. By all reports, she was adored by everyone who knew her and it wasn't hard to see why.

"¡Hola, Isabella!" she said as they stepped onto the deck. "¿Podemos sentarnos al lado de las flores?"

Rapp understood enough to know that Azarov wasn't dictating where they sat and that the table near the flowers, while a great spot for an early dinner, was a tactical death trap.

Claudia stiffened but managed not to look back. "Is that them?"

"Uh-huh."

"Why didn't you tell me?"

"I didn't want you to spill your drink on your funeral dress."

"You're so funny. Maybe comedy was your calling, no?"

He just smiled, ignoring Cara and Azarov as they ordered drinks. After a convincing interval, the Russian looked directly at him and whispered something in his companion's ear. A moment later they were up and walking in Rapp's direction. Claudia seemed to think it was a good time to finish her second glass of wine and get a firm grip on her third.

"Mitch?"

"Grisha?" Rapp said, feigning surprise as he stood and shook the man's hand. "What are you doing here?"

"I live only a few kilometers away."

"Really? I had no idea."

Azarov turned toward Cara. "I'd like you to meet Mitch. We know each other from Saudi Arabia."

"Hi," she said, extending a hand. "I'm Cara. So you're in the oil business, too?"

"I am."

They had actually met once before. It had been dark, though, and he'd had a silencer pressed to her boyfriend's head. It'd be interesting to know how Azarov had explained that one away.

"And this is Claudia," the Russian said.

She twitched visibly at the fact that he knew who she was, but managed to look reasonably relaxed as they exchanged greetings. Her B-plus grade moved to a tentative A minus.

"Have you been on the trail behind the restaurant yet?" Azarov asked. His accent had softened noticeably, taking on a bit of the Spanish that surrounded him.

"I haven't," Claudia responded.

"Why don't you take her on a tour, Cara?"

"Sure. The toucans are usually out this time of the afternoon. Grab your wine. It's easy walking."

Rapp watched the two women descend from the deck and disappear into the jungle.

"May I join you?" Azarov asked.

"Please."

They sat and Rapp took the opportunity to examine the man. The cuts from the glass that had shattered in his face were long healed and whatever scars remained were obscured by his tan. He'd put on a few pounds, taking the edge off the gaunt, professional endurance athlete look he'd had before. Rounding out his new softer image was a blond head of hair about the same shade as Scott Coleman's.

Most of the change, though, wasn't physical. The

man was extraordinarily talented and well trained, but had lived most of his adult life as little more than a slave to Maxim Krupin. Now he looked . . . happy. In fact, he looked happy enough to make Rapp wonder if he'd made a mistake coming there.

"Vacation?" Azarov said, sipping an ice water. "Or have you managed to bring in a team that I missed?"

"No team. Just us."

"Why? You've had two opportunities to kill me and you've taken neither. I assume your people are watching me, and if that's the case, you know I'm no longer in contact with the Russian government."

It was true as far as anyone had been able to tell. Azarov's first order of business after divesting of most of the foreign property that he no longer needed was learning to surf. The fact that he'd been an Olympic-level biathlete and was sleeping with a full-time instructor hadn't hurt. With the exception of a run-in with three territorial Hawaiian locals—one of whom was still relearning how to walk—his pursuit of the sport had gone spectacularly.

Recently, though, he'd reconnected with the successful consulting company he'd used as a cover operation, appointing a new CEO and taking over as chairman of the board. It wasn't a particularly demanding position, but it also wasn't one he in any way needed. As far as the Agency could tell, he had a net worth of more than one hundred million dollars and spent less than two thousand of it every month.

Rapp's silence caused the Russian to become wary. "I trust your friend Scott Coleman is still doing well?"

"Yeah. Should be back in a year or so. That's not why I'm here."

"What, then?"

"How's the quiet life?" Rapp asked, not yet ready to answer the man's question.

"I enjoy it. I enjoy my time with Cara. The freedom. And how about you? I have to admit that, based on your history together, a relationship with Claudia Gould is surprising."

"Sometimes you have to let things go."

"An enlightened attitude, but not one I would have ascribed to Mitch Rapp. How is her daughter? Anna, isn't it? After your late wife. She must be what? Six?"

"Seven."

"Ah," he said noncommittally, and then took another sip of his drink.

"So," Rapp said, glancing behind him to make sure Cara hadn't reappeared. "You wouldn't be interested in a small side job."

Azarov's initial surprise was obvious but then he gave an understanding nod. "I took out the head of your backup team. You need a replacement and you feel I owe you."

"No. I've gotten tangled up in something Scott and his boys can't be involved in."

"I see. And if I say no?"

"Then we'll have dinner and I doubt we'll ever see each other again."

Azarov looked past him at the clouds building on the horizon. "How long?"

"A few weeks. Certainly no longer than a month."

"Details?"

"There's someone I want to talk to."

"Can I assume that he doesn't want to talk to you?"

"Safe assumption."

"But your government doesn't agree about the importance of you meeting with this person."

"Fair to say."

"Not a personal vendetta, though. That would be something you'd handle yourself."

"I'm looking forward to the conversation," Rapp said honestly. "But the goal here isn't personal satisfaction."

"I'm intrigued. Payment?"

Rapp shrugged. "I can offer you a lot of money, but the most expensive thing you bought in the last six months was a new board."

Azarov's brow furrowed, considering the issue. "U.S. citizenship?"

"Sure. But it'd be easier to just make Cara an honest woman and get it that way. Besides, you live in Costa Rica. Why pay the taxes?"

"True, but I think we would agree that someone with my skill set shouldn't be expected to work for free."

Rapp pulled out his wallet, extracted a single dollar, and laid it on the table. The Russian stared at it for a few seconds, finally reaching out and stuffing it in his pocket. "But you're picking up the dinner bill."

CHAPTER 21

THE phone on Aali Nassar's desk buzzed and he snatched it up. "Yes?"

"Aali, how are you?" King Faisal said. "Are you all right?"

Nassar let out a relieved breath. Perhaps premature, but at least the waiting was over. He'd called the palace multiple times since his return to Riyadh only to be told that the king was indisposed. Generally these periodic breaks in communication were the result of the man's failing health, but that had now become a dangerous assumption. Had Faisal been avoiding calls because he'd heard about the disastrous meeting with President Alexander? Had he been made aware of the Americans' suspicions regarding Talal bin Musaid?

"I'm well, Your Majesty. And you?"

"Me? Let's not speak of me. I'm told that you suffered serious injuries defending yourself against those cowards in Mauritania."

"I assure you that the reports have been wildly exaggerated."

In fact, they had been entirely fabricated. The story was that Nassar had been drawn personally into a desperate fight with the terrorists. Accounts of his heroics were beginning to cross the line into the improbable, but no one had any reason to question them.

"Exaggerated? Modesty doesn't suit you, Aali. The terrorists themselves are corroborating accounts of your actions."

Mullah Halabi's doing, of course. The fact that the ISIS leader was already using his influence to increase Nassar's stature in Saudi Arabia was an encouraging sign.

"I did only what was necessary, Your Highness."

The king laughed. "Well, Aali, if this is too trivial a matter for you to discuss, why don't you tell me about your meeting with the president?"

Nassar actually smiled at that. The old man hadn't heard. Perhaps Nassar's initial analysis had been correct. President Alexander was indeed too spineless to pursue the matter.

"It turned out to be much more difficult even than the attack, Majesty."

"What? How so?"

Nassar allowed for an appropriately dramatic pause, given the news he was about to deliver. "The Americans believe that Talal bin Musaid recently went to Morocco to make a payment to ISIS."

"What are you talking about? That's outrageous!" the king said, before descending into a coughing fit. It was violent enough that Nassar wondered if the old fool was finally going to drop dead.

Unfortunately, Faisal managed to regain his breath. "Is there any truth to this, Aali?"

"In my opinion, there is not, Majesty. The accusation relies entirely on the account of a single mercenary and a laughably poor photograph. While it's true that the prince was in Morocco at the time, I've spoken to his security people and embassy personnel, all of whom are willing to testify that he was nowhere near the site of the alleged exchange."

"Have you spoken to *him*? Have you spoken directly to Talal?"

"I haven't, Majesty. We—"

"I'll summon him to the palace immediately."

It was the expected reaction, but a potentially disastrous one. What were the chances that the idiot prince wouldn't let something slip under questioning?

"Sir, I'd strongly recommend against that. Given some time, I believe I can prove his innocence to the Americans. And if that's the case, the entire matter will go away without anyone ever knowing about it.

"I'm not convinced, Aali. President Alexander wouldn't make this kind of an accusation lightly."

"I agree, Majesty. He's an impressive and thoughtful man. But not infallible. If I'm wrong and my investigation doesn't clear the prince beyond a shadow of a doubt, then he should be called upon to explain himself. But why humiliate him with an accusation that I'm convinced is false?"

Faisal didn't immediately respond, but Nassar could hear his ragged breathing on the other end of the line. "You've never failed me before, Aali. And your heroism in Mauritania has once again demonstrated that you were the right man to oversee our intelligence efforts. I'll do as you advise. I'll wait for your report."

"Thank you, Majesty."

Faisal disconnected the call and Nassar leaned back in his chair. The conversation had gone as well as could be hoped. He had time to carefully consider the problem that bin Musaid posed and how to best solve it. Further, at this point, it was unlikely that the Americans would contact the king to protest the tone of Nassar's meeting with the president. But if they did, he could always excuse his performance by citing the shock he'd felt at a royal being the target of such an accusation.

There was a knock on his office door and a moment later the bearded face of Mahja Zaman peeked around the jamb. "I hear you're off the line with the king. Do you have a moment to speak with a common peasant like myself?"

Nassar's parents had been servants in the Zaman household, and because he and Mahja were the same age, the two of them had struck up a friendship. They'd attended the same madrassa in their youth, and it was Mahja's father who had recommended Nassar for the university scholarship program created by the king. Mahja and Nassar continued their lifelong friendship, rooming together at Oxford and exploring Europe during school breaks. Upon their return to Saudi Arabia, Nassar had joined the military—the best way for the son of a working-class father to move up in society—and Zaman had taken over his family's wildly profitable construction company. Despite their divergent paths, the friendship endured.

"You look healthier than I expected," Zaman said as Nassar came around his desk to embrace the man.

"It was nothing."

"Nothing? I read that you were forced to jump onto an armored vehicle and kill those dogs yourself! Praise Allah that you escaped with your life."

Nassar indicated for his friend to sit and then took the chair next to him. The office door was closed, but still he scooted close so that they could speak in whispers.

"Once again, I must ask for your help, Mahja."

Zaman's expression turned conspiratorial. "You know that I am always at your service and at the service of God."

The lessons of the madrassa had influenced Zaman even more than they had Nassar. He had remained devout, but his life of privilege had left him yearning for something more meaningful than the acquisition of more and more wealth. Like Prince bin Musaid, this nagging emptiness made him useful, but the analogy ended there. Whereas the prince was a spoiled boy in the throes of a tantrum, Zaman was strong, devoted, and clever. Those qualities made him an effective soldier, but also made it necessary for Nassar to tell him more than he would have liked. Zaman was not a man who would tolerate being a simple pawn, and his intelligence allowed only the most careful lies.

"Fortunately, while critical, it's not a complicated matter."

Zaman nodded. "What, then?"

"We need to make another cash payment."

"Where?"

"Brussels. You'll take the money in your private

plane, transfer it to a car, and then drive to a designated location in the Molenbeek neighborhood."

"And after that?"

"Nothing. That's the end of your involvement. Take the keys and leave. The car will be driven away a few hours later. No face-to-face contact will be necessary."

"Cameras?"

"No coverage where you'll leave the vehicle."

"How much?"

"Five million euros."

Zaman was surprised by the amount. "Five million? Does this mean that you've made contact with Mullah Halabi?"

"I have," Nassar admitted.

"Excellent! And do you think your new relationship will bear fruit?"

"Perhaps."

In fact, it already had. Beyond the ISIS-generated story about his superhuman actions during the Mauritania attack, there had already been a quantifiable reduction in antimonarchy sentiment on social media. After the five million euros was transferred, Nassar expected the rate of that reduction to accelerate. It was a strategy that worked on two levels. His fabricated heroics played well with the general population, and the attenuation of antiroyal Internet bile played well with the king.

"Will it be used in an attack against the Americans?"

"I can't be certain, but that would be my assumption."

Zaman grinned. "I wouldn't be surprised to see you as caliph one day. The leader of lands that stretch from Mali to Tajikistan."

"If Allah calls on me to fill that role, I will of course do His will."

Zaman slapped him on the shoulder. "Always so smooth, Aali. Those English girls at school never had a chance."

CHAPTER 22

DONATELLA Rahn moved through the alley-way, carefully avoiding puddles swollen from the rain. Her long, dark hair was piled under a hat and she wore sunglasses that obscured a face that had at one time made her a great deal of money.

She maneuvered around a cascade of water coming from a broken gutter and took an opportunity to glance behind her. While the rain had done a good job of clearing the streets of pedestrians, there was no reason to be exposed any longer than absolutely necessary. Savoring the moment—while tempting—was a mistake made only by amateurs.

She slipped into a shallow alcove and pressed her back against the dirty bricks. The rain was coming harder now, obscuring her field of view more than she'd anticipated. On the positive side, it worked both ways. In the unlikely event that someone saw her, they would only register a vague human outline taking refuge from the storm.

At the center of the alley she could see her victim huddled next to a dumpster. The man with him flicked a lighter to life, and its flame glinted off a spoon used to prepare the drugs they had scored that afternoon. Having spent much of her youth doing similar things behind similar dumpsters, she knew how long it would take, the procedure, and the necessary paraphernalia. Not that it mattered. The drugs weren't what she was there for.

And that begged the question: Why *was* she here?

For so many years she'd led a charmed life. Italian runway model, Mossad assassin, private contractor. She'd killed terrorists, well-trained enemy soldiers, and captains of industry. She'd been respected, sought after, and feared—by peers, by governments, and by the world's billionaire aristocracy. Now she was getting drenched stalking a filthy and meaningless little creature named Jimmy Gatton.

He was a drug addict, small-time dealer, and hustler—none of which was of any concern to her. It was his work as a petty thief that had attracted her attention. Three weeks ago she had returned to the home that had been forced on her and found it torn apart. Her stereo, television, and laptop were gone. The contents of every cabinet and drawer was strewn across the floor, as was the contents of her refrigerator.

Donatella's anger had flared, but only briefly. None of it was really hers. None of it meant anything. Besides, it wasn't like she hadn't been involved in similar jobs to feed a similar habit when she was young.

She'd begun walking from room to room, picking up the necessities that made existence possible—pans, a toothbrush, a thermostat ripped from the wall—and leaving the rest. As she continued, she began to feel an increasing queasiness in the pit of her stomach.

The job was sloppy and unnecessarily destructive, but there was also a strange thoroughness. She made her way into the master bedroom, feeling her stomach tighten further. As expected, her closet door was open and its contents shoveled onto the carpet. Not expected, though, was the open door to a hidden storage room at the back. The latch had been hacked away with a meat cleaver that was now stuck in the drywall.

Donatella had frozen, her mouth suddenly going dry. When she finally managed to begin inching forward again, her horror grew with every step. Her magnificent designer clothes and shoes, most made specifically for her in her previous life, weren't just discarded like the other things in the house but utterly destroyed. The thief, after working so hard to get inside the secret room, had undoubtedly expected far greater treasure. Jewels. Weapons. Art. Perhaps even drugs. Instead he found decade-old Valentino, Gucci, and Louis Vuitton.

In his rage, he'd torn them apart and, judging by the smell, urinated on them. She'd stared down at all that was left of who she once was and, for the first time since her homeless teenage years, felt like she was fading away. How much more of this could she endure before she disappeared altogether?

Donatella remembered looking up at the cleaver, suddenly mesmerized by its polished surface. She kept it razor-sharp, as she had always done with her blades. Was that the answer?

She didn't know how long she'd pondered that question, but, like so many times before, her rage had saved her. It wouldn't end like this. Not after everything she'd been through in her life.

She'd survived Mitch Rapp abandoning her to the
FBI's witness protection program. She'd survived
being imprisoned in bland suburban hellhole after
bland suburban hellhole. She'd even survived a few
brief experiments with honest work. Hell if she'd let a
petty thief break her.

After another quick scan of her operating environment, Donatella stepped from the alcove and started
through the rain toward the center of the alley. It
wouldn't be long before the drugs being prepared
would go from spoon to vein, and she wanted to make
sure that Gatton experienced what was to come with
perfect clarity.

The two men glanced up as she appeared from the
mist, confused at first and then intrigued. Gatton was
the first to stand, moving to block her path. His hair
was matted but his features were immediately recognizable from his mug shot.

The police had been largely uninterested in the
break-in and she certainly couldn't go to her FBI handlers. They would be furious to discover that she'd
been clinging to mementos from a past that they'd
worked so hard to eradicate. So Donatella resorted to
the power she'd always had over men to get a local
detective to admit that he knew who had done the
job. Over drinks in an intimate little restaurant, he'd
been eminently understanding—sympathizing with
her sense of violation but explaining that he didn't
have evidence that would stand up in court. In the
end, his advice was to take the insurance payout and
move on.

"You're a pretty lady," Gatton said. The rain swallowed the sound to the point that no one outside of

the alley would hear him even if he shouted. Even if he screamed.

She angled to get around him but he sidestepped and once again blocked her path. His companion was still crouched behind the dumpster, paying only partial attention. The drugs were what he cared about.

"What have you got in your hand?" he said, pointing to the eight-inch cylinder clutched between perfectly manicured nails. "Maybe something I want?"

Gatton had obviously made the same calculation that she had. What happened in this alley would stay in this alley.

He took a step toward her. "I bet you got a lot of things I want."

Donatella pressed the button on the spring-loaded baton, extending it to its full length. Gatton didn't even flinch. People were typically slow to process things that were utterly unexpected, and he was slower than most. She swung the weapon, slamming it into his ribs instead of going for the more obvious head shot. His grunt was audible through the roar of the rain, as was the satisfying snap of collapsing bone.

He staggered right and she spun, swinging the baton hard enough into the back of his legs to take his feet out from under him. His face twisted in pain when he hit the wet asphalt, but he couldn't take in enough air to make a sound.

In her peripheral vision she saw Gatton's companion pull a knife from his pocket. She turned and met his wide-eyed gaze with a dead one of her own. His confusion was even deeper than Gatton's had been. The fact that she had a weapon and had used it to defend herself would be comprehensible, but her refusal to run for the safety of the street would be completely unfamiliar.

"Do we have business together?" she said, just loud enough for him to hear.

Apparently, they didn't because he just gathered up his drug paraphernalia and fled.

Donatella shook off her umbrella and entered the parking garage. Her heart rate was still slightly elevated, but that was all that remained of what had happened. Her hair was still perfectly arranged, her makeup was unblemished, and her clothes were free of both wrinkles and blood.

She slipped into the gray Ford Focus the FBI had given her—out of spite, she assumed—and inserted the key in the ignition. She started to turn it, but then froze when a gun was pressed to her ear by someone in the backseat.

A cop? Could she have been seen? If that was the case, what should she do? Killing the man would be a trivial matter, but it wouldn't play well with her FBI handlers.

No. What was she thinking? Police didn't hide in backseats waiting for a suspect to get in their car. A former enemy? Doubtful. As odious an organization as the FBI was, it had hidden her identity quite competently. A mugger? A rapist? That would be interesting. After all this time, two men in one day.

"What the fuck was that all about?"

Despite the years, the voice was immediately recognizable.

"Mitch?" she said, turning slowly.

"You didn't answer my question."

"He stole from me," Donatella said. The anger that had faded long ago erupted again. "Like you did."

She pushed the gun aside and lunged over the seat, wrapping her hands around his neck and squeezing with everything she had. "You did this to me, you bastard! I had beautiful men. Beautiful women! A beautiful flat in Milan! I am what you made me!"

He dislodged her hands and shoved her back against the dashboard hard enough to knock the wind out of her.

"You did this to yourself, Donatella. How many times has the Bureau had to relocate you? Twice now? And from what I just saw, you're going for a hat trick."

"What are you doing here, Mitch? You don't care about me. You haven't for a long time."

"That's not true and you know it. But, *damn*, you're a pain in the ass."

"Are you going to send me to Iowa?"

It was the FBI's favorite threat. And after what had happened two years ago in Dallas, they'd made it clear that it was no longer an idle one.

He shook his head. "I have a job you might be interested in."

"A butcher shop that needs a new manager?"

"You're never going to let that go, are you? It was just a suggestion. You like food and you're good with knives."

His phone rang and he put it to his ear. "No, the alley north of that. Uh-huh. I don't give a shit. Bury him in the woods, feed him to some pigs. Just get rid of him. Yeah. . . . One, but he doesn't seem like the type who's going to go to the cops. Forget him. I know she is. I already said I owe you, what more do you want? Fine. . . ." He disconnected the call. "Where were we?"

"You were talking about a job," she said, her eyes narrowing slightly. "Why would you be coming to me? Is this something Scott and his Boy Scouts can't handle? No. They walk on water. Something that needs a feminine touch?"

His eyes shifted in a way that most people would have missed. They'd been together in their younger years and she could still read him. A smile began to play at her lips. "No, not a feminine touch. You're into something too ugly for them. You're isolated."

"Something like that."

Her smile broadened and she leaned back against the dash. "What's in it for me?"

"What do you want?"

"I want to go home to Italy. And I want funding to start my own fashion line."

"Cut the crap, Donatella. You know I can't do that."

"You can do anything."

"The Mossad wants you dead."

"You and Irene could take care of that with a phone call."

"Yeah, but we can't take care of Hamas. Those guys really know how to hold a grudge. And we can't do anything about the enemies you made when you were working private. Try again."

"Why don't you make me an offer?"

"Don't you want to know what the job is first?"

"Not really."

"All right. New face, new identity. A nice condo in New York overlooking Central Park. You stay away from the fashion industry, but I bankroll you in an art gallery."

"Art?" she said. It was something she'd never considered. "I like art."

"I remember," he said, slipping his Glock into the holster beneath his arm. "You used to drag me to those openings."

"I thought you could use a little culture. Apparently it didn't take."

CHAPTER 23

ANTHONY Staton moved along the shattered wall, finally getting a glimpse of his target in the moonlight. The building was constructed of concrete and had sustained a fair amount of damage from the war and ISIS's recent takeover of the city. The bottom floor was burned out, but the entire top floor had apparently been renovated into a luxury flat. It was hard to believe from where he was standing. Great care had been taken to leave no outward evidence that it was habitable, and blackout shades went down every afternoon just before sunset.

Now that the Agency had located it, there was nothing he would have liked better than to see the whole structure disappear in a pillar of flame. Paint it with a laser, wait for a drone to come overhead, and then slink out of there in the ensuing dust and chaos.

Unfortunately, that wasn't the plan. The former Iraqi general who had planted his fat ass in this cut-rate penthouse was apparently too important to vaporize. Irene Kennedy wanted him alive, and that left Staton wandering around ISIS-held streets with nothing more than a bare-bones team to back him up. Fast and light was undoubtedly the best strategy in this situation, but that didn't make him feel any less exposed. This was an op that he would have gladly let someone else handle, but the Agency was an operational clusterfuck right now. Scott Coleman was damn near in a wheelchair, Joe Maslick had dug in his heels, and Mitch Rapp had hung up his Glock. Who would have thought he'd live long enough to see that last one happen?

"This is Forward One," came a voice over his earpiece. "I'm in position. Still quiet. Looks like we might get lucky."

Staton wondered. He couldn't help thinking of the cliché from the cheesy Westerns he liked so much. *Quiet. Too quiet.*

They hadn't wanted to move in when the streets were all but abandoned because the team would stand out too much. Instead, they'd picked a time of night early enough that there were still a few people wandering around, but late enough that they were more interested in getting home than asking questions.

Still, pedestrian traffic was far lighter than he'd expected and he'd only seen two patrols—both easily avoided. Either this was shaping up to be a cakewalk or the other shoe was about to drop. In his experience, it was always the latter. There were no gifts in this life.

He reached up and activated the throat mike hidden beneath his traditional garb. "I have eyes on the line and I'm moving into position. Stay on your toes. I don't have a great feeling about this."

"You never do, Tony. Copy."

There was a clothesline that ran from the top of the target building to an abandoned one across the street.

An advance team had managed to replace it with a Kevlar one that they swore looked and felt exactly the same. Staton had been skeptical but, judging by a pair of pants hanging from it, he'd been overly pessimistic.

Three of his men would zip-line across it to the roof. From there, they'd cut through the lock on the access door and slip down into Fares Wazir's apartment. They'd pop the guards, dart the family, and then take the former general back across the line. The best they'd been able to come up with for getting him to a viable LZ was a wooden handcart. Reasonably common in the area, but still risky. The whole thing—the zip line, the uncertain number of security men, the cart—was a little seat-of-the-pants for his taste. Scott Coleman would have loved it, but Staton saw it as a fuckup waiting to happen.

"Is everyone in position?" he asked. The team confirmed.

"Then we're a go."

There was a lone man walking up the street in his direction, but Staton largely ignored him. He looked to be about a hundred years old, hobbling forward with none of the urgency felt by the other people out at that time of night. He probably figured, at his age, screw ISIS.

Above, a dark figure crossed the Kevlar line, moving quickly enough to be invisible to anyone not specifically looking. A second followed, and then a third.

A voice crackled in his earpiece. "We've gained the roof. Looks clear."

"Copy that," Staton said. "Go ahead and reposition the cable."

"On it," another voice responded.

The end attached to the abandoned building would be moved down one floor to reverse the slope and give them an even faster ride on the way out. It made the landing a little tricky—particularly with the deadweight of Wazir—but it was worth it to reduce their exposure time.

"The lock is what we expected," one of his men said over the radio. "It won't—"

Staton ducked involuntarily at the sudden flash and deafening concussion of an explosion. It took him a moment to process the fact that the roof his men were on had been transformed into thousands of flaming concrete shards arcing through the air. The old man in the road stopped, glancing back at the massive fireball, before continuing on his way as if nothing had happened.

"Pull back!" Staton said into his throat mike. "I repeat, pull back!"

He ran forward, trying to figure out what the fuck had just happened. Did his men trip a booby trap? It seemed impossible—they were specifically looking for one and had instructions to tell him before they started cutting through the lock.

Flashes of gunfire appeared in the building across from their target, precisely where his man handling the cable would be.

Staton broke away from the wall at his back, sprinting north toward his remaining team. He'd made it only about ten yards when more flashes lit up the road. He tried to pinpoint where the fire was coming from, but it was impossible. It was coming from everywhere. Every window. Every rooftop. Every doorway. The old man went down and Staton swerved right in a futile search for cover. The first round hit him in the new hip that everyone thought would retire him. After that, impacts started coming so fast, he couldn't distinguish them. The overwhelming sensation was of their momentum, shoving him sideways and finally slamming him to the ground. The darkness was gone now, driven away by thousands of muzzle flashes.

He spotted the carcass of a car shimmering in the artificial light and tried to crawl to it. The force of the bullets impacting his back seemed to be pinning him to the ground, though, grinding him mercilessly into the dust. He squeezed the trigger of his own weapon and the roar of it joined the rest before everything went silent.

Aali Nassar laid his phone on the limousine's seat and allowed himself a rare smile. The king had called personally to express his gratitude for the reduction in antimonarchy trolling on social media, still blissfully unaware that it was Sayid Halabi's doing.

Further, the five million euros demanded by the mullah was at this moment being loaded onto Mahja Zaman's private jet. He had provided half himself, while two other men loyal to Nassar had made up the balance. All of the arrangements were complete and there was no reason to believe the transfer wouldn't go smoothly.

Even the problem posed by Talal bin Musaid was showing signs of improvement. Reports were that he was on his way to Monaco to visit his brother. Having him outside of Saudi Arabia would be helpful, as Nassar had decided that the benefits of killing the prince now outweighed the drawbacks. While it was unlikely that President Alexander would have the courage to move against bin Musaid in a way that would jeopardize the precarious relationship between their two countries, it was conceivable that the CIA or Mossad would attempt an unauthorized rendition.

And while all these developments were undoubtedly gifts from Allah, they were hardly sufficient to elicit a smile from a man unaccustomed to the expression. No, only the news of Mitch Rapp's resignation had the power to do that. The extent of the injuries suffered by the CIA man in Saudi Arabia were apparently far worse than the intelligence community had been told.

A chime on his phone sounded and he glanced down at it. An encrypted email from Irene Kennedy. He opened it and, instead of text, found only a link to an ISIS propaganda site. Intrigued, he clicked on it and waited for the video to load. When it began playing, he felt the breath catch in his chest.

It was a slickly edited film of an attack on a small group of U.S. operatives. The location was immediately recognizable—Fares Wazir's home in Iraq. Nassar rewound it and watched again, his fist clenching around the phone as the roof blew off the top of Fares Wazir's apartment and gunfire erupted from every direction. The overhead shot zoomed onto a man running across the street, jerking wildly as he was impacted by what seemed like an infinite number of rounds. He finally fell, firing his own weapon uselessly into a stone wall before going still. The video then began quick cuts accompanied by loud revolutionary music—dead Americans being carried from buildings, the barely recognizable remains of the ones from the roof being collected, a bloody corpse being dragged through the streets.

He finally shut off the video and dialed a number Mullah Halabi had given him. He had never imagined he'd be forced to use it so soon, and in response to such crushing stupidity. Surprisingly, the ISIS leader picked up personally.

"You're up late, Director."

"I just saw the video of the raid on Fares Wazir's home."

"Glorious, isn't it?"

"Glorious?" Nassar said, glancing at the glass separating him from his driver, although he knew it was soundproof. "It's insanity! I gave you that information to allow Wazir to escape before the Americans arrived. Irene Kennedy just sent me an email with only the link to the video—no text at all. I can assure you that her lack of diplomacy was intended to make a point. To make it clear that she suspects that the leak came from my organization."

"Yes, I imagine you're right."

"Then why would you do this? Why would you jeopardize my position and my ability to provide you with intelligence?"

"Because you needed this, Aali."

"What? I *needed* it?"

"You portray such strength, but inside you're weak. Of course, you would say that you grew up poor, but in fact you lived the lifestyle of your family's wealthy benefactors and attended Oxford. And I'm aware of your military service, but your carefully planned operations were acts devoid of any real risk or passion. Now you feel the danger. You feel the Americans' eyes on you, the anxiety of wondering if one of their drones is circling you right now. Will they discover your betrayal? And if so, what action will they take?"

"If they kill me, all the money and intelligence I'm providing you will disappear. The king—"

Halabi began to laugh, drowning out Nassar's words. "I suspect you'll be fine, Aali. Particularly now that the CIA is trying to deal with the departure of Mitch Rapp. But I'm not certain of it. And neither are you. You're now in a position that will test your faith in God. Will you pass that test? Are your actions in His service? Or your own?"

There was no point in fighting with the man. Nothing would come of it.

"I serve God."

"Good, Aali. Good. And of course I sympathize with the difficulties the general has caused you. So tell me. What is it I can do to balance the scales?"

Nassar was both surprised and relieved by the offer. Already, Halabi was beginning to understand his value and the importance of maintaining his loyalty.

"Prince Talal bin Musaid is on his way to Monaco," Nassar said.

"Ah. Can I assume that his usefulness to you is at an end and that you're concerned about the risks of dealing with him yourself?"

"Yes."

"Then I'll contact my people in Europe and have the matter put to rest."

CHAPTER 24

EAST OF JUBA
SOUTH SUDAN

_THIS sucked.

No, that was the understatement of the century. This had catastrophe written all over it. In blood. Ten feet high.

Kent Black's foot suddenly felt too weak to depress the accelerator and he let the truck's speedometer drift. Outside, dust was enveloping the vehicle, confining him to the suffocating heat of the closed-up cab.

The road he was on was little more than a tracked-up strip in an endless plain of sunbaked dirt. His GPS said he was headed in the right direction and kept counting down to his arrival, but he wasn't sure that was a good thing.

He despised South Sudan. When he'd been an army sniper, he'd spent a lot of time fighting in Iraq and Afghanistan, but that had been different. Sure, both countries were dry, dusty shitholes, but at least he'd had backup and a few geographic features to hide behind. The empty landscape he was penetrating into had a hazy, overexposed-photograph feel that Black found disorienting. Undoubtedly why Kariem had chosen it as the location for their meeting.

Arms dealing had never been high on his list of careers, but what choice did he have? His lucrative job as a five-thousand-dollar-suit-wearing, supermodel-dating contract killer had recently run into an impassable roadblock named Mitch Rapp. Their business together had ended with Rapp agreeing not to kill him but making it clear that, the next time they met, the outcome would be different.

So Black had grabbed a map and searched for corners of the world that were both remote and in need of a man of his talents. South Sudan, which was teetering in and out of civil war, seemed to fit the bill. He figured he'd do a little mercenary work for the government while Rapp forgot about him. Unfortunately, the government proved to be only slightly less crazy than the rebel forces it was fighting. In the end, supplying both sides from way behind battle lines turned out to be not only more lucrative but a hell of a lot safer.

Until now.

Kariem was the most psychotic of the rebel leaders he dealt with—a guy who would set a man on fire for putting too much cream in his coffee. If human history taught any consistent lesson, though, it was that the biggest psycho usually came out on top. So while their relationship had a lot of potential upside, it was also extremely precarious. Which was why Black always had one of his lackeys make the physical deliveries.

Again, until now. Yesterday, Kariem had requested that Black be personally involved in their transaction—a shipment of surplus AKs and a few RPGs that were as

likely to blow up the person using them as the people
they were aimed at.

The question was why. To reward him for his service to the cause? Probably not. To cut him up with a
chain saw? A better bet. It wouldn't be the first time
one of the rebel leader's suppliers ended up in pieces.

A line of military vehicles—all supplied at a tidy
profit by him—appeared on the horizon. He accelerated to a more confident pace, finally skidding to
a stop in front of the rebel contingent and throwing
open the door.

"General!" he said, using the title the man had given
himself. "It's great to see you! How's the war going?"

Kariem was a disconcertingly large man with
deep-black skin setting off eyes that had turned a bit
yellow. One tracked reasonably well while the other
wandered a bit. The result of a childhood head injury,
apparently.

"Have you brought the weapons?"

"Of course."

"They're good?"

"They're okay."

Kariem nodded. He'd never been all that concerned
with a few guns failing or exploding in his soldiers'
faces. Men were cheap. Weapons were expensive.

Black scanned the faces of the rebels surrounding him with an easy smile. Some were sitting on
the burning hot hoods of their vehicles, while others
milled around eyeing him. There were around twenty
in all. Probably a third were either drunk or on something. All were armed.

If things went south, he was definitely going to be
killed by a bullet that he'd overcharged these assholes

for. Before that happened, though, he'd punch a few holes in General Douchebag's head. While close-contact fighting wasn't Black's specialty, it didn't have to be. All he had to do was draw and pull the trigger before one of Kariem's inebriated minions could figure out how to get his rifle off his shoulder.

"It's my understanding that you're selling weapons to my enemies," Kariem said. His face was a lifeless mask—like one of those Old West bandits propped up in his coffin. It was fucking unnerving.

"I don't know what you're talking about," Black lied. "Who told you that?"

"One of my men. He used to fight for Abdo and he says you are providing him with equipment."

"Wait a minute, now. You and Abdo are allies," Black said.

It had been true up until about a month ago, but that alliance had fallen apart over something even his troops didn't fully have a handle on. No one could blame an American new to the area for not being able to keep up with the ever-shifting landscape of African rebellion. At least, that's what Black hoped.

Kariem stared at him for a few seconds and then began reaching for his waistband. Black swatted at an imaginary fly in order to get his hand next to the Beretta he had stuffed in his waistband. It turned out to be unnecessary. The African just pulled out a small leather pouch containing a diamond nearly the size of a golf ball.

Two minutes later Black was standing in a cloud of dust with that stone safely in his pocket. He leaned against the jeep he'd been left, watching the truck full of weapons struggle to keep up with the general's motorcade. The cold sweat of fear turned into the hot sweat of being stuck in the desert with nothing but a piece-of-shit jeep and a pair of flip-flops for transportation.

Fucking Mitch Rapp.

The rebel jeep was still holding together as Black crossed the White Nile and headed into Juba. After hours of nothing but dust and rock, the landscape turned green, with majestic trees and tended fields dotting the landscape. Not that any of those things were easy to make out. The on-again, off-again civil war had done a job on the city's power infrastructure, leaving it in a permanent gloom.

He had to rely on his one working headlight to navigate the roads, weaving through pedestrians, bicycles, and the occasional farm animal. Finally he turned onto a quiet street that dead-ended into an old church. Its faded yellow walls were still structurally sound, as was most of the roof, but that was about it. The windows were boarded up, the steeple was listing badly, and the cross that had once topped the bell tower was lying broken by the perimeter wall.

It wasn't much, but it was home.

He pushed a button on the remote in his pocket and the heavy doors that once welcomed the city's Christians opened enough to allow him to drive inside. He parked the jeep amidst the overturned pews and headed for his living quarters at the back. The crates that he normally would have had to navigate were conspicuously absent. The sale to Kariem had wiped him out of merchandise and he'd need to sell the diamond to his fence in New York before he could bring in any more. On the bright side, his demonstrable lack of inventory would give him time to figure out what he was going to do about his client list. The under-the-table sales to the government still seemed safe, but the situation with Abdo was tricky. The problem was that while Abdo was far stupider than Kariem, he was just as vicious. He wasn't going to just sit quietly by while his weapons supply dried up.

Best to consider the problem with the assistance of a few of the beers he kept stashed in the fridge behind his desk. Hopefully, the power had been on all afternoon. There was nothing worse than getting back from nearly being dismembered only to find a fridge full of warm brew.

He pushed through the door, but then froze when he saw a man sitting at his desk. He had a dark complexion beneath shaggy hair and a slightly more presentable beard. It didn't take long for recognition to kick in.

Black spun and sprinted back into the nave, leaping what was left of the altar before spotting the shadow of someone in his path. He tried to get around it, but without being quite sure how it happened, his feet were taken out from under him and he found himself rolling uncontrollably across the rubble-strewn floor. He was about to get up and start running again when a woman slipped a blade under his chin.

Where the hell had she come from? The bitch was wearing white pants and a blouse that was completely free of dust and sweat stains. How was that even possible?

She stared down at him with her dark hair hanging down on either side of his face. Black usually went for girls who were young and easy to impress, but this woman was gorgeous. Her age was impossible to determine—the athletic shape looked late twenties but the face had a few subtle lines that suggested early forties.

He heard footsteps and tried to spot the approaching man without causing the blade to cut into his throat. Finally he came into view, looking down at Black with an expression of vague disappointment.

"Mitch! Come on, man. Don't let me get killed by a chick. Especially one this hot."

The woman eased the pressure of the blade against his skin and looked up at Rapp. "I like him."

"This is the best you could do? Arms dealing to both sides in a civil war?" Rapp dropped behind Black's desk again and fished a beer from the refrigerator.

"Come on, man. You said to stay out of your way. How much more out of your way can I get? I'm off the edge of the fucking earth."

It was hard to argue. The kid could follow instructions.

"Have a seat, Kent."

He did as he was told, looking a little hopeful at Rapp's rare use of his alias.

His real name was Steve Thompson. The Kent Black bullshit was an effort to make him sound more like the jet-set private contractor he'd always wanted to be. In truth, he was a poor Montana kid who had grown up with fewer creature comforts than he had here in Africa. His father had been a crazy survivalist who'd spent half his time preparing for the end of the world and the other half beating on his son. That was, until he'd disappeared. There hadn't been so much as a hint of foul play and no body was ever recovered, so the younger Thompson—now Black—had been cleared and shuffled off to a foster home.

He'd eventually become an Army Ranger and top-notch sniper. The problem was that he'd seen his father in every commander he'd ever had and eventually was booted out of the military for insubordination.

Rapp had actually considered taking Black on when he hit the street, but it wasn't an idea that lasted long. The kid was gifted, but also unpredictable and in possession of a seriously broken moral compass. So, while perhaps not CIA material, he was just the man for the shit detail the president had handed out.

"Seriously, Mitch. You don't want me in South Sudan? I'll disappear. How about Borneo? Or Siberia. I could—"

"Shut up."

He fell silent, fidgeting in his chair like a schoolkid called in front of the principal.

"Do you want a job?"

The young man didn't bother to hide his surprise. "What do you mean?"

"Was I not clear?"

"Word on the street is that you left the Agency."

"That's right."

"So you've gone private?"

"Something like that."

"And you want to work with . . . me?"

"I did, but now I'm starting to change my mind."

"Don't do that!" Black said, leaping from his seat. "I'm in."

"Do you want to know what the job is?"

"Not really."

That was starting to become a theme. "How about the pay?"

"I'm not worried. You always take care of your guys."

He took a few steps in no particular direction, a wide grin spreading across his face. "Fuckin' A. I'm working with Mitch Rapp."

CHAPTER 25

THE PRINCIPALITY OF MONACO

PRINCE Talal bin Musaid stepped from his brother's jet and walked unsteadily down the steps. He didn't even bother to berate the men handling his expensive leather luggage, instead focusing on getting to the tarmac safely. His arrival in Monaco and numerous glasses of Hennessy had failed to calm him.

He'd been forced to lie about his plane being in for repairs to prompt his brother to send his own. In fact, it was in perfect working condition, but bin Musaid had no way to fuel it or pay landing fees. His bank accounts—even the hidden ones—had been completely drained. His credit cards had been canceled due to fraudulent activity. His lines of credit had been maxed out and most of his significant assets had liens against them—either from the loans he'd used to buy them or for taxes he couldn't be bothered to pay. If his brother had refused to fetch him, it was unlikely he could have put his hands on enough cash to buy a ticket on a commercial carrier.

A black Mercedes pulled up in front of him, but

instead of his brother appearing from the back, his brother's wife stepped out from the driver's seat.

"Your Highness," she said with a polite smile. "It's so good to see you."

He hadn't laid eyes on her in more than a year and that was very much by design. When his brother had begun seeing this Spanish commoner, bin Musaid had understood. She was young, stunningly beautiful, and, he assumed, good in bed. But then he'd married the bitch. She was his only wife and, as far as anyone knew, he didn't even keep a mistress.

Bin Musaid watched in silence as she oversaw the loading of his luggage and then indicated to the passenger seat. Instead he got in the back. His brother had been disinherited for his relationship with her, but he cared little. He'd made an enormous amount of money in European real estate and had no need of the family's support.

"I'm sorry that Hossein couldn't pick you up personally," she said, starting the car and pulling away. "He's stuck at the office."

Her Arabic was still barely intelligible, and listening to it made his anger grow. He had no choice but to swallow it, though. His brother had been largely estranged from the family for more than a decade, and in that time it had become clear where his loyalties lay. With this infidel and their three Westernized children.

"What brings you to Monaco?" she asked. It was likely that his brother was aware that he came there often but never contacted them. He'd undoubtedly put the woman up to finding out what had changed. Bin Musaid didn't bother to respond.

Aali Nassar had done a skillful job of sowing doubt about bin Musaid's involvement in the Rabat affair, but the king was not entirely convinced. That doubt put the prince in a very dangerous position and made his brother's independent life in Europe a gift from Allah. Bin Musaid was unwilling to tell either the king or Nassar about what had happened to his fortune out of fear of what a criminal investigation might find. His brother's lawyers and accountants would be in a position to make discreet inquiries, and bin Musaid could use what they learned to plan what came next. If this was a simple matter of hackers, the king could exert considerable pressure on the relevant financial institutions to return the money lost through their incompetent security measures. If it was something more, then other arrangements would have to be made.

"Will you be staying long?" his sister-in-law probed.

"Be still, woman!"

He immediately saw the error of his outburst and softened his tone. "I'm sorry. It was a long flight. No. Not long."

It was likely a lie. The more he considered it, the more improbable it seemed that this was the work of hackers. Not only was the attack too thorough, but some of it seemed designed solely to anger and humiliate him. Most of his money had just disappeared so completely that it seemed to have never existed. The exception was the three million or so dollars that had been donated in his name to Jewish charities and girls' schools.

No, the answer would likely be much more dangerous and needed to be hidden from his brother for as long as possible. He wouldn't tolerate any risk to his wife and children in order to hide a brother he barely spoke to.

Bin Musaid gazed out the window at the opulent cityscape that he knew so well. What would his brother's people discover? The CIA was the most obvious perpetrator, but Aali Nassar seemed convinced that the pathetic American president would never authorize a move against a prominent Saudi royal. The Jews? The Iranians? Or was he being naïve? Nassar had been angered by his personal involvement in the Rabat operation but had become enraged when he discovered that the CIA had been tracking the exchange. Was it possible that this was his doing? A punishment for Rabat? And, if so, had it been authorized by the king?

While it was hard to imagine, it was even feasible that he was actually in physical danger. This was another reason his brother was a gift from God. He maintained a security detail and the presence of his wife and children at the house would discourage at least the Americans from making a move. Unfortunately, it also meant that bin Musaid would not only have to tolerate their presence but court it.

He forced himself to lean forward between the seats. "How have you been, Carmen?"

"Me? Uh, fine," she sputtered, understandably surprised by the question.

"And the children? I'm very much looking forward to spending time with them while I'm here."

CHAPTER 26

RAPP opened the door to the office at the back of Kent Black's church and felt a blast of cold air. Still interested in testing Claudia's abilities, he'd put her in charge and she continued to impress. Not only did she have a projector hanging from a bloom of wires in the ceiling, she'd managed to fix the AC.

Chairs were lined up along the wall and contained the rogues' gallery that had replaced Scott Coleman's flawless and unwaveringly loyal team. The desk had been cleared of Black's junk and now held a bucket filled with ice and beer. Where she'd found ice in a city that couldn't even keep the lights on was beyond him, but why look a gift horse in the mouth? Rapp grabbed a bottle and took a seat at the rear. He still wasn't comfortable having these people behind him.

Claudia nodded in his direction, looking a little nervous. He didn't react other than to twist the top off his brew. At that moment she wasn't the woman he was sleeping with. She was his logistics coordinator. Time to get this briefing rolling.

She dimmed the lights and used a remote to turn

to the projector's first image. "This is a three-month-old shot of Prince Talal bin Musaid. He's the nephew of King Faisal—the son of his favorite sister. She and bin Musaid's father are both dead, and he was left with access to a considerable fortune. Sadly for him, that fortune disappeared a few days ago and is now in accounts controlled by Mitch."

"No shit?" Black said. "How much are we talking about?"

Rapp was about to tell him to shut the fuck up but then decided to see if Claudia would let him sidetrack her meeting.

"Let's stay focused, okay, Kent?"

She switched to an image of an impressive mansion built into a steep hillside. It was surrounded by a wall and had an imposing gate, but both were more architectural statements than security measures.

"We've gotten lucky. Bin Musaid left Saudi Arabia recently and is staying here with his brother in Monaco. It appears that he's told his brother what happened, because he's assembled a team of investigators to try to trace the missing money."

"Will they be successful?" Azarov asked.

"No."

"What do we know about the brother and the house?" Donatella said.

"By all reports, Hossein bin Musaid is a successful and honest businessman. Relatively secular, married to a Christian, three children of early school age. He gives a lot of money to charities, none of which are political or religious in any way. As far as the house goes, there are two security guards and another man who seems to function primarily as a driver. None are former military or particularly well trained. Basically, what you'd expect from a wealthy, well-liked man involved in legal enterprises."

"So, civilians," Black said. "How are we treating them?"

"Like gold," Rapp responded. "None of them gets so much as a scratch."

"That isn't going to make life too easy. Does bin Musaid ever leave the house?"

"Not since he arrived," Claudia responded.

"What are we talking about then?" Black said. "Breaching in broad daylight when the kids and the brother aren't there? Maybe drugging the guards? You'd need a calculator to count all the things that could go wrong."

"We're not taking him at the house," Rapp said.

"But Claudia said he never leaves."

Rapp finished his beer and went for another. "Talal bin Musaid isn't going to spend the rest of his life playing with his nieces. He's going to want booze and he's going to want women."

"I tend to agree," Azarov said. "And if he's a wealthy Saudi, it's likely that he's spent a great deal of time in Monaco. Do we have any information on his habits when he's been there in the past?"

"I'm glad you asked," Claudia said, switching to a slide of a building surrounded by obscenely expensive cars. "This is Terry's—a very exclusive club on a hill overlooking Monte Carlo. The prince is a member and it's normally where he spends his evenings."

"I've been there a number of times as a guest of my consulting company's clients," Azarov said. "There are a few armed bouncers out front, but their role is more to keep out undesirables than to handle any-thing serious. Cameras inside. No other security that I'm aware of."

"Can we get in?" Rapp asked.

"Not without being a member or being accompa-nied by a member."

"Then let's get a membership."

"Impossible," Claudia said. "There's a waiting list a hundred people long and most of them have more money than bin Musaid did."

"If you're so sure he's going there, why not snatch him off the road?" Black said.

"I know how you men like to break things," Dona-tella interjected, "but let's not make this any harder than it is. Unless this is very different from the clubs I've been to, beautiful women don't need a mem-bership. I'll go in, strike up a conversation with the prince, and he'll invite me to a hotel. Then it's just a matter of a quick jab with a needle."

"I don't think that's going to work," Claudia said.

"Why not?"

"Because while you're right about beautiful women getting around the membership rules, those women tend to be half your age."

Rapp tensed, but the ice pick stayed in Donatella's designer purse. Instead she just waved a hand dismis-sively. "Bland children."

She was right, Rapp knew. No one was going for some gangly kid if Donatella Rahn was showing them attention. Unfortunately, there was no way in hell he could say that out loud.

"I don't like the idea of you going in alone," he of-fered instead.

She reached back and put a hand on his knee, a move that was undoubtedly intended to get Claudia's attention. And, based on her expression, it worked.

"Maybe you should come in with me, Mitch. It would be like old times."

"I believe Donatella's plan to be a reasonable one," Azarov said. "But with one change. It should be me, not Mitch, who goes with her. The clientele of Terry's includes a lot of people in the extraction industry. It won't be long before someone appears that I know. When they do, I can just go in with them."

"I'm not convinced," Claudia said. "Based on my research, the women bin Musaid's been involved with tend to be a lot younger and a lot blonder."

"Probably less Jewish, too," Donatella said. "It's not a problem."

"But—"

"What are we arguing about?" Black said, unintentionally bailing Rapp out. "There isn't going to be a guy in there that wouldn't cut his left nut off to get Donatella in the sack. This is a no-brainer."

"And if you're wrong?" Claudia asked.

"Then we'll move on to plan B," Rapp said. "But I don't see any drawbacks here. If Donatella blows it, she and Grisha have a couple of drinks and we go home."

"How are we going to cover . . ." Her voice faded at the sound of vehicles roaring up to the front of the church. Everyone got to their feet, and Black went for the door.

"Claudia, you're going out the back," Rapp said. "Donatella, go with her."

"What are you talking about?" Donatella protested. "I—"

"Shut up! I'm holding you personally responsible for Claudia's safety. Are you listening? Do you understand what I'm saying?"

She frowned and looked over at the younger woman. "Don't worry. I won't let anything happen to your little French girl."

By the time he and Azarov entered the main section of the church, Black was already unlocking the main doors. He started to pull one back and it was immediately shoved inward with enough force to almost knock him off his feet. A flood of locals in dirty fatigues rushed in, spreading out and aiming their assault rifles in what seemed to be random directions. They were smart enough to worry about potential threats, but too young and poorly trained to know where to look for them.

A few moments later, a more senior man in slightly less grimy camo entered. He was obviously in charge but had the look of someone who had gained his rank by being older and more brutal than the children he led instead of being more competent. Either way, his ragtag troops were clearly afraid of him. While their guns had settled on Rapp, Azarov, and Black, their attention remained on their commander.

"NaNomi!" Black said after he'd regained his balance. "Great to see you! How's Abdo doing? They tell me he has a touch of malaria."

"He heard you met with Kariem," the African said. "That you are going to stop selling us guns."

"Why would I do that? You're my best customer and Kariem's an asshole. I've got you guys covered like always."

"Then I want to buy."

Black let out a low whistle. "My inventory's wiped out right now. But I have a shipment coming in soon, and when I do, you'll be the first guy I call."

The African grabbed Black by the hair and yanked his head back. Rapp moved his hand subtly toward the gun beneath his shirt but didn't reach for it. In his peripheral vision he saw Azarov do the same.

"Or maybe you won't call!" the African shouted. "Maybe you're trying to starve us of weapons so Kariem can massacre us!"

He pulled out a massive combat knife and held it to Black's neck. Rapp didn't react. It was all for show. NaNomi wasn't there to kill his boss's arms dealer. Just to provide him with a little motivation.

"That's not true!" Black said emphatically. "In fact, those two guys back there are my suppliers. I was just placing an order when you showed up."

The African released him and started toward Azarov as Black fell to the floor.

"Who are you?" he demanded.

Azarov bowed his head respectfully. "I'm Grisha."

"A Russian."

"Yes, sir."

"And is what Kent says true? Are you here to sell him weapons?"

"I am, sir."

NaNomi turned and strode toward Rapp. "And you? Who are you?"

Rapp just stared back at him.

"I asked you a question!" he said, bringing the knife up.

They didn't have time for this shit. The details for the Monaco op needed to be finalized and all the logistics needed to be ironed out before bin Musaid ventured out of his brother's house. None of that was going to be possible with this tool nosing around.

The silence drew out long enough that Black finally filled it. "That's Mitch. He's an American. They're bidding against each other. I'm trying to get Abdo the best price."

"Is that true?" NaNomi asked.

By way of an answer, Rapp grabbed the man's wrist, yanking his arm out and snapping it at the elbow. When NaNomi dropped the knife, Rapp caught it, then drove it into the top of his skull hard enough that the point came through his chin.

The room's reaction was easily predicted. Azarov just stood there, watching calmly. Black ran and dove over an overturned pew. NaNomi's men froze.

It was unlikely that any one of the young guerrillas had ever made a decision on their own in their lives. Now they were faced with an impossible one. Did they avenge NaNomi even if it meant killing the men who supplied their leader with weapons? Did they just ignore what had happened and go report back? Did they grab the white men and take them?

No, what they desperately wanted was for someone to give them an order to follow. And Rapp was happy to oblige.

"Get out," he said. "Tell Abdo he'll have his weapons next week and we're going to give him forty percent off his normal deal."

They just stood there for a few seconds. Finally, one on the right started for the door. The movement seemed to break the others from their trance and they began to follow.

"Hold on," Rapp said, pointing to the corpse at his feet. "Aren't you forgetting something?"

Two of the boys scurried over and dragged what was left of NaNomi outside. A few moments later they were speeding back up the road.

"What the *fuck*?" Black said, dropping the rifle he'd had stashed behind the pew. "Why did you do that?"

When Rapp didn't answer, Azarov spoke up. "NaNomi wasn't sent here to threaten, Kent. He was sent to get weapons. He would have stayed and held us until your shipment arrived. We don't have time for these kinds of distractions."

"Distractions? That's easy for you to say—you don't live here. You don't work with these psychos. Do you know what Abdo did to the last guy who screwed him on a deal? He smeared meat on the guy's dick and then turned a hyena loose on it. And not just any hyena. His *pet* hyena. That's right. The guy keeps a fucking hyena as a pet."

Rapp turned and started for the office. "You worry too much, Kent. You need to learn to relax."

CHAPTER 27

"WHAT do you think?" Claudia said, stopping at the edge of the dock and spreading her arms wide.

The yacht was a good hundred and fifty feet, its three decks glowing white in the setting sun. A gangway was connected to the back, but Rapp could see no evidence of anyone on board.

"Subtle," he said.

She led the group into an expansive living area that was a sea of polished brass, gleaming wood, and immaculate furniture. There was even a futuristic wet bar along the port side.

"Before everyone starts thinking I'm insane," she said, turning to face them, "this actually *is* pretty subtle in the context of Monaco. And it doubles as a getaway vehicle. Plus, should we need to get rid of any evidence, I have a chart of some of the deeper waters in the area. There's a helicopter pad and a speedboat that can be quickly deployed if necessary. Finally, it has enough bedrooms and bathrooms to accommodate all of us."

"Crew?" Rapp said.

"Congolese. They'll be arriving tonight. I've worked with them before. Good sailors, discreet, and between all of them they probably speak no more than ten words of English."

"Very thorough," Azarov said.

Claudia's smile was a little forced. She was still terrified of the man.

"I have to admit," Donatella said, "the little French girl has come through."

"Hell, yeah," Black agreed. "This is what I'm talking about."

"I've had people watching Terry's and have photos of everyone going in and out," Claudia said. "There's a tablet on the bar with the pictures. Grisha, could you take a look and see if you know any of them?"

He sat on one of the stools and slid the device toward him.

"We've had one change in the situation since the briefing in Juba," she continued. Two bodyguards have come in from Saudi Arabia. They're both former Saudi army and have worked for bin Musaid before. They're with him at his brother's house now and I think we can assume they'll go with him if he leaves the compound.

"How are they getting paid? I thought we got everything."

"He had them on retainer. There was nothing I could do about that."

"So are we considering them civilians?" Black asked. "Or can we take them out?"

"Claudia?" Rapp said.

"No terrorist ties. Just former soldiers making a living."

"There's your answer," Rapp said.

"Great," Black grumbled.

"That could make getting bin Musaid out of the hotel room more complicated," Rapp said. "If they stay in the car or in the lobby, it's not an issue; but if they decide to post in the hallway, we've got problems."

"Agreed," Claudia said, turning on a big-screen TV and connecting her laptop. A picture of a luxurious hotel suite appeared a moment later.

"We've rented this room at the Metropole for Donatella to take the prince back to. We also have the one next door."

"Do we have a shot of the hall outside?"

"Of course." She switched the view and Rapp took a few steps forward, examining the details.

"I wouldn't stand next to the door if I were them. I'd go to one on either end of the hall. Access?"

"The emergency stairs are on the left of the passage. On the right is the elevator."

"Cameras?"

"Yes, but I can disable them."

Rapp nodded. "Okay. Grisha and I can handle this. We'll stun gun them and drag them into the room when Donatella gives us the signal."

"How are we getting the body out?" Black asked.

"I didn't see any reason not to just stick with the classics," Rapp responded.

"Laundry cart?" Donatella said.

"Exactly."

Claudia switched to a shot of a woman in a maid's uniform pushing a cart large enough to cram bin Musaid into.

"This will be in Donatella's room and I'm having

a uniform made for her." She glanced in the former model's direction. "Size eight?"

Donatella's eyes narrowed dangerously.

"Is it common for one of those carts to be on that floor?" Rapp asked. He knew the answer but was anxious to break the death stares the women had fixed on each other.

"No," Claudia responded, turning back toward him. "But all we have to do is get it to the elevator. Then I can send you nonstop to the basement."

"What about me?" Black said.

"You have a top-floor flat to the west of Terry's. There's a good-sized private terrace for you to set your rifle up on. The range is just over five hundred meters, but light winds are forecasted throughout the week."

"Doesn't sound like there will be anything to shoot at," he said, disappointed.

"The hope is that you'll just be spotting for us," Rapp said. "But you know what hope's worth."

Claudia turned toward the Russian, who was now perusing the bar's bourbon selection. "Any luck, Grisha?"

"I know two of the men in these pictures. One more I have a passing acquaintance with."

"Okay," she said. "Can you show me which ones? I can start getting background on their movements and find out if they have reservations at the club going forward. Why don't the rest of you go pick out your bedrooms?"

Black grabbed his duffle and disappeared almost immediately. Donatella took her time, pausing next to Rapp as she passed. "It's a very romantic boat, no? Perhaps we should meet on the upper deck later. Say, midnight?"

"Give it a rest, Donatella."

"Ah, yes. The little French girl. She's quite beautiful. Why don't you ask her to join us?"

Rapp leaned against the bow rail and stared out at the city lights. Fifty yards to his left, a yacht even larger than theirs was crawling with noisy kids who looked to be in their early twenties. The champagne was flowing and an increasing number of girls were abandoning their bikini tops. When he was that age, he'd thought a scholarship to Syracuse, a suburban girlfriend, and a six-pack of Busch was a pretty good deal.

He heard footsteps coming up behind him on the deck but didn't bother to turn. He'd been living with Claudia long enough to know her gait.

"Everyone's asleep," she said, slipping her arms around him. "Are you coming to bed? Or are you going to join the party on the other boat?"

"It's a nice night. I thought I'd enjoy it for a while. Did you talk to Anna? How is she?"

"Good. She's on her way to see Tommy's lacrosse match with Irene but asked me to remind you to wear your seat belt."

They'd told her that the injuries he'd suffered in Pakistan were the result of a car crash. Now she was obsessed with what she perceived to be his unsafe driving habits.

"Have you ironed out all the details?" he asked.

"Almost. The parking garage cameras are the last thing. Oddly, they're more difficult to access than the ones in the building. It'll be taken care of by tomorrow afternoon."

"With a little luck, this could actually go smoothly."

"Oh, I doubt it."

He turned toward her. "Are there issues we haven't talked about?"

"With taking the prince? No."

"Then what?"

"I'm concerned, Mitch. This isn't a black op. You've got no official standing. Have you considered the possibility that you might spend the rest of your life on the run from your former friends and colleagues?"

"They wouldn't find me. Most of them wouldn't want to."

"Even if that's true, your life would never be the same. I lived that way for years—the constant moves, the aliases, the lack of anything lasting. And for you, the loss of your country."

"I can handle it."

"I wonder."

"Is that all?"

"No."

"How did I know that?"

"I'm worried about your team. They're all very talented—particularly Grisha—but they're not reliable or loyal. They're not Scott."

"They'll hold together."

"Are you sure? You have a Russian assassin who cares only about one thing: the woman he left behind in Costa Rica. If he sees any risk of not being able to return to her, he'll abandon us. Then you have a sociopathic woman who is doing this for the new life you've offered her, but also because she wants you back. And, finally, you have a boy who doesn't want to work with you—he wants to *be* you. How long until he decides he's ready to test the great Mitch Rapp?"

"When you put it that way, it does sound pretty bad."

"I'm being serious."

"I know. It's your job to think about this stuff and I agree with everything you said. But it's the only hand we've got to play."

She looked up at him, clearly wanting him to say more.

"Look, Claudia. I haven't seen Donatella in more than ten years. We had a short relationship that we both knew wasn't going anywhere. Don't let her get to you. She just likes to make trouble."

Claudia examined his face for a few more seconds and then took his hand. "Let's go to bed. We can take our minds off our problems for a little while."

CHAPTER 28

DONATELLA Rahn walked up the steps to the yacht's upper deck, sipping a sparkling water. She had a light wrap over her dress but didn't need more. Despite the fact that it was almost 10 p.m., temperatures were still in the low seventies.

The rest of their haphazard team was already there but, somewhat tellingly, all were occupying their own space. She did the same, settling into an empty lounge chair and taking an opportunity to study the people around her.

Kent Black was near the railing doing another endless set of push-ups. He was purported to be an excellent sniper but seemed impossibly young and desperate to impress. It was clear that he idolized Mitch almost to the point of deification. Saint Rapp. The Great and Terrible Oz. She'd known him when he was just another boy getting into the business. Talented, to be sure, but who could have guessed what he would become?

Grisha Azarov had his back to her, talking quietly into a satellite phone, as he did often. He was quite an intriguing figure, exuding calm confidence and that hint of clinical depression that she'd come to associate with Russian operatives. Claudia did a mediocre job of hiding her fear of him, while Rapp made no attempt to hide his respect. Donatella's eavesdropping suggested that Azarov always talked to the same person but a name had proved difficult to make out. Probably Cara, but the fact that he never gave Donatella so much as a glance suggested that it could also be Carl.

She turned her attention to a table where Rapp and the little French girl were discussing something in hushed tones. What on earth did he see in her?

Unfortunately, the answer was obvious. There was the youth, of course—she was certainly no more than midthirties. And then there was the beautiful face and flawless body. Moreover, she appeared to be irritatingly competent. The name Dufort was complete nonsense, of course. There was little question that this was the woman who had played a significant role in the success of the late Louis Gould. While pulling a trigger could be quite difficult, equally difficult was making sure you were standing in the right place when you did it. Gould was always standing in the right place, and it was common knowledge that he had his wife to thank.

Finally, Donatella focused on Rapp, the man responsible for bringing them together. He'd never understood that they were made for each other. Instead, he'd left and taken up with that idealistic little reporter Anna Reilly. While she could understand what attracted him to Claudia Gould, what he'd seen in that Goody Two-shoes was a mystery.

Donatella turned to gaze out over the city lights but kept Rapp in her peripheral vision. What if something were to happen to the little French girl? Would getting rid of the competition create an opportunity for them to rekindle the romance that had been so powerful in their youth?

She took a sip of her water and finally looked fully away from her former lover. No. He'd find out and then she'd experience what so many had experienced before—the very brief and very final view down the barrel of his Glock.

The chime of a phone sounded and Claudia picked up, speaking a few unintelligible words into it before disconnecting.

"The prince has left his brother's compound and is driving in the direction of Terry's."

Azarov looked between the front seats as Rapp eased into the crowded parking lot of Monaco's most exclusive club. The former CIA man was wearing an inexpensive suit and had pulled his hair back into a neat ponytail. Combined with his general build and constantly sweeping eyes, he looked much like all the other bodyguards shuttling their employers to Terry's. Of course, those similarities were an illusion. He was unique. And, as such, utterly fascinating.

Azarov had done very little in his life beyond training. His athletic talent had been identified at a young age and he'd been taken from his home in favor of a Soviet biathlon camp. Later he'd joined the Russian special forces, where he'd learned and applied an entirely new skill set. Finally, he'd gone to work directly for President Krupin, continuing to hone his abilities with some of the most accomplished coaches in the world.

Rapp had enjoyed few of those advantages—lacrosse and track in his early years, then a relatively short involvement in triathlon. No, he was a far rarer animal. A pure talent. How Azarov had been bested twice by the American despite his haphazard training history, age, and almost comically thick medical file was difficult to fully understand. What he did understand, though, was that Rapp could be as good a friend as he was deadly an enemy.

It was this realization that had torn him from Cara and the life they had made together. An opportunity to observe Rapp up close and the excitement that he missed more than expected were just ancillary benefits. The American was someone who could be trusted to stand with those who showed him loyalty, and there could be no better ally than the one man better at this game than himself.

"Can you see, Grisha?" Rapp said, veering away from the valets and finding a space that allowed a view of the people entering Terry's.

"Yes, but I don't know any of those men."

Rapp spoke into a phone patched through the BMW M5's audio system. "Claudia, do you have an ETA on the prince?"

"A little less than two minutes if he makes the lights."

"Kent. Give me a sitrep."

"I'm setting up now. Thirty seconds and I'll be ready to rock."

"For God's sake," Donatella said in a typically exasperated tone. "None of this is necessary. I can just walk in there right now and in a few minutes bin Musaid and I will be on our way to my hotel suite. Instead, we're sitting here waiting for someone who can get Grisha in. I've done this a thousand times, Mitch. And guess what? I somehow managed without you."

Azarov glanced over at the woman in the backseat with him. She was unquestionably one of the most alluring creatures he'd ever seen. But that came at a price. Her magnetism wasn't produced just by her beauty—there were many equally stunning women. It was the sense of danger she exuded. The sharp edge that became a bit more ragged with every passing day. There was little doubt that at one time she and Rapp had been involved, and it was even more obvious that she would like to see that relationship rekindled.

The fact that Rapp was so tightly tied to Claudia was unnerving the woman more than she was willing to admit. Donatella was at an age where her irresistible power over men would soon begin to fade—a painful realization that would be magnified by the way Rapp looked at the younger Claudia Gould.

Would those issues translate into recklessness? Could she be trusted in a fight? Interesting questions, but not ones worth asking at this point. While he wasn't in the habit of relying on other men's judgment, he made an exception for Rapp. If the American felt she deserved a place on this team, it was likely that she did.

Kent Black's voice came over the phone again. "I'm set up and have eyes on the prince's vehicle. Give me a second and I should be able to get a head count."

Donatella Rahn only half listened to the ensuing discussion, instead watching two girls walk across the parking lot toward the door. Both were in their early twenties, thin, tall, and expensively dressed. The one on the left, while wearing this year's Chanel, didn't seem comfortable in it. The other was even worse, looking dangerously unsteady in ancient Jimmy Choos.

Fresh off an Eastern European farm, she suspected. Looking to use the gifts nature had provided to build a better life. They entered without challenge but ultimately would be of little interest to anyone outside of the bedroom. And even then, she suspected their talents leaned more toward slopping pigs.

"Okay," Black said over the speakers. "We've got two men in front and one in the back. They're about to take the left into the club's entrance."

"Roger that," Rapp said.

They watched bin Musaid's car pull in front of the club as a valet rushed to open the back door. The prince stepped out, not exactly keeping a low profile in his red-checked headdress. The attendants were obviously familiar with his habits and none made a move to park the car. Instead, the bodyguards pulled into a space close to the door.

"Did you get a good look at him, Donatella?"

"He's hard to miss."

They waited another five minutes before Azarov tapped the back of Rapp's seat. "There. That's Klaus Alscher. I've known him for years."

He got out and crossed the lot, feigning surprise at running into Alscher. After a warm handshake and a few introductions, he disappeared inside.

"You're up, Donatella," Rapp said. "Be careful."

"This isn't the Gaza Strip," she said, opening the door and stepping out.

Unlike the girls who had entered earlier, Donatella

neither teetered nor looked uncomfortable. She moved gracefully across the lot, aware of how the light played across her silk dress and of the men watching her approach. She gave one of the bouncers a seductive smile and he stepped aside to open the door.

The interior was what she expected—marginally stylish and wildly expensive. Girls like the ones she'd seen in the lot were everywhere, on the prowl for a wealthy man who might be interested in lavishing them with gifts. Or perhaps even setting them up in an apartment for a secret long-term relationship. She understood these women better than Claudia ever could because, for a time, she'd been one of them.

Azarov had managed to maneuver his companions into a tactically viable position and was getting a fair amount of attention from the young women around him. They'd be probing, trying to determine his wealth and station in life. If they succeeded, he would quickly become the most sought-after man in the bar. Not only rich but a marked improvement over the potbellied Arabs who made up the majority of the clientele.

Laughter burst out from the east corner of the room when a young man jumped onto his chair and began gyrating wildly to the sedate music. Donatella allowed herself a bemused smile and moved toward the bar. Bin Musaid was standing at one end, surrounded by friends and the requisite contingent of women. He glanced in her direction, and she met his eye for a moment before turning her attention to the bartender. He brought her a martini that she sipped while intermittently engaging and dismissing the men who approached her. Whenever she sent one away, she would steal a glance in bin Musaid's direction. And every time she did, he paid increasing attention.

The truth was that the girls in this bar were sheep. And while hunting sheep could be mildly amusing, bin Musaid was a man who would find hunting a tigress far more diverting.

CHAPTER 29

I AM Prince Talal bin Musaid."

Both Donatella and Azarov had microphones on them that fed through the BMW's sound system. Rapp glanced at his watch when he heard bin Musaid introduce himself to Donatella. Eight minutes forty-two seconds since she'd walked into the place. She hadn't lost her touch.

He cut back the volume on Azarov's conversation about Venezuela's economic meltdown and half listened to her coy banter. There was no reason to worry or second-guess. She'd play with him for a while, get him worked up, and then inside of forty-five minutes they'd be on their way to her hotel suite.

Rapp watched the flow of traffic in and out, memorizing the positions of drivers waiting for their clients. It was impossible to know how many were armed and how many just handled the wheel, but it paid to learn as much as possible about the operating environment. Even if his role turned out to be nothing more than watching Donatella sashay to bin Musaid's car.

The conversation droning from the speakers was

the most interesting thing on the menu until two Volvo S90 sedans cruised up to the entrance. The light from the building passed through them, illuminating an interior that caught Rapp's attention. Each contained two men in front and three wedged into the back. All were bearded and appeared to be between twenty-five and forty. An advance security team for some heavy hitter? Rapp glanced back, hoping to see a limo hanging back. Nothing.

"Kent. Are you seeing these two Volvos?" he said into his radio.

"Yeah, I got 'em. What's up?"

"Probably nothing. But stay sharp."

The valets opened the doors and the men began stepping out, taking pains to stay facing the car. What were they hiding?

"Finger on the trigger, Kent."

"Who are these assholes? A bunch of Arab soccer players?"

"I don't think so," Rapp said, opening his car door a couple inches.

Finally, one of the men was forced to move away from the vehicle in order to let the next one out. When he did, he opened his coat and swung an assault rifle into firing position.

"Take them!" Rapp shouted, throwing the door fully open and leaping out.

The bouncers went down with the first bursts of automatic fire, followed quickly by three men and a young woman congregated at the entrance. The terrorist who had pulled his gun first was slammed against the vehicle by what seemed to be an invisible force but was in fact a round from Black's fifty-caliber sniper rifle. Another was spun around when Rapp hit his right shoulder blade, spraying rounds across the parking lot before dropping behind the lead Volvo. Black took out another just as a group of the drivers Rapp had identified earlier—including the ones who had arrived with bin Musaid—started running toward the building with guns drawn.

"Too soon," Rapp said under his breath.

Six of the surviving terrorists were going for the door, leaving one behind the vehicles in anticipation of the bodyguards coming up behind them. He fired on full automatic, mowing down all of them before they could get within fifteen yards. One of the drivers had hung back and was shooting over the hood of his car, but fear was getting the better of him. He ducked down to reload as Rapp took careful aim at the man firing around one of the Volvo's rear bumpers, but was forced to dive back into the car as three of the men about to enter the building concentrated fire on his position.

"Donatella, Grisha! You've got six men coming in on you," Rapp said. "All armed with assault rifles."

He slid back out of the car and aimed between the window and the pillar at the lead Volvo. The driver east of him had reloaded and was shooting again, but still not managing to hit anything. On the bright side, he was giving the terrorist remaining outside something to shoot at.

Finally, the tango went for better position and was forced to break cover for a moment. Rapp's round hit him in the face while Black's impacted his torso, dropping him on top of a dead parking attendant.

"Kent," Rapp said. "See that bodyguard shooting

from the cars east of my position? Pin him down. I don't want him coming up behind me."

By way of answer, Black rammed a fifty-caliber round into the edge of the door the man was hiding behind. A good third of it was ripped off, and shrapnel sprayed across the asphalt. Apparently that was enough. He ran for the trees at the edge of the lot while Rapp sprinted toward the building.

He kicked one of the doors and looked inside. Two bodies lay on the floor in the opulent entryway but it was otherwise empty. Gunfire echoed from deeper inside, with enough rounds expended to create a gunpowder haze in the air. He leapt over the bodies and passed two more corpses before coming out into the main bar area. Most people were on the ground or seeking cover behind overturned furniture. The scene seemed to slow as Rapp swept his Glock from right to left. One shooter was down, likely the work of either Azarov or Donatella, but he could spot neither of them.

A man appeared from around the corner and began sprinting across the room. His extraordinary speed made him easy to identify.

Rapp fired toward Azarov, missing his ear by only inches. The Russian didn't flinch or bother to look behind him to see if Rapp had hit the terrorist who had been coming up behind him. Instead, he swung his gun awkwardly toward a man shooting at a group of young people huddled in a corner booth. The seemingly desperate shot fired from beneath his arm hit the man in the neck, spraying blood across a massive mirror and crumpling him.

There were only three shooters left, and they seemed

to recognize that the momentum of the battle had reversed. Instead of continuing to fire at every viable target, they were shouting at one another to spread out. This wasn't a random terrorist attack. They were looking for someone.

Rapp ran toward the bar, grabbing an injured girl as he passed and shoving her beneath a table. He finally spotted Donatella and bin Musaid in the southeast corner of the building. She was screaming her head off while the prince cowered behind. Her right hand was in her purse, undoubtedly wrapped around the Beretta Nano inside, but for the time being she seemed content to play the damsel in distress.

A barrage of automatic fire began pounding the polished wood trim near her and Rapp dove to the floor as she fired, hitting the tango in the leg. Rapp didn't bother to check his momentum, instead sliding toward the terrorist zeroing in on bin Musaid, who was so focused on his target that he didn't even notice Rapp coming to a stop only inches away. The CIA man was actually able to press the barrel of his weapon against the back of the tango's head before pulling the trigger.

In his peripheral vision, Rapp saw another terrorist using a young man as a human shield while he tried to get a bead on a fast-moving Grisha Azarov. The Russian had a clear head shot but didn't take it, instead firing through the hostage's stomach and into the shooter's left hip. Not ideal but understandable. The hostage would survive and Azarov's cover as an energy consultant wouldn't be jeopardized by a one-in-a-thousand combat shot.

With no similar concerns about anonymity, Rapp hit the tango in the back of the head as he was falling away from his hostage. That left one alive by his count. He was out of view, though, so that meant he was Azarov's problem.

Rapp sprinted to where bin Musaid was now trying to wrestle the gun from Donatella's hand. He grabbed the Saudi by his silk collar and shouted at him in Arabic. "Forget the whore, Your Highness. We have to get you out of here!"

"Who . . . who are you?"

"The king charged me with your safety, Highness. Now get up. We have to go!"

Rapp pulled the man to his feet and they started running toward the front door. Bin Musaid was terrified and unaccustomed to moving fast, causing him to stumble with nearly every other step. They were only a few feet from escaping when a shot sounded—not the undisciplined automatic fire that had been echoing off the walls since he'd entered, but a single, carefully aimed round. Bin Musaid's feet went out from under him, and Rapp was forced to drag the man across the polished floor.

He was still conscious, but the wound in his lower back was bad enough that he wasn't going to be able to continue under his own power. Rapp lifted him into a fireman's carry and headed for the door, talking into the microphone hidden in his shirt cuff.

"Kent, I'm coming out carrying the prince."

"Roger that. You're clear to the car. Don't try to get out of the parking lot the way you came in, though. It's a complete clusterfuck. Back straight up and go through the bushes. If you don't hit any trees, it's about twenty yards to the road.

"Copy."

Very few people had managed to escape the build-

ing, but most of the ones who had were forgoing their
vehicles and running for the edges of the property.
That left Rapp a clear path to his car and a welcome
amount of privacy as he shoved the wounded Saudi
through the passenger-side door. A few moments later
Rapp had the engine started and was reversing through
Terry's expensive landscaping. When the BMW finally
jumped the curb into the street, he drifted it 180 degrees and slammed it into Drive.

"Mitch, you've got a vehicle coming hard at you
from the southwest corner of the lot. Might just be
someone looking to tag along on your escape route,
but I wouldn't bet on—"

Black's voice was drowned out by the sound of automatic fire and the ring of impacts against the BMW's
rear end.

"Can you do anything about them?" Rapp said.

"No angle. You're on your own, man."

Rapp pressed his foot to the floor and was shoved
back in the seat as the vehicle accelerated down a
sweeping hill.

The stench in the car suggested that one of bin
Musaid's intestines had been punctured, and Rapp
glanced over at him. The pallor was obvious even
in the dim glow of the instrument lights, as was the
amount of blood that was soaking into the upholstery.
More concerning, though, was the Volvo in his rearview mirror. There was a man standing up through the
sunroof, and Rapp could see the gleam of his weapon.
So far they were out of range, but the driver was taking
insane chances, nearly rolling over the steep embank-
ment to the right every time he cornered.

"Did you hear those men speak, Your Highness?"

Rapp said. "They sounded Iraqi. And there's no question that they were after you personally."

"Hospital," he responded weakly. "Hospital . . ."

Rapp had seen enough people in similar shape to know that he wasn't going to make it. This would be a short interrogation and he needed to focus the man. To that end, he eased up on the accelerator and let the Volvo get close enough for the shooter to shatter their rear window.

Bin Musaid's feeble scream mixed with the roar of the M5's engine as Rapp accelerated again.

"Your wound doesn't look serious," he lied. "And I think I can lose the men chasing us, but it'll be hard to hide you from them—they know that I have to take you to a hospital. Who are they? Do you know anything I can use? The king has made it clear that you're to be kept safe at all costs."

Bin Musaid started to cry. "I . . . I betrayed him."

"Who? Who did you betray?"

"I gave money to ISIS. I supported their effort . . ." His voice faded. For a moment Rapp thought he was dead, but a volley from behind jerked him back to consciousness.

"Nassar! It has to be."

"Nassar? Do you mean Aali Nassar?"

Bin Musaid nodded and then coughed violently, spraying the steering wheel and Rapp's right hand with blood. "He drained my bank account, knowing that I'd seek my brother's help. He knew it would be easier to kill me in Europe than at home."

"That makes no sense, Highness. If he suspects that you are involved with ISIS, why wouldn't he go to the king? Why wouldn't he just arrest you?"

"You don't understand," bin Musaid responded, weakening quickly. "I was just the messenger. He's afraid that if the CIA takes me, I'll reveal that he was behind all of it."

"Behind all of it," Rapp repeated. "Are you telling me that Aali Nassar is coordinating support for ISIS?"

Bin Musaid nodded.

"Who else is involved?"

The prince didn't respond.

"Answer me!" Rapp shouted. "The king will take care of Nassar, but if I don't know who the others are, I can't stop them from killing you."

"I don't know," bin Musaid sobbed.

"He must have said something. Wealthy businessmen? Other royals? Government employees?"

"The hospital," bin Musaid said in a voice that was barely audible. "You have to get me to the hospital."

He didn't have much more time, and it was likely he was telling the truth about not knowing more. Why would Aali Nassar tell this useless piece of shit anything?

Rapp tightened his hands on the wheel and focused on putting a little distance between him and the chasing vehicle. He wasn't going to be able to shake them completely, though. The Volvo was a surprisingly capable car, and the man behind the wheel was either going to stay on their tail or die trying. This situation was unusual in a fundamental way, though. For once, they weren't after him.

He hammered his foot onto the brake pedal, slamming bin Musaid against the dashboard. Rapp kept his eyes on the headlights growing in his rearview mirror as he reached for the passenger-door handle.

"What are you doing?" bin Musaid managed to say before Rapp threw open the door and shoved him out.

"Stop! What—"

Rapp accelerated away, turning on the stereo and leaving bin Musaid lying in the road. In his rearview mirror, he saw the Volvo come to a stop in front of the prince, illuminating him in its headlights as the man in the sunroof emptied a full magazine into him. After that, they hooked a U and disappeared back up the road.

With his immediate problems solved, Rapp dialed Claudia.

"Mitch! Are you all right? I'm not getting a GPS signal from you."

"I'm fine. The transmitter probably got shot."

"Where are you?"

"About seven miles south of Terry's, getting ready to head back."

"No, don't. All the terrorists are down and Grisha and Donatella are out."

"Do they need a pickup?"

"They're fine on foot."

"What about Kent?"

"He's okay, but he had to get out of the apartment fast. There's just no way to make that rifle quiet. I heard you have the prince. Is that true?"

"I lost him."

"What do you mean, 'lost him'? He's not a set of keys! How could you have lost him?"

Rapp slowed to the speed limit and opened a window to try and clear the smell of bin Musaid's damaged bowel. "Long story."

CHAPTER 30

RAPP eased the BMW to the edge of the dock and looked both ways. It was empty of pedestrian traffic at this hour, and most of the yachts moored near his were dark. The inevitable exception was the one inhabited by the tireless rich kids. They were on another tear, but it wouldn't be a problem for him. Even if they noticed the BMW and managed to make out the small-arms damage, they'd never remember it in the morning.

He turned left, trying to keep his engine noise down. Claudia was standing on the yacht's stern and the gangways were in place.

He was barely on board before she started retracting them and closing the stern railing. Living up to his reputation for efficiency, their Congolese captain immediately began motoring out to sea.

Claudia opened the car's passenger door and backed away at the sight of the blood. "Did you do this?"

"He got hit in the bar," Rapp said, stepping out and talking quietly over the top of the vehicle. "They were chasing me because of him, so I tossed his body out."

Not entirely the truth, but close enough.

"But *you're* all right? And by that I mean completely uninjured."

He nodded. "What about the others?"

"Same. Kent is on his way to France on a motorcycle. Donatella is on a train to Italy, and Grisha's company is sending a jet for him. He'll take it to his house in London. Then, after things calm down, they'll all make their way back to Africa."

"And us?"

"We'll detour over some deep water to get rid of the car and rendezvous with them next week."

It took some effort, but he finally managed to get bin Musaid's blood off him and down the drain. Leaning into the hot water, he let it pound on the back of his head, forcing Claudia to raise her voice to be heard. She was sitting on the granite counter with a portable computer on her lap.

"It's on pretty much every television channel in the world, Mitch. There's some shaky cell phone footage from the parking lot, but nothing of you yet. That's not going to be true of the interior security cameras. I'm sorry that I wasn't able to shut them down."

It was another drawback to having left the government. Kennedy could have seriously limited access to that security video. Now it was likely that the local police were already watching it, and by dawn Interpol, the FBI, CIA, MI6, and Saudi intelligence would have copies. It wasn't going to be long before he was identified.

"Sixteen dead," she continued. "More than that wounded. The authorities are holding back the names, but an unofficial list is starting to circulate. There are some very wealthy and powerful men on here, Mitch. This is going to get a lot of attention. Do you know who the shooters were?"

"Iraqis."

"Not a coincidence, I assume."

"No. The fireworks were just for show. They were after bin Musaid."

"Who sent them?"

His initial reaction was to lie. Not because he thought she didn't know how to keep her mouth shut, but because he wanted to protect her. Unfortunately, it was a little late for that now.

"Aali Nassar."

"The Saudi intelligence chief?"

Rapp turned off the water and grabbed a towel. "He's behind the Saudi financing of ISIS. Bin Musaid was just one of his delivery boys."

"Why?"

"Bin Musaid died before he could say. My guess is that, with all of Saudi Arabia's internal problems, Nassar thinks ISIS is going to come out on top. He wants to be on the winning side."

"Did the prince live long enough to give you the names of anyone else involved?"

"No. And he wouldn't have known anyway. Nassar would play that pretty close to his chest."

"What about King Faisal?"

"I doubt he'd be part of this. I've known him for years and he's just looking to run out the clock. But wealthy businessmen who want to cut deals, royals who want Faisal's throne, government officials looking to move up the ladder? The list of Saudis who have reasons to sympathize with ISIS isn't exactly short."

"All right. I'll start working on Nassar's history, known associates, and financial condition. Any chance you'd consider contacting Irene? I'm good, but I don't have her resources."

He shook his head and pulled on the clothes she'd laid out for him. "The only evidence I have against Nassar is the word of a little pissant who's getting scraped off the road right now. I agreed to get myself into this. But she didn't agree to come along."

"Okay. I'll handle it."

"Carefully, though, right, Claudia? Nassar might be a terrorist son of a bitch, but he's a smart one with an army."

CHAPTER 31

THE knock on Aali Nassar's bedroom door was hesitant but insistent. Not his wife. Even in an emergency, she would go to the staff before disturbing him. The clock read 3 a.m.

He rolled from bed and put on a robe before striding through the darkness to the door. As expected, the head of his security detail was standing on the other side.

"What is it?"

"Your assistant just arrived, Director. He says it's critical that you speak."

Nassar nodded. "Show him to my study. I'll be there in a moment."

"Right away, sir."

Nassar pulled on a pair of slacks and a collared shirt before starting for the office he kept at the back of his home. Enough lights had been turned on to allow him to navigate, but not so many that the activity in the house would be obvious. These kinds of surprise meetings were kept as quiet as possible.

What was so important that it couldn't wait another three hours until he arrived at the office? A successful terrorist attack on the homeland? An action by the president of the United States? The death of the king?

When Nassar entered the office, he found Hamid Safar pacing its length.

"Sir, we have reports that Prince bin Musaid has been killed."

Nassar felt a profound sense of relief but didn't show it. "How?"

"A terrorist attack at a private club in Monaco."

"A terrorist attack? Do we have details?"

"There appear to have been ten men in total, all armed with assault rifles. They took out the security people and forced their way in, then proceeded to kill or wound a significant portion of the clientele before being killed themselves."

"By authorities?"

"No, sir."

"Then whom?"

"That's a difficult question to answer," he said, placing his laptop on Nassar's desk and opening it. "We just received raw footage from the security cameras. Can I go through it with you?"

"Of course."

It started with an outdoor feed depicting the terrorists getting out of their cars and beginning the assault. All was proceeding as expected until one of them was thrown violently back into one of the vehicles.

"What happened there?"

"Three of the men were killed by fifty-caliber rounds fired from the upper floor of an apartment building five hundred meters to the east. European authorities have identified the apartment and found the weapon, but they don't think they will be able to trace it. We have some poor security camera footage of a man leaving the building, but it would be impossible to use it for identification purposes."

"Why would there be an unknown, highly skilled sniper set up to fire down on a terrorist attack that no intelligence agency was aware was going to take place?"

"The authorities are working under the theory that the shooter was a member of one of the patrons' security details."

"It seems like a rather extraordinary measure for someone going to a nightclub."

"Agreed. Further, we have a list of the members who were there that night, and none of them would have security that elaborate."

Safar started the video again, depicting a terrorist being hit in the side and spun around.

"That wasn't a high-caliber round," Nassar commented.

"No, sir. There are two effective shooters. The sniper and one of the drivers in the parking lot."

Nassar watched the gunfight play out. When all the terrorists outside had been killed, a man appeared and ran for the doors. Safar paused the video. "We assume that this is the other successful shooter."

"A security guard for one of the men inside?"

"We're not sure."

The video switched to an interior view, displaying the chaos in a steady flow of changing angles. "Six terrorists entered. One is already dead at this point, but it's unclear who fired the shot. Watch the left side of the screen."

A man ran at incredible speed across the frame, one hand over his head and the other holding a pistol. He aimed awkwardly and fired, surprisingly taking out a terrorist firing at a booth full of young people.

"Have we identified that man?"

"Yes, sir. His name is Grisha Azarov. A well-regarded energy consultant from Russia. Have you heard of him?"

"The name is vaguely familiar. His company has done work for Aramco, no?"

"That's correct."

The man who had crossed the parking lot came into the frame, sliding on the floor toward an injured terrorist and calmly pressing a Glock to the back of his head before pulling the trigger.

The camera angle changed and finally Prince bin Musaid came into view. He was wrestling with a woman whose purse appeared to be on fire.

"Who is she?"

"We don't know. Most likely one of the whores who frequent the establishment."

A moment later the man from the parking lot appeared and began pulling the prince toward the door.

"Here," Safar said, slowing down the video. "This is where bin Musaid is hit."

The impact was obvious, but it was difficult to tell exactly where the bullet had penetrated. The man from the lot threw bin Musaid over his shoulder and ran, eventually getting picked up by the exterior camera before disappearing into the parking lot.

"So the wound the prince suffered was fatal?"

"We can't be certain, sir. He was driven away and

later found riddled with bullets in the middle of the road."

"Was the man who took him from his security detail?"

"No, sir. They were both killed in the parking lot."

Safar's nervousness seemed to be growing and Nassar's agitation grew with it. Mullah Halabi had said he would deal with bin Musaid but had made no allusion to the fact that it would be done in the context of a terrorist attack targeting some of the wealthiest men in the world. And to make matters worse, his lackeys hadn't killed the prince cleanly. It was possible that he had survived for some time with his rescuer.

"If he wasn't part of bin Musaid's detail, then who was he? Even with limited footage, it's obvious that he's highly trained and has significant combat experience. A man like him would be known to the world's intelligence community."

Safar minimized the video and brought up another. Instead of being designed to give an overview of the attack, this one had been spliced together to focus on that one shooter. The additional footage confirmed Nassar's initial analysis. Even in his years in the special forces, he'd never seen anyone who could match the man's speed, accuracy, and flawless instincts. He didn't hesitate, he appeared to be immune to the confusion of battle, and he never missed. Unfortunately, he also seemed to have a gift for keeping his face from lining up directly with the establishment's cameras.

Safar switched to an unrelated video that appeared to depict an American military operation in an unidentifiable Middle Eastern village. The shaky footage—probably from a helmet-mounted camera—detailed an ambush and the desperate battle that ensued. All the soldiers fought well, but there was a man who stood well above the others. Despite the poor quality of the image, it was clear that he was the same size and build as the man in Monaco and that he wore his hair and beard the same way. More important, he had the same icy calm and the same graceful, economical way of moving.

"What you're watching now," Safar said, "is a rare and highly classified video of Mitch Rapp in combat."

Nassar felt his mouth go dry. "How long was bin Musaid in the car with him? Tell me!"

Safar fumbled with the computer, pulling up Google Maps and making the calculations based on where they'd found the Saudi prince's body. "No more than four or five minutes."

Nassar pressed his palms against his temples, feeling them begin to throb. If bin Musaid had been conscious, he would have been confused, terrified, and in pain—an easily exploited situation. Rapp would have told the prince that he'd been sent there to protect him but that he couldn't do so unless he knew who was behind the attack. How much could bin Musaid have revealed over the course of five minutes?

"We need more than speculation," Nassar said, trying to keep his voice even. "I'll be at the office in one hour and I want facts, names, and options. Further, we're going to have to calculate how to present this to the king. Obviously there will be no mention of Rapp's potential involvement. Eventually the other agencies will identify him, but for now we have some time."

Safar was already packing up his computer. "I'll see to it immediately. Is there anything else?"

"Find Azarov and use our contacts at the CIA to get a location on Rapp."

Safar disappeared through the door as Nassar eased himself unsteadily into the chair behind his desk. By all reports, Rapp had resigned from the Agency. Was it possible that he'd gone rogue? That he had been following the prince of his own volition and thus had been present for the attack by Halabi's men? Or was it something far more dangerous? Was his retirement just disinformation created by a CIA that was supporting this operation?

His phone rang and he immediately recognized the number. His decision to pick up, though, took another few seconds.

"Yes."

Mullah Halabi's voice sounded uncharacteristically upbeat. "I understand that you've been briefed on recent events in Monaco."

The fact that the man knew this so quickly added to Nassar's anxiety. Did he have people watching the house? Was it possible that Nassar's personal guards—perhaps even his trusted assistant—were among the man's many disciples?

"I have," was all Nassar could get out.

"A magnificent operation, wouldn't you say, Aali? Not only is your prince dead but all those infidels as well."

"Bin Musaid wasn't killed."

"You're misinformed, Director. When my men left him in the road, he was little more than a piece of meat."

"But he wasn't killed *immediately*," Nassar said angrily. "The man who got him out . . ."

"Yes?"

"We believe it was Mitch Rapp."

"Indeed?" the mullah said, sounding even more gleeful. "Wonderful! Can you feel him, Aali? Can you feel Satan's breath on your neck? I can. Every second of every hour. The day that you lose your sensitivity to that searing wind is the day that God no longer sees you."

CHAPTER 32

"WHAT happened to the BMW?" Claudia said as she walked into the yacht's galley.

"Bottom of the sea," Rapp responded, sliding a cup of coffee toward her.

"That was *my* job."

"You were dead asleep. I also called your pilot. He'll have the jet waiting for us in Malta."

She pulled her robe up around her neck and pointed to the potato he was chopping. "*And* you're making breakfast? I feel like I'm not earning my money."

"I'm not paying you."

"In that case, I'll have an omelet."

He walked to the refrigerator and began digging around for some eggs. She'd been up half the night putting together everything she could on Aali Nassar, although they hadn't yet discussed what she'd found. Rapp had considered telling her about the deal that was struck with the Saudis after 9/11 but quickly abandoned the idea. It was one of the ugliest skeletons in America's closet, and she didn't really need to know.

"Maybe I should do that," she said, watching him pile ingredients on the counter.

"Have a little faith."

"I'm skeptical by nature."

"Did you find anything interesting on Nassar?"

She took a sip of her coffee while he looked for a pan. "I did, but then I considered throwing it all into the sea."

"Why?"

"Because this wasn't the mission, Mitch. You were going to coerce bin Musaid into pointing a finger at high-level Saudis involved with ISIS and—"

"He did that."

"But it isn't a group of minor royals or wealthy businessmen. It's the director of Saudi intelligence. That's a fundamental shift in the mission."

"It's not a shift. Just a change in scale."

"Mitch, we—"

"Do you want out?" he asked. It would be impossible to hold it against her. While she'd worked some fairly high-profile targets in the past, none were anything like Nassar.

She stared at him for a few beats before speaking again without directly answering the question. Whether that was because she wasn't sure or because she was insulted by the question, he didn't know. Probably best to let it go for now.

"I wasn't focused on Nassar's personal history because I assume you're already aware of it—his modest upbringing, his education in the madrassas and then Oxford. His time in the Saudi special forces . . ."

"Yeah. The Agency's been keeping an eye on him since he was a young officer. He was always going places, though I don't think any of us would have guessed that he'd replace a royal as head of the Intelligence Directorate. I assume you looked into his associates?"

She nodded.

"And?"

"I've come up with a good list, I think. The most important name on it is Mahja Zaman."

"Who's he?"

"A childhood friend and his roommate at university. They continue to maintain a close friendship, and Zaman is both extremely wealthy and extremely religious. By all reports, he's also quite intelligent."

"So a completely different animal than bin Musaid," Rapp said, cracking a couple eggs into the pan he found.

"Absolutely. While Nassar would have tolerated the prince to access his money, his relationship with Zaman would be very different. He'd have to treat the man as an equal."

"So Zaman might actually know something about Nassar's network and methods."

"If anyone does, it would be him."

"Any other front-runners?"

"A few. But one is of particular interest. Ahmed el-Hashem, the number two man at the Saudi embassy in Paris. He's rich, well-connected, and seems to have an unusually close relationship with Nassar. He's also heavily connected to the bin Laden family and was a close friend of Osama when they were young. Just the kind of man I would recruit if I were Aali Nassar."

Rapp lowered the heat on the stove. "In order to move against someone like Nassar, I need more than bin Musaid's deathbed confession. At this point we have to assume that the CIA and MI6 have IDed me from the Monte Carlo security camera footage. If that's the case, it won't take long for that information to filter to Nassar. And when it does, we need to be paying attention. If he's guilty, he's going to start getting rid of anyone who can finger him."

"They're not the only people he's going to try to get rid of, Mitch. We're on his radar now."

Rapp tossed some grated cheese in the pan and shook it to release the egg from the surface. "Do we know where Zaman and el-Hashem are?"

"Zaman's in Brussels, staying in an upper-floor hotel suite. He doesn't have a checkout date, so I can't tell you when he's planning on leaving or where he's going when he does. El-Hashem is at his house in Paris and working his regular job at the embassy. He has two full-time security men living on the premises, both of whom also act as drivers. There's a wall around the property as well as cameras and alarms—about what you'd expect. Nothing special."

"What about Nassar?"

"On his way to London."

"Why?"

"I don't know."

Rapp slid the omelet onto a plate and put it in front of her. She examined it for a few seconds before digging in.

"Not bad," she said, sounding a bit subdued. Given the situation, it was understandable.

"I'm a man of many talents."

"I suppose so. Now tell me what you want to do about the things that don't involve breakfast."

"First, get in touch with Grisha and tell him he might

have a run-in with Nassar in London. After that, we're going to prioritize Zaman. I want to get face-to-face with him before Nassar can get rid of him or pull him back to Saudi Arabia. "

"And el-Hashem?"

Rapp would have liked to move simultaneously against the man but, without access to the Agency's manpower, it wasn't going to happen.

"He's going to have to wait. Can you get surveillance on him? Maybe try to get his personal phone and email?"

He hated relying on her people, but there was no other option. His contacts were more reliable, but they were also connected to intelligence agencies across the globe. A lot of them owed him their lives and would be willing to repay that debt, but he wasn't looking to call in those markers.

"I have someone good in Paris," Claudia said through a full mouth. "What about the others on my list?"

"Do what you can, but keep it low-key. We don't need to spook anyone. Not yet."

The muffled sound of a phone ringing interrupted him and he waited for her to dig it out of her robe. After a quick look at the screen, she picked up.

"Bonjour, chérie! Comment ça va?"

Unquestionably Anna. Claudia insisted that they communicate with her only in French in an effort to ensure her continued fluency.

"Why can't you sleep? No . . . I find that hard to believe. Irene has a great deal of security and her people would sweep for closet monsters every afternoon. It's standard procedure. Yes, but— Have you brought this up with Tommy? Oh, he does. I see. I don't— Yes, he is, but— Sweetie, you— Okay. Fine."

Claudia held out the phone. "She wants to talk to you. She says you know how to handle these kinds of things."

CHAPTER 33

"AND now I'm told I shot an innocent man," Grisha Azarov said, leaning forward and putting his face in his hands.

The psychologist sitting across from him wore a perfectly calibrated expression of sympathy. As he should at the prices he was charging.

"But, Grisha, that man is going to survive and the terrorist holding him was gravely injured by the same bullet. The authorities have given me access to the files describing what happened in Monte Carlo, and your actions were nothing short of heroic. Your cool head saved lives. You need to focus on that."

Azarov didn't bother to look up, having already examined every detail in the bland office. What else was there to do during these mind-numbing meetings?

"Grisha?"

He tried to come up with something convincing to say. These sessions were critical to the fiction he'd created in Monaco and there was no guarantee that a foreign intelligence agency wouldn't get hold of the notes from them. He'd done everything possible to look like an amateur—awkward sprints, suboptimal shots, and terrified expressions.

There was no telling if it would be enough, though, so now he was here dealing with nonexistent feelings of fear, guilt, and lingering panic. It was really quite laughable. His ability to conjure these emotions was so limited that he'd been forced to spend hours watching footage of people with PTSD and practicing in the mirror. Cara would have been quite impressed with his performance, he imagined. She was always trying to get him to share feelings that existed only in her imagination.

"It's not just the hostage," Grisha said finally. He would have liked to get some tears flowing, but the only thing that had the power to do that was onions. "It's the terrorists."

"Please go on."

"I know they're evil. I've spent my career in the Middle East. But they're also human beings. How can I understand where they came from? What they've been taught from the time they were children? I don't even know if they fully understand their actions. And I killed them."

"Taking a human life is one of the most traumatic things a person of conscience can do. But you have to acknowledge that those men had no intention of ever leaving that place. They . . ."

Azarov tuned the man out and glanced at the clock. Ten more minutes until the session was finished. He'd soon leave London, arguing that he needed a change of scenery and to avoid the potential spotlight. The authorities had agreed to keep his identity confidential, but there was always the concern that cell phone footage would surface.

Kent and Donatella were already taking a circuitous route back to Africa. Mitch and Claudia would soon follow.

The question was: Would he do the same? He still wasn't sure the benefits of his involvement outweighed the risks. Unquestionably, Mitch Rapp's gratitude might prove valuable one day. But there was more. On some level he missed the excitement. No, "excitement" wasn't the right word. The challenge. The thrill of being able to do things that only three or four men on the planet would even attempt.

But maybe it was time to consider going home. Rapp wouldn't be pleased, but he was a man of honor. They would shake hands and part ways amicably.

He pondered the issue while his therapist continued to drone on, finally deciding to stand with Rapp and his people. After the operation was done, he would return to his life with Cara. He'd surf and work on his house. He'd make normal friends and tour all the places he'd been to but never really seen. He'd let her give away a significant portion of his hard-earned fortune to the poor. And he'd forget everything he'd once been.

"I think we're reaching the end of our time," the psychologist said.

The man's words pulled Azarov back to the present and he stood, extending a hand. "Thank you, Doctor. I'm finding these sessions to be very helpful."

"Same time tomorrow, then?"

"I look forward to it."

He strode from the office and exited into a light

London rain. The narrow side street was choked with parked cars but otherwise empty as he started along the sidewalk. When he came up on a black limousine, the rear window opened.

"Mr. Azarov? May I have a moment of your time?"

"Who are you?" he said, displaying the expected confusion.

"My name is Aali Nassar. I'm the director of Saudi intelligence."

Claudia had emailed about this. Prince bin Musaid had been killed, but apparently not before naming Nassar as the man behind the financing of ISIS. She'd been concerned that he might try to make contact while he was in London, and it seemed that her concerns were well-founded.

Azarov let recognition slowly register in his expression. "Of course. I work with your colleague the energy minister."

"I'm aware of that," he said, opening the door. "Would you like to get out of the rain for a moment?"

Azarov shrugged and slid into the vehicle's luxurious interior.

"First," Nassar said, "how are you? Praise Allah that you survived your ordeal in Monaco. Still, it must have been a very difficult experience for you."

His tone suggested that he wasn't entirely convinced by the explanations of Azarov's success against a group of heavily armed terrorists.

"Thank you for your concern. But I'll be fine."

"Good . . . That's good." Nassar paused for a moment. "Your performance was quite impressive. I imagine that the Russians will be quite disappointed that you went into consulting and not the military."

A leading comment that couldn't be ignored.

"Because I do much of my work in unstable countries, my company has spent a great deal of money teaching me to defend myself. And I was an athlete in my youth. A heart condition kept me from turning professional, but I still train recreationally. It proved quite helpful."

"And the weapon you used? My analysts were intrigued."

"It was made for me by a gunsmith recommended by my shooting instructor."

"Do you have it with you? I'd love to see it."

Azarov shook his head. "I have a special permit to carry it in Monaco. Getting a similar permit in England is next to impossible. However, I can give you the name of the woman who made it if you'd like. Her work is second to none."

Nassar fell silent and Azarov met the man's intense stare with a softer one of his own. The intelligence director was trying to let the silence become uncomfortable enough for Azarov to offer more, but he wasn't going to play that game. The less he said, the better.

Finally, Nassar pulled out a tablet and held it up. The photo was of Donatella standing at the bar, speaking with Prince bin Musaid.

"Do you recognize either of these people?"

"I remember the woman. It would be difficult not to. Did she survive?"

"Yes."

"And the man?"

"Prince Talal bin Musaid. I'm afraid he did not."

"I don't recognize the name. Please give my condolences to his family."

Nassar flipped to another photo and Azarov allowed a hint of fear to register. It depicted Rapp dragging bin Musaid toward the door. The photo was blurred from movement, and Rapp was doing everything possible to keep his face out of the camera.

"I have trouble sleeping," Azarov said. "When I wake up, it's this man and not the terrorists I see. He aimed right at me and fired. I thought I was dead, but he missed." Azarov looked away for a moment as though he was struggling to get his throat to produce sound. "Do you . . . do you know who he is?"

"We have suspicions. If I were to bring you a better photo, do think you could identify him?"

"Yes. I believe so."

Nassar tapped the glass next to him. "It appears to have stopped raining. I appreciate your time, Mr. Azarov. And your heroism."

Nassar watched the Russian go, studying his athletic gait as he hurried along the sidewalk.

It seemed extraordinary that he could have done what he had in Monaco, but everything he said checked out. He was indeed the semiretired CEO of a highly respected energy consulting firm and a personal friend of Saudi Arabia's oil minister. He had spent a significant amount of time at combat shooting school, and his athletic prowess as a youth was well-documented. Add a little luck and it wasn't impossible. It was, however, improbable.

He looked down at the tablet just as the photo of Mitch Rapp went black. They now had incontrovertible evidence that bin Musaid was alive when he left the bar. And that forced Nassar to assume that Rapp knew of his involvement. What would the CIA man do? Was he indeed rogue or did he have the clandestine support of the Agency? Would he dare attempt to assassinate the director of Saudi Arabian intelligence?

It was possible but unlikely that even Rapp would be that rash. It seemed more likely that he'd first look for proof. And with bin Musaid dead, that meant moving against Nassar's closest associates.

He reached for a button between the seats and lowered the glass separating him from his driver. "Are our people in place in Brussels?"

"They're still making preparations, sir. But I've been assured that all will be ready when you arrive."

CHAPTER 34

THE rain in Brussels was coming down much harder than it had been in London. Heavy droplets fell on the windshield, threatening to overwhelm the nondescript Citroën's wipers. An ideal environment for the tragic but necessary event to come.

Having completed the money transfer to ISIS, Mahja Zaman was staying in a hotel a few kilometers to the north. Nassar's staff had created a plan to bring him back to Saudi Arabia, where he could be protected, but that strategy required a careless arrogance that was not one of Nassar's failings. How many times had Mitch Rapp's targets been put behind impenetrable security only to end up missing or dead? As difficult as the decision had been to make, Zaman had to be moved permanently beyond Rapp's reach.

His driver dialed a phone with one hand and spoke quietly. "One minute out."

When the call was disconnected, he glanced over at Nassar in the passenger seat. "With due respect, sir, there's no reason for you to be personally involved in this. My people can deal with it quickly and quietly without putting you in danger."

"Noted."

They pulled into an alley that ran behind the hotel and Nassar stepped out. The service door immediately opened and he entered a utilitarian corridor. To his right, one of his men was closing a door leading to the security guard charged with monitoring the hotel's myriad security cameras. The recording function had been disabled and the man was lying facedown at his desk with a bullet hole in his head.

They entered a service elevator and Nassar tried to maintain his calm façade as it rose. He was allowing his personal feelings to force an obvious error. His people should have been handling this while he made his way back to Saudi Arabia. Zaman would have felt nothing as he was sent on his journey to paradise. And when he arrived, he would understand that his death was necessary in the battle against the enemies of God.

The doors slid open and Nassar's man checked the hallway before motioning him forward. Fortunately, the entrance to Zaman's suite wasn't far and, as in the alley, the door opened just before Nassar arrived.

"Aali," Zaman said, embracing him. "I'm happy to see you so soon after our last meeting."

"As am I, old friend. I understand everything went smoothly?"

"It was a simple matter," he said, ushering Nassar and his man into the room.

"In affairs like these, Mahja, I'm afraid nothing is simple."

The man's smile faded. "What do you mean?"

"I'm sorry to be the one to tell you this, but we have reason to believe that the CIA is aware of your involvement."

"The CIA! How? I followed your instructions to the letter!"

"It had nothing to do with a failure on your part. Just the fortunes of war."

"Are you here to take me back to Saudi Arabia?" he said, starting to sound a bit panicked. "The CIA kidnaps people from Europe! We must—"

"Mahja! Be calm. We've had a long and close friendship. More than that, you've been of great service to me and to God. I would never allow you to fall into the hands of the Americans."

Nassar gave a subtle nod to the man who had taken a position three meters to Zaman's left. When he pulled a silenced Glock from his jacket, Zaman registered the movement in his peripheral vision. Fortunately, there was hardly even enough time for surprise to register on his face before a round hit him in the temple.

Nassar stood motionless as his man lifted Zaman's corpse into a chair and began securing it there with a roll of tape.

"Sir," he said. "There's no reason for you to be part of this. You should go."

Nassar nodded and turned toward the door. The war against Mitch Rapp had begun. The former CIA agent was aging and suffering from a lifetime of injuries that would have killed a normal human being. More important, he appeared to be isolated—not only from Scott Coleman and his team, but also from the brilliant strategist Irene Kennedy.

Would it be enough? Would Aali Nassar be remembered by history as the man who finally defeated the American? Or would he just be another entry on the list of his victims?

Claudia parallel parked the car at the mouth of the alley and turned off the ignition. The rain immediately filled the windshield, and she left the headlights on to dazzle anyone who might glance in their direction.

"My people have been through the hotel's service area a number of times. The corridor you'll be walking through isn't well traveled, but even if you do pass someone it shouldn't be a problem. The hotel has over a hundred employees, with a fair amount of turnover—no one will give you a second look. Four security guards in total, none with any combat or law enforcement background. Three of them will be on the move and one will be watching the monitors. He'll be in a room to your right as you walk in."

She handed Rapp a key card. "This will open every door in the building."

"You're sure?"

"Of course I'm sure. I've done this before, you know."

He did know, and so far she performed flawlessly. But that and his feelings for her didn't obscure the fact that it took only one mistake. How many of his friends and enemies were dead because of a jammed gun, faulty radio, or wrong turn?

"What about Zaman's security?"

"Just the one driver, and he's on the other side of town buying gifts for Zaman's family. I have a man tailing him, so we're getting real-time updates on his location. If he starts coming in our direction, I'll let you know. Now, let's test your phone link."

She dialed and he picked up on the Bluetooth headset in his ear. It was one of the benefits of the modern world. Tactical communication devices had become common in the civilian population.

"Can you hear me?" she asked.

"Yeah, you're good. How's the signal inside?"

"Four bars in the area you're entering and the service stairs. Five everywhere else."

"Then we're ready." He reached for the door, but she grabbed his arm.

"Mitch, I think this is a mistake."

She was probably right, but they didn't have a lot of options. Nassar already knew enough to have paid Azarov a visit, and that made it almost certain that he had enough intel to know that bin Musaid wasn't dead when Rapp carried him out of Terry's. The Saudi intelligence director would err on the side of caution and assume the prince had given him up. That meant he was either going to get rid of Zaman or put him under lockdown in Saudi Arabia. Their window of opportunity was closing fast.

"It'll be fine. Just keep your eye on Zaman's driver."

Rapp pressed the key card against the reader and, as promised, the lock slid back. He pulled the rain-soaked fedora a little farther down his forehead and went inside.

The passage was as described, but the level of activity wasn't. Instead of being empty, with an overweight rent-a-cop sequestered in a monitor-lined room, there were two men on their knees, trying to get the security office door unlocked. They were speaking Dutch, but it was clear that they were concerned that they couldn't raise the man inside. If this had been a CIA op, he'd have aborted, but he wasn't working under Agency protocols anymore. He was a criminal. And a desperate one at that.

"Entering the stairwell," he said quietly. "I just passed two men trying to get access to the security office."

"Trying to get access?" Claudia responded immediately. "The door was closed and locked? Get out of there, Mitch. Now, while there's still time."

"Negative. I'm proceeding up."

The possibility that the malfunctioning door was a coincidence was a thousand to one, but you never knew when you were going to get lucky. All he needed was a few minutes alone with Zaman. He might be a fanatical ally of Aali Nassar, but at his core he was a rich piece of shit who had probably never spent a night on unmonogrammed sheets. It was unlikely that it would take more than a few slaps to give him diarrhea of the mouth.

Rapp arrived at the door leading to the top floor hallway and paused for a moment. "Exiting the stairwell."

Claudia acknowledged but didn't say anything further. He knew she was scared, but she was dealing with it. Another check in her plus column.

There was a single man coming down the hallway toward him. Middle Eastern, dark suit, athletic build. The bad signs just kept piling up.

He didn't seem to want to make eye contact, so Rapp went with it, reaching up to shake some water off his hat in a way that obscured his face further. There was a window at the end of the hall and Rapp followed the man's reflection in it. He disappeared around the corner without ever showing any interest.

The presidential suite was on the left and entry went smoothly with Claudia's key card. When the door was only half-open, Rapp spotted Zaman's body lashed to a chair. He considered chasing the man he'd just passed, but he was probably already in the elevator. There might still be time to catch him with a sprint down the stairs, but then what? A shootout in the lobby with no backup or political cover?

Rapp opened his mouth to tell Claudia to follow the man but then closed it again. If Nassar was behind this, there was no telling what kind of resources he had and how much he knew. She wasn't Scott. She could get hurt.

"Are you in?" came Claudia's voice over his earpiece.

Rapp stepped inside and closed the door behind him. "Zaman's dead."

"You're getting out, then, right? Tell me you're on your way back to the stairs."

"That's an affirmative."

"Don't lie to me, Mitch. I'm the only person you've got right now. I need to know where you are."

"Two minutes and then I'm out."

Zaman had been tied and killed with a single shot to the head. That was only the tip of the iceberg, though. Another bullet had shattered his kneecap and three of his fingers were lying on the floor. Had someone really been forced to work this hard to get information from a wealthy middle-aged real estate developer? The likely answer was no. And that meant serious trouble for him.

"Get in touch with the man you've got setting up surveillance on el-Hashem in Paris," Rapp said. "Tell him to watch his ass. If Nassar's willing to take out his best friend, he'll go after the others."

"I'm going to call him off, Mitch. He's a thief, not a shooter."

"Your asset. Do what you think is right."

A quick search of the suite turned up nothing and he was already exiting back into the hallway when Claudia told him his two minutes were up. He'd made it about halfway to the stairs when two security men appeared around the corner.

"Sir?" one said in English as they closed in. "May we have a word with you?"

"Pardon?" Rapp said in native French. The man he'd passed earlier had called security on him. Clever little bastard.

The guards stopped in his path and the one on the right repeated the request in French.

"Is there a problem?" Rapp said, smiling easily.

"Are you a guest of this hotel?"

"Yes. Why?"

"May we see your key?"

Rapp fished around in his pocket and held it out. He despised dealing with men like this. Killing was quick and easy, but incapacitating was complicated and time-consuming.

"What room are you—"

Rapp grabbed him by the front of the shirt and pulled him into a half-speed elbow strike. He crumpled to the floor as his partner looked on wide-eyed. Instead of attacking, he turned and tried to run. Rapp kicked his back foot and followed him down. A careful blow to the back of his neck had the desired effect and a moment later Rapp was running down the hall.

"Mitch," Claudia said over his earpiece, "are you all right?"

"Yeah. But I'm going out through the lobby. Security's onto me, and I'll be better off mixing with the crowd."

"Understood. I'm on my way to pick you up."

He dropped the coat and hat that he assumed security had a description of and hoped to hell that Nassar's people had done a thorough job of sabotaging the hotel's cameras.

He stepped into the elevator and pressed the button for the lobby. It stopped halfway down and a couple in their seventies got in. He asked them if they were familiar with any good restaurants in the area, starting a conversation that continued after the doors were open. Security would be looking for a lone man in a coat and hat, not a man in a gray sweater who was part of a group of three.

He thanked them for the advice when they exited into a covered driveway and walked to the curb as Claudia pulled up. The attendant opened the door and Rapp slipped him five euros before getting in the car. An average tip for a hotel of that quality—nothing he'd remember one way or another. Claudia gave him the expected kisses on both cheeks and then eased the car back onto the street.

CHAPTER 35

THE leafy street was empty of traffic this time of night, and Julien Moreau walked casually along it. Streetlights were widely spaced, and because the mansions that lined the avenue were set back behind walls, the environment was pleasantly shadowed. Normally that would have put him in danger of stepping in one of the piles of dog shit so common throughout the city, but the wealthy residents kept their avenues spotless. In truth, it probably wasn't that arduous a task. Arabs were about the only people who could afford to live in this neighborhood, and they didn't much care for dogs. A cultural quirk that made his job so much easier.

An ancient stone wall appeared to his right and he ran his hand along it, counting steps. It was well maintained but had been left rustic, with the jagged edges and receding mortar lines that thieves like him deeply appreciated. Cameras were also conspicuously absent except for over a gate more than fifty meters away. The obsession people had with looking at people arriving at their entrances never ceased to amaze him. If someone pulls up to your fucking gate and rings your buzzer, there's a good chance they're not coming to steal your daughters.

When Moreau counted his thirteenth stride, he turned and grabbed a protruding stone in the wall. The shoes he was wearing were favored by climbing guides—tight and sticky enough to scale cliffs but not so uncomfortable as to make it difficult to run. He moved quickly up handholds he'd memorized from a laser scan done the day before. In less than five seconds, he was at the top and looking for a way down.

The inside had been stuccoed in order to complement the modern house beyond, but it wasn't a problem. The landscaper had placed trees in ideal positions for anyone trying to gain access. Moreau slithered down one and crouched behind its trunk, taking in his surroundings.

The house was basically a big glass box—one of those homes that looked very prestigious in architectural drawings but that no one in their right mind would want to live in. The lights were on, providing a view right through it. The kitchen was empty, with a similarly uninhabited pool area glowing behind. Ahmed el-Hashem, Saudi Arabia's assistant ambassador to France, was sitting at a desk on the upper floor, writing in longhand. Apparently he could afford to live in this neighborhood but couldn't afford a laptop.

Or a decent security system, as it turned out.

According to Moreau's source—namely, the man who did the install—it was all off-the-shelf crap. Even better, the owner had insisted that it not be obtrusive, which wasn't easy in a fishbowl where everything was visible. So, basically, nothing that would come even close to challenging a man of Moreau's talents. In fact, it was unlikely he would have even taken a mind-numbing job like this one if it hadn't been for two irresistible factors. One, it had finally given him an excuse to use the 3-D laser scanner he'd stolen from the university. And two?

Claudia Gould.

What words were sufficient to describe the woman? Sublime? Brilliant? Stunning? Mysterious? He could go on all night and never even scratch the surface. Those eyes. That body. And, okay, the kid. But that's what boarding schools were for.

Moreau had done a fair amount of work for her in the past but figured he'd never hear from her again after her husband died. Then, out of nowhere, the phone rang and the voice so indelibly imprinted on his heart flowed into his ear. A new job, a new relationship, and new possibilities.

He had no idea what she'd seen in Louis Gould. Sure, he'd been good-looking. Then there were the rippling muscles and wealth. He'd also had that whole international super spy thing going on. Some chicks were into that, Moreau supposed. But if you took all those things away, he was just a violent dick. Maybe she was ready for a change? Perhaps something with a cultured, intellectual thief? A man who could enjoy art and food and wine? Someone who could show her the world through a lens not smeared with blood?

He let out a quiet breath. But before he started planning his future with her, he needed to get this job done. He didn't get to steal anything—his instructions were just to set up some surveillance. Video was simple—the stupid glass house again—but audio would be a bit more interesting. He'd have to get in close enough to do some hand drilling, and as easy as it was to see into the building, it would be almost equally easy to see out.

Moreau crept forward a few meters and then stopped again for another quick scan of his surroundings. The landscaping was spread out and tasteful. Unlike most of his countrymen, el-Hashem had resisted installing gilt statues of cherubs peeing into fountains.

Moreau avoided increasingly bright splashes of light as he closed in on the structure. El-Hashem was still writing away and one of his guards was in the living room—a fit-looking man of the type who wore sunglasses at night. Where was the other? Likely somewhere in the house, but making an assumption like that would be an amateurish mistake. Could he be patrolling the exterior? Had he seen Moreau go over the wall, and was he now creeping up from behind?

Unlikely, but still his absence added a little spice to the drudgery of this gig.

The Frenchman followed a deep shadow to a tree he'd found with a drone flyover. It was one of four surveillance angles he'd need, and the branches looked sturdy enough to support his sixty-five kilos. Six or seven meters would be high enough to make the camera invisible from the ground and to keep the solar panel in the light.

He began fishing a unit out of his backpack but then stopped when he saw the security man inside head toward the stairs. A changing of the guard? Would he finally discover the location of the other man? Confirmation that he was inside would allow Moreau to move much more quickly and remove all danger of being late for his dinner reservation.

The guard went up the steps, walking with a level of caution that seemed a bit odd. Maybe el-Hashem was one of those rich assholes who didn't like to see or hear his staff. Moreau himself had once worked in a similar environment. He'd left that job with his employer's Bentley and the contents of his safe.

The guard stopped in the doorway of the room occupied by el-Hashem, raised his gun, and fired a single round. It hit the Arab in the head and pitched him forward onto his desk.

Moreau froze. Had that really just happened? Was he having a flashback from the drugs he'd been so enamored with at university? Were flashbacks really even a thing?

The guard walked calmly over and yanked what was left of the dead man's head back. It was enough to break Moreau from his trance and he panicked. Scooping up his pack, he began sprinting toward the perimeter wall. Coming around the thick stump of an ancient tree, he suddenly found himself skidding face-first through the dirt. When he glanced back to see what had tripped him, he vomited into the dry leaves. The guard he'd been looking for was lying on his back, staring up at the sky with part of his head missing.

Moreau forced himself to his feet and stumbled to the tree he'd used to access the compound. He shot up it, pausing reluctantly on top of the wall to ensure that the street was still empty. A moment later he was walking with an awkward, hurried gait toward his vehicle. It was the longest six minutes and twelve seconds he'd ever spent, but finally he slid behind the wheel and pulled out.

His breath was coming too fast, making him light-headed. But not so much that he couldn't dial Claudia. She picked up on the first ring.

"Julien! Where—"

"They killed him!" he screamed. "You screwed me! You didn't say anything about anyone getting murdered."

Her voice carried its normal sensual calm. "Do you ever check your messages?"

He glanced at the phone's screen. Three from her.

"Fuck!" he said, unable to come up with anything more relevant.

"I need you to calm down, Julien. Tell me what happened."

"Are you deaf? They killed him!"

"Who killed whom?"

"One of the guards. He killed el-Hashem. I saw it. He did it right in front of me. In that fucking glass house. It was like watching a movie."

"I understand. But you—"

"The other guard's dead, too! Part of his head was gone. I tripped over him."

Moreau suddenly bolted straight up in his seat. "Oh my God. His blood. I think I have his blood on me!"

"Julien, stop talking and breathe, okay? I need you to go through with me exactly what happened."

"Have you not been listening? Don't ever call me again." He disconnected and pulled onto a more heavily traveled street. For some reason the cars moving around him brought back a little of his calm. He glanced at the phone in the passenger seat but resisted reaching for it. After another minute he caved. How could he stay mad at such a magnificent woman?

Not surprisingly, it didn't take her long to answer. "Are you all right, Julien? Are you hurt?"

"I'm fine."

"Where are you now?"

"In the car. Headed back to the city center."

"Okay. Good. Now tell me this. Were both men shot in the head?"

"Yes."

"Could you see the kind of gun?"

"What the hell do I know about guns? I've never shot one in my life!"

"Because you know about everything," came the soothing answer.

Flattery? Really? Did she think he was that easy? Shit. Of course she did. And she was right.

"I was pretty far away. It had a silencer for sure. If I had to guess, I'd say a Glock."

"Did you leave anything behind? Were the cameras installed?"

"No. Nothing."

"Good. I've tripled your fee. You'll find the money in the account we discussed. I'd suggest you get out of France for a while. And that you forget you ever heard of me or Ahmed el-Hashem."

CHAPTER 36

RAPP fished around in the tiny refrigerator, finally finding a beer at the back. His plan had been to ease up on the drinking until he managed to pull his life together. But since things seemed to be rocketing in the other direction, fuck it.

The door to the cockpit was closed, but he glanced in that direction anyway. The man inside was another one of Claudia's—a drug runner out of Colombia. Not Scott Coleman by a long shot, but a solid pilot with a set of torture scars that suggested he knew how to keep his mouth shut.

"Everyone's back in Juba, but there seem to be some problems," Claudia said as he sat down in a facing seat.

"What kind of problems?"

"The man you killed. Apparently, the rebel leader he works for wasn't happy. He has people watching the church. According to Kent, it would be suicide to go back. They've rented an empty safari hotel outside of town and are holing up there until we arrive."

"Fine."

She leaned forward in her seat with a concerned expression. "We need to talk about what happened in Brussels and Paris."

It wasn't a subject that was going to improve his mood, but there was no getting around it. Aali Nassar was making his play, and it was a good one. A decision had to be made about what to do. The president had asked him to find the highly placed Saudis allied with ISIS and kill them. Rapp intended to carry out that request, but the question now was how. Did he try to get clever and save himself, or did he just move forward with the hammer?

"Zaman was killed with a single shot from a nine-millimeter. To authorities, it will also look like he was first tortured for information. El-Hashem died the same way, and unless I miss my guess, he'll be found tied to a chair with the same kind of injuries. Sound like anyone you know?"

"Doesn't ring a bell."

"And there are witnesses, Mitch. The security men you put down in the hotel as well as the people you talked to in the elevator. I'm also guessing that the bodyguard who took out el-Hashem is giving the police your description and telling them about how he barely escaped with his life."

"Is that all?"

"No. There are still the cameras in Monaco as well as all the eyewitnesses who survived the attack." She leaned back. "*That's* all."

"It's hard to complain about Nassar doing my job for me. At this rate, he'll have his entire network wiped out by next week."

"He's framing you, Mitch! If someone showed me all this, even *I'd* think you were killing wealthy Saudis and shooting up nightclubs. We need to shift our focus to clearing you. We can easily argue that you discovered the threat to Terry's at the last second and were trying to stop the terrorists and save the prince. It's not airtight, but it will play. I can probably patch together some reasonably convincing evidence that you weren't in Paris at the time el-Hashem was killed. That just leaves Brussels. It's a harder problem, but if we can demonstrate a pattern of—"

"That's all fine and good, Claudia, but what about Nassar?"

"What about him?"

"He's partnering with ISIS. In all likelihood he's going to use their power in the region to help him take over when King Faisal dies. Then Mullah Halabi won't be flailing around with assault rifles and suicide vests—he'll be backed by Saudi Arabia's military and intelligence capability. He could conceivably use that to march straight across the Middle East."

"How is any of that your problem, Mitch? Tell Irene what you've discovered and let the Americans handle it."

"I think you're missing the fact that I *am* the Americans. I'm not your husband. I'm not a contract killer. My job is to stop millions of people from being murdered by a bunch of fundamentalist psychos."

"No, it isn't. You don't work for the CIA anymore. We've talked about this, Mitch. Everyone's going to walk away from you. All the people you've kept from harm, all the politicians you've made look good, all the operatives you've bled with. By this time next week I wouldn't be surprised if Scott's men are chasing us around the world."

"It's not just my job, Claudia. It's what I believe in. It's who I am."

"Well, stop believing in it and be someone else!" she said, her voice filling the tiny plane. "You've given enough of yourself to these people."

"Maybe it's time for you to move on."

She folded her arms across her chest and tried to stare him down. "I've been in worse situations."

"Really?"

"No. I was just trying to sound positive."

"I appreciate the effort."

"Mitch . . ." she started, choosing her words carefully. "I think this might be harder for you than you expect. I know the physical danger matters very little to you. But are you ready for your country to turn on you?"

"I don't suppose I have much of a choice."

"But the others do. Their motivations are different than yours. You asked them to help you capture a Saudi prince. Donatella would seduce him, he'd be drugged, and they'd be paid. Now you're about to ask them to go after the Saudi intelligence chief while being opposed by America and all its resources. I know people like this, Mitch. They're not going to hold together much longer."

"Then we'll have to move fast."

"Fast . . ." she repeated under her breath. "Would you at least do one thing for me? Open a channel to Irene? Tell her what you've found and ask her what her plans are?"

He shook his head. "I'm not going to get her involved in killing the intelligence director of an ally, Claudia. If it ever came out that she even knew about it, she'd end up in jail and our partnerships all across the Middle East would collapse. If she wants to talk, she has my number."

CHAPTER 37

ALI Nassar stood next to King Faisal on the tarmac, waiting for a set of stairs to be pushed up to his private Airbus A380.

The plane had been in a holding pattern for over two hours to allow the sun to set. The aging monarch could no longer tolerate the afternoon heat. It was an ironic weakness for a man who ruled a desert kingdom and yet another indication that the order of things would soon be changing.

A group of formally dressed men appeared in the doorway, carrying a coffin draped in a Saudi flag. They descended with a level of care and solemnity that bordered on the comic. Beyond having been born to the king's favorite sister, Prince Talal bin Musaid had lived his life as a spoiled, useless child.

It was odd that a man whose life had been so inconsequential could be so dangerous in death. The actions against Zaman and el-Hashem had been forced by bin Musaid, as was the continued dismantling of the network Nassar had so carefully built. The Saudi intelligence apparatus was in turmoil as the royals shrank in horror at one of their own being targeted by the radical forces they themselves had created. The vulnerability the nobles suddenly felt had put a strain on his relationship with the king, instantly reversing the gains he'd made by convincing ISIS to attenuate its public criticism of him.

Strife and chaos always traveled hand in hand with opportunity, though. It was just a question of whether one was strong and clever enough to take advantage.

Faisal began to shuffle forward and Nassar followed at a respectful distance. The pallbearers stopped and allowed the king to run a hand over the flag. His face was uncharacteristically hard to read. Was he feeling grief for a self-indulgent boy who had betrayed him? Anger at the fact that the royalty, and not just its subjects, were now at risk? Or was this just a reminder of the mortality that he felt more keenly with every passing day?

Faisal finally stepped back, allowing the men to continue to the hearse as he returned to his limousine.

"Who were these murderers?" the king said as Nassar slid in next to him.

"Former Iraqi soldiers who joined ISIS."

"I want them destroyed. I want ISIS destroyed. No more middle ground. No more cowering behind the Americans. I want their heads and the heads of anyone who has even hinted at supporting them."

"Your Majesty—"

"What, Aali? Are you going to say that this is a delicate matter? That we have to proceed with caution? That I have to hide behind the walls of my palace while these cowards plot how to put a knife in my back?"

"It's not *just* a delicate matter, Highness. It's a complicated one."

"Complicated how?"

"We now have sharpened video composites from MI6 and, based on them, we're reasonably certain that Mitch Rapp was the man who carried bin Musaid out of the nightclub."

"Mitch Rapp?" the king said, twisting toward him. "How certain?"

"Seventy-five percent."

Faisal faced forward again and nodded knowingly. "I wonder, Aali. You seem to have a personal animosity for Mr. Rapp that I don't share. He risked his life to save my kingdom from a nuclear holocaust. Without him, I doubt we would have a country to discuss."

The implication was clear—that Nassar had provided no service in his lifetime that could rival those of this vile American. The king was dazzled by the man, rapt with tales of his exploits and seduced by the illusion of being under his protection. It would be a difficult task to break the old fool of his obsession with Rapp, but not an impossible one.

"Your Highness, I think you have to consider the fact that Rapp's appearance in that nightclub just as it was attacked is coincidental to the point of absurdity."

"Perhaps the CIA became aware of the threat and he was there to thwart it. I've watched the video, too, Aali. And it's quite apparent that his primary objective was to save the prince."

The monarch's tone was defensive enough that Nassar had to suppress a smile. The man was aware that his argument was ludicrous. He just needed to be forced to admit it.

"Our analysts do not believe this to be the case, Highness. First, as we both know, Mr. Rapp has left the employ of the CIA, and as far as we can tell has cut off all contact with his former colleagues. Second, we know that he suspected the prince of financing terrorists. The idea that a man like Rapp would try to protect the prince stretches credibility to the breaking point."

"And what else do your clever analysts say?" Faisal asked coldly.

"We think it's feasible—perhaps even likely—that Rapp was behind this attack."

The king let out a laugh strangled by his deteriorating lungs. "That's insane, Aali. It's everything he's fought against his entire life."

"True, but consider the following, Your Highness. We know that as a young man he was violently opposed to the pact our governments made to bury the evidence of Saudi involvement in 9/11. And, at a minimum, he would have seen Prince bin Musaid's activities as a betrayal of that pact. More likely, he would have seen it as an indication of a larger conspiracy."

"Your point, Aali?"

"Why would Mitch Rapp, one of the most powerful and effective cogs in the American intelligence machine, suddenly quit? We suspect that it's because he wanted to investigate bin Musaid's actions further and was blocked by the president, who would be concerned by the potential fallout from such an investigation."

"I'm not convinced, Aali."

"Then let me provide you with additional evidence."

He retrieved a tablet from his briefcase and Faisal looked down at the photo on it with red-rimmed eyes. "Ahmed."

"Yes, sir. Details of Assistant Ambassador el-Hashem's

murder are now coming in from French authorities. As you can see, he was tied to a chair, tortured, and then shot in the head with a single nine-millimeter bullet." Nassar swiped to the next photo. "And this, though unrecognizable because of the blood and damage, is Mahja Zaman, a businessman I believe you're acquainted with."

Faisal looked up at him. "One of your closest friends. Isn't that true, Aali?"

"Yes, Highness. We've known each other since we were children."

"What happened?"

"Precisely the same thing. He was bound, tortured, and killed with a bullet to the head."

"And you suspect Mitch Rapp."

"This goes far beyond simple suspicion, Your Highness. El-Hashem's guard barely escaped with his life, and his description of the man who attacked the ambassador matches Rapp. Further, a man leaving Zaman's hotel room was confronted by two security guards. He subdued them both in a matter of seconds. They, as well as a French couple who actually spoke with the man, describe someone very similar in appearance to Rapp."

"But why Zaman and el-Hashem? Do we have any reason to believe that they were involved in aiding ISIS?"

"No, but we're looking deeper. Be mindful of the fact that they wouldn't necessarily have to be involved for Rapp to come for them. He's no longer bound by American laws or CIA regulations. All he would need is some vague suspicion that they had information—even unwittingly—that could help him."

Despite the cool interior of the limousine, sweat began to glisten on Faisal's face. It wasn't surprising. He had been the driving force behind the deal struck with the Americans after 9/11. And, more important, he was responsible for making sure that the Saudi end of the agreement was honored. At that moment he would be wondering if he might be Rapp's next target.

"Your Highness," Nassar said, softening his tone, "this entire matter is easily resolved. We simply need to speak with the American authorities and request a meeting with Mr. Rapp. If he's not responsible for any of this, it should be a trivial matter for him to prove it."

Faisal didn't react for a long time, but finally he spoke. "You're right, Aali. With the evidence we have, it is entirely reasonable that we would want to speak with Mitch. I imagine that Irene Kennedy and the president feel the same. All he has to do is provide evidence of his whereabouts during these attacks. As you say, a simple matter."

"Precisely, Highness. And if the Americans are unable to produce Mr. Rapp, I think it's also reasonable that we solicit their help in finding him. Wouldn't you agree? I'm sure they're as anxious to clear this up as we are."

CHAPTER 38

"TURN left up here," Rapp said, glancing at the GPS on the dashboard.

His Glock was resting in his lap, but so far there was no sign of the rebels that Black had warned them about.

"There *is* no left turn. Just a bunch of stalls," Claudia said, weaving through the pedestrians clogging the dirt street.

Instead of going directly to the abandoned safari hotel his people had retreated to, they were taking a circuitous route to a building behind Black's repurposed church. The fact that the instructions he'd provided didn't match the GPS map wasn't all that surprising—Google's cartographers had good reason to avoid Juba. It did, however, add to the suspicion lodged in the back of Rapp's mind.

Could Black be leading him into a trap? Was it possible that Nassar had somehow managed to locate the young sniper and make him an offer he couldn't refuse? Or, even more likely, had Black initiated contact with the authorities himself? He wasn't the sharpest tool in the shed, but he was sure as hell sharp enough to know that Rapp's scalp was about to become a very hot commodity on the world market.

"Mitch? What do you want me to do?"

They could just find their own path, but that had its own risks. Rapp's knowledge of the town was limited and its layout was constantly evolving. Impromptu markets sprang up and disappeared, buildings collapsed and were replaced with temporary structures. Roads were rerouted and commandeered. He assumed that the Agency had updated maps, but he didn't have access to them anymore.

"Just take the next left you come to."

He checked again for signal on his cell and again got nothing.

"Do you think Kent's betrayed us?"

"Maybe, but I'm betting against it. It's possible that he could get lucky and take out Donatella, but Grisha? More likely it's just Africa."

"Likely, but not certain," she said, looking a bit worried.

"This job just keeps getting worse, doesn't it? I—"

"I know. You warned me."

She swung the car onto a narrow path between buildings and the GPS recalibrated. They were back on the right track.

After about a hundred yards a man ran out of a doorway to their right and jogged toward the car. The white face was immediately recognizable, and Rapp tightened his grip on his Glock as Kent Black yanked open the back door.

"Where have you two been?" he said, ducking inside. "I was sweating my ass off out there."

"Your directions took a little artistic license," Claudia said.

"You can't find shit in this town from one day to another. Just keep going. Next right. There's an old gate. We'll be going through it and parking on the other side."

The barrier opened as they approached, and Rapp spotted Grisha Azarov behind it. By the time they'd parked, the Russian had the gate locked down again.

"We've got a decent view of the church from the top floor," Black said, getting out and leading them into a building that looked to be on the verge of buckling. Many of the walls had crumbled and about half of the third floor was now lying on the second. Despite that, a number of people had taken up residence—mostly families, some cooking over fires, others trying to stay out of the sun, but all paying a lot of attention to the four white people in their midst.

"What's the story with the people living here?" Rapp asked, slowing to let Azarov pass. He still didn't like having the man behind him.

"They've got no love for Abdo, if that's what you mean," Black said. "He's the reason most of them are homeless. And we're paying them ten times more to keep quiet than that scumbag would ever pay them to talk. We're good."

They came out on the top floor and found Donatella standing in the shade on the north end.

"Mitch!" she said, throwing her arms around him. "I was starting to worry."

Claudia's expression hardened. She was wearing dusty cargo shorts and a sweat-soaked T-shirt, while Donatella looked like she'd just come from the queen's garden party.

"Show me the church," Rapp said, leaving the two women to stare at each other.

Black led, dropping to his stomach a few yards from the edge of the floor and slithering toward a missing section of wall. There was a pair of Zeiss binoculars hanging on a column, and Rapp used them to scan the area around their former headquarters.

Abdo's men weren't wearing their customary dirty fatigues, having changed into civilian clothes. Still, they stood out. While everyone else in town seemed to have something to do or somewhere to go, they were just standing around, scanning the passing faces.

"How many in total?" Rapp said.

"We've made five. Three on the ground and two in buildings east and west. Probably at least one inside, but there's no way to know. Twelve-hour shifts, ending around midnight and noon. I told you, Mitch. You shouldn't have killed NaNomi. These guys don't mess around, and they know how to hold a grudge."

"Is there anything inside the building I need to worry about?"

"What do you mean?"

"I mean did you leave anything in there about us?"

"Nothing about you. Just my whole life. That's all."

They slid back to where the others were waiting.

"It looks like we're going to have to leave this horrible place," Donatella observed. "May I suggest Sardinia? Easy to get lost in, good food, and the weather's lovely this time of the year."

"We're staying here," Rapp responded.

"But, Mitch, we—"

"Those security videos from Monaco are making their rounds to the world's intelligence agencies, and

I'm guessing I've already been IDed," he said, cutting her off. Once she got to complaining, it was almost impossible to get her to stop. "Claudia and Kent aren't on them, so they're probably okay. Grisha, are you confident you talked your way out of this?"

"For now," the Russian responded. "But as a consulting company executive, it would be better if I'm not filmed in a similar performance anytime soon."

Rapp nodded. "That leaves you, Donatella."

"Me?"

"You think the Mossad isn't going to recognize you?"

"Of course they will. I've hardly aged a day. But the people I worked for are dead or retired. There would be no profit in moving against me."

"And if the video goes public?"

"Then some people from my past will know I'm alive. Not ideal, but manageable with your help."

Rapp turned to Claudia. "We'll stay at the safari hotel and see how much shit hits the fan over the next few days. But I need you to work out an alternate location for us."

"I'll have it taken care of by tomorrow night."

Rapp folded his arms across his chest and scanned the faces staring back at him. Claudia was right. He was moving into uncharted territory with a group of misfits whose motivations were all over the place. It was a problem that needed to be acknowledged before they continued.

"This job was about getting Talal bin Musaid and transporting him to a location where I could question him. We've now moved well outside of those operational parameters. It appears that the Saudi intelligence chief, Aali Nassar, is the one calling the shots.

Now he's killing the people close to him and doing a pretty good job of framing me for it. I don't have to tell you that politicians don't like these kinds of scenarios. The amount of money, influence, and potential embarrassment we're talking about is going to make them scramble for cover."

"What does that mean, exactly?" Black said.

Donatella answered. "It means that all of the people who used to be Mitch's friends are now his enemies. We're about to have the CIA, the U.S. military, MI6, Saudi intelligence, and the Mossad come down on us like a ton of bricks."

"That's pretty accurate," Rapp said. "At the scale we're talking about now, I become expendable."

"And if you're expendable," Donatella continued, "then we're just bugs to be stepped on without second thought."

Rapp nodded. "Look, it wasn't my intention to sign you on for anything like this, and if you want to walk away, I'll understand. You'll be paid whatever we agreed on and I'll never give up your names."

"When you say 'walk away,'" Azarov said, "walk away from what? What do you plan to do?"

"Deal with Nassar. He's been busy cleaning up after himself, but now he's going to turn his attention to me."

"So you want to kill him," Azarov said.

"I definitely want to kill him. But it's going to be complicated."

"Complicated how?" Black said. "Why don't I just fly to Saudi Arabia and put a bullet in him from half a mile away?"

"I don't think he's going to make it that easy," Rapp said.

"And it would blow back against Mitch," Claudia added. "So far, he actually *is* innocent. Executing the Saudi intelligence chief would very much alter the chessboard."

"Then what?" Azarov said.

"I'm still working on that."

"How confidence inspiring," Donatella said.

The Russian disagreed. "I've been involved in a number of these kinds of operations, and acting rashly is a recipe for disaster. Mitch is right to consider every possibility before making a move. Aali Nassar isn't a Taliban enforcer or suicide bomber. He's a brilliant man with virtually unlimited resources."

"So who's in and who's out?" Rapp said.

Donatella was the first to speak. "After everything we've been through, I'd never abandon you."

The implication was clear—that he'd abandoned her. And maybe it was true. But that was a reflection for another time.

"Hell, I live for this shit," Black said with his customary bravado. "I'm in for whatever you figure out."

Azarov remained silent for a few seconds before speaking. "I like to finish what I start. And, frankly, I'm not sure that Nassar won't have more questions for me about what happened in Monaco. I'd prefer to see him neutralized."

Rapp looked over at Claudia.

"You know my answer."

CHAPTER 39

THE WHITE HOUSE
WASHINGTON, D.C.
U.S.A.

WANT to be perfectly clear, Irene. You believe that was Mitch in the Monaco video."

President Joshua Alexander gazed at her over the *Resolute* Desk. His expression was serious, perhaps even grave, but something in it hinted at fear. As it should.

Irene Kennedy had always liked and respected the man. He was pragmatic, understood the threats facing the country, and listened to advice. When necessary, he was also willing to look the other way. That said, it was her experience that people could change very quickly when their backs were against the wall. It was a transformation that tended to occur even faster in politicians.

"My people put the likelihood at ninety-five percent."

She herself put it at a hundred, but there was no reason to say that. Alexander was unaware that she knew about his early morning meeting with Mitch Rapp. And while Rapp had said nothing about what had been discussed, he also had done nothing to prevent her from coming to the obvious conclusion.

"What was he doing there, Irene? I was told he left the CIA. Is that not the case? Is he working for you?"

She found this charade a bit insulting and considered telling the president that she was perfectly aware that it was he who had set Rapp on this path. As satisfying as that would be, though, it would also be extraordinarily unwise. As usual, she had no choice but to swallow her anger and play the games that politics required.

"Mitch gave me his resignation and I have not been in contact with him since. To the best of my knowledge, no one at the Agency has."

"So you don't know where he is?"

"I have no idea," she responded honestly.

"Well, that piece of shit Aali Nassar is going to be here in less than two minutes, and he's not going to be happy with that answer."

"Mitch Rapp is no longer my concern nor the concern of the Central Intelligence Agency. He's a private citizen who happened to be in a European establishment when it was attacked by terrorists. I saw nothing in that video to suggest that Mitch—if that's indeed who it was—did anything criminal. If Director Nassar wants to talk to him, then he's free to find him and request a meeting."

"You're not going to seriously sit there and tell me it was just a coincidence that Mitch was there when those terrorists attacked," Alexander said.

She just took a sip of her tea.

The enhanced video from Monaco had been three of the most interesting minutes of film she'd ever watched. Kennedy was extremely surprised by the presence of Grisha Azarov, whom everyone had dismissed as the luckiest extraction consultant in history. Seeing him work was quite extraordinary and went a long way to explaining how he had managed to injure Scott Coleman so badly.

Even more shocking had been the presence of Donatella Rahn. She still hadn't been identified and even the CIA's analysts were speculating that she was nothing more than an Eastern European prostitute.

And that left the unknown sniper who had been ensconced on the top floor of an apartment to the west. All they had of him was poor security camera footage depicting a man of average height and build wearing a bulky coat, a hat, and large eyeglasses opaque to surveillance equipment. She'd quietly looked into a number of men whom she thought Rapp might have recruited but, to her old friend's credit, had come up empty. Was it possible that he'd solicited the help of Kent Black? She knew that the former Ranger was selling arms in Africa, but there had never been any reason to keep tabs on him.

"You seem even more guarded than usual, Irene. Is there something you're not telling me?"

"Is there something *you're* not telling *me*, Mr. President?"

She regretted the words the moment they came out of her mouth. The unwavering control that had served her so well in her career was beginning to fail. One of the most courageous, patriotic, and effective American operatives ever born had been put in a position that was likely fatal, and there was very little she could do to change that.

Alexander refused to acknowledge it, but there was only one course this meeting could take. Mitch Rapp, the man who was like a brother to her and who had sacrificed everything for his country, was going to be thrown to the wolves.

"What are you trying to say, Irene?"

She was saved from having to answer by the president's assistant poking her head in. "Sir? Director Nassar has arrived."

Alexander stood behind his desk. "Show him in."

Nassar looked a bit less smug and significantly more tired than the last time they'd met. He shook hands with Alexander but decided to dispense with that pleasantry when turning to face Kennedy. "King Faisal wants to know what your involvement with Mitch Rapp is and what is being done about him."

"Could you be more specific, Director?"

"You know exactly what I'm talking about. His involvement with the terrorist attack in Monaco and the kidnapping—perhaps even murder—of Prince Talal bin Musaid."

She allowed an intentionally unconvincing expression of shock to cross her face. "You're suggesting the man in that nightclub was Mitch Rapp?"

"There's videotape!"

"Really? And is that videotape conclusive?" she said, quoting Nassar's own words when he'd been faced with the existence of photographic evidence that bin Musaid was financing terrorists in Morocco.

"We believe it is," Nassar said, a brief flash in his eyes registering the insult. "We—"

"Director, why don't we sit for a moment?" the president interrupted.

He led them to a seating area and they all settled in. Alexander should have been enjoying turning the tables on the Saudi. Instead he was calculating every possible way Rapp's actions could blow back on him. It wasn't lost on Kennedy that it would be far better for him if the former CIA agent disappeared forever. As Stan Hurley had been fond of saying, dead men tell no tales.

"I demand that we dispense with these games immediately," Nassar said. "Everyone in this room knows that the man in that video is Rapp."

"I know no such thing," Kennedy retorted. "And even if it is, the man in that video is killing the terrorists and appears to be trying to *save* the prince."

"Save him? He threw His Highness into the street, where he was gunned down like an animal!"

"Gunned down by the men in the pursuing car. Perhaps the prince was already dead. I think it's fair to say that it would be quite disturbing to have a dead body in one's passenger seat."

"Disturbing? Don't be absurd! A man like the one in that video wouldn't be bothered by the presence of a dead body in his car."

She just shrugged.

Nassar pulled two photos from the portfolio he was carrying and handed them to her.

"Since you're not satisfied by the quality of the pictures captured from that video, Director Kennedy, perhaps you'll find these more convincing."

Each depicted a bloody corpse secured to a chair. She tapped the top one. "Ahmed el-Hashem."

"We were very sorry to hear about your assistant ambassador's death," the President interjected.

"I'm sure you were," Nassar remarked in an openly disrespectful tone. "He was tortured—likely for information—and then executed with a single shot to the head from what my people are saying was probably a Glock. The second man, Mahja Zaman, suffered the same fate."

"Mahja Zaman?" Kennedy said. "Who is he?"

"A Saudi businessman."

She pulled out her phone and Googled the name as he continued. It was just for show, though. She was extremely familiar with Mr. Zaman.

"He was killed at a Brussels hotel, as was one of the hotel's security people. Further, the murderer—who fits Mitch Rapp's description—incapacitated two more security guards on his way out of the building before being driven away by a Caucasian woman."

"Do you have photographic evidence?" Kennedy asked.

"Rapp disabled the cameras when he killed the security guard."

"So, a six-foot, bearded, dark-complected male in his forties. That narrows it down to about a quarter of a billion people."

"Don't be a fool! You know as well as I do that this is Mitch Rapp's doing! He believed that Prince bin Musaid was involved with ISIS, and he's interrogating and murdering men he perceives to be connected."

"And why would he perceive these men to be connected?"

He didn't reply, and Kennedy continued to scroll through her phone. "This is interesting. It says that Zaman is about your age and went to Oxford. Did you know him?"

"We were roommates."

"Really," she said, looking up and affecting an expression of sympathy. "Then I'm very sorry for the loss of your friend."

"This is all irrelevant," the Saudi said, trying to regain control of the conversation. "Whether this is or is not the work of Mitch Rapp is a matter that's easily resolved. All we need to do is speak with him."

"Then I'd encourage you to do that," Kennedy said.

"Where would I find him?"

"I'm not in the habit of keeping track of my former employees."

Nassar finally turned his attention to the president, who, for obvious reasons, was content to let his CIA chief take the lead. "Sir. You know as well as I do that Mitch Rapp is involved in this. The man was always unstable and violent, and now he's gone rogue. King Faisal demands that he be found before he can kill any more of our citizens. If we discover that he wasn't involved, of course we'll provide both you and him a formal apology. Until then, though, I think we can make the assumption that he'll keep killing until he's stopped. Because of the king's deep respect for you and his acknowledgment of Mr. Rapp's past contributions to our security, we're willing to keep this quiet. If you refuse to help, however, we'll be forced to make this information public and seek the help of the world's law enforcement agencies."

Even Alexander couldn't hide his increased apprehension at the word "public." He turned to Kennedy.

"Irene, can you get in touch with him? Ask him to come in for an interview?"

"Probably not," she said, vaguely.

Nassar's jaw clenched. "Mr. President, I am formally asking for your government's help in finding Mr. Rapp. If he's innocent, he'll have an opportunity to clear his name. If he's not, his capture will prevent any further bloodshed."

Checkmate, Kennedy knew. Refusing the perfectly reasonable request would be a political disaster and would force Alexander to manufacture a rationale for that refusal that would be too far-fetched to play on the world stage. It's what she had feared since the day the president sent Rapp on this fool's errand.

"What is it you need?" Alexander said.

"For you to provide my task force with a man who can assist and who can act as a liaison between my people and yours."

Alexander looked at Kennedy. "Irene? Could you provide someone?"

"Of course. Perhaps—"

"With all due respect, sir, I already have someone in mind."

"Who?"

"Special agent Joel Wilson of the FBI."

Kennedy's heart sank at the name. Wilson was the former acting deputy director of counterintelligence, a twisted little man who hated Rapp with the same intensity as many of his terrorist enemies. Worse, he was an extremely competent and obsessive investigator. Nassar had once again proved his cunning. Wilson would abandon all common sense, all perspective, and all national loyalty for an opportunity to exact revenge on Rapp.

"I don't know him," the president said, standing. "But if that's who you want, fine."

Nassar stood as well, shaking the man's hand and giving a curt nod to Kennedy before heading for the door. When it closed behind him, Alexander turned to her. "Joel Wilson? Who the fuck is that?"

"You remember him, sir. He worked with Senator Ferris against us when—"

"That little prick? The idiot who the Pakistanis used to try to take out the CIA's clandestine services?"

"Yes, sir."

"I still can't understand why you didn't put that bastard in jail and throw away the key."

"It was less complicated not to. We didn't want to give the FBI a black eye, and tensions with Pakistan were already bad enough. We demoted him and agreed to let him keep his pension. To the best of my knowledge, he's working at one of the FBI's resident agencies. Montana, maybe? Or it could be Alaska."

Alexander dropped back into the couch. "What do you know about all this, Irene? I'm not buying that you came up with Zaman and Nassar going to school together from your phone."

"No, sir, I didn't."

"Give me your best guess on this, Irene. What's Mitch's involvement?"

She smiled easily, hiding her anger at Alexander for having the audacity to so calmly ask her that question. "It seems self-evident that Mitch was at that nightclub, watching bin Musaid. Based on our analysis of the video, what happened there wasn't a random terrorist attack. They were there to get bin Musaid. Rapp saw it happening during his surveillance and intervened."

"So what about el-Hashem and Zaman? Is it possible that bin Musaid fingered them when he was in the car with Mitch and that Mitch decided to deal with them on his own? We both know how opposed he was to the arrangement that was made after 9/11."

"It's possible but unlikely. Leaving aside el-Hashem for the moment, Zaman's death in Brussels implies that Mitch murdered a security guard. There's nothing in his history to suggest he'd do something like that."

"But then he's never gone rogue before, either."

She let that go, but her anger notched higher.

"If you don't think it's too immoral for Mitch, sir, then I'd argue that it's simply too sloppy. Once that guard was killed, the clock would be ticking on his body being discovered. There would be no time to carry out an effective interrogation."

"So what, then?"

"A much more likely scenario is that whoever was behind Prince bin Musaid's actions in Morocco is getting rid of everyone who knows his identity and framing Mitch for it."

"Are you sure you're not letting your friendship with him cloud your judgment?"

"Let me ask you something, sir. How many times have I told you I was certain of something?"

"Never. You're the master of the hedge."

"Well, I'm certain Mitch is not responsible for the death of that hotel security guard. And if *he* didn't do it, someone else did."

"Okay. Who?"

"If I had to guess? Aali Nassar."

"Is that a joke?"

"Not at all. Nassar is an ambitious man. He'll want to be on the winning side when Faisal dies, and he might see ISIS as a critical backer. Frankly, he might be right."

"Can you contact Mitch in a way that no one can track?"

"I don't know if Mitch would take my call, and there's no such thing as completely secure communications—particularly if Nassar knows more than he's telling us."

"Then don't. You can't be seen as having any involvement in this." He sank a little deeper into the cushions and let out a long breath. "I can't believe that Mitch would do something like this without authorization, Irene."

She stared directly at him when she answered. "Neither can I."

For the first time in their relationship, the most powerful man in the world wouldn't meet her eye.

CHAPTER 40

ALI Nassar stayed in the car, looking past his driver at the endless horizon. He had sent his security detail back to Saudi Arabia and replaced them with a team of Secret Service men provided by the president. All were too young to have much experience, but also too young to have a relationship with Mitch Rapp. The fact that the CIA man had appeared at Zaman's hotel virtually guaranteed that he was aware of Nassar's role in the financing of ISIS. And if that was true, he would be coming.

Nassar was now engaged in mortal combat with a man who had never lost such a confrontation. It had been proved over and over again that brute force would fail against Rapp. The only hope was to outmaneuver him, and the Secret Service men were an effort to do just that. Rapp would be reluctant to use deadly force against the American security detail, while they would have no such misgivings where he was concerned. It was far from being an assurance, but it was the most logical course of action while he was on U.S. soil.

The Secret Service agents had spread out on the

street and were scanning the light traffic with practiced eyes. Finally, two of them disappeared into a coffee shop to the north.

Nassar had wasted no time getting to Bismarck, going directly to his plane from his meeting at the Oval Office. Despite this, it was certain that Irene Kennedy knew of his whereabouts. Was that duplicitous bitch involved? Had she quietly sent Rapp Nassar's flight plan? Was the CIA assassin out there, clean-shaven and blending in with the slack-jawed farmers?

Nassar's phone rang, and he looked at the secure number, initially moving to dismiss it but then thinking better. He needed a distraction and would have to speak to the man soon anyway. Nassar slid down in his seat a few more inches and picked up.

"Hello, Qadir."

"Zaman and el-Hashem are dead and you haven't been returning my calls!" came the panicked response. "Rumors are that Mitch Rapp was involved. Is there any truth to this?"

"I'm afraid there is."

"What action are you taking?" he screeched. "I demand that—"

"Qadir! Be calm!"

"Calm? How can you even say this to me? I'm told that you're in America with heavy security. I'm at my home with my wife and children. He could walk in here at any moment and—"

"You think I'm safer in America?" Nassar cut in angrily. "In his home country? Quit acting like an old woman. Are you afraid to meet God after having done His work? Is there some reason for you to fear His judgment?"

The man didn't respond and Nassar softened his tone. He needed Qadir to hold together for just a bit longer.

"I already have a security team watching you, your house, and your family. But because this situation is escalating, it's going to be necessary to move you. A safe house is being set up for you near al-Ghat. You'll be collected tonight and moved there until I can deal with the Rapp situation."

"'Deal with the Rapp situation'? How many people have said that in the past, Aali? Just how do you intend to 'deal with the Rapp situation'?"

Qadir Sultan was the last man who knew of Nassar's direct involvement with ISIS and, as such, was currently the second greatest threat to him. While it was true that two Saudi intelligence officers would retrieve him that night, neither they nor Sultan would ever arrive at the safe house. Instead, their bodies would be discovered by the side of the road, each with a single bullet wound to the head. "I said I'm dealing with it, Qadir. How is not your concern."

One of the Secret Service men exited the coffee shop and signaled that it was secure, prompting Nassar to disconnect the call. He got out of the car, fighting the urge to crouch as he walked. The sense of relief he felt when he stepped off the exposed street and into the building was palpable.

The tiny restaurant was only about half full and Joel Wilson was eating a sandwich near its center. Nassar approached and leaned down in order to speak to him at a level that would be inaudible to the other patrons.

"Special Agent Wilson? I wonder if I might have a word with you."

He looked up from the tablet he was reading and spoke with a full mouth. "I'm having lunch. What do you want?"

"I'm Aali Nassar."

"Is that supposed to mean something to me?"

"I don't guess it would. I'm the chief of Saudi Arabia's General Intelligence Directorate."

That captured the man's attention, but he remained understandably skeptical. "Just out touring the Dakotas, are you?"

"I assure you that I am who I say I am, Joel. May I call you Joel?"

"Whatever works for you."

"Could we move to a booth and speak for a moment?"

"What's wrong with right here?"

Nassar leaned in a little closer. "I'd like our conversation to be private, and because I'd feel more comfortable with my back to the wall."

"Why?"

"Because Mitch Rapp is trying to assassinate me."

Skepticism was replaced by fear at the mention of the CIA man's name.

"I don't know who that is."

"Please," Nassar said, pointing toward the back.

It was the first test. Wilson was not a stupid man, and after everything he'd been through, he had every reason to decline the invitation. But would he be able to? He had become obsessed with Rapp during an investigation into the accusation that the CIA man had been misappropriating government funds. It had turned into a self-righteous crusade that had collapsed on him when it became clear that those accusations had been disinformation from Pakistan's ISI.

Men like Wilson, though, could never admit they were wrong. He believed with religious certainty that he had been undermined by corrupt forces inside the U.S. government. That he had been made a scapegoat in an effort to save the Washington elite from embarrassment. The question was whether that righteous indignation had been beaten out of him or whether every demotion, insult, and threat had instead fanned its flames.

Wilson passed the test when he picked up his things and walked to the back of the building. Nassar took a position to the right of him and nodded toward the man's tablet. "I assume that's connected to the Internet. May I first suggest you confirm my identity?"

He was impressed by the man's thoroughness. Wilson pulled up multiple websites containing photos of Nassar, then repeated the search using a British proxy server. Undoubtedly he was concerned that this was a sting operation designed to see if he'd left his Mitch Rapp obsession behind him.

"Okay. You're who you say you are," he said finally.

In response, Nassar pulled out a photograph of Rapp and slid it across the table. "Do you recognize this man?"

"Not a very good photo."

"It was stitched together from a number of different stills to create as clear an image as possible. We believe it to be Rapp."

"If you say so."

"Obviously, all this is highly confidential, but he took Prince Talal bin Musaid out of the Monaco nightclub that was just attacked and may have murdered him. We also believe that he's responsible for the deaths of at least two more Saudi citizens."

Wilson's face went blank again, and he slid the photo back to Nassar. "Then I'm guessing Irene Kennedy wanted them dead. You should be talking to her."

"Is it possible that you're not aware of Mr. Rapp's resignation from the CIA?"

"Bullshit."

"It's hardly a secret. Perhaps information like that takes time to filter to this part of the country?"

The man took the photo back and stared down at it for a long time. "What's this have to do with me?"

"I'm forming a task force to track him down before he can do any more damage. I need a man with outstanding investigative abilities, courage, and unimpeachable integrity. You came to mind."

"No."

"No?"

"I've been down this road before. It's why I'm sitting in a North Dakota coffee shop. Mitch Rapp has a lot of enemies, but he's also got a lot of heavy political cover. I think I'll just stay here and keep my pension, if you don't mind."

Nassar took the photo back and put it in the breast pocket of his jacket. "I think your understanding of Mr. Rapp's position is a bit dated, Joel. He's left the CIA and begun murdering civilians, one of whom was King Faisal's nephew. Your government has authorized you to join my task force as my second-in-command."

Wilson actually laughed at that. "You want me to believe that you got Director Miller to agree to that?"

"What Director Miller wants or doesn't want is irrelevant. I'm working directly with President Alexander."

"The president?" Wilson said, his demeanor suddenly changing. It was an easily predicted transformation. Wilson would find the idea of going over the head of the man who had banished him irresistible.

"I assume you'll want to confirm that," Nassar said. "Just call the White House and tell them who you are. They'll put you through."

"To who?"

"To the president, of course."

Wilson chewed his lower lip, his eyes turning distant. It was almost possible to see the grandiose scenarios playing out behind them. Him being honored at the White House. Him refusing to inform Director Miller of the Rapp investigation's progress. And, finally, him putting Mitch Rapp behind bars while the people who had halted his prior investigation were accused of a cover-up. At long last, the nation would recognize Joel Wilson for the hero he was.

"What about Kennedy?"

"It's been her inability to control Rapp over the years that created this disaster. She has no say in this matter whatsoever."

"Yeah? Well, in my experience she has a way of deciding herself what she does and doesn't have a say in."

Nassar nodded. "You're right to be afraid of her, Joel. You live in a lovely city, have a safe job, and you'll soon be eligible for retirement. I can't be blamed for trying, though."

He started to stand but Wilson grabbed his arm.

"Sit down. I didn't say no."

"Then you're considering it?"

"What exactly are you offering?"

"I don't understand the question."

"If I help you, I want my career back."

It would have been expedient to simply make that promise, but Wilson wasn't stupid. The delicate balance of believability and fantasy had to be maintained.

"I'm a Saudi bureaucrat, Joel. I can't guarantee something like that. But I can tell you that the president is anxious to have this matter dealt with before it can cause an international incident. It's hard to imagine how having his gratitude could hurt your career."

Wilson stared out the windows at the front of the building, watching widely spaced snowflakes fall in the street. "Bringing him in is going to be a hell of a trick. He's not going to surrender. And even if he did, can you imagine the shit he has locked up in his head? What are they going to do? Put him on trial? Just let him sit there and spill everything he knows all over the courtroom floor?"

"I agree. Mr. Rapp will strongly resist being taken alive."

The implication was clear, but, instead of recoiling, Wilson smiled.

"So, are you interested, Joel?"

"Hell yes, I'm interested."

Men like him were so easily manipulated. So easily blinded. Mitch Rapp and his people were among the few things standing between the survival of the Western world and chaos. Wilson's indignation was made possible by the freedom that Rapp risked his life to protect.

"Then tell me what our first move should be, Joel."

"I hear that he built a fancy house outside of D.C. I say we tear it apart and see what turns up."

"Getting a warrant will be difficult," Nassar said. "What I've told you is all true but probably wouldn't meet the standards of evidence required by your legal system."

The FBI man smiled cruelly. "Remember how I said Rapp has enemies? Well, some of them are judges."

CHAPTER 41

ALL progress had now officially ceased.

It was a situation that normally would have irritated the hell out of Joel Wilson, but tonight it didn't bother him a bit. The weather was clear and still, with a sky full of stars hovering over the house—compound, really—in front of him.

The gate was a modern copper construction new enough that the green patina was still subtle. The walls were white stucco, rising a little taller than aesthetics demanded. And all of it was perched on the top of a low summit that looked out over the surrounding countryside.

He and his team had passed a barn on the way in, as well as a few home sites in the beginning phases of construction. They were nothing but a distraction, though. This hilltop had one purpose and one purpose only—to provide a location for Mitch Rapp's castle.

A young FBI agent was standing at the keypad that opened the gate, working with a screwdriver and alligator clips to gain access. He'd been there for more than ten minutes—significantly longer than Wilson ordinarily would have tolerated without intervening. But not tonight. Tonight he'd just savor the moment.

Earlier that day he'd spoken directly to Joshua Alexander. The president had confirmed Aali Nassar's story and made it clear that Wilson would be provided whatever resources were necessary. If he called the FBI, the local cops, the CIA, the NSA, or Jesus Christ himself, and they didn't jump, he was to use Alexander's private number immediately.

The turnabout from exile to having the president's personal contact information had happened at disorienting speed. His official reprimands, his demotion and transfer to North Dakota, his wife leaving him— even his brief flirtation with suicide—were already fading from memory.

What he hadn't shared with the president was how far he intended to take this investigation and how bad it was going to get. This was about more than Mitch Rapp going off the reservation—something a complete moron could have seen coming a mile away. It was about Kennedy's protection of him. It was about Senator Ferris abandoning Wilson and becoming one of Kennedy's most ardent supporters. The only things that could have brought about that betrayal were the threat of public disgrace or treason charges. How many other politicians were in her pocket? How many other government officials had she allowed to keep their pensions in the hope that it would prevent them from blowing the whistle?

His phone rang and the screen displayed a number that was still immediately recognizable. It had been a long time since Director Miller had called him, and he wondered whether he should even bother picking up. He didn't answer to Miller anymore. If anything, Miller answered to him.

In the end he couldn't resist.

"Hello?"

"I understand you're at Mitch Rapp's house with some of my people."

"I thought it'd been made clear that they're *my* people, Director."

"Joel . . ." the man said in an exasperated tone Wilson remembered well. It was like hearing his father all over again. But Miller wasn't his father. He was one of the men who had been subverted by Irene Kennedy. One of the men who would be exposed before all this was over.

"I know you want revenge against Rapp and Kennedy," Miller continued. "And that you want to take us all down for corruption and God knows what else. But you need to put your personal feelings aside and think about what you're doing."

"Are you afraid I'm going to dig too deep? That I'm going to find out what's really been going on? Because that's the job the president gave me."

"It's the job the *Saudis* gave you, Joel. We don't work for the Saudis. The enemy of your enemy isn't your friend. Aali Nassar is a treacherous, fundamentalist son of a bitch who would slit his own mother's throat for . . . hell, for damn near anything. You've been in this exact same position before with the Pakistanis. Here's what I can guarantee you, Joel—"

"Are you about to threaten me, Director? Because I should warn you that I'm recording this call."

"Shut up for once in your life and listen. Nassar and the Saudis have a hidden agenda here. What it is,

I don't know. But don't trust them, Joel. Stay neutral, stay professional, and you might get out of this with your skin."

"Then you *are* threatening me."

"Damn it, Joel!" Miller said, raising his voice for one of the few times in their relationship. "If Rapp really has gone rogue, then this isn't about you losing your pension or getting transferred. He's going to kill you. Can you get that through your thick skull?"

"Can I quote you on that?"

The line went dead and Wilson smiled. It had been a good try, but Miller's call reeked of desperation. He wondered how many more like it he'd receive before all this was over.

The man working on Rapp's keypad suddenly turned and began walking in Wilson's direction. The gate was still closed.

"What? Why aren't we in?"

"I'm not getting through that, sir."

"So when the Bureau told me you were competent, that wasn't true? Is that what you're saying?"

"Sir, I've never seen a unit like that. It doesn't have any brand markings or a model number. I couldn't even tell you what country it was made in."

"Then go home."

"Sir, I—"

"If you can't do your job, then you're just in the way, aren't you? Now, get the hell out of here."

Wilson turned his attention to an FBI SWAT team standing behind a massive vehicle fitted with a battering ram. "We can't get through the electronics, so we're going to have to tear the gate down."

The team leader looked at him and then at the gate. "I don't think that's a good idea, sir."

"What do you mean, not a good idea?"

"That's Mitch Rapp's gate."

"I'm aware of whose gate it is."

"Maybe we could call the Agency. They might have a way to get in."

Wilson just stared at him. "Are you afraid of damaging Rapp's gate?"

The men all looked at one another. A few actually nodded.

"Sir," the team leader started again. "Do you see those cameras up on the wall? They're still filming." He thumbed behind him. "And have you noticed that?"

Wilson squinted through the darkness toward the barn. It took a moment, but he finally made out a lone human figure leaning on a cane. "Who is he?"

"That's Rapp's closest friend, Scott Coleman. He once jumped out of a second-story window onto a suicide bomber and beat the guy to death with a car jack. A fucking car jack, sir. And he's known as one of the more easygoing people Rapp works with."

Wilson knew exactly who Coleman was. He was the man who had set up the listening devices that had recorded Wilson's meeting with Senator Ferris. He was the man who had provided the audio that had destroyed his life.

"Get in the vehicle and take down the gate. That's an order."

"With all due respect, sir. Fuck you. Keys are in it."

Wilson was stunned by the man's insubordination, but now wasn't the time to deal with it. They needed to gain access, and if he had to do it himself, so be it. He climbed in and, after a minute of examining the controls, figured out how to get it started. Depressing the accelerator, he aimed the ram at the center of the gate. The cameras on the wall watched silently and he found himself hoping they could see through the windshield. That Rapp would know exactly who had done this.

He hit hard, expecting the enormous vehicle to sail through, but instead the gate flexed, absorbing the impact. He was thrown against the seat belt, his head snapping forward with enough force to momentarily daze him. When he regained his equilibrium, he let out a lengthy string of expletives, reversed fifty yards, and floored it. This time the gate gave way spectacularly and he slammed on the brakes, skidding to a stop in front of a modern structure completely devoid of windows.

He had to wait for the men to come up cautiously behind him, but when they finally did, he leaned out the window. "Take down the front door!"

"Sir, I—"

"Shut up! You're either taking down the door or I'm taking down the whole wall."

The SWAT leader thought about that for a few seconds before pulling a ram out of the back. It took a few minutes, but they finally defeated the door and disappeared inside. The lights attached to their weapons flashed haphazardly around the entryway before going dark again as they penetrated deeper. Wilson lit a cigarette. He wouldn't put it past Rapp to have the place booby-trapped. Not his problem, though. That's what the SWAT guys got paid for.

What would he find inside this vault of a house? Cash skimmed from government accounts? Souvenirs from illegal assassinations? Materials Rapp used to blackmail government officials into supporting him? If he found the latter, Wilson wondered what he should do with it. Certainly not hand it over. No, he'd hold on to it until he'd built a case so airtight that half of Washington would have to get behind him while the other half threw themselves out of windows. And he'd be there at the center of it all, the media's new darling.

Finally a voice came over the walkie-talkie on the seat next to him.

"We're clear."

Wilson jumped down from the vehicle and entered, walking over the smashed door and flipping a light switch. A tasteful glow grew around him, illuminating expensive woodwork, Asian-inspired furniture, and a bold painting of a flower that looked like it cost more than he made in a year.

"Tear the place apart," he said, throwing the painting to the floor in search of a hidden safe. Or at least that was what he'd tell anyone who asked. He began yanking drawers out of the sideboard as the sound of similar activity began filtering down the hallway.

When he was finished in the entry, he skirted a glass wall that looked into an interior courtyard and entered what looked to be a child's room. One of his men was sifting gingerly through the contents of a shelf and Wilson pushed him aside, dumping everything onto the floor. "Move your ass! I don't have all week."

The man stared nervously at the mess before following orders and picking up the pace. The reverence they afforded a psychotic CIA thug was both insulting and an impediment to getting anything accomplished. Wilson was looking forward to hearing their mumbled apologies when he shined a bright light into who and what Mitch Rapp really was.

He heard running feet in the hallway and went out to see what was happening. A man with an iPad rushed up and held it out. "I found this in the master bedroom, sir. It's password protected, but I think you'll be interested in the wallpaper image."

Wilson woke it and stared down at three smiling people looking back at him. One was a little girl, laughing as she tapped a croquet ball across the yard of a Cape Dutch house. Standing next to her was a woman in her midthirties, dark hair and eyes, stunningly beautiful. Most interesting, though, was the man sticking his foot out to block the ball from finding its target. Mitch Rapp. A current photo, in living color.

Wilson grinned and looked up, scanning the junction between the wall and ceiling for a security camera. When he found one, he approached it and raised the tablet toward the lens.

CHAPTER 42

THE power was out again, but the breeze coming through the open windows kept the heat down. The fifty-year-old mansion had been converted into a hotel years ago, but after Sudan's split, it had been largely shut down. The owner had been endlessly grateful when they rented the entire property, and he'd been working ever since to demonstrate that gratitude. Not only was the place spotless, but a sideboard in the living room was arranged with hard-to-get premium liquor.

Azarov was reading the label on a bottle of bourbon while Rapp scanned the landscape beyond the windows. According to Black, this area was under the iron-fisted control of a rebel group that Abdo counted among his most dedicated enemies. The young sniper seemed confident that they were momentarily safe from the locals, and Rapp had no reason to question that conclusion. The kid seemed to understand the intricacies of the fighting around Juba.

"I haven't been able to find much information that I have confidence in," Claudia said, grazing on a platter of vegetables provided by their host. "I'm certain that Nassar is in the U.S. and ninety percent sure that he had a meeting at the White House."

"What about now?" Rapp asked.

"The best I could determine is that he went to North Dakota."

"That seems kind of unlikely," Black said. He was on his fourth beer and looked like he was starting to feel them.

"I agree. I'm working to corroborate, but it's difficult."

"If he's in the States, he's vulnerable," Black said. "It would be a hell of a lot easier to operate there than in Saudi Arabia."

"I wonder," Azarov said. "If I were him, I'd have requested an American security team. Mitch would hesitate to attack out of fear of injuring one of them."

"A frontal assault isn't feasible anyway," Claudia said. "Even if it succeeded, it would play into the narrative that Mitch has gone insane and is running around the globe, killing people. He'd be hunted for the rest of his life, and anything he had to say about the Saudis would be completely discredited."

"It's like being teamed up with a bunch of old ladies," Black said. "I'll do it. I'll go to North Dakota or Iowa or wherever and pop that asshole right in the head. No muss, no fuss, no collateral damage. And Mitch can be three thousand miles away with an airtight alibi."

"They'd still assume he was behind it, based on what's happened so far," Donatella said.

Black grabbed another beer. "But Claudia said she could get Mitch off the hook for killing Nassar's two buddies—"

"Three," Rapp said, causing the others to turn toward him. "Qadir Sultan was found dead last night along with two security men from the Saudi intelligence ministry."

"Let me guess," Donatella said. "One shot to the head from a nine-millimeter bullet."

"That matches the early reports."

"He's destroying his own network in an effort to keep it from leading back to him," Azarov pointed out. "Is it possible that this is good for us?"

"Sultan was the last of the men that we've identified as being close to him," Claudia said. "It's likely that his network extends further, but Mitch and I don't think anyone left would have direct knowledge of Nassar's involvement. He would have interacted with them through intermediaries."

"Then punching a few holes in Nassar is the way to go," Black said. "He's taken out his lieutenants for us. With him dead the whole thing collapses. Job done, Mitch hangs out a shingle and makes an obscene amount of money taking contracts. How is this not a good plan?"

"Because the rest of us are experienced enough to know we don't want to spend the rest of our lives being hunted by the world's governments," Donatella said. "It's not as romantic as it sounds, Kent."

"Then we need to demonstrate Nassar's involvement," Azarov said. "Prove that he killed those people and that he's financing ISIS."

"Agreed, but it's easier said than done," Claudia replied. "The man doesn't leave behind a lot of loose ends."

Rapp's phone chimed as a heated discussion of their

situation broke out among the others. He opened a hidden app and watched a series of jerky images being broadcast via a satellite connection.

The gate he'd spent so much money on turned out to be worth every penny, surviving the first attempt at a breach before succumbing to a SWAT vehicle traveling at reckless speeds. His front door had held longer than expected, too, noticeably fatiguing the men who were now fanning out in his entryway. A man wearing a suit instead of combat gear appeared after the area had been secured and Rapp squinted down at the image.

Claudia would be pleased to know that she'd been right about North Dakota. It was where the FBI had sent Joel Wilson.

Wilson began tearing up the room, ostensibly in a search but really just to cause as much destruction as possible. Rapp had told Irene Kennedy that they should bury that piece of shit in the woods somewhere, but she'd thought moving against him would cause more problems than it solved. He wondered if she still felt that way.

"Mitch?" Claudia said. "Mitch? What are you doing? Are you listening to us?"

He didn't respond, so she broke up the meeting, finally coming alongside him while the others wandered off.

"Are you all right?" She glanced at the phone and put a hand on his shoulder. "You must have expected this."

"Yeah."

He concentrated on Wilson as the man held a tablet up to one of the interior security cameras. He recog-

nized the wallpaper picture as one taken of him playing with Anna and Claudia in front of her house in
South Africa. Now the man had a current picture of
all of them as well as a shot of Claudia's home.

"Who is he, Mitch?"

"An old enemy that I didn't deal with when I had a
chance."

"CIA?"

"FBI."

"So now Nassar's solicited the help of the American
government. I hate to bring this up again, but is it time
for you to contact Irene?"

He didn't respond, instead freezing the image and
continuing to stare down at it.

"Mitch?"

"How hard will it be for them to get into your tablet?"

"Hard. It would take even Marcus at least a week.
There's nothing on it, though. I use it mostly for reading magazines."

"Can you access it remotely?"

"No. It's not set up that way. Why?"

"What about the computer at your house in Cape
Town? Could you access that remotely?"

"Sure. What are you thinking?"

"I'm thinking that, with that picture, it's not going
to take them long to show up on your doorstep."

She shrugged. "We're not there, and accessing the
information on my computer would be extraordinarily difficult, Mitch. I have confidential files on it
from my time working with Louis. It would take years,
even with the help of the NSA."

"But you could get in remotely and make it easy,

right? Wipe the sensitive information and change the password to Anna's birthday or something."

"Sure. But why?"

He ignored the question. "Would it be possible to create some fictitious emails between you and me and backdate them?"

"Not too difficult, but they wouldn't be entirely convincing, particularly combined with the simplistic password. If someone looked closely, I'm not sure the scenario you're talking about would hold up."

Rapp nodded slowly, only partially hearing her. Nassar had to be dealt with whether it blew back against him or not—that was a decision Rapp had already made. But if he could lead Nassar into a trap and get someone else to do the wet work, his life would be a lot simpler. And probably a lot longer.

He tossed his phone onto the table in front of him. "It doesn't need to hold up. I know Joel Wilson, and I can guarantee you that he only sees what he wants to see."

CHAPTER 43

IRENE Kennedy closed the thick file on Aali Nassar's life and considered what she'd read. His early schooling had come from the Saudi madrassa system, but he'd moved on to an English university after that—an educational background that could create both radical Islamists and secular moderates. He was extraordinarily competent and ambitious, traits that defined both great men and evil ones. Which was he?

In the world of intelligence, nothing was black-and-white. This situation, though, was more murky than most. Unfortunately, if she pieced it together in the most logical way, the picture that emerged was as ugly as any she'd ever seen.

She was virtually certain that President Alexander had set Mitch on his current course without considering the consequences. And now that those consequences were making themselves known, he was scrambling for cover. It was a game that had been played by powerful men for thousands of years.

The Iraqis who had attacked the nightclub in Monaco were associated with ISIS, and their pursuit of Prince bin Musaid after he'd escaped suggested that this wasn't the random terrorist attack that the public believed it to be.

After acknowledging those two things, though, she was forced to step onto far less stable ground. It seemed likely that Rapp had sent Donatella into that club in an effort to lure bin Musaid to a location where he could be interrogated. The terrorist attack was a violent and messy interruption of an operation that should have been clean and quiet.

Assuming that Nassar was indeed behind bin Musaid's terrorist activities, what would he think of Mitch Rapp's rescue of the prince? The answer was obvious. He would have no choice but to assume that bin Musaid had given up everything about Nassar's network, forcing the intelligence chief to get rid of anyone who knew of his involvement. The three men who had been killed so far all had unusually strong connections to Nassar.

It was there that the web became even more tangled. She certainly wouldn't put the torture and deaths of those men beyond Rapp. But would he have had the resources to move so quickly? Doubtful. Would he have killed the security guard at the Brussels hotel? Absolutely not. It seemed much more likely that it was all Nassar's doing. His survival now depended on cutting ties to ISIS and getting rid of Rapp.

The question now was what action should she take. What action *could* she take? President Alexander had washed his hands of Rapp, but she wasn't Joshua Alexander. She very much appreciated Rapp respecting her wishes and keeping her out of this. But how long could she remain in the background? They'd been through too much together for her to abandon him.

There was a quiet knock on the door, followed by one of her assistants entering. "Dr. Kennedy? There's a Special Agent Joel Wilson here to see you. He doesn't have an appointment."

She'd expected a call, but a surprise visit? Wilson was enjoying himself even more than she'd anticipated. "Thank you. Send him in."

By the time she could stand, he was already striding across the carpet.

"Hello, Joel." She began to extend a hand but he just dropped uninvited into one of the chairs in front of her desk.

"I assume you've heard?"

"That you managed to get a search warrant for Mitch's house? Yes."

A smug smile played at his lips. "Word in this town travels fast."

Which was exactly what he wanted, she knew. Wilson desperately needed for everyone to know that he had been vindicated. That he now wielded the power of the White House in his crusade to vanquish the corrupt forces lined up against him.

She also knew that he blamed her as much as Rapp for what had happened to him. What he would never accept was that he had done this to himself and that the penalties for his actions could have been much worse. If it hadn't been for her and Director Miller, Joel Wilson might have ended up in jail. Or dead.

"We've been able to determine with nearly one hundred percent certainty that Rapp was the man in Monaco."

She sat, resigning herself to the fact that this meeting wasn't going to be as brief as she'd hoped. "He's retired, Joel. He's allowed to go to nightclubs."

"I figured you'd say that. We've also been able to determine that he was the man who attacked the two security guards at that Brussels hotel. Tell me, Irene. Is he allowed to do that?"

"What about the one who was killed?" she said, genuinely curious.

"He covered his tracks better on that. But we're working on it."

She nodded. "And what does all this lead you to believe?"

"That he's finally completely lost his fucking mind. I don't know what did it—the stress, the concussions, watching his wife get blown apart. . . . Doesn't matter, though, because he's running around the world, murdering innocent people. And I think we can both agree he isn't going to stop unless someone makes him. He likes the taste of blood, Irene. He's addicted to it."

There was so much that could be said. About bin Musaid's involvement with ISIS. About Nassar's connections to the dead men. But mostly about Mitch Rapp himself. In fact, he despised the taste of blood. His entire life had been nothing but one sacrifice after another. None of it would make any difference, though. Wilson saw only himself.

"You're a talented investigator, Joel. You always have been. But your judgment's being clouded by your personal feelings. I'd urge you to clear your mind and apply it to the problem. If you do, you'll see that none of what's happened makes sense."

He actually laughed at that. "*My* personal feelings? You're so blinded by him, you can't see the bodies piling up around you. Hell, I just got testimony that last year he shot an unarmed Iraqi girl named Laleh Qarni."

Kennedy stiffened. "Let me offer you a piece of advice, Joel. If you should ever come face-to-face with Mitch, don't mention that name. I've known him for most of my life, and even I wouldn't dare say it out loud in his presence. Do you understand?"

Whether it was what she'd said or how she'd said it, the FBI man's arrogance faltered. As a cover, he pulled out a photo and slapped it on her desk. It depicted Mitch, Claudia, and Anna playing croquet in South Africa.

"Forget Laleh." He tapped the photo. "Who's *this* woman?"

He didn't have clearance to know her real identity, so Kennedy used the one the CIA had created for her. "Claudia Dufort."

"What's her relationship to Rapp?"

"Personal."

"And where can I find her?"

"Presumably with Mitch."

"And the girl?"

"Her name is Anna."

"Did he take her on his killing spree, too?"

"No, she's not with him." There was no way Kennedy could lie. As odious as this investigation was, it was authorized at the highest level. "She's staying with me."

"Excuse me?"

"Was I not clear?"

"You kept this secret?" His eyes lit up at the potential chink in her armor.

"Just because you don't know something doesn't mean it's a secret, Joel. Claudia told me she and Mitch needed to get away and asked me to keep her daughter so her school year wouldn't be interrupted."

"But you're still going with the story that you have no idea where they are and no way to contact them. So, if the little girl gets sick or falls down a well, you can't get in touch with her mother?"

"I have email addresses for both her and Mitch. I'm happy to share them with you."

He leaned forward in his chair and stared directly into her eyes. "You know that I'm coming for you, too, right, Irene?"

"Of course I do. Now, if you'll excuse me, I'm late for a meeting."

CHAPTER 44

"WHY are we just sitting here?" Joel Wilson said. "We should be following them in."

Nassar watched the scene through the windshield of the SUV they'd hired. On the surface it wasn't much different from Wilson's breach of Mitch Rapp's home, but beneath the surface the differences were considerable. The men working to open the gate on Claudia Dufort's house weren't a well-trained FBI SWAT team. They were a random collection of his own people, local police, and men supplied by Mullah Halabi.

It was a dangerously unpredictable mix, but it was Halabi's people he was most concerned about. While they were reasonably disciplined by terrorist standards, the contrast between them and his General Intelligence Directorate operatives was still rather stark. It made sense to limit Wilson's exposure to the ISIS men as much as possible.

He glanced over at the impatient American and felt his fears diminish. The man had eyes, but they were glassy with a fervor that Nassar normally equated with Islam. While those men saw only God and their duty to Him, Wilson saw only Rapp and the revenge that was so close at hand.

"The presence of the African police creates an unstable situation, Joel. And the chances of Mr. Rapp hiding at the home of a woman he's known to be involved with is far-fetched in the extreme. This is a job for soldiers, not generals."

As if to punctuate his words, two shots rang out. Wilson went for the door handle, but Nassar grabbed his shoulder and activated his headset. "Report."

"Two guard dogs," came the reply in his earpiece. "We're clear."

"Copy. The compound is secured, Joel. We can go in now."

"What about those shots?"

"It was nothing."

Nassar pulled through the gate, parking in a courtyard overflowing with palm trees and bougainvillea. Mullah Halabi's men were near the front door in what seemed to be a wary détente with Nassar's team. Wilson was blind to the obvious tension, instead focusing on irrelevant matters that so easily distracted Americans. In this case, it was the two dead guard dogs and the local policeman pinning a terrified African woman against a tree. When one of them slapped her, Wilson jumped out and ran in their direction.

"Stop!"

Nassar followed, keeping Halabi's men in his peripheral vision as Wilson pushed the policeman aside.

"Who are you?" he said to the woman.

Her words came out in an unintelligible jumble, so

the policeman spoke for her. "She says she works here. That she lives in the servants' quarters at the back."

"Is there any reason to believe that's not true?"

The man shrugged.

"Calm down," Wilson said. "We're not here to hurt you and you're not under arrest. Now tell me. Where is Claudia Dufort?"

"I . . . I don't know. She hasn't been here in many months. I care for the house." She looked past him for a moment at the dead animals lying in the grass. "And the dogs."

He pulled out a photo and held it up to her. "Do you know this man?"

She nodded. "Mitch. He's an American."

"When was the last time you saw him?"

"When he came to help get Claudia and Anna's things."

"So months ago."

She nodded.

"How do you communicate with them? Do you have a phone number?"

"No. An email address."

"Okay. Go back to your quarters and stay there until I tell you to come out."

She rushed off and he turned to Nassar. "Her story matches what we already know—that Dufort and her daughter have been living with Rapp in the U.S."

"Agreed. Questioning this woman would be a waste of time. Rapp wouldn't reveal anything to a servant."

He followed Wilson into the house and a brief search turned up an office at the back. It was only three meters square and contained little more than a desk, a computer, and a single chair. Wilson immediately sat and turned on the computer. Not surprisingly, it requested a password. He swore quietly and rebooted it from a thumb drive.

"Your computer experts still haven't been able to access her tablet," Nassar pointed out. "What makes you think you can get into this?"

"People are funny," he said. "They feel safe in their homes. So while they secure the hell out of their phones and tablets, they tend to be lazy with their desktops. They want it to be easy, they want their kids to be able to get on, and they figure no one will ever have physical access to it."

Nassar riffled through a stack of papers but found nothing more than notes from the girl's school and receipts for inconsequential household products. Finally, he wandered back out into the main part of the house as his and Halabi's men tore the space apart. Normally it wasn't his practice to get personally involved in these kinds of operations, but there was little choice. His life depended on the American FBI agent finding Rapp. Every minute that passed without success increased the danger.

After about thirty minutes a shrill laugh filtered through the home, reaching him as he passed through Dufort's wrecked kitchen. He jogged back to the office and found Wilson grinning like an idiot at the computer screen.

"I found her daughter's birthday on the calendar and reversed it for the password," he said. "I hope she's one hell of a piece of tail, because she isn't the sharpest knife in the drawer."

"Is there anything of value on the hard drive?"

"I'm less interested in the drive than the email,"

Wilson said. Nassar watched as he searched for all the correspondence with Rapp.

"Okay, let's start on the date we know they left the U.S.," Wilson said. "Yeah, there's an increase in email frequency, so they may not be together. Or at least they haven't been for the entire time."

"I doubt Mitch Rapp would discuss something as sensitive as his location on a commercial account," Nassar said.

"No," Wilson replied, opening and closing successive individual emails. "But he might not have to. Don't give this asshole too much credit, Aali. He's not an intel guy. He's just a killer." The FBI man suddenly jabbed a finger into the screen. "Right there!"

"What?"

"It's a bunch of bullshit about Anna, but then look at what he says. 'It hit ninety three degrees today but the sun finally went down a half an hour ago.'"

Wilson dialed his phone and put in an earpiece. "Yeah, it's me. September twenty-seven. Where in the world did the temp top out around ninety-three and the sun set around three forty-five GMT. Uh-huh. Yeah, I can wait."

He continued scrolling through emails, closing most within a few seconds, but occasionally minimizing one instead.

"Central Africa? You're sure? Are you going to narrow it down? Okay, I've got something else for you. On October fifth, there was audible shelling in the morning. Yeah, it uses the word 'shelling' specifically, so some kind of active war zone. Right . . ."

Nassar left the man to his work and exited the house, crossing the lawn to a stand of trees near the rear wall. He glanced around him to make certain no one was within earshot and then dialed his sat phone.

"Peace be upon you, Director," Mullah Halabi said.

"And you." He deeply resented having to check in with the man, but it would be unwise to refuse the request.

"I understand you're at the home of one of Rapp's women. Is the search proving fruitful?"

Nassar's jaw clenched, but it was hardly a surprise that Halabi's men were reporting back to him. Having the volatile mullah tracking his movements so closely, though, unnerved him. As with Rapp, it was often hard to distinguish between the hunter and the hunted.

"We believe that he may be in central Africa. We're working now to pinpoint a location."

"Excellent. I have many devoted men in the region. I'll be happy to make them available to you."

Nassar wanted to reject the offer, but there was no practical way to do so. Pointing out that the ISIS leader's African followers would be unpredictable and poorly trained would be an insult. And admitting that their presence made him uneasy would make the mullah question what he had to hide.

"That's most generous."

"Of course, Aali. My resources are always at the disposal of my loyal disciples."

Nassar bristled at being lumped in with the illiterate cannon fodder that made up Halabi's cult of personality, but he did nothing that would hint at his displeasure. The ISIS leader was a critical tool in the subjugation of the Middle East and would have to be deferred to until an opportunity to replace him arose.

Joel Wilson appeared around the edge of the house and began rushing toward him.

"I'm afraid I'm going to have to go," Nassar said respectfully. "The American FBI man is coming."

"May Allah be with you," he said, and then severed the connection.

"I've got something!" Wilson shouted, showing no interest in who Nassar had been talking to.

"Really? That's surprising, Joel. We've been here less than an hour."

In fact, it seemed quite incredible. While Mitch Rapp undoubtedly had a gift for violence, it was likely that Wilson was underestimating his intellect. Strength, speed, and steel nerves alone couldn't explain the trail of dead the man had left over the last twenty years. Was Rapp capable of making obvious mistakes?

The FBI agent smoothed out a single sheet of paper on an outdoor table and motioned him over. Nassar looked down at the crude map of Africa and the various markings on it.

"The red circles indicate everywhere our satellites picked up significant explosions on the day Rapp talked about shelling. Combining that with the temperature and sunset data gives us a ninety percent probability that they're in South Sudan."

"Impressive, but that's an entire country."

"I'm not done," Wilson said. "There was active fighting in a number of places in that country, but he mentioned in a later email that he was getting provisions from the main market and that it was more trouble than it was worth to drive. That means he's close enough to a main market to walk and hand carry food back to where he's staying. Then he made his fatal slip. He called the place he was staying 'the church.'"

"And that's enough information for you to locate him?"

"I'm still cross-referencing with MI6, but I think there's a good chance. 'Main market' suggests a town big enough to have more than one, which rules out a number of villages with shelling close enough to hear. My gut says we're talking about Juba."

"And the church?"

"I don't know yet, but I'm guessing my people will have a bead on it before we go wheels up. How many nonoperational churches can there be a few minutes' walk from the central market?"

Nassar nodded, examining the map. "Excellent work, Joel. I was always confident that you were the man for this job, but now I have no doubts at all."

All true, but something in the back of Nassar's mind remained suspicious of the man's success. It was bordering on being too easy. And this suggested two scenarios. First, that Rapp would be aware that his emails to his woman could be accessed and used to locate him, in which case he was already a thousand miles from Juba. Or, second, that those emails were the bait for an elaborate trap.

Of course, Nassar recognized that it was also possible that he was just being paranoid, but it wasn't something he was willing to bet his life on. Wilson's life, though, was of less importance. While it would be inconvenient to lose him, he was hardly irreplaceable. And his death at Rapp's hands would do a great deal to further the narrative Nassar had been crafting.

"I was speaking to the king earlier, and I've been recalled to Riyadh on an urgent matter," he lied. "I tried to explain to His Majesty that I was needed here, but he wouldn't be deterred. My men and my plane are at your disposal, Joel. I'll take a commercial flight home and return as soon as I can."

CHAPTER 45

THE darkness in the alley went from deep shadow to impenetrable darkness and back again every few feet, but Kent Black kept inching forward. Juba's electricity was out again, and all he had to work with was a few battery-powered lamps glowing in distant windows.

It wasn't the safest time to be skulking around town, but the possibility of being jumped by a bunch of drunk rebels wasn't why he wanted to get the hell out of there. All that mattered was that he got back to the safari camp before Rapp figured out he was gone.

Black came to the mouth of the alley and was able to make out the vague shape of the church's listing steeple against the stars. It was only another seventy-five yards to the east pedestrian gate, then five minutes inside and then he was out. Easy, right?

One of the men Abdo had sent to watch the place was sitting in an open jeep across the street, but he was dead asleep with an AK clutched to his chest like some

kind of security blanket. Based on his age, he'd probably only recently traded up.

The next fifty yards went pretty well. Quiet, good
cover, and no more of Abdo's men. The gods of war
had taken pity on him.

Or so he'd thought. When the church's east wall
came into view, he saw a lone figure standing next to
the gate. The sheer size of him and the slightly crooked
stance acquired when a bullet had crushed his right
femur a few years back made him easy to identify.
Barnabas Malse.

Black froze. He'd had some training in hand-to-
hand combat in the army, but that had been a long
time ago. As far as he was concerned, getting any
closer than three hundred yards to a target was just
plain stupid. If God had wanted people to fight with
knives, he wouldn't have given them sniper rifles.

Skirting the building next to him, Black managed
to leave the glow of a distant fire behind. He was wearing tattered fatigues and had smeared his face with
dirt in an effort to blend in, but the effect was marginal. With a little backlighting, though, it might get
the job done.

He shook out his shoulders to loosen up and then
started walking casually toward Malse. The man separated himself from the wall he was leaning against
but didn't make a move for his sidearm.

If there was one thing the African didn't lack, it
was confidence. And that conviction didn't just come
from his freakish bulk and the terror he instilled in
everyone for five hundred miles around. He was also
in the habit of kidnapping and eating albino children.

When Black had first heard the stories, he'd thought they were just a bullshit legend. It turned out that they were true. Malse believed that his unusual diet made him invincible in battle.

The African said something and Black just pointed to his ear in a way that suggested he couldn't hear. It wouldn't register as being unusual. A significant percentage of the rebel population was about half deaf from the constant shooting and explosions.

His heart felt like it was trying to fight its way out of his chest by the time he got within ten feet of the man. Malse still hadn't recognized him or made a move for his weapon, but he did speak again. Black nodded vigorously at whatever the fuck he'd said, hoping to draw attention away from the knife appearing from his pocket. When he got inside of five feet, he lunged, driving the eight-inch blade into the man's stomach. Malse looked surprised, but other than that the knife didn't seem to make much of an impression. He grabbed Black by the front of his fatigues and lifted him off the ground, throwing him into the church's perimeter wall. The former Ranger managed to keep his head from impacting but still hit hard before dropping gracelessly to the ground. He'd barely managed to get to his knees when Malse grabbed him again— this time with one hand on his throat and the other on his thigh. Black found himself being lifted again but managed to grab hold of the hilt of the knife protruding from Malse's stomach on the way up. He yanked it sideways, opening a long slit that poured blood down the front of the African's grimy blue jeans. He still didn't seem to notice.

This time Black hit the wall upside down and almost seven feet up, impacting the ground a moment later face-first. He saw Malse coming for him again but was too dazed to do anything but lie there wondering if the magic really worked. If all those murdered children really had made him immortal.

A human figure appeared from the shadows behind the African and Black squinted at it, trying to make sense of what was happening. A hand clamped over Malse's nose and mouth and he was dragged out of sight. After that, there was a quiet crunching sound and then nothing.

Black tried to push himself to his feet, failing the first time and then managing to regain enough equilibrium to succeed on his second try. When he did, the dark figure was standing in front of him, backlit as he had been before. Not Malse. Way too small and straight. Still fuzzy, there was nothing Black could do when the man grabbed him by the hair and dragged him into the same dark alcove he'd dragged the African.

Black fell to his knees and looked down at Malse. His previously good leg was bent sideways at a ninety-degree angle and his head was twisted all the way around backward. Somewhere, there was a witch doctor who owed him a refund.

"Couldn't sleep?"

The quiet voice sent a surge of adrenaline through Black, bringing him back to full alertness.

"Mitch? What are you doing here?"

A gun appeared and a moment later there was a silencer pressed to Black's forehead.

"I was about to ask you the same thing."

A thousand lies passed through his mind, but he

knew that every one of them would end with his brains splattered over what was left of Malse.

"There's information on you and the others inside the church, Mitch. I don't think anyone would be able to find it, but I didn't want to take chances."

"I asked you about this a few days ago. You told me the place was clean."

"That wasn't entirely accurate."

"What kind of information?"

Black didn't answer.

"You have one chance to convince me you're just an idiot, Kent. Because if I start thinking that you're playing both—"

"It's an entire dossier on everyone involved and what we're doing," Black blurted. "I'm sorry, Mitch. I told an old friend that if I were to disappear, he should come get it and release it on the Internet."

"Why would you think that you were going to disappear?"

"I don't know, man . . . because why would someone like you give a shit about someone like me? Particularly when you've got Donatella and the fucking Russian terminator to watch your back. I'm pretty sure that next to the word 'expendable' in the dictionary, there's a picture of me."

"No one on any of my teams has ever been expendable, Kent."

"I understand that now. That's why I'm here. I was going to get the stuff and destroy it. I didn't tell you because I didn't want you to think . . . you know . . ."

"That you're an idiot?"

"Yeah. That."

As much as Rapp wanted to put a bullet in this

little dipshit, there was no point. When he'd started out, he'd made similarly boneheaded moves that Stan Hurley would have been justified in burying him for.

"What exactly are we talking about?"

"A single eleven-by-fourteen envelope."

"No electronic files? Nothing on a server somewhere?"

"No way, man. I swear. That shit's too hard to control."

He lowered his weapon. "Okay."

"What do you mean, 'Okay'? That's it?"

Rapp didn't answer. The ringer on his phone was turned off, but he'd felt it vibrate three separate times over the last few minutes. When he pulled it out, he found multiple messages from Claudia. Not a great sign. She wasn't a woman prone to calling repeatedly to deliver good news.

He dialed and, not surprisingly, she picked up immediately.

"Mitch! Where are you? I've been trying to get in touch."

"I'm at the church. What's up?"

"I found Joel Wilson."

"Where?"

"I'm sorry, Mitch. My man at the airport let me down. Wilson's on the ground and bearing down on your position with four cars.

"ETA?"

"Call it five minutes."

"Can you slow him down?"

"I have people along every route to you. We can probably improvise something."

"Do what you can. Kent and I are going into the church—"

"Going in? Why would you—"

"Don't talk, Claudia. Listen. Put Grisha on the north roof with a rifle. Put Donatella east."

"Okay," she said reluctantly. "I'll do it."

"And don't worry. I'll see you in a few hours."

Black, still on his knees, started to protest before Rapp could even disconnect the call.

"Donatella on the east roof? That should be me, Mitch. She's crap with a rifle. She says it herself."

Rapp shook his head. "You're coming with me."

"What, to help you find the envelope? I can tell you right where it—"

"No, so I can use you to stop bullets when this thing goes to shit."

CHAPTER 46

H ow much farther?" Wilson asked.

"We good," his driver responded enigmatically. It was likely that he hadn't understood the question and that those two mangled words were the only English he knew. Nassar had handed over his entire team and arranged for Wilson to be met by a further contingent of men at the airport. The dilapidated SUV he was riding in was at the center of a three-car motorcade picking its way through the city of Juba. While the local team's English skills were lacking, all the men were well armed and all seemed familiar with the operating theater.

Still, it was less than ideal. The lack of U.S. personnel—an FBI team at least, but even better some SEALs—added to the sense that he had stepped off the edge of the world. Despite the demands of his former job, he'd never much liked traveling. Even vacations to places like London and Paris had made him feel vaguely uncomfortable. The loss of control that went along with being in a foreign land never sat well with him.

Intermittent intel was still filtering in, but he probably wasn't going to get anything else that was useful. The problem wasn't that sources weren't available, it was that he couldn't bring himself to trust most of them. Irene Kennedy had her hands in everything, and half the world's intelligence community was either loyal to her or afraid of her. That left him with no choice but to rely on a patchwork of people who either hated her or were too long retired to be influenced by her.

It appeared to have been enough, though. They'd managed to sift through all of Claudia Dufort's emails and tease out every piece of relevant information they contained. A friend at Immigration had provided the critical piece in all this—the names of former residents of Juba now residing in the U.S. They had independently confirmed the location of the church Rapp had referred to and given a fairly detailed description of its surroundings. Combined with satellite maps and a series of photos they'd found on a travel blog, Wilson had a reasonable sense of his tactical situation.

The lead car turned down a side street and Wilson twisted around, looking through the dust at the vehicle behind. Normally he relished being in command, but this was something different. His lack of knowledge about this part of the world and his difficulty in communicating with the men working under him made him feel less like the captain of this ship than someone caught in its wake.

As much as he hated to admit it, he wished that Aali Nassar hadn't been called back to Saudi Arabia. Unlike Irene Kennedy, Nassar had a straightforward manner that instilled confidence in everyone around him. He had combat experience and a reputation for backing up his comrades in arms.

Wilson faced forward again as his driver turned to follow their lead car. What would it be like to capture the infamous Mitch Rapp? To drag him back to the U.S. in chains? To expose him and Kennedy for what they were? There would be the massive media circus, of course, and the political posturing that always came with it. Then there would be the endless hearings and the inevitable vicious attacks by the people who benefited from the status quo. Even as the hero of this story, Wilson knew it would be a difficult couple of years. At the end, though, he would be able to write his own ticket.

Returning to his position as an FBI executive had its benefits but seemed like small thinking. While he'd never fancied himself a politician, it was impossible not to consider that as an option. With the Saudis' financial backing and his newfound notoriety, it was hard to imagine that a Senate seat wouldn't be his for the taking. Was it feasible that he could take Carl Ferris's place as chair of the Judiciary Committee? He'd love to see the look on that backstabbing old prune's face if he did.

Wilson was blinded by a sudden flash ahead of his lead car. A moment later the sound of the explosion reached them, mixing with the static of machine-gun fire.

"Go right!" Wilson screamed, all thoughts of his future suddenly extinguished. "Right, you idiot!

He crammed himself onto the floorboard as his driver spun the wheel and jammed the accelerator to the floor. The sound of gunfire faded, and Wilson rose just long enough to confirm that his motorcade was still intact. Arabic chatter was audible over the walkie-talkie lying on the seat next to him and he picked it up.

"What the hell was that? Report!"

"It is fine," a voice responded. He recognized it as belonging to one of the men who had been with him in Cape Town—the only one of a handful of English speakers he had.

"What the hell are you talking about? You call that fine?"

"Just a skirmish between two of the factions trying to control the city. We can route around. It won't be a problem."

"Are you sure? Do we know where we're going? We could end up heading down a dead end and getting pinned down."

"Be calm, Special Agent Wilson. It's nothing. Much like your Chicago, no?"

CHAPTER 47

RAPP kept Kent Black in front of him, taking in the grounds of the church as they moved through the gate and toward the rear entrance. Abdo hadn't stationed a man inside the wall, probably out of fear of spooking them if they returned. The precaution was negated by a dim flicker visible around one of the boarded windows. Black didn't seem to notice, instead focusing on getting through the courtyard without making any noise.

They arrived at the door leading into the office and took positions on either side. Rapp had his Glock drawn, but Black hadn't brought a sidearm. Even a silenced one would have been too loud to use against Abdo's men, and he was smart enough to admit that he couldn't hit much with one anyway.

Rapp gave a short nod and Black slid his key into the lock. It clicked, and the door swung open on quiet hinges. The younger man seemed surprised when Rapp thumbed him inside. Apparently, he'd thought the part about him being there as a human shield was a joke.

Unarmed, he swung around the doorjamb and disappeared into the gloom. Rapp followed, scanning over the sights of his weapon. There was just enough illumination for him to confirm that the room was empty.

He moved to the door leading to the nave and immediately spotted two men huddled around a small fire near the middle. One was sitting in a pew sideways to Rapp's position, and the other was directly facing him. The night had turned cool and both were leaning forward, warming their hands. They seemed to have settled in for the evening, so Rapp signaled for Black to retrieve the envelope. Instead, the former Ranger crept over to him.

"It's not in the office, Mitch. It's out there."

Rapp swore under his breath.

"I'm sorry. I really am."

There wasn't much Rapp could do about the man facing him. Fortunately, he was staring directly into the fire and it was reasonable to assume that he wouldn't be able to see beyond the ring of warmth and light. There were no guarantees, though.

With little choice, Rapp moved through the door, keeping movements painfully slow. When there was no reaction, he allowed himself to pick up the pace a bit, finally escaping the man's line of sight and angling in on them. He stopped just beyond the circle of firelight and holstered his Glock. While the noise from the silenced weapon wouldn't be a problem inside the structure, the flash would penetrate the cracked boards covering the windows.

Neither of the men was carrying a sidearm, and their rifles were just outside of easy reach. Killing them was doable, but killing them silently was going to be a trick. If he'd been with Azarov, they could each take one. Involving Black, though, would likely cause more problems than it solved.

Rapp's eye moved to a machete leaning against the end of the pew closest to him. He'd initially registered it as a potential threat but now it was starting to look like an opportunity. A little more slasher flick than he'd normally go for, but this was no time to get picky.

He pulled a thin cord from his pocket and strode casually into the light. The man in the pew spotted him first, spinning as Rapp picked up the machete. The African threw his arms up but was too slow. The machete connected with the top of his head, penetrating a good two inches before getting lodged in his skull.

As expected, the other man went for his AK. The most practical way to get his hands on it was to simply turn onto his stomach and reach out. He did exactly that, presenting his unprotected back. Rapp slipped the cord around his throat and dropped onto him.

The African was young and powerful, managing to fight his way to his knees as he clawed at the cord. Rapp secured his legs around his waist and twisted back, flipping him into the fire. The flames had the intended effect, splitting the man's focus between his lack of air and the coals igniting his fatigues. The battle intensified and then was suddenly over. Rapp dragged the body off the campfire and rolled it across the floor, making sure the flames were out.

"Damn," Black said, approaching hesitantly from behind. "Have you ever thought about working in a hockey mask?"

"Get the fucking file, Kent."

Rapp went to one of the windows and looked through a gap as Black started pulling up floorboards. There was no sign that any of the men watching the church had noticed anything. But it was hard to be sure. If they were aware of what had happened, would they attack immediately or call for backup?

Behind him, Black had gained access to a floor safe and was using a red penlight to work the combination. A moment later he came up with the envelope he'd described. Rapp pulled the flap and looked inside, scanning a few surreptitiously taken photos and a one-page explanation of what and who was involved.

"You know I should kill you for this," Rapp said.

"Yeah," Black responded, looking at the floor.

Rapp tossed the envelope on what was left of the fire and pointed toward the rear entrance. "Go relieve Donatella. But remember: Unless it's absolutely necessary, don't do anything. We're just spectators."

"You got it," he said, obviously thankful to have a second chance. "What about you?"

"I'm staying here."

It hadn't been the plan, but now that he'd gone through the trouble of getting into the church, why not? Nassar, Wilson, and their people would be arriving soon, and Abdo would assume that they were connected with Black's operation. Then the shit was going to hit the fan. With a little luck, Nassar would be killed in an attack by South Sudanese rebels who had nothing to do with Mitch Rapp or ISIS. After that, Claudia could focus on putting together enough intel to clear his name and to strong-arm King Faisal into excising any remaining conspirators from his country.

Then again, maybe it wouldn't be that easy.

His phone vibrated and he inserted an earpiece.

"Mitch, are you there?" Claudia's voice.

"Yeah."

"I managed to detour Wilson's motorcade once, but that was all. They're two minutes out. What's your situation?"

"I'm in the church."

"Do you have time to get out?"

"I'm staying," he said, starting to climb a ladder into the balcony. "I've got good position here."

"And Kent?" Her tone suggested that she thought he might be dead.

"On his way to relieve Donatella."

"I don't need that boy's help," Donatella chimed in.

"Don't argue. Just give him the rifle," Rapp said.

Azarov's voice came on. "I have eyes on three cars approaching the front gate. Moving fast. I can't see inside them, though."

"Donatella?" Rapp said, moving to a partially intact stained glass window and peering through one of the clear panels. The sun was coming up, casting the city in a deep-orange glow. "What have you got?"

"I can't see in the cars, either, but we have a lot of activity from Abdo's sentries, and the civilians in the street are all running for cover."

Rapp spotted the approaching vehicles in the dawn light. They skidded to a stop at the front gate, and four men got out of the lead car, fanning out as one of them went to work with a set of bolt cutters.

"I've taken over Donatella's position," Kent said. "Ready to rock."

The gate was pushed open and the remaining passengers stepped out as the cars eased inside. To Rapp's practiced eye, a few looked extremely well trained, but the others were a mess. Not what he'd expect from a team assembled from Saudi spec ops. Further, there were two men who looked like locals.

"Give me a sitrep on Abdo's men," Rapp said.

"They're in the process of surrounding the building, staying out of sight," Azarov responded.

Rapp pulled out his Glock and checked it. He wasn't sure if any of this was going to work but, at the very least, it was going to be interesting.

CHAPTER 48

JOEL Wilson leaned forward between the SUV's seats, scanning through the windshield. The sunrise was still just a weak glow on the horizon, but it provided enough illumination for him to watch his men spread out in the courtyard. A few seconds later they had breached the peeling front doors and disappeared inside the church.

What they would find was a complete unknown. He had no assets in Juba and there had been no time for meaningful reconnaissance. In a city full of war-weary and suspicious Sudanese, the presence of an advance team would have been reported throughout the region in a matter of hours. There had been no choice but to roll into town like a hurricane in an effort to stay ahead of the informants that Rapp undoubtedly had on the payroll.

His fingers gripped the seats as he anticipated the telltale bursts of automatic fire followed by the individual volleys of Rapp's pistol. The clock in his head ticked steadily, each movement of the imaginary second hand reducing his hopes further. Finally a heavily accented voice came over his earpiece. "The building is clear."

"Fuck!" Wilson said, throwing himself back in the seat.

"We go in?" his driver asked.

"Of course we go in, idiot! Now, move!"

They accelerated through the gate and Wilson got out into the rising heat of the morning. Where the fuck was that CIA son of a bitch? Gone to murder more innocent Saudis? Or had he been tipped off? And if it was the latter, who was responsible? Someone at the local airport? Someone back in Washington? One of Wilson's own men? He knew little about them other than the fact that they had Nassar's confidence.

As impressive as the Saudi intelligence chief was, moving this quickly and joining forces with locals was always dangerous. Loyalties in this part of the world were bought and sold almost hourly.

Wilson jogged inside and pushed the doors closed behind him. "Cover all the entrances and get men up into the balcony. I also want men on the outside wall spotting in every direction. If Rapp doesn't know we're here, he might be stupid enough to walk into a trap. And if he does know we're here, he might be stupid enough to attack."

"Understood," came the response over his earpiece, although no one seemed to be moving.

The sunlight coming through the building's cracks was sufficient to illuminate the interior, but there wasn't much to see. Rotting pews strewn across the floor, the remains of an altar, and piles of debris created by the structure's slow collapse.

"Sir!" a man near the center called. "Here!"

Wilson ran to him and looked down at what he had found—a doused campfire. He crouched and held out a hand, feeling a jolt of excitement at the heat still emanating from it. The fire had recently been put out, explaining the water on the floor. But why was the pew next to it so wet? He ran a hand over the top and then did the same underneath. It came back stained with blood.

He bolted to his feet and drew his gun for the first time in his career. "We've had recent activity in here. Talk to me. What are we seeing from the walls?"

"Be calm," came the response from Nassar's lead man. "We have no—"

His condescending response was drowned out by the shouts of two men standing next to a pile of debris in the northeast corner of the building. Wilson started in their direction but then stopped short when he saw the bodies. One still had the cord that had killed him wrapped around his neck. The other was far more gruesome. A machete had nearly cut his head in half and the handle was still jutting from the bridge of his nose.

Wilson stumbled back a few steps, suddenly very aware that he wasn't a combat operative. He was an investigator with a talent for office politics. Beginning to panic, he started toward the main door. "Pull back. Bring whatever evidence you've found, but I want everyone back in the vehicles in one minute. We're—"

A voice speaking rapid-fire Arabic came over the comm, followed by a response from Nassar's commander, who no longer sounded so cocksure.

"What is it?" Wilson said. "What's going on?"

Two men ran past him and out the door while another climbed into the balcony and took up a position near a broken window.

The voices in his earpiece became increasingly desperate and he found himself frozen. "What's happening?" he screamed into the microphone on his headset. No one bothered to respond.

Rapp remained completely still, using only his eyes to track the men running along the west side of the church. He was sitting on a beam jutting thirty feet above the side courtyard. There was significant damage to this section of roof and he blended perfectly into the visual chaos.

Shouting was audible through the plastic sheet that kept rain from penetrating to the building's interior. Mostly Arabic, but also an unintelligible African dialect and a panicked American voice that undoubtedly belonged to Joel Wilson.

According to Black and Azarov, the cars that made up Wilson's motorcade were now empty and Nassar hadn't appeared. The Saudi intelligence chief continued to prove that he was in no way stupid. While Wilson was blind to anything but revenge and transforming himself into the great American savior, Nassar apparently had no such delusions. Despite the fact that his life was very much hanging in the balance, he could still see clearly enough to be suspicious of the information on Claudia's computer. Hats off to the terrorist son of a bitch.

"Here we go," Black said over the comm. "Two pickups coming in hot. Most of Abdo's spotters seem to be backing off, so the main force is going to be the men in those vehicles."

"How many?" Rapp asked, dangling his feet over the edge of the roof to loosen his stiff right knee.

"Moving too fast to get an exact head count. You know the drill, though. Small trucks packed to the point that they're damn near dragging the ground."

"Copy that," Rapp said.

"They're moving out of my line of sight," Black said. "Grisha? Are you picking them up?"

"Yes. I'd estimate twenty-three men, including the drivers. Assault rifles, mostly AKs. The front vehicle is swerving a bit. It doesn't look like a mechanical problem. I'd guess that the driver's impaired either by alcohol or drugs. ETA to the gate is fifteen seconds and they aren't slowing down. It conceivable that they're going to try to ram the doors."

"What? No plate numbers?" Black said.

"They didn't seem relevant," Azarov responded, not picking up on the sarcasm.

"Mitch," Donatella said. "I have eyes on you from the southwest. There's no one in the courtyard below you. Can you climb down and get out the back? Kent can give you cover."

"I might take you up on that, Donatella. But not quite yet."

Joel Wilson heard the growing roar of an engine outside but couldn't work out what that meant until a pickup crashed through the church's front entrance. The doors were flung across the floor along with most of the men who had been riding in the bed. The FBI man froze, looking at the African soldiers strewn out in front of him. Some were dazed, some were getting to their feet, and others were either dead or unconscious. Had their brakes failed, or had they come through the doors on purpose? Who would do such a thing?

Successive bursts of automatic fire pulled him from his stupor, and he sprinted toward the back of the building, diving behind an overturned pew along the west wall. From around the side, he saw a second pickup come through the hole made by the first. The men in the back jumped out and began running in every direction, spraying rounds haphazardly in the general direction of Nassar's men.

Wilson drew back farther behind the pew, unwilling to fire his weapon out of fear that it would give away his position. Who were these men? Had Rapp hired them? He'd referred to himself as "we" in the emails. Was this his team? A group of suicidal African mercenaries? Would a man famous for his precision—someone who almost always killed with a single shot to the head—work with people like this?

He dropped onto his back and peered out from beneath the bench. At least for now, Nassar's men seemed to have the tactical advantage. They'd taken cover at strategic points around the church and were firing controlled bursts, in contrast to their attackers, who were shooting wildly from a run. Would it be enough of an advantage? They were outnumbered and there was no way to know if this was the entire opposing force. There could be hundreds of similar soldiers closing in from the courtyard. The image of the man with the machete in his head flashed through his mind and he fumbled for his satellite phone, dialing a private number the Saudi intelligence chief had given him.

It rang a few times before Nassar came on. Wilson was halfway through a babbling plea for backup when the phone beeped and a woman's voice asked him to leave a message.

CHAPTER 49

RAPP continued to work his right knee, swinging his leg out over the courtyard as the battle raged on inside the church. He heard a scream behind him and glanced back in time to see one of Wilson's men stagger into the plastic covering a hole in the roof. He slid down it, leaving a streak that glowed crimson in the dawn light.

"Mitch," Kent Black said over his earpiece. "Are you just going to sit there all day? Can I have some coffee delivered?"

"Napoleon said, 'When your enemy is doing something stupid, don't interfere.'"

"I think the attribution is apocryphal," Azarov commented.

"The point's valid, though."

"Agreed."

The frequency of gunfire had leveled out and was now declining, indicating that the running battle inside had turned into a skirmish between forces with cover. Unfortunately, it wouldn't turn into a war of attrition. Abdo probably already had reinforcements on the way.

Nassar wasn't there, so Rapp had resigned himself to the fact that his carefully laid trap was a bust. In light of that, did he care what happened in that church? It wasn't his nature to walk away from fights, but what was there to gain from going in there? He could kill Wilson and a few of Nassar's men, but it seemed that Abdo had that well in hand. The only thing he could accomplish was to be seen or, worse, have someone snap a cell phone picture of him.

He missed the involvement of Irene Kennedy even more than he'd thought he would. The role of strategist was unsatisfying as hell.

"Kent, is there a way I can get off of here from the outside?"

"Not unless you're Spider-Man. The walls are dead smooth and I wouldn't trust any of that roof structure."

"Copy," Rapp said, feeling strangely relieved for an excuse not to slink out of there like the criminal he supposed he now was. "Looks like I'm going to have to go out the way I came in. Grisha, can you reposition so you can cover that line of retreat?"

"Affirmative. Two and a half minutes."

"Two and a half minutes," Rapp repeated, setting the timer on his watch. "Do it. I'm going in."

He drew his weapon and slipped through the blood-smeared plastic. Only one of Nassar's men had managed to set up in the balcony, and a series of bullets had stitched their way up through the floor, killing him. He was lying at the edge with his rifle hanging partially over it.

Rapp plucked the weapon from his lifeless hands and lay down on top of him. The fact that none of the rounds had come through the man's back suggested he would provide sufficient protection.

Below, it looked like a bomb had gone off. Men were strewn across the floor, some taken out by gunfire and others by the impact of the pickup when it had crashed through the doors. Two of Nassar's men were still alive and shooting from cover near the altar. Abdo's force was down to three—two hugging the west wall and one just out of sight beneath the balcony overhang. Rapp scanned for a sign of Wilson but couldn't see any.

"Has anyone come out?" he said into his radio.

All responses came back negative.

Could the FBI man be holed up in Black's office? It seemed unlikely. There was a door leading to the outside, and if he knew Joel Wilson, he would have taken the opportunity to escape.

Rapp's questions were answered a moment later when the man beneath the balcony broke cover and ran for the east wall. Nassar's remaining shooters were too busy with the other two to worry about him, but a familiar white face popped up from behind a pew near the back wall and fired a few rounds that didn't get within twenty feet.

Abdo's man threw himself to the ground and began crawling toward Wilson. Rapp watched for a few seconds but then reluctantly reached for his silencer.

"Mitch," Black said over the radio. "The spotters I can see are starting to move away."

"I'm seeing something similar," Azarov said.

"Me too," Donatella confirmed.

"Copy," Rapp said, screwing on his suppressor.

If he were an optimist, he'd think that they'd had enough and were retreating. It was much more likely, though, that Abdo had a secondary force moving in and that they were pulling back to join it. As much as he would have liked to wait until a few more of the people below had killed one another, there was no more time.

Rapp fired a carefully aimed round into the head of the man crawling toward Wilson, followed by a round to the ribs of one of the men along the east wall. Nassar's shooters saw him go down, and one broke cover, going for position on Abdo's last surviving man. The African guerrilla saw him and fired, taking him out before being cut down himself. Then everything went still.

"Joel!" Rapp shouted. "You still alive back there?"

"What? Who is that?"

"It's Mitch."

The FBI man didn't respond immediately. Finally, "What are your intentions?"

It was a good question. The CIA assassin Mitch Rapp would kill him and Nassar's last man, then leave Irene Kennedy to clean up the mess. The question now was: What would Mitch Rapp the international fugitive do?

"Now that I've saved your ass, I'm surrendering," he called. "I want to go back to the U.S. so I can clear my name."

"Mitch," Claudia said over his earpiece. "What are you doing? He isn't—"

"What do you say, Joel?" Rapp said, cutting her off. It was time to show Wilson whom he was working for. It was a long shot, but maybe the FBI man could be useful.

"Why should I believe you?"

"Because I've got the high ground. If I wanted you and your last man dead, we wouldn't be having this conversation."

A few more seconds passed before Wilson rose slowly into view. He motioned for his man to do the same and, surprisingly, he obeyed.

Rapp slid his weapon down the back of his pants and stood, walking deliberately toward the edge of the balcony. "Does your friend speak English?"

"Yes," the man answered for himself.

"Then you understand not to shoot. That I'm surrendering."

"I understand."

"What the fuck are you doing?" Black said, sharing Claudia's confusion. "Blast those assholes into the next time zone and let's get the hell out of here."

It probably wasn't bad advice, but Rapp ignored it. He was curious about what would happen. While he was confident that Wilson really did want to march him in front of the cameras in chains, Nassar would be far less excited about the prospect of a bunch of congressional hearings.

Rapp inched into view, ignoring Wilson, who was aiming at him with a shaking hand, and instead focusing on Nassar's man. His accent and mediocre performance during the fight suggested that he wasn't one of the Saudi General Intelligence Directorate's crack operatives. And if that was the case, who was he?

"Okay, everybody, take it easy. I'm coming down."

Nassar's man sighted over an AK-47 as Rapp moved toward the ladder. The distance between them was about thirty yards, and that, combined with the angle, would make a clean shot difficult. The Arab looked smart enough to wait, but for how long? Would he take the doable but difficult shot at Rapp when he started down the ladder? Or would he risk letting the CIA man get close enough for a sure thing?

Those questions were answered when Rapp reached for the first rung. The man's stance suddenly stabilized, and he pulled the butt of his assault rifle more firmly into his shoulder. Rapp jerked back just as a short burst chewed through the ladder an inch from his hand.

"Cease fire!" Wilson shrieked, as Rapp dropped to the floor. "Cease fi—"

The sound of the rifle changed subtly as the shooter adjusted his aim and squeezed off another burst. Rapp rolled to absorb his impact with the floor and rose to one knee in time to see Wilson throw himself over a pew. Impacts from successive rounds pounded the wood for a few seconds before Nassar's man began swinging his weapon back in Rapp's direction.

The CIA man's position wasn't ideal, and it took more time than it should have to line up. The shooter was backing away as he fired, going for the cover of the altar. Rapp squeezed off a round and hit him in the stomach, causing him to lose control of his rifle. The barrel rose and rounds started punching holes in the roof as Rapp sprinted across the floor, grabbing the weapon and taking the wounded man's legs out from under him. He tossed the AK and used a foot to pin the Arab to the ground, ignoring the fact that Wilson was approaching with his pistol held out in front of him.

"I told him not to shoot," the FBI man stammered. "And then he . . . he tried to kill me."

Rapp grabbed the injured Arab by the collar and began dragging him toward what was left of the church's front entrance. "Do you have a phone with a camera, Joel?"

"A phone," he mumbled. "Yeah. I have one. But I—"

"Get pictures of all of Nassar's men. Do it now."

The careful recording of crime scenes was very much in the FBI man's wheelhouse, and the task seemed to revive him. He moved hesitantly at first but gained confidence as he flipped the bodies and lined his lens up with their faces.

"Change of plans. I'm coming out the front," Rapp said into his radio. "Wilson will be following. Don't shoot either of us."

Black, who had line of sight on the front courtyard, acknowledged.

"Where are you going?" Wilson said, running up behind him. "What just happened? Who attacked us? Were they your people?"

Rapp dropped the wounded man behind one of the vehicles in Wilson's motorcade and popped the trunk.

"You're under arrest," the FBI man said in a voice that was completely devoid of conviction. He didn't seem to be able to think of anything else to say.

The injured man managed to find the strength to swear in Arabic as Rapp lifted him into the trunk. It was a tight fit and he had to slam the lid a few times to get it to latch.

"You have a shooter moving toward you from the rear courtyard," Azarov said over his earpiece. "He appears to be one of Abdo's men."

"Can you handle it?"

"I should have a shot in a few seconds."

"Mitch," Wilson said, once again aiming his service pistol. "Did you hear me? You're under—"

Azarov's rifle sounded and Wilson dropped to the ground. "Shit! Someone's shooting at us!"

Rapp slid into the vehicle's driver's seat, leaned out the window, and looked down at the man lying in the dirt. "Get in the car, Joel."

Wilson thought about it for less than a second before jumping to his feet and scrambling for the passenger door.

CHAPTER 50

MALIK! Respond!"
But there was only silence where moments before desperate shouts and gunfire had reigned.

Aali Nassar removed his headset and stared blankly across his desk. He'd considered the possibility that this was a trap and for that reason had not accompanied Wilson to South Sudan. Even in his own mind, though, his return to Riyadh had been cautious to the point of paranoia. The idea that someone like Rapp would be capable of backdating emails and mining them with a series of innocuous clues that, in their entirety, were just barely enough for Wilson to find that warehouse . . . It was unthinkable.

Despite the air-conditioning, Nassar could feel the sweat beginning to run down his forehead. One thing was certain. Four of his most loyal men were dead. Worse, so were the men supplied by Sayid Halabi. Men like Malik. Could they be identified and traced to him? What about the Africans the mullah had provided? Finally, what if they weren't in fact all dead? What if some were in a condition that would allow interrogation?

His hand hesitated for a moment over his phone and then he picked it up, dialing his assistant.

"Yes, Director. What can I do for you?"

"I need you to contact Jean-Paul Jayyusi."

"Sir? Are you—"

"Just do it!" Nassar said. "Have him call me on this line."

His man's reluctance wasn't surprising. Jayyusi was the head of the loosely defined South Sudanese intelligence apparatus and a man who was best avoided at all costs. Until the recent formation of his country, he had been nothing more than a sadistic criminal with a gift for gathering and brokering sensitive information. Since then, little had changed. He had loyalty to no one and nothing beyond feeding his own insatiable desire for wealth, power, and women.

Nassar waited for almost half an hour in unbearable silence before his phone rang. Jayyusi couldn't be trusted and there was no question that the details of their conversation would be up for sale before it had even ended. But what choice did he have? If he accepted that a thug like Mitch Rapp couldn't have planned a trap this clever, then he had to consider the possibility that Irene Kennedy was involved. And if that was the case, the game he was playing was far more dangerous than he could have ever dreamed. He couldn't afford to leave any information on the table, even if it meant hinting at the true nature of his involvement.

"General Jayyusi," he said, putting the phone to his ear. "I appreciate you getting back to me so quickly."

"It's not every day that I receive a call from someone of your stature and your"—his voice faded for a moment as he searched for the right word—"resources."

Normally political pleasantries would be exchanged, but Nassar had no interest in speaking to this man any longer than necessary. They both understood their roles in this transaction and there was no point in pretending otherwise.

"I'm interested in a gun battle that occurred in Juba today."

"There were many such incidents," the man probed. "Can you be more specific?"

"It just ended and was centered around a church."

"Ah, the well-armed foreigners. Your people, Aali?"

"I had men attached to the detail, as did the Americans. We were trying to locate a terrorist who has recently murdered a number of prominent Saudi citizens. Information came to light that he might be hiding in South Sudan."

"And you're just calling me now? If you told me sooner, I could have helped you."

More likely the man would have played both sides, charging an outrageous sum to support Nassar's men while selling information of their arrival to anyone interested.

"We had to move quickly," Nassar said. "My apologies."

There was a lengthy silence before Jayyusi spoke again. "Neither of us has any interest in wasting valuable time, so let me be direct. I have information and you have money. Am I mistaken, or is an exchange desirable?"

"It is."

"One million U.S. dollars."

"We both know that's an unconscionable sum."

"Indeed. And my information isn't even that good.

But you brought a team into my country and created a deadly confrontation in the middle of my capital city. Under the circumstances, and considering the obscene wealth that your country holds, I see this as a fair price."

"Do you have account information for the wire?"

"Those details can be handled by our people at a later time. I have no reason to believe that you're not a man of your word."

"Then we have an agreement. What do you know about what happened in Juba?"

"The church was the headquarters of an American arms dealer."

"Name?"

"Jason Blaze. Obviously an alias."

"And do you know his actual identity?"

"No. It was never something that interested me."

Undoubtedly because Blaze was paying him to look the other way. "Please continue."

"Recently a group of white people joined his business. Two men and two women."

"Do you have descriptions?"

The tapping of computer keys was audible over the marginal connection. "The women are both quite attractive and dark-haired. One midthirties, the other perhaps ten years older. The younger of the two appears to be a native French speaker. The men are both athletic in build and around six feet. One is blond and tanned, but probably naturally fair-skinned. Likely Eastern European. The other has nearly black hair, long, with a beard and dark complexion. He speaks English with an American accent and, we think, fluent Arabic. He did something that no one else has been able to—he killed a local rebel leader named NaNomi. Apparently by driving a knife through his skull."

Nassar nodded to himself. Mitch Rapp. And it could be assumed with reasonable confidence that the young Frenchwoman was Claudia Dufort. But who were the others?

"After that incident, they were forced to run," Jay-yusi continued. "The rebel group sent scouts to watch the church in case they returned."

Nassar felt some of the tension in his shoulders easing. Jayyusi's information was proving to be worth its exorbitant price. The Rapp it portrayed was the one that Nassar was familiar with. A violent man who had been unable to control himself when confronted with a meaningless African guerrilla, thus forcing his team to flee an ideal base of operations.

"So my men—" Nassar began, but Jayyusi anticipated his question.

"Walked into an ambush meant for Blaze and his associates."

Nassar turned the man's words over in his head for a few moments. "Were there any survivors?"

"One of the cars your men arrived in was seen leaving the scene, but we have no information as to who was inside."

A rebel fleeing the battle? One of Nassar's own men? None had contacted him yet, but it was possible that they just hadn't had the opportunity.

"Was there a white man among the dead, General? An FBI agent named Wilson was in command."

"I don't have those kinds of details yet. My people are just now moving in."

"And you'll provide me with that information as soon as you have it?"

"Of course."

"Then I have only one last question for you, General. Do you know where Blaze and his people went?"

"I'm afraid that I don't have the ability to share that information with you, Aali."

It was a strangely constructed response. "Is that because you don't know or because our financial transaction isn't satisfactory?"

"Neither. It's because of what Blaze's new associate did to NaNomi. I see no profit in making an enemy of him."

CHAPTER 51

THE city of Juba was thirty miles in the rear-view mirror, and Joel Wilson still hadn't spoken. Rapp glanced over and saw him staring through the windshield in a state that bordered on catatonia. Was it feasible that he was reevaluating the things he'd done? Could he actually be facing the fact that, after being duped by the Pakistanis, he'd just fallen into an identical trap set by the Saudis?

Rapp was still fifty-fifty on leaving the man's body in the desert, but his enthusiasm for the idea was waning. The risks of counting on Wilson to pull his head out of his ass were astronomical, but the benefits might be, too. This kind of complex plotting was Irene Kennedy's sphere of influence and he'd never seen any reason to get involved. With her out of the picture, though, a hammer couldn't be the only tool in his box.

There was a poorly defined dirt track to his right and he took it, climbing a steep slope out of the scrub and into the trees. The change in scenery broke Wilson from his trance.

"Where . . . where are you taking me?"

"Relax, Joel. I need to talk to the asshole in the trunk before he bleeds out. Is there anything you can tell me about him?"

Wilson nodded. "His name is Malik. One of Nassar's men."

The road petered out in a small clearing surrounded by dense vegetation. Rapp stopped in the middle, stepping out and going around to the trunk. Any concerns he had that the man was dead from blood loss or heatstroke were put to rest before the trunk lid was even fully open. Malik swung a car jack at him with a piercing shout, missing by at least a foot.

Rapp didn't bother to disarm the man, instead grabbing him by the hair and dragging him out into the dirt. The terrorist took another swing, but it passed harmlessly in front of Rapp's shins.

"Get a photo."

Wilson retrieved his phone and snapped a shot of the man's face.

"Can you record audio on that thing?"

"Sure."

"Then do it," Rapp said, turning his attention to the man trying unsuccessfully to push himself to his feet. He'd been bleeding for a good forty-five minutes now and wouldn't last much longer.

"Who are you?"

Malik spit a mouthful of blood in Rapp's direction, answering in Arabic. "I don't have to tell you anything."

"Interesting accent," Rapp replied. "Not Saudi Arabia. Iraq?"

He didn't answer.

Rapp looked over at Wilson. "You try."

"I don't think he's going—"

"Don't make me tell you again, Joel."

The FBI man took a hesitant step back in the face of Rapp's sudden anger, but complied.

"Where are you from? Are you Iraqi?"

The man spit another crimson glob but didn't otherwise respond. Out of the corner of his eye, Rapp spotted movement at the edge of the clearing and brought his hand closer to his Glock.

"We want to get you medical attention," Wilson said. "But in return we need information."

"Fuck you!"

Rapp continued scanning the tree line but, rather than spotting the camouflage of a local rebel, he saw flashes of reddish-brown and black fur. Not as bad as a contingent of Abdo's men, but better to move things along. The scent of the dying man's blood was obviously carrying on the wind.

Rapp shoved Wilson out of the way and stepped down on the bullet hole in Malik's stomach. The man screamed in pain and grabbed Rapp's ankle, futilely trying to escape.

"You have to answer!" Rapp shouted down at him. "You work for him."

"I work only for the glory of Allah."

"I saw you!" Rapp said, grinding his heel into the wound. "You betrayed your god. Why are you working for this man? Why are you working for the FBI? Are you a Christian?"

His expression of agony was replaced by one of horror at the suggestion.

"Or was it just money? Did you sell out your god for a few American dollars? That's it, isn't it? You're just a whore."

Now the Arab was backed into a theological corner. He knew that his time on this earth could be measured in minutes. Would he meet Allah having not defended his faith?

"My allegiance is to Mullah Halabi! God's representative on earth!"

Wilson stared down at him, stunned by the revelation.

"Don't lie to me," Rapp said, rewarding the man's response with a slight reduction in the pressure on his stomach. "Nassar hates ISIS. It's a threat to the Saudi royalty."

"You're a fool. The royalty have become tools of the West. They aren't true followers of Islam."

"That may be true, but they *are* Nassar's power base," Rapp said, easing his foot back a bit more. "And that son of a bitch loves his power."

"The weaker we look in Saudi Arabia, the more complacent Faisal becomes. The old fool thinks we've stopped our propaganda campaign because of the Intelligence Directorate."

Rapp loved these ISIS pricks. It was a serious pain in the ass to get the al Qaeda guys to talk, but their dumber, crazier cousins would run their mouths all day if you let them.

Nassar, on the other hand, was neither dumb nor crazy. Teaming up with Halabi to tamp down ISIS propaganda in Saudi Arabia was a cunning move. The fact that Faisal had one foot in the grave made him willing to delegate to anyone who looked like they could hold the kingdom together. As he became weaker, Nassar became stronger. With the help of Halabi and his millions of Saudi sympathizers, the king's death could set the stage for a coup. The royal family would be chased into exile, leaving their massive financial and military resources in the hands of radicals.

Wilson licked nervously at his lips, the realization that he'd been working for ISIS finally starting to sink in. The decision not to leave him for the scavengers might work out after all.

Rapp stepped over Malik and slid back into the car. Movement at the edge of the clearing was becoming less hesitant, and a few dark-ringed eyes were starting to appear.

Not sure what was happening, Wilson ran around the other side only to find the door locked. He dove through the window when Rapp began pulling away, getting stuck halfway in. "Stop! You can't leave m—"

Rapp grabbed him by the back of the head and slammed his face into the console between the seats. The padding made the act a bit unsatisfying, so he repeated it a few more times before shoving Wilson back through the window. The FBI man fell into the dirt, dazed and bleeding badly from his nose.

"There aren't a lot of second chances in life," Rapp said, leaning across the passenger seat. "Do the right thing, Joel. Or I'll be coming for you."

He turned the car and was about to floor the accelerator, but instead paused to point toward Malik and the pack of wild dogs he was desperately trying to crawl away from. "And you might want to consider running."

CHAPTER 52

THINK you're completely insane."

"I know," Rapp said.

Claudia was sitting on the edge of the bed, wearing exactly the expression he'd expected. She hadn't really been a citizen of any particular country since she was a child. Her life had been about moving around the world in search of jobs or to stay ahead of whoever was chasing.

His history was different. Sure, he'd originally joined the CIA out of anger and hate, but those emotions had been replaced over the years by a sense of duty. At the end of the day he believed in what he did. He believed in America and the idea that everyone had a right to life, liberty, and the pursuit of happiness. Where Jefferson had gone wrong was in thinking that those rights were inalienable. In truth, they had to be fought for every hour of every day.

Claudia motioned with her head in the general direction of the door. "As your logistics person, I feel like I have to point out that when the team you built is gone, your only ally other than me is Joel Wilson.

A man who spends his nights dreaming about how to destroy you."

"Uh-huh," he said, leaning back against the wall.

"I can make us disappear, Mitch. We can get Anna and fade away. The only person who would have a chance at finding us would be Irene, and she wouldn't be looking. Even if some other intelligence agency got lucky, what would they do? Any of the people they'd send probably owe you their lives. And the three or so private contractors good enough to take the job are also smart enough not to."

"What about what's happening in Saudi Arabia?"

"What about it?" she said in an exasperated tone. "They brought this on themselves. If Nassar and ISIS want it, let them have it."

He wasn't surprised that she'd see it that way, but the truth was far more complicated. While it was a fact that this was a wound the royalty had inflicted on themselves, it was the average person who would suffer. What would happen to *them* when ISIS rolled across the Middle East? He didn't have to ask because he'd seen it with his own eyes. And what about America's soldiers, who would be sent when the U.S. could no longer stand by and watch the horrors that would be created by a Saudi-ISIS alliance? How many of *them* would bleed out in the sand?

"I can't just let this go, Claudia."

"Then I'm going to ask you again to call Irene."

He shook his head. "I can't drag her into this. She has to make that decision on her own. We'll wait and see what Joel does."

She snatched up a throw pillow and flung it at him, missing his right ear by less than an inch. "Joel Wilson is probably in Aali Nassar's office right now, plotting how to find you! Or he's in Washington telling Senator Ferris that you murdered his entire team!"

"Maybe."

"Stop being so calm!" When she reached for the alarm clock he moved in. She had a pretty good arm, and the heavy plastic looked like it could do some damage.

She resisted for a moment when he wrapped his arms around her, but then rested her head on his chest. "I haven't had much of a life, Mitch. Except for Anna, I wish I could forget everything that happened before I met you. But now . . ." Her voice trailed off for a moment. "You're the best at what you do. But even you can't survive with the whole world against you."

Rapp stepped out onto the safari camp's terrace to find the rest of his team waiting. Donatella had retreated to the shade of a flowering arbor and Kent Black was tanning in a lounge chair next to a pyramid of empty beer cans. Predictably, Azarov was sitting with his back to the building, sipping sparkling water.

"All of you have lived up to your reputations," he began as Claudia took a seat. "And I want to thank you for everything you've done."

"What's next?" Black asked, slurring a bit.

"There is no next. You've already stayed on a hell of a lot longer than I had a right to expect."

"What about that towelhead who's trying to frame you, Mitch? I thought we were going to pop him."

"It'd be better for all of you if I handled that myself."

"So you're releasing us?" Donatella said.

"Yeah. And that brings us to the subject of payment. After expenses, Orion Consulting still has bank balances of . . ." He looked over at Claudia.

"Just over fifty million U.S. dollars."

"Okay. Fifty million. Grisha, I know you got your cash up front, but do you want a cut?"

The Russian shook his head.

"Then Claudia and I are going to keep ten to finish what we have to do. That leaves forty. Split between Kent and Donatella, that's twenty each."

Black's head rolled forward off his lounge chair. "What? Did you just say that you're going to transfer twenty million dollars into my account?"

"Yeah. And you're free to start contracting again. Or you can sit on a beach for the rest of your life. Just stay out of my way."

"Not a problem," he said, getting up and making rounds, shaking everyone's hand. When he got to Rapp, he just backed away cautiously. "It's been real, man."

Rapp waited for him to disappear around the corner before he spoke again. "Donatella. I don't have a lot of pull at the CIA right now, but it doesn't matter. Claudia's as good as anyone at this. It'll take a couple of months, but she'll put a clean identity together for you and get you set up in New York. Obviously you're going to have to get some work done to your face."

"I have someone in Buenos Aires."

"No contracts, no fashion industry, and no Italy," Rapp reminded her.

She nodded. "I assume we won't meet again in this lifetime?"

"Not unless something goes very wrong."

She glided up to him and gave him a lingering kiss on the mouth. "If you ever need someone to watch your ass again, don't hesitate to call."

Stepping back, she looked at the others. "It's been a pleasure working with all of you. Claudia, I'll send you my contact information when I get to Argentina."

"I'll look forward to it. And while you're there, ask them if there's something they can do about your nose."

Rapp tensed but, to his surprise, Donatella grinned and the two women hugged before she wandered off.

The sound of Kent Black's motorcycle speeding away reached Rapp just as he turned to the last man left on the terrace. "I assume you want something more than the dollar I paid you in Costa Rica."

Azarov set down his drink and stood. "It'll probably turn out to be nothing."

"But?"

"Should any of the enemies I made in Russia ever decide to come back into my life, I might need help."

"I'll be there."

He nodded respectfully and then walked over to Claudia. She looked a little nervous when he kissed her hand, but the naked fear that was so obvious at their first meeting had faded.

When Azarov was gone, she turned toward Rapp. "Just the two of us."

He popped the top off one of the unopened beers Black had left. "Yeah. Just the two of us."

CHAPTER 53

IRENE Kennedy glanced over her reading glasses as her office door opened and her executive assistant slipped through.

"I know you asked not to be disturbed . . ."

"Is everything all right, Jamie?"

"I'm honestly not sure how to answer that question. Joel Wilson is here to see you again."

"I'm sorry. Did you say Joel Wilson?"

"Yes, ma'am."

The FBI agent had been last seen in Juba, where he and his team were ambushed. Intelligence was still piecemeal, but the best information circulating was that it was a case of mistaken identity. A local rebel leader thought Wilson and his people were a group of arms dealers led by someone called Jason Blaze.

She, however, knew a bit more. Blaze was really a former Army Ranger who answered to the name Kent Black. Further, she had a description of his associates that bore an uncanny resemblance to Mitch Rapp, Claudia Dufort, Donatella Rahn, and Grisha Azarov.

In all likelihood, Rapp and Claudia had led Wilson

into a trap—the goal of which was to kill Aali Nassar without their direct involvement. Unfortunately, Nassar wasn't there. A tragedy, really. Not only was he a man who very much needed killing, but she hated to see such a beautifully conceived plan go wrong.

"Irene? Should I send him in?"

"Absolutely," Kennedy said. She'd been working under the assumption that Wilson was dead. And in her experience conversations with dead men tended to be extremely illuminating.

She stood but didn't immediately come out from behind her desk when Wilson appeared in the doorway. He was normally put together with a sterile meticulousness that very much embodied who he was. The hesitant gait, filthy clothing, and blackened eyes of the man entering her office were completely unfamiliar.

"Dr. Kennedy. Thank you for meeting with me without an appointment." He offered his hand but then seemed to realize how grimy it was and withdrew it.

"Are you all right, Joel? Should I call a medical team?"

He shook his head and she pointed him to a seating area at the corner of her office. He sat and she handed him a bottle of water before taking a position across from him.

"My understanding is that you and Director Nassar's men were attacked in South Sudan. Could you tell me what happened?"

"We tracked Rapp there through some emails he sent to Claudia Dufort. I don't know who attacked us. But it wasn't him."

She was intrigued. Historically, Wilson blamed

Mitch for everything bad that happened to him. "How do you know that?"

"Because he saved my life. One of Nassar's men— who wasn't really one of *his* men—tried to kill Mitch. When I yelled at him to cease fire, he turned on me. If Mitch hadn't shot him, I'd be dead."

"Joel, I want you to slow down. What do you mean it wasn't one of Nassar's men?"

"We questioned him. I think he was ISIS. But I don't know if that means he infiltrated Saudi intelligence or if Nassar knew the whole time."

He pulled a phone from his pocket and almost dropped it trying to place it on the coffee table between them. She'd seen this before in her career. The man was broken. He'd spent his entire life as a narcissist who believed that he was always right—always on the side of the virtuous. Now reality had imploded that self-image. Most people in his condition never recovered from the cognitive dissonance. A rare few managed to absorb their new position in the universe and adapt. Which category did Joel Wilson fall into?

"There are pictures on there of all of Nassar's men and a recording of our interrogation of the one who survived."

She picked up the phone and began flipping through the photos as he continued.

"Nassar was playing me. The more I think about it, the clearer it becomes. He was counting on my hatred of Mitch to blind me to everything else that was happening. And he was right."

Kennedy set the phone down and appraised the man. His head was hanging loosely on his shoulders with a blank stare focused on the carpet.

"In this business, it happens to us all eventually, Joel. The question is what you do about it."

"I want to help," he said without hesitation. "I want to find out if Nassar is connected with ISIS. And if he is, I want to take him down."

It was an interesting offer. Even more interesting, though, was whether it was an offer that Mitch Rapp had anticipated. Had he consciously forgone killing Wilson at the risk of allowing the FBI man to continue his vendetta? It was a level of restraint and strategic thinking that she wouldn't have necessarily attributed to her old friend.

There was no question that Wilson was a gifted investigator. In some ways it was his weakness. His ability to see the big picture was compromised by his obsession with fine detail. In this case, though, it was those fine details that needed attention. The big picture was her job.

"Is that a sincere offer, Joel?"

He finally met her gaze. "Of course it is."

"Does anyone know you're here?"

"What? Why?"

"Answer the question."

She could see the wheels of his mind turning. He was wondering if she was involved with Rapp and desperate to hide that involvement. More to the point, he was wondering if answering in the negative would end with him buried in Langley's basement.

Finally his body sagged. "No one knows. I came here first. I haven't talked to anyone."

She pressed a button on a phone sitting next to her and her assistant reappeared.

"Jamie, I need to make sure that there's no record

of Agent Wilson leaving Juba or arriving in the U.S. Also, call General Jayyusi in South Sudan. Ask him if he's spoken with Aali Nassar. If so, ask him if it's not too late to have him confirm Agent Wilson's death and to destroy the bodies that were left behind."

Wilson didn't even react to what she was saying. Apparently he'd decided that he deserved whatever fate she had planned for him.

"That's not going to be cheap," Jamie said. "Is there any limit to what I can pay him?"

"No. But I want you to be clear that we're buying an exclusive. If I hear that he's sold any of this information again, I'll be . . ." Her voice faded for a moment as she chose her next words. "Inconsolably disappointed."

"I think he'll understand your meaning. Anything else?"

"That'll do for now."

She disappeared and Wilson watched the door close as though he were in a gas chamber.

"What about Mitch?" she said. "Do you know where he is?"

Wilson shook his head. "He left me a long way outside of Juba. Last time I saw him, he was driving back toward the city."

It seemed clear that Rapp had seen the same thing in Joel Wilson that she did. He could have killed the man with little fear of repercussion. Instead, he'd left him with a phone full of intelligence and the freedom to use it as he pleased.

"What are you going to do with me?" Wilson said, becoming uncomfortable with the silence drawing out between them.

"For now, I think it's in our best interest to let the world think you're dead. Of course, we'll call Director Miller and tell him that's not the case. If it's acceptable to you, I'd also like to ask him to let me use you to lead the effort to identify the men on your phone and their connection to Aali Nassar. I have good intelligence analysts, but what we need here is an investigator."

He just stared at her, stunned.

"You were expecting something else?"

"Yes . . . no. I mean, I'd love to be involved in getting Nassar."

"Then why don't you have one of my assistants send for some clothes for you and show you where the showers are. In the meantime I'll assemble your team."

CHAPTER 54

SAUDI ARABIA

THE basement had been lined with cubicles, and the overhead fixtures were dimmed, causing each workstation to glow with the light of its computer monitor. Ironically the secret to effective intelligence analysis was the sharing of ideas, but in this case that kind of an exchange was impossible. Aali Nassar's goal was neither truth nor accuracy. What he needed now was to conjure an alternate reality so convincing that it persuaded even the analysts who had created it.

As he walked across the room, the people who noticed him stood, some even attempting an awkward salute. He ignored them. They weren't soldiers or the disciplined operatives he'd surrounded himself with since graduating from university. They were the young technology experts who now reigned supreme in the intelligence-gathering field.

Nassar was wary of them, not only because he lacked any real understanding of how they did what they did, but because their talent was always inversely proportional to their faith. For these men, God, country, and authority were meaningless when compared to what they saw in those screens.

The most gifted—and thus least devoted—of the analysts assigned to this detail had been placed along the back wall. He swiveled in his chair when Nassar stopped in the open door of his cubicle but didn't stand as the others had.

"What have you discovered?" Nassar said, ignoring the lack of respect.

"We haven't been able to get confirmation, but our suspicion is that all our men are dead."

"Why no confirmation?"

"The only thing we have to go on is interviews of people who witnessed the battle, and most seem unreliable. Either they were trying to get away from the fighting or they're so war-weary that they didn't pay much attention. We've matched up the different accounts to create the most probable chain of events, but I still can't guarantee accuracy."

"What have you put together?"

"After Abdo's men attacked, it quickly turned into a melee. It was impossible to tell who was shooting at whom and most of the fighting was done inside the church. One car left the scene with an unknown number of passengers, but we don't know where it went and we haven't heard from any of our people. Most likely it was one or more of Abdo's men escaping the fighting and now they're on the run. He has a reputation for punishing cowardice pretty harshly."

"And the bodies of my men?"

"They were burned along with the church."

"The rebels did this?"

"No, sir. It appears to have been done by government troops. We're not certain why. The chain of command in Juba is hard to follow. It might have just been a decision by low-level police."

Nassar nodded. While the fire made it impossible to confirm that all his men were dead, it also made identifying the corpses difficult. In that way, the fire had been a gift. If photos of the men he'd sent had been taken and given to a foreign intelligence agency, they would be quickly identified as not working for the Saudi General Intelligence Directorate. And after that, it was possible that they could be associated with ISIS.

"Do we know if the FBI man Joel Wilson was among the dead?"

"It appears that he was. The local police said that one of the men was white and they took his wallet before the fire started." The young man used his mouse to pull up a photo of Joel Wilson's North Dakota driver's license.

In his peripheral vision Nassar saw his assistant appear and motion him to a conference room along the wall.

"Carry on. I want to be updated immediately with any new information."

"Yes, sir."

"We've finally made direct contact with Abdo," Hamid Safar said as Nassar entered and closed the door.

"And?"

"He confirmed that it was his men who attacked and that they did so because they believed our men were associates of Jason Blaze. He's also agreed to have his people swear that an American fitting Mitch

Rapp's description killed Wilson, though he wants a significant amount of money to do so."

"Pay him what he asks," Nassar said.

While the story wasn't without flaws, no one would expect concrete evidence in that part of the world. All he needed to do was generate enough suspicion to motivate the Americans. Now the murdered man in question wasn't a Saudi national with potential ties to terrorism. It was an American FBI agent doing the president's bidding.

The Americans would have no choice but to dedicate a significant amount of resources to this manhunt. It would also have the effect of frightening any U.S. operatives involved. A Mitch Rapp willing to kill American agents would create a great number of nervous trigger fingers and would likely muffle any criticism if attempts to take him alive failed.

"Contact your counterpart at the FBI, Hamid. Tell them about Rapp's involvement in Wilson's murder and put them in touch with Abdo."

"Understood."

"Has there been any progress in finding Rapp and his people?"

"None. But the Americans trained him and are familiar with his associates, methods, and finances. With improved cooperation from them, he won't stay invisible for long."

Nassar sat at the small conference table and dismissed his assistant with a wave of the hand.

How much had Rapp learned, and did it matter? Everyone who knew of Nassar's involvement was dead—all in a way that would strongly implicate the CIA assassin.

Now Rapp had fled his base in Juba and was on the run. More important, the entire Western world would soon be hunting him. He knew far too much about their clandestine wars to ever be allowed to defend himself in a hearing. Even Irene Kennedy, his stalwart supporter for decades, would be forced to abandon him. She was loyal, but not stupid enough to commit political suicide and potentially end up in prison.

Despite all this, it would be a mistake to underestimate the man. Wounded animals could be extraordinarily dangerous, and Mitch Rapp was no exception. Nassar had already doubled his personal security detail, but now it seemed wise to move to an undisclosed location. Rapp was the most talented assassin of his generation, but he couldn't kill what he couldn't find.

Nassar's phone rang with an immediately recognizable number. As always, he considered rejecting it, but the conference room was soundproof and swept for listening devices daily. There was no better place to have this unavoidable conversation.

"Yes," he said, picking up.

"Is Rapp dead?" Mullah Halabi's tone suggested he already knew the answer to the question.

"No. I—"

"It's my understanding that my men are."

"As are mine," Nassar shot back. He hadn't asked for Halabi's men, and their constant presence was becoming a significant problem. Reminding the mullah of this, though, would be counterproductive. He was a dangerous man and it was clear that he had infiltrated all levels of Saudi Arabia's government.

"Joel Wilson's investigation led him to South Sudan. Rapp was already gone and he was attacked by a local rebel group. The area is in the midst of a civil war, which is undoubtedly why Rapp chose it."

"And yet you survived."

"I was called back to Riyadh."

"Allah must have great plans for you."

"I am his servant."

"Indeed," the ISIS leader said with an obvious lack of conviction.

"This may turn out to be an ideal situation," Nassar started. "We've begun a disinformation campaign that will cause the Americans to believe that Rapp was there and that he killed Wilson. We know—"

"Perhaps death isn't Rapp's immediate destiny, Aali. If he's taken back to America in chains, what havoc might he wreak? Certainly the political enemies of the CIA would line up against him. Would there be public hearings? If so, Rapp might reveal secrets that would shake his godless country to its core."

"Yes, but in that kind of a hearing, my relationship with you would be uncovered."

"And then the king would put you to death. It is a man's greatest hope to have the privilege of being martyred."

The line went dead, and Nassar slammed his phone against the table. It was easy for that cave-dwelling goatherd to speak of the glory of martyrdom. Nassar, however, had no intention of dying or ending up in one of Faisal's dungeons. He had a great many things left to do in this life, and Mitch Rapp was the last great obstacle to accomplishing them.

CHAPTER 55

R EMEMBER when I told you I thought you were insane?" Claudia said, looking through the jet's window at a private airstrip cut into the desert. "Now I'm sure of it."

Rapp was dozing on a sofa near the back of the plane. "It's going to be fine."

"How is it going to be fine?" she said. "Aali Nassar is desperate to see you dead, and now we're flying into his backyard. Do you think King Faisal's going to save you? It doesn't matter what you've done for him and his country in the past, Mitch. He's an old man and Nassar will have poisoned him against you. He's probably personally sharpening the sword they're going to use to behead you."

"Faisal never does anything himself," Rapp said, adjusting into a more comfortable position. "He's probably just overseeing the sharpening."

"Stop trying to deflect."

"Stop worrying so much."

"I'm your logistics coordinator. It's my job."

"And you're good at it."

"Don't patronize me, Mitch. Just don't."

Rapp had hoped his relationship with Claudia would achieve the balance and ease he'd been searching for. She was pragmatic and adaptable, lacking both his late wife's naïveté and Donatella's violent unpredictability. Unfortunately, it seemed that anyone he got close to was eventually sucked into the chaos and darkness that swirled around him.

And it was time to admit that he was making it worse. He just couldn't stop testing her. From the standpoint of logistics, she was virtually flawless—one of the best he'd ever worked with. But he was still concerned with how she dealt with the stress of life-and-death situations and how their relationship would affect her judgment.

Or was that just a copout? Maybe he was testing himself. Hell, maybe he was trying to drive her away. The idea of losing someone again constantly lurked at the back of his mind. Thoughts of his own death didn't concern him all that much, but the idea of another funeral and the emptiness and rage that followed was the one thing that had the power to scare him. On the other hand, one day he'd be forced to look back and assess his life. Was "numbness" the word he'd wanted to use to summarize it?

"Mitch?" she prompted. "You better not have fallen asleep during this conversation."

Once again he was reminded of how much he missed Scott Coleman. The former SEAL would be sitting silently at the front of the plane, cleaning his weapon and waiting for orders.

"I'm awake."

"This is too much of a risk for not enough reward.

If you want to convince someone of your innocence, it should be the Americans. And even then you should let me set up a neutral meeting place. Somewhere with a back door if things go—"

The wheels hit the ground and the engines reversed, causing her to fall silent. Too late.

Rapp rose to his feet and walked toward the cockpit. The pilot was scanning an empty building to the north as he brought the aircraft to a stop. His hand was white-knuckled on the throttle, waiting to slam it forward again if necessary.

"Take a left after that hangar," Rapp said, pointing through the windscreen.

"It says that's a restricted area."

"Just do it, Paco."

As he eased the aircraft forward, a military contingent appeared. The pilot began to slow, but Rapp took a seat next to him and pushed the throttle forward again.

"I think they're serious," Paco said, pointing at four machine gunners tracking them from the top armored vehicles. "Are you sure about this?"

"I'm sure."

While there had never been any formal introductions, it was likely he'd figured out who Rapp was by now. And in light of that, he'd decided it was better not to question orders.

"Stop by that building up there," Rapp said, slipping out of the seat and heading toward the back. He pointed at Claudia. "We're up."

"What? What's that mean?"

The plane came to a stop and he opened the door before lowering the steps. She followed him into the heat and glare of the sun, looking around nervously at the soldiers watching them.

Normally, Rapp would have been wearing a hat and sunglasses in an effort to thwart the cameras that had become so ubiquitous in modern society. Today, though, he walked slowly, scanning the airstrip with his face completely exposed.

Claudia put a hand in his back and pushed him forward. "What the hell are you doing? I don't know where you think you're going, but could we at least get there?"

He adjusted his trajectory toward a Gulfstream G550. David Graves, wearing a dark suit and seemingly unaffected by the heat, was standing at the base of the steps leading onto the aircraft. He watched them carefully, moving his hand toward the weapon holstered beneath his left arm.

His reaction drove home for Rapp the seriousness of his situation. They'd known each other for years and still got together at the range every month or so, usually grabbing a beer afterward.

By the time they made it to within ten feet, his hand was wrapped around the grip of the SIG P226 that Rapp himself had shot many times. It wasn't surprising. Word was going around the intelligence community that Joel Wilson was dead and that Rapp was responsible.

"What are you doing here, Mitch?"

"I'm not here, Dave."

"There are about fifty Saudis behind you who might disagree."

Graves glanced at Claudia but then pressed a finger to his earpiece, suggesting that he was receiving a transmission.

"Are you sure?" he responded into the microphone on his wrist. "Do you want me to come in? I think you should have at least some— Yes. Understood."

He stepped aside and Rapp followed Claudia as she moved toward the steps. When they entered the aircraft, she stopped short.

Irene Kennedy rose from her chair and approached, giving Claudia a short embrace as Rapp chose a seat near a section of fuselage with no windows.

"I'm so glad to see you, Claudia," Kennedy said. "I've been worried. Are you all right?"

"Yes, but what are you doing here? Mitch kept refusing to call you."

"I called *him*," she said, indicating the chair next to Rapp's and taking a facing seat. "And I'm looking forward to hearing about what you've been doing over the past month. Grisha Azarov, Donatella Rahn, and Kent Black . . ." She shook her head. "Desperate times . . ."

"Word is Joel Wilson's dead," Rapp said. "Last time I saw him, he looked okay. You didn't—"

"No, of course not." She twisted in her seat. "Joel! Could you come out here, please?"

The FBI man appeared from the secure communications space at the back, looking a bit sheepish.

"Joel's been working to identify the men who were killed in Juba and helping to clear you in the deaths of the Saudi nationals you're accused of killing."

"Are you making any progress?" Rapp asked.

"It's hard to get anything concrete," Wilson replied. "But we're building a pretty decent circumstantial case for your innocence."

Rapp pulled out the fake passport he'd been using

and tossed it to the man. "It's not exactly ironclad, but you might be able to get some mileage out of it."

Wilson flipped through the pages, looking at the entry and exit stamps. "Every little bit helps. Let me go back and get some scans."

Rapp returned his attention to Kennedy. "Is our meeting with the king still on?"

"Yes," she responded, glancing at her watch. "In fact, we're running late. Claudia, why don't you wait here for us?"

"I think I should come," she protested. "I have all the details of what we've done—times, dates, places, transportation. I could help fill in anything that Joel hasn't been able to figure out."

"I understand, and we'll need you to coordinate with him later, but for now I'd like to keep you out of this as much as possible. And besides, it will give you a chance to give Anna a call. She and Tommy are having a wonderful time together, but she misses her mother."

The lights of the Erga Palace's fountain had come on, bathing the pillared entrance in a warm glow. Guards were plentiful, all carrying assault rifles and all very interested in the limousine gliding past them.

"Stop here," Rapp said in Arabic to the driver.

"What?" he responded. "Why? I've been told to take you to the entrance where the king's assistant is waiting."

"Stop here," Rapp repeated. The man had no choice but to do so. Rapp was the king's guest and, as such, his wishes were to be carried out to the letter.

"You don't mind a little walk, do you, Irene?"

"An excellent idea," she said, following him out into the quickly cooling evening.

"What are we doing?" Wilson said, looking around at the guards before leaving the relative safety of the limo.

"Relax," Rapp said, putting a friendly hand in his back and ushering him toward the palace entrance. "I just needed a little air."

In truth Rapp wanted to make sure this little visit was as public as possible. He needed the guards—many of whom would be loyal to Aali Nassar—to see not only him and Irene Kennedy walking freely into a meeting with the king but also the late Joel Wilson strolling along with them.

They met Faisal's assistant on the palace steps and, after some strained pleasantries, were led to a marble-and-gilt audience room near the back of the palace. As expected, the king wasn't there. He liked to make an entrance and they were forced to wait. The only seat was a gold-and-red-velvet throne on an elevated platform, so they had to stand.

After five minutes Faisal appeared and struggled into his seat. The platform had been getting progressively shorter as he aged, and Rapp noted that it might be about time for another adjustment.

"I have agreed to this meeting and excluded Director Nassar at your request, Dr. Kennedy. I do this out of respect for you and in acknowledgment of what Mr. Rapp has done to defend my kingdom in the past. But I want to be clear that I believe him to be a murderer."

Despite their long relationship, Faisal didn't look at him. Yet another reminder of how quickly political loyalties could change.

"Your Highness," Kennedy said. "I'd like to introduce Joel Wilson, the FBI agent who was helping Director Nassar try to find Mitch."

"I'm quite familiar with Agent Wilson," Faisal said. "Though I was told you were dead."

"No, sir. One of Director Nassar's men tried to kill me, but Mitch managed to prevent it."

"That's a very serious accusation. Do you have proof?"

"Is the equipment we requested available?"

The king pointed toward an ornate cabinet against the wall. Wilson opened it, docking his laptop and retrieving a remote control. A moment later the lights dimmed and his screen was projected on the wall.

"This first image is a list of dates and places where Mitch has traveled since leaving the CIA. They are corroborated by his passport. You can see that it would be impossible for him to have killed your man in Paris or Qadir Sultan in Saudi Arabia."

"You're offering entries in a forged passport as proof?" Faisal asked.

"Please, let him finish," Kennedy said.

"Thank you. We have corroborating evidence from various cameras in airports and other locations, all time-stamped."

He scrolled through them, but Rapp's natural ability to keep his face out of photos worked against him. When Wilson brought up an image of a lengthy telephone record, Rapp had had enough.

"Stop."

Wilson looked over at him. "I was just getting to—"

Rapp stepped forward and locked eyes with the aging monarch. "You know damn well that I didn't kill those people because I'm telling you I didn't kill them. Why would I lie? Why would I be standing here in front of you instead of putting a bullet in your head and hoping the next asshole who sits in that chair is better?"

Faisal jerked back, alarm and confusion reading on his face. It was probably the first time he'd ever been spoken to that way.

"Mitch . . ." Kennedy cautioned, but the old man pushed himself to his feet and spoke over her. "You tell me all this, but then you insist that Aali not be present to defend himself. He's been unfailingly loyal to me and worked tirelessly against ISIS."

"Listen to yourself," Rapp responded. "Even you don't believe what you're saying. You either need to run this country or turn it over to someone who can. Because you've been played and I can't tell if you're too stupid to realize it or too old to care."

"Guards!" the king shouted, and a moment later two men armed with HK G36s burst through the door. Kennedy took a few steps back while Wilson scurried for the edge of the room. Rapp held his position. He wasn't finished yet.

One guard took a position to his right, unsure what Faisal wanted him to do. Rapp took advantage of the confusion and swept his legs from under him while grabbing the barrel of his gun. He jerked it out of his hands and rammed the butt of it into the head of the second guard, whose knees buckled. Rapp dropped the rifle and snatched the Browning Hi Power from the man's holster before he dropped to the marble floor.

The remaining palace guards registered the commotion and he could hear their shouts as they fanned out behind him. They were even less inclined to act, though. Rapp had his weapons lined up on Faisal's forehead and the slightest twitch of his finger would put an end to their king.

"Are we going to continue our conversation, Highness? Or are we going to end it?"

The events of the last few seconds had come too fast for the man and it took him a beat to process what had happened. When he did, he dismissed his guards. Rapp kept the weapon lined up as they dragged the two unconscious men away. When he heard the door close, he dropped the gun on the floor.

"Twenty years ago, would you have put this much trust in a power-hungry piece of shit like Aali Nassar?"

Faisal sat and let a good thirty seconds pass before he responded. "No."

"You've been playing a dangerous game—blinding your people with religion and hoping that you could control them. But now you've lost that control and you're too old and weak to get it back. Is this the legacy you want to leave? Do you want to be remembered as the last king of Saudi Arabia?"

Faisal seemed to lose the strength to sit fully erect in his throne. "So, instead of the radicals, I should turn my kingdom over to the Americans? To the Christians? Why? Because you believe I've been betrayed but offer no real proof?"

"We have a great deal more than what you just saw," Kennedy said, returning to Rapp's side. "We have a tape of one of Nassar's men pledging allegiance to ISIS. We have photos of a number of his people that we've been able to associate with Mullah Halabi. We have information putting Director Nassar in Brussels when Mahja Zaman was killed. But I suspect none of this will be enough for you. And in light of that, I believe that you should give Director Nassar an opportunity to prove his own innocence."

"How?"

"By doing nothing. Mitch and I would like you to walk us to our car behaving in a friendly and grateful manner. After that, we'd like you to have your people pick up Nassar's assistant, Hamid Safar, and hold him in solitary confinement."

"Then you're asking me to interrogate an intelligence official with no evidence against him?"

"Not at all, Your Highness. If you like, invite him here as your guest. Just make sure it's impossible for him to communicate for a few days."

"And you expect this to prove something?"

She nodded. "We've diverted significant human and electronic surveillance resources to track Director Nassar, who's currently in a safe house outside of Bisha. If he's innocent, I'd expect him to contact you and demand to know where his man is and why you were meeting with Mitch. If he's guilty, then he may present us with an interesting opportunity."

CHAPTER 56

ALI Nassar went through the photos again, putting them in chronological order and expanding them to fill the computer monitor. Taken in their entirety, they told a story that couldn't be denied.

The first depicted Mitch Rapp and Claudia Dufort deplaning outside of Riyadh and then entering a Gulfstream G550. He deplaned again shortly thereafter, this time with Irene Kennedy and a man who was unmistakably Joel Wilson. He stared at the blurry image of the FBI agent's face for a long time, trying to calculate what it meant. Had he been working with Kennedy the entire time? Impossible. His career had been destroyed by her and Rapp. His hatred for them was both well-documented and well-founded.

The only answer was that the attack in South Sudan had indeed been a trap set by Mitch Rapp. Was it he and Wilson who had escaped in the car seen leaving the scene? Had they taken a prisoner for questioning? Was that why the bodies had been burned?

He scrolled forward, pausing at the photos of the three Americans entering Erga Palace, but then moving on to the much more telling images of them leaving. Rapp and Wilson showed no signs of animosity and King Faisal not only shook the CIA assassin's hand but then walked him to a waiting limousine. None of Nassar's people had been close enough to overhear their conversation, but the gratitude in the old man's body language was impossible to miss.

What did the Americans know? It seemed almost certain that they had identified some of the ISIS men sent to Juba. Had they found evidence of his involvement in the death of Mahja Zaman? Of his involvement in financing terrorism and undermining the Saudi government?

The king wasn't aware of his location, but he did have Nassar's phone number. Yet he hadn't used it to summon him for an audience. Why? Was the evidence the Americans possessed so damning that he wouldn't even be afforded the opportunity to defend himself?

Questions were infinite but answers were nonexistent.

He dialed his assistant for the fifth time since receiving the photos and for the fifth time got no answer. It was beyond unusual. With perhaps three exceptions over the years they'd been working together, Safar had picked up his calls within a few rings. Now there was nothing but silence.

Nassar could feel his time running out, and as it did, his rage intensified. He refused to accept that he had been outmaneuvered by a thug like Mitch Rapp. This had to have been a concerted effort by Irene Kennedy and multiple foreign agencies. Perhaps even the king.

He reached for his phone again, this time dialing the number of his assistant's wife. Unlike her husband, she picked up immediately.

"I've been trying to contact Hamid," Nassar said. "Is he with you?"

"No. He was taken away hours ago. What's happening, Director? I—"

"Be quiet! Who took him away?"

"King Faisal's men. They—"

"Where is he now?"

"I don't know. They didn't tell me anything. I've been trying to call him, but he won't answer. I'm—"

Nassar disconnected the line and closed his eyes, trying to control his breathing. If Faisal had taken his man, there could be no more confusion about his own situation. Safar was strong and dedicated to the cause, but no man could hold out forever. If he was being interrogated by Faisal's men, he would break after three or four days. If he was being questioned by Rapp, the time would be significantly shorter.

Nassar dialed a number he'd been given and listened to it ring. The time seemed to stretch into infinity as he waited. Finally, a now familiar voice came on.

"What can I do for you, Aali?"

Mullah Halabi gave nothing away, but it seemed likely that he had received similar photos of Rapp's visit to the palace.

"It appears that the Americans have discovered our relationship and informed King Faisal."

"That's unfortunate."

Nassar waited for him to say more, but the man remained silent.

"If I fall into Mitch Rapp's hands, I'll be questioned."

"I'm quite sure you will be. But what will you tell him? That I'm determined to destroy the Saudi royalty by any means necessary and claim their land for the caliphate? I hardly think this would come as a surprise."

"I can do a great deal for you."

"This was true when you were Saudi Arabia's intelligence chief. But now you're just a man on the run. I have many men on the run at my disposal. Every one of them loyal zealots who want nothing more than to die for me."

"Martyrs are of little strategic value," Nassar said, trying to keep his voice even. He knew that the outcome of this conversation would determine whether he lived or died. "I have intimate knowledge of military operations and intelligence methods that will be impossible to alter quickly. I also still control significant financial resources. Bring me in and allow me to make my case. If you're not convinced, you can kill me."

He heard muffled voices—Halabi speaking to someone else in the room.

"You'll be sent an address," the mullah said finally. "I suggest you begin your preparations to leave."

The line went dead and Nassar swept a hand across his desk, knocking most of its contents to the floor. A glass mug shattered loudly on the tiles, prompting one of his men to burst through the door to his left.

"Is everything all right, Director?"

"Bring my car around. We're leaving in ten minutes."

"Where are we—"

"Don't question me!" Nassar shouted. "Just carry out my orders!"

The man disappeared as Nassar slid a USB drive into one of his computer's ports. The worm it contained would download thousands of critical files before covering the theft by wreaking havoc on the General Intelligence Directorate's computer system. Most important, though, it would drain a number of government accounts and deposit the money into anonymous ones he controlled.

It was a protocol he'd set up years ago when he took his first hesitant steps toward undermining the Saudi royalty. He'd never expected to have to use it or to have to flee the country he believed he was destined to rule. Again the rage washed over him. Rapp was back safe in the arms of his country. And he was laughing.

Nassar looked past his two security men at the lights of Mecca shining through the windshield. The journey there had taken almost five hours, but he still found it impossible to collect his thoughts. All he could feel was an increasing sense of disorientation.

It was all gone. His position and prestige. His opulent home and private aircraft. His sons and the powerful friends he had so carefully cultivated. He would spend the rest of his life in squalor, surrounded by fanatics and at the pleasure of a religious zealot who believed that Allah spoke through him and him only.

Nassar tried to clear his mind and focus on the immediate steps that needed to be taken. The only thing that mattered now was convincing Halabi of his value.

Soon, though, he found his thoughts drifting to the future. The former Iraqi officers whom Halabi had surrounded himself with presented an opportunity. While they were far more competent than the rank-

and-file ISIS fighter, they were also far less fanatical. They continued to be concerned with such worldly trappings as power, survival, and money. Subverting their loyalties would be no small task but, if done carefully and over time, it might be possible. With their support and the convenient martyrdom of the mullah, the fanatics could be brought into line.

Patience would be the most difficult part, straining even his iron discipline. The thirst for revenge—on Rapp, on the king—was burning inside him with an intensity that would have to be temporarily quenched. He had the knowledge and contacts to use ISIS to its maximum potential now, but with every hour that passed, those advantages would fade. Intelligence was a commodity with a very short shelf life. He would have to resist letting his passions overpower his reason. Mullah Halabi would be watching for any hint of disloyalty and would deal with it quickly and permanently.

"Director," his driver said. "The address you gave us is just ahead."

Nassar squinted at a garage door lit by a single security lamp. As he was searching for signs of life, the door began to open.

"Pull in."

"Do you want us to clear—"

"Just pull in."

The interior was poorly illuminated, but Nassar was able to make out a lone man standing at the back of the building. It looked like some kind of shipping depot, and there were a number of trucks lined up in the space. It would be sufficient to hide a significant force, although there was no sign of that kind of activity.

Another decision point had been reached. Did he

exit the car with his men in case this was an ambush? Or did he use this as an opportunity to display his fealty and submission?

There was little choice. His immediate survival and eventual success depended entirely on the mullah's trust.

"Do you see that man, Director? Should we get out?"

"Let's wait a moment," he said, pulling a Browning pistol from its holster. The two men in the front seats had been with him for years and had fulfilled their duties impeccably. It was a shame that their service had to come to an end.

He lifted the weapon and fired in quick succession, putting a single round into each man's head. They slumped forward and he stepped from the vehicle, leaving his gun on the seat.

CHAPTER 57

H E'S still on course toward your position. One klick out."

Rapp remained motionless, lying partially buried by the sand in an elevated position over a roadbed. The steady voice of Marcus Dumond in Langley inspired even more confidence than he remembered.

Not that Claudia and the group of misfits he'd put together had been bad, but there was something to be said for a team of professional, motivated, and patriotic government agents armed with cutting-edge technology. The less drama the better, as far as he was concerned.

"They should be right on top of you, Mitch. I'm using thermal on the surveillance drone, so I'm not sure if they're running headlights."

"Copy."

They weren't. The hum of an engine was the first thing to reach him. It was a moonless night, but a sky full of stars was just enough for Rapp to make out an SUV emerging from the blackness. He followed it with his eyes as it passed and continued north. According to the Agency's maps, there was nowhere for it to get off until a small village about ten klicks farther on.

The hope was that it was their final destination, but hope had never been worth much in Iraq. Just as likely, they would pass through the village and climb into a mountain range pockmarked with caves that no one knew anything about. If that was the case, this was going to turn into another of the clusterfucks that he'd spent his career dealing with.

Rapp gave them a two-minute lead and then stood, picking up the dirt bike Scott Coleman had lent him. It was an all-electric model made by Zero and, as advertised, it didn't make a sound when he started it. Slipping on a pair of prototype night-vision goggles, he twisted the throttle and was treated to a disorientating combination of acceleration and silence.

"Are you getting the overhead feed, Mitch?"

All he could see was the hazy green terrain in front of him. "I've got nothing."

"Shit. Hold on."

He heard something that sounded like Dumond banging on his extremely expensive electronic equipment and was rewarded with an overhead map in his peripheral vision. It displayed speed and direction for both him and his target, as well as their relative positions.

"Five by five."

"Told you it would work."

Unfortunately it was one of a thousand things that had to. Tracking Aali Nassar to Mecca had been easy, but after that things had gotten complicated. Sayid Halabi might be a psychopath, but he was a thorough one. He'd run Nassar through tunnels and markets, transported him on foot, on trains, and in cars. There had been more than a few moments of panic—most notably when the Agency had been temporarily fooled by a double in Sakaka—but they'd always managed to reacquire him.

The cost, though, was unprecedented. Satellites had been retasked, allies' arms had been twisted, and resources had been diverted from a very pissed-off military. Rapp had even been forced to bribe a Taliban group that would undoubtedly use the money for guns they'd eventually shoot at him with.

In light of that, coming up empty wasn't an option. Nassar had been allowed to drain off an enormous amount of data and money from the Saudis, and letting him walk with it was a huge risk.

"Your speed looks good, Mitch. You're paralleling them at about five hundred yards."

"Copy. What's that ahead, Marcus? Before the village. The infrared's picking up something I can't ID."

"It's a newly constructed bridge. Went up over the last few days."

Rapp maneuvered the bike around a deep sand drift and then throttled across what looked like an ancient lake bed. The light amplification wasn't ideal for picking up ruts in the dried mud, and he was forced to keep his speed below twenty miles an hour.

"It looks perpendicular to the road Nassar's vehicle is on. Are they going to cross it or go under it?"

"The road leading to the village passes under it. Actually, there *is* no road that connects to the bridge. It's just there. Our guys think the builders put it in first and that they haven't started grading in the road yet."

"Where would it go?" Rapp said, starting to get suspicious.

"They don't know. Not much out there. Kind of weird, actually."

He cut left and goosed the bike up to twenty-five, hearing only the dull chatter of the tires as they hammered against the cracked earth.

"You're drifting off course, Mitch. Look at your overhead display."

"Are they still headed for that bridge?" Rapp said, ignoring Dumond's warning.

"Yeah. Probably a minute out. And you're going to intersect the road in about thirty seconds if you don't correct."

"Will I come out far enough behind them to stay out of sight?"

"With no lights? Yeah. Easy."

Rapp lifted the front wheel as he dropped three feet onto the poorly maintained dirt track.

"Where are they now?"

"Ten seconds from the bridge."

"Have they slowed down?"

"I have their speed at twenty-two miles an hour."

About the maximum the rutted road surface would handle, Rapp calculated.

"They're through and out the other side," Dumond said.

"Any chance someone got out?"

"No way in hell. The bridge is only about fifteen feet wide and they held their speed. Still heading for the village. Maybe five minutes out."

"Copy."

The road cut started to deepen, causing steep banks

to grow up on either side of him. He didn't want to get funneled into the low ground like this, but there was something about that bridge that didn't feel right. Over the last three days Halabi had proved to be even more cunning than they'd given him credit for—nearly defeating the surveillance capabilities of the entire Western world with nothing more high-tech than a pickup truck. Was this another one of his tricks?

Rapp ditched the bike and continued on foot. The bridge was visible ahead, a hazy horizontal line against the glow of stars. He pulled his Glock from his jacket and screwed on the silencer as he continued. The darkness beneath the bridge was deep enough to significantly reduce the effectiveness of his goggles, forcing him to slow and drop to a crawl.

"Are you all right, Mitch? Why did you leave Scott's bike?"

He didn't respond, instead inching through the blackness beneath the structure. He could make out vague outlines but none took on a human form. What he could see, though, were a number of mattresses laid out on the ground with a vertical cargo net set up at one end. Rapp slid over them, finding a hole in the rock face on the other side. It measured probably three feet wide by five feet high and was filled with darkness that completely defeated his equipment.

"I think Nassar might have bailed out when they passed under the bridge," he said into his throat mike. "There's a cave entrance under here."

"Shit," Dumond said. "And I've got more bad news. Nassar's car blew through the village and it's headed for the mountains. Do you want me to pull the guys back to your position?"

Joe Maslick had a team in the foothills, but the risks of this operation were starting to push the limits of what was acceptable. The hope was that Nassar would lead them to Halabi and maybe a few of the former Iraqi generals he was using to brutalize the region. But even with a reward like that on offer, their primary concern was to make sure Nassar never saw another sunrise. If that meant passing up a chance at Halabi, so be it.

"That's a negative," Rapp said finally. "It's time to pull the plug. Tell Mas to take out that vehicle and check if Nassar's in it. In the meantime, I'm going to go into this hole and see what I turn up."

CHAPTER 58

ALI Nassar crouched, feeling the already ago-
nizing pain in his back flare to the edge of what
he could bear. He guessed that he had at least three
broken ribs and, based on the bone straining against
the skin above his right shoulder, a separated collarbone.

The fact that the SUV he'd been transported in was
missing its rear doors and seat belts hadn't registered
as unusual. ISIS scavenged what they could from the
locals, the Americans, and their victims. Comfort was
hardly the concern of men whose goal was to be martyred while visiting misery and death upon everyone
around them.

It wasn't until he was unceremoniously shoved
through that gaping doorway that he realized the vehicle had been specifically chosen for its condition.
Despite a pile of fetid mattresses, he'd landed hard,
rolling at almost forty kilometers an hour before becoming hung up in a cargo net.

It had been the last piece of an elaborate effort to
ensure that no one could follow Nassar's movements

across the Middle East. Even he had to admit that the thoroughness of Halabi's protocols was impressive and almost certainly sufficient to defeat the efforts of even the Americans.

The stone roof rose again and he straightened his injured body, grinding his teeth in response to the pain. The natural cavern was roughly cylindrical, two meters in diameter, and descended at a shallow angle into the earth. The ground was covered with a thick layer of sand, muffling their progress as they continued forward by the glow of a single flashlight.

The passage turned left and Nassar used the opportunity to glance back. The man behind him had stopped, posting himself at the bend and fading into the darkness as they moved away.

It was impossible to judge distance, but Nassar counted off another three minutes before he heard voices filtering to him from ahead. Individual words were muddled by poor acoustics, but the gravity of the hushed tones was clear.

The passage finally opened into a cave more than ten meters square, illuminated with battery-powered work lights. Mullah Halabi was sitting on a stone outcrop, elevated above a group of middle-aged men kneeling in two lines in front of him. At the edges of the space, younger men armed with assault rifles melded into the shadows. Undoubtedly, they were members of Halabi's famously devoted private guard.

Nassar recognized a number of the older men from information shared by the Americans and Europeans—soldiers from Saddam Hussein's disbanded army. Most of the high-ranking officers had been either captured or killed, but in many ways these lower-ranking officers were more useful. Their superiors had left the details of war to them while they focused on the much more critical activity of currying favor with Hussein.

Halabi's predecessor had begun recruiting these men in an effort to turn his motivated but undisciplined forces into an army capable of holding territory. After he died in a drone strike, Halabi took over with the much more ambitious goal of standing even against the powerful Saudi and Egyptian militaries.

"Welcome, Aali. I trust your journey wasn't too uncomfortable."

"Not at all," he said, hiding the pain that speaking caused him.

"I understand that you have something for me?"

The thumb drive Nassar was carrying had been discovered when he was searched for tracking devices in Mecca. He'd been allowed to keep it and now he retrieved it from his pocket. When he stepped forward to hand it to the ISIS leader, the men at the edges of the cave came to life.

"Don't give it to me," Halabi said, pointing to a man to Nassar's right. "Give it to him."

He did as he was told and watched the man slip the drive into a laptop.

"It's asking for a password."

"Of course it is," Halabi said. "But I suspect that the director will be reluctant to give us that password."

"The intelligence and bank account information on that drive are yours," Nassar said.

The mullah smiled. "A meaningless response. Perhaps politics was your true calling."

"Perhaps."

"Can we break his encryption?" Halabi asked.

The man shook his head. "Unlikely. Torturing him for it would have a higher probability of success."

Halabi nodded thoughtfully. "I wonder. It seems likely that there's a password that would put the information forever out of our reach. Isn't that so, Aali?"

"It is."

Halabi rubbed his palms together in front of his face. "The money that drive gives us access to will quickly slip through our fingers, and the intelligence will just as quickly become dated. Is it the information it contains that's valuable, or is it the guile and experience of the man who brought it here?"

The question was clearly rhetorical, but one of Halabi's people answered anyway. "Do those qualities make him valuable or do they make him dangerous? He's betrayed his king and country. Why? For the cause? For Allah? Or is it for personal gain? Can he be trusted, Mullah Halabi? Is he here to assist you, or is he here to replace you?"

"I had power," Nassar responded. "I had wealth. I had the respect of the king and the Americans. But I jeopardized it all. I—"

"The king is old and weak," the man interrupted. "You feared the collapse of the kingdom and were playing both sides. The Americans discovered your treachery and now you've had to run."

Once again they were better informed than he'd hoped.

The man who had spoken did so with an arrogance that suggested he had the confidence of his leader. Someone like Nassar would be a significant threat to his position in the ISIS hierarchy.

"They discovered my allegiance to Mullah Halabi,

yes. Regrettable, because while I can be of great assistance to you from here, I would have been much more effective at the king's side. The effort that went into gaining his trust isn't something that I'd expect a simple soldier to understand."

The man stiffened at the insult, but Nassar ignored it. "I've worked closely with the Americans on their homeland security protocols and in preventing terrorist attacks on their soil. It's given me an intimate knowledge of their borders and immigration policy, their power grid and nuclear plants. Even their water supply. If we strike surgically, we can turn the tide of the war. We can make the Americans lash out against all Muslims and turn your thirty thousand soldiers into a billion."

Rapp strapped his night-vision goggles to his Camel-Bak and slid a combat knife from the sheath at his waist. The darkness inside the underground passage was too deep for light amplification, and the sound from even a silenced pistol would bounce endlessly off the walls.

He passed through the cavern's entrance and found himself completely blind. His other senses strained to compensate, but there was nothing for them to cling to other than the scent of earth. He kept his pace agonizingly slow, dragging his fingers along the left wall for reference. There was a significant risk of slamming his head into a rock outcropping and he had to test every footfall to ensure complete silence.

Despite these precautions, he cut his face on something jutting from a wall and nearly tripped twice, barely managing not to fall. He still hadn't plummeted down a thousand-foot shaft, though. So that was something.

Because of the sensory deprivation and the focus necessary to remain silent, it was impossible to track time. For some reason he wanted to know how much had passed, but illuminating his watch was out of the question. In this kind of darkness it would look like an explosion.

Rapp slid his toe forward, but stopped when it touched rock. He brushed his fingers along the stone above him, confirming that it maintained its height but that the passage bent left. He altered his trajectory appropriately but barely made it two feet before again bumping into something. Not rock, though.

He brought his hand down and drove the man back, generating a mental map during the struggle that allowed him to get his palm over his opponent's mouth. The metallic rattle of the man trying to bring his weapon to bear would have been almost inaudible under normal circumstances, but in this situation it assaulted Rapp's ears, overpowering even the sensation of teeth sinking into his hand.

Rapp shoved the man's head into the rock as a fist repeatedly slammed into his side and shoulder. The muffled thumps were way too loud, but there was still the possibility that no one had noticed the mortal battle taking place in the confined space. If his opponent's finger found the trigger of his weapon, though, that anonymity would be gone forever.

He brought the knife up to what he thought was the man's throat but missed, snapping the point off on the stone wall. It sparked, creating a split-second flash that finally allowed Rapp to drive what was left of the tip into the man's neck. The dulled weapon didn't penetrate as deeply as it should have, forcing him to follow his opponent into the dirt, holding on to him until he finally went still. Rapp lay there for another minute or so, listening for anyone bearing down on him. Nothing but the nearly imperceptible drip of blood from his wounded hand.

He ripped a piece of cloth from the bottom of his shirt and used it to secure the thick flap of skin that the man's teeth had torn loose. Satisfied that the bleeding was at a manageable level, he continued his slow journey through the passage.

The sound of voices reached him first, followed by a dim glow. His movements quickened as his eyes, starved for so long, began picking out the walls and obstacles he'd been struggling to avoid.

The muddled conversation slowly separated into three distinct voices, all speaking Arabic. One calm, one angry, and one on the defensive. He didn't recognize any of them, but the context suggested that the one making a case for himself was Aali Nassar. Much more interesting was the calm, superior tone of the man officiating. Was it possible that the last-minute plan he and Kennedy had hatched was going to work? Was he about to come face-to-face with Mullah Sayid Halabi?

It turned out to be even better than that. Rapp stopped ten feet from where the passage opened up, spotting Nassar as well as a number of men sitting on cushions on either side of him. Based on their ages, there was a good chance they were the officers whom Halabi had assembled from Saddam Hussein's military. It was feasible that a significant portion of the ISIS command-and-control structure was in that cavern.

Nassar wasn't moving around much, and his right collarbone was protruding noticeably—likely injuries he'd sustained in his leap from the vehicle. He was, however, swaying enough as he spoke to reveal glimpses of the man presiding over the meeting. Rapp's heartbeat increased when he confirmed the man's identity. Halabi.

Unfortunately, there was no clear shot at the ISIS leader from his position, and he could see only a portion of the chamber the men were set up in. Three armed guards were posted along the right wall and he suspected that there were at least that many just out of sight. Based on the slight movement of air, it was also probable that there were other exits.

If he fired a shot, all hell was going to break loose, and he was at a significant disadvantage—not only from the superior numbers of the enemy but from his confined operating environment.

That left a low probability of success and an even lower probability of survival. His first shot would have to be at Nassar to get him out of his line to Halabi, but after that everything was the luck of the draw. Would Halabi be able to make it to cover before Rapp got a clear shot? Was there someone at the chamber entrance who would immediately block it? Even in a best-case scenario he'd only have time to get Nassar and Halabi before he was forced to bolt for the cover of the corner behind him. Then it was just the not-so-simple matter of making it to the exit before the passage filled with ricocheting lead.

Rapp removed his CamelBak and crouched, digging a penlight and a grenade out of it. He laid them neatly in the sand and then pulled the Glock from his shoulder holster. A quick glance around him at the rock walls suggested that they were more hardened mud than stone. Not as structurally solid as he'd have liked.

With no better option, he pulled the grenade's pin and tossed it toward the cavern. While it was still in the air, he snatched up the Glock and fired a single round, hitting Nassar in the back of the head. The round did what he needed, which was less killing the Saudi and more distracting the ISIS men from the explosive that had landed in the sand a few feet inside the chamber. Everyone went into motion, but instead of hitting the deck they stood and ran.

Three guards jumped on Halabi before Rapp could get a clear shot, so he turned and sprinted away. Even with his exceptional speed, there wasn't time for him to reach the bend in the passageway. He heard the explosion and felt the sudden increase in air pressure before going down in a choking cloud of dust.

Rapp regained consciousness slowly, confused as to where he was. Home? Asleep next to his wife in their house on the bay? His throat felt raw and he was about to get up to find something to drink when he remembered that she was dead and the bay house demolished.

There was a surprising lack of physical pain—not much more than a bad headache that was probably a by-product of what he calculated to be his ninth concussion. The numbness worried him until he managed to wiggle his fingers and toes, ruling out paralysis. Much more movement than that was impossible. His legs were completely pinned, as was his right arm. His left was free and he used it to search for the penlight he'd been carrying. After almost a minute of feeling around, he gave up and started digging. The makeshift bandage came off his hand and he could feel the bite wound fill with dirt. Not exactly sanitary, but avoiding infection was pretty low on his priority list at this point.

After what seemed like about half an hour he was able to free his right arm enough to illuminate his watch. It provided sufficient light to see that the space above him went all the way to the original roof of the passage, but the length wasn't much more than three feet. His legs were buried to his upper thighs but the weight didn't feel too bad. He probably could have pulled them out if his head wasn't wedged against the rubble in front of him. He tried to clear some space but managed only to cause a secondary collapse that filled what little air he had left with dust.

Rapp illuminated his watch again but turned it off after a few seconds. There wasn't a whole hell of a lot to look at, and it just magnified his mild claustrophobia. On the bright side, the fact that he'd never made arrangements for his burial wasn't turning out to be a problem.

He actually laughed out loud at that before letting the silence descend again. Finally he laid his cheek against the ground and stared into the darkness. His hope was that his mind would latch onto all the things he'd accomplished. The people he'd saved. The country he'd strengthened. Instead it got mired down in his failures. The relationship with his brother that he'd let turn into a couple brief phone conversations around holidays and birthdays. A world he'd seen through the sights of a gun. His hopelessly brief stint as a husband and his recent hesitant steps at acting like a father.

It had been a hell of a ride, though.

When Rapp woke again, his confusion had deepened. The air supply was giving out. He lifted his head and a cascade of dirt and rock hit him in the face. Maybe the start of a collapse that would put him in the express lane to hell. He smiled weakly. It'd be good to see Stan Hurley again.

"*Mitch!*"

He ignored the voice, assuming it was just a figment of his oxygen-deprived imagination.

"*Mitch!*"

This time the voice was accompanied by a light that penetrated his eyelids and the rush of air. A massive hand grabbed the back of his head, protecting it from a cascade of dirt and rock.

"Mitch, it's Joe! Say something, man!"

His throat was too caked with dust to get anything out, but he managed to grasp the man's forearm in a weak grip.

"Wick! He's alive! What's the ETA on that fucking chopper?"

Rapp wasn't able to make out the response.

Maslick withdrew his arm and hammered a shovel into the dirt next to Rapp's shoulder. "You gotta stop doing this to yourself, man. You're not as young as you used to be."

EPILOGUE

THE bottom of the couch had been sliced through during the search of Claudia's home, but it wouldn't show. Rapp flipped it back upright and swore under his breath when he saw similar damage across the top. She was already looking to cut Joel Wilson's balls off, and this wasn't going to help. As much as he'd like to be there to hold him down, Wilson was continuing his extraordinarily meticulous efforts to clear Rapp's name. The guy was a complete jackass, but he was competent as hell. His balls were going to have to stay attached for the time being.

Rapp gently lifted an overturned lamp and swore a little less cautiously when it snapped in half. Anna was immersed in the task of cleaning up her bedroom, well out of earshot. It wasn't hard to pick up on the mood of her mother, and the kid was perceptive enough to lie low.

He picked up the pieces of the lamp and headed outside to toss it on the growing pile of unsalvageable items. His phone began to ring as he started back, and

a quick glance confirmed that it was the heavily encrypted number that had gotten him into all this.

"Yes, sir," he said, turning and walking toward the
shade of the wall that surrounded the property.

"How are you doing?" President Alexander asked.

"Good. I think Mas got more beat up digging me
out than I did getting buried."

"I swear you have nine lives, Mitch."

"Yes, sir," he said, not mentioning that by his count
he was already on eleven.

"Look, I wanted to personally give you an update
on Iraq. The guys we sent to confirm your kills started
taking fire and I pulled them out. They tagged the
spot, though, and we dropped a bunker buster on it.
If anyone survived the collapse, I can guarantee you
they're dead now."

"Unless there was another exit."

"Let's just call it a win for now, okay, Mitch? All evidence suggests that you killed Halabi and most of the
ISIS brass."

Rapp wasn't so sure. He'd been burned too many
times to count on unconfirmed kills. Until someone
scraped DNA from the shit stain that used to be Sayid
Halabi, he'd reserve judgment.

"Yes, sir."

There was a pause that felt too long for a man who
had every second of his day mapped out ahead of time.
"I wanted to apologize face-to-face, but Irene says
she's not sure when you're coming back."

"Apology, sir?"

"I didn't want to turn my back on you, Mitch. Sure as
hell not for the Saudis. You know how I feel about them."

Rapp walked to his car and unlatched the trunk,

pulling a large, garishly wrapped box from it. "You gave me fair warning, sir. I wasn't under any illusions about how this was going to go down."

"Still, when I say I owe you, I mean it. The meeting we had . . ."

Unwilling to talk about it even on an encrypted line, his voice faded. "Well, let's just say it wasn't my finest hour."

"What meeting?"

"Thanks, Mitch. And not just from me. King Faisal also wants me to convey his gratitude."

"So he's going to thank me through back channels while he quietly throws me under a bus at home?"

"Oh, it's worse than that. We're going to call what happened in Iraq a joint operation. And I know how you like your anonymity, so we needed someone to give the credit to."

"Nassar," Rapp said, starting back for the house.

"He dies a hero and the king doesn't have to admit that a traitor got that close to him. Now isn't the time for him to look weak. You probably know that better than I do."

"Another half-assed political accommodation stacked on top of a bunch of other half-assed political accommodations."

"No one's ever summarized my job more eloquently. Enjoy your time off, Mitch."

The line disconnected and Rapp set a course for Anna's room. It was still a complete disaster, and she was sitting on the bed, reading.

"How's it going?"

"Done!" She waved a hand around at the hard work she imagined she'd completed.

"Looks good," he said, stepping inside. "I got you something."

"What is it?" she asked, looking over the book and eyeing the box under his arm.

"Why don't you open it and find out?"

She bounded off the bed and tore into the box, shredding the paper and pulling out a squirt gun nearly half her height.

"It's for those closet monsters."

"Awesome! Can I fill it?"

"Sure. Doesn't do much good unless it's loaded."

She darted into the bathroom and he heard a clank that sounded suspiciously like a toilet lid going up."

"The sink, Anna. Use the sink."

"Okay," she said, sounding a little exasperated.

When she reappeared, she was struggling under the weight of her new weapon.

"You think he might be in there now?"

"It's a she. And I don't know."

Rapp slunk to the side of the closet, pressing his back against the wall and giving her a silent countdown as she lined up on it.

He threw open the door, but before she could take down her target, a shout froze them both.

"STOP!"

What was it about mothers and their uncanny timing? Rapp's own had been the same way. The second he and his brother had lit a fuse, tied something to the cat, or climbed onto the roof, she would magically appear.

Rapp could see Claudia in his peripheral vision but kept his eyes locked on Anna, who was trying not to laugh.

"Is there not enough damage for the two of you? Really? Since I can't count on you to help, could you at least not make more work for me?"

Apparently her mood hadn't improved.

"We were taking out a closet monster," Anna explained.

"Your teddy bear is in the closet."

"Collateral damage," she responded.

Rapp winced. Where had she picked that up?

"Put the gun down," Claudia ordered. "We're going to dinner. Somewhere nice. And we're going to have a good time. Is that clear?"

Anna bolted for the bathroom to clean up and slammed the door behind her. Rapp tried to squeeze past Claudia, but she caught him by the arm. "Collateral damage? I look forward to having a long conversation about that later."

Pocket Books
proudly presents

RED WAR

VINCE FLYNN

Available Now

Turn the page for a sneak peek at the latest
Mitch Rapp thriller by Kyle Mills, *Red War* . . .

1

EAST OF MANASSAS,
VIRGINIA, USA

M ITCH Rapp slowed, letting Scott Coleman's lead extend to ten feet.

They were running on a poorly defined dirt track that switchbacked up a mountain to the west of the one he'd built his house on. By design, it was late afternoon and they were in full sun. Temperatures were in the high eighties with humidity around the same level, covering Rapp in a film of perspiration that was beginning to soak through his shirt.

Coleman, on the other hand, looked like he'd just climbed out of a swimming pool. He was pouring so much sweat that the trail of mud he left behind him would be visible from space. His breathing was coming in random, wheezing gasps that made him sound like the soon-to-be victim in a slasher flick. On the brighter side, his pace was steady and he wasn't tripping over the roots and loose rocks beneath his feet.

So, three quarters of the way to the summit, he was moving about as well as anybody could expect under the circumstances. Rapp wasn't anybody, though. It was time to see what the former Navy SEAL could do.

He crashed through some low branches to Coleman's left, pulling back onto the trail a few feet ahead. After about a minute of matching his old friend's pace, he started to slowly accelerate. Behind him, the rhythm of footfalls rose in defiance. Like they always did.

Coleman had just spent more than a year focused entirely on recovering from a run-in with Grisha Azarov, the nearly superhuman enforcer who worked for Russia's president. Azarov had finally walked away from his country and employer, but unfortunately not in time to save Coleman a wrecked shoulder, a knife blade broken off in his ribs, and multiple gunshot wounds. The blood loss alone would have killed a man half his age, but the former SEAL managed to beat the odds and stay above ground.

That had turned out to be the easy part. When he'd finally been hoisted out of bed, it had taken him almost a month just to relearn how to walk. And then there was the mental side. Going from being stronger, tougher, and faster than almost everyone around him to someone who needed a motorized cart to navigate the grocery store had been a tough blow. Even worse was coming to terms with the fact that Azarov had torn through him like he wasn't there. Coleman was still struggling to regain the confidence he'd always possessed in well-deserved abundance.

So it had been a surprise—of the rare good kind—when he'd showed up on Rapp's doorstep and invited him on a trail run. It was good to see a hint of the old swagger. He'd been Rapp's backup for a long time and the truth was that the year without him could have gone better. In this business, you were only as good as the people you surrounded yourself with.

Rapp glanced at the heart rate monitor strapped to his wrist. One sixty-five—a hard, but comfortable pace that he could hold for around three hours before blowing up. Behind him, Coleman's breathing was becoming desperate and his footfalls were losing their steady temp. Stumbles, followed by awkward saves, were increasingly frequent as his thigh muscles began to give up. But no falls. Not yet.

They broke out of the trees and Rapp pushed the pace a little harder as the summit came into sight. Coleman tripped and went down on one hand, but managed to get back to his feet without losing momentum. He was running purely on determination and pride now, but that was okay. He had serious reserves of both.

One hundred and seventy-one beats per minute read out on Rapp's monitor.

Coleman was starting to wheeze, a sick whistle from deep in his chest. Something caught in his throat and he started to choke, causing Rapp to hesitate for a moment. Then he started to sprint. If his old friend was going to drop dead, better now than in Afghanistan or Syria when people were counting on him.

Rapp slowed to a walk when he reached the top of the mountain, squinting as he scanned the rolling carpet of green below. He could see the gleaming dot that was his house to the east, surrounded by a few homes erected on similar widely spaced lots. His obscenely rich brother had bought the entire subdivision and sold the individual parcels for a dollar to Rapp's colleagues, ensuring that his older sibling would always be surrounded by shooters loyal to him.

To the south of Rapp's gate, a contemporary house of wood and blast-resistant glass was nearly finished. Whether its owner would survive the last hundred yards of this run to take occupancy, though, was an open question.

Fortunately, it was a question that didn't take too long to answer. Coleman crested the hill, lurching toward Rapp and finally collapsing to the rocky ground. He managed to rise to all fours but didn't stand, instead keeping his head down and concentrating on not throwing up. After about a minute, he regained enough control of his breathing to get out a single word.

"Time?"

Rapp glanced at his watch. "One hour, sixteen minutes, thirty-three seconds. Pick it up a little bit and you might qualify for the senior Olympics."

In fact, the pace they'd sustained on the climb would have shaken off a third of active duty SEALs. Not too bad for an old sailor the doctors said would need a cane for the rest of his life.

Coleman managed to lift one hand off the ground and raise his middle finger. "What's your best?"

Rapp considered telling the truth but quickly discarded the idea. The amount of work Coleman had put into his recovery and the progress he'd made was incredible. No point in discouraging him.

"Hour eleven forty."

"What would Azarov have done?"

"How the hell would I know?"

"Don't bullshit me, Mitch. You worked with him."

Rapp had recruited Azarov to help him with an operation that he didn't want to involve Coleman's men in. The former SEAL understood Rapp's rationale for using the man who had nearly killed him—it had been a straight up illegal action that he didn't want to blow back on the men who had been so loyal to him over the years. But that didn't make Coleman any less competitive.

"All he does these days is drink beer by his pool and surf with his girlfriend."

Coleman pushed himself to his feet. "Okay, Mitch. If you won't tell me that, at least you can stop lying to me about your real personal best."

"Fine. Hour four flat."

"Shit," Coleman said, lowering himself onto a boulder and staring out over the landscape. "I'll never be as fast as I was before. Too many years and too much mileage."

"Fighting's not just about running up hills, Scott. You know that. I'm more concerned about your head."

Coleman nodded, not taking his eyes off the horizon. "Over the last year, I've had a lot of time to think. Maybe too much."

"And?"

"I'm not afraid, if that's what you're wondering. When your number's up, it's up. And I've made peace with what Azarov did to me. He was a young guy pumped full of performance-enhancing drugs. An Olympic-level athlete with surprise on his side."

A barely perceptible smile appeared at the edges of his mouth. "And he damn near took you out, too."

It was a true statement. Rapp won his battle with the Russian, but that win had ended with him getting blown off an oil rig with his hair literally on fire. Too many more wins like that might kill him.

"It's gonna get dark, Scott. And I want to take it easy on the way down. My knee's bothering me."

Coleman's smile widened at the obvious lie.

And that was another thing that would be impossible to replace if he decided not to come back to active duty. They always knew what the other was thinking and could anticipate each other's moves. They'd grown up in this business together and had a connection that Rapp doubted he could ever replicate with someone else.

"I'm okay with where I stand now," Coleman said, looking up him. "The question is, are you? You can't be out there worrying about me leaving you hanging."

Rapp's cell phone rang and he pulled it out of a pocket in the back of his shirt. Claudia.

"What's up?" he said, connecting the call.

"How's Scott? You didn't hurt him, did you?"

Claudia Gould had recently gone from being the woman he was living with to being the woman he was living with who was also the logistics coordinator for Coleman's company. Her late husband had been one of the top private contractors in the world before Stan Hurley tore his throat out. Not an ideal start to a relationship, but it seemed to be working for both him and Coleman. She'd helped Rapp start living something that could pass for a life and she'd held SEAL Demolition and Salvage together while Coleman spent his days with personal trainers and physical therapists.

"He's sitting right here."

"Upright and under his own power?"

"Tell her you're fine," Rapp said, holding out the phone.

"I almost took him at the top, Claudia! Don't let him tell you any different."

Rapp frowned and put the phone back to his ear. "See?"

"Is he ready to come back to ops?"

"I think he's ready to come back and run the whole thing. Ops and logistics."

She switched to French, as she always did when she was irritated. "You can wish all you want, Mitch, but he's not firing me. I'm running that side of the business now. And it's a good thing for us, because it pays a lot better than the CIA."

There was no winning this fight, he knew. Claudia had taken a lot of pressure off Coleman and he had precisely zero desire to go back to coordinating details. Besides, she was better at it—something Coleman was fully willing to admit. The problem for Rapp was getting used to having the woman he was sleeping with on the comm when things went south. Boundaries between their personal and professional relationship were complicated and still in flux.

"Now's not the time to talk about this, Claudia. Scott and I are going to start down, but it might take a while. Go ahead and feed Anna if she's hungry. We can do dinner when I get back."

"Actually, you aren't coming down and we're not having dinner together. Look to the north."

He turned and squinted into the horizon. It took a few seconds but he finally made out a small dot over the mountains.

"There's a laptop on board with a full briefing. Be careful, okay?"

She disconnected the call and he put the phone away before pointing to the approaching chopper. "So what's the story, Scott? Are you back or not?"